THE LIMITS OF THE WORLD

ANDREW RAYMOND DRENNAN

Cargo Publishing

The Limits Of The World
Andrew Raymond Drennan
First Published in 2015
Published by Cargo Publishing
SC376700
Copyright © Andrew Raymond Drennan 2015

ISBN 978-1-908885-36-4

Printed and Bound by Bell & Bain in Scotland
Cover design by Allan Sommerville at Blok Graphic

www.cargopublishing.com

Also available as:
Kindle Ebook
EPUB Ebook

For Raymond Drennan (1945-2014)

'The book is a silent teacher and a companion in life. People should carry books with them at all times and read various good books zealously.'

> *– Kim Il-sung, Eternal President of North Korea, from a sign hanging in a North Korean library containing only books written by or about him and his son, Kim Jong-il*

'A man will be imprisoned in a room with a door that's unlocked and opens inwards; as long as it does not occur to him to pull rather than push.'

> *– Ludwig Wittgenstein*

'The Welcoming Party; British Ben And Yankee Hal; And The Importance Of Photographs'

Pyongyang city limits, 15ᵗʰ December Juche 99 (2011)

Han was a hungry man in a starving country, trundling down the deserted highway in his rusting Seventies BMW, towards the grey, slowly beating heart of Pyongyang. The sun was pale and low and still, as if it couldn't muster the resolve to rise any higher, and wanted just for one day out of billions of years to have a day off bringing light to dark corners of a lonely planet. In the distance the city's high-rises were crowded and hassled by morning mist, and Han felt a tremendous sadness sitting with him in the car. His return to the city now at the age of twenty-eight didn't feel like a homecoming. He knew there were no family or friends waiting for him outside whatever anonymous apartment block the Party had assigned him to, creeping up on tiptoes with the Doppler sound of each approaching car. After the past ten years in the countryside of Pyonganbuk province he was returning as he had left: alone.

The car strained under the weight of his luggage, an upturned two-seater sofa and plywood coffee table glistening with overnight frost strapped to the roof with rope-ties, the cold cracked-leather interior in back filled with clothes (almost all a uniform brown the colour of roadside dust, folded sharply into compact slithers as if they would at some point be required to pass through a tight letterbox), pots and pans with scraped innards from years of vigorous stirring over inadequate heat, cardboard boxes of his paperwork from the Propaganda and Agitation Department (their corners dented from frequent packing and unpacking as he moved from one promotion to the next), and boxes of books by the Great Leader Kim Il-sung (dead seventeen years) and the Dear Leader Kim Jong-il (very much alive), their spines all uncracked. None of these actually – legally – belonged to him, they were the Party's. The only things Han owned were inside him, in his head: that sacred piece of real estate that could at once both imprison and set a man free, its padlock hidden away from both intruder and owner.

He pulled over by the side of the road, under the Arch of Reunification at the edge of the city limits, two giant concrete female figures embracing from one side of the highway to the other, holding a unified Korea between them. The view ahead was dominated by the Ryugyong Hotel – by some distance the tallest building in Pyongyang – rising out of an otherwise modest skyline like a single beat on a heart rate monitor. He reached in back for his Kim Il-sung biography *A Great Mind*, digging out a small worn notepad and snapped-down pencil nestled in its hollowed centre pages. Hidden under *A Great Mind*, among Han's illicit trove of Western novels, was a copy of Joseph Conrad's *Heart of Darkness*, its pages yellowed from years idling on dusty bookcases across South East Asia before travelling thousands of miles through various networks of Chinese tourists and North Korean smugglers, to the illegal market stalls where Han had purchased them, under cover of darkness and only ever from villages he knew he would never return to. Inside he had listed page references along with brief codas of what he would find there. He consulted the page marked '*Another thing about loneliness*' (his Chosongul script soft and fat from a blunt pencil nib, the letters forming little buildings down the side of the page), then opened a clean page in his notebook.

'*I'm about to drive into Pyongyang but I've had to stop. I keep thinking about that line in Conrad from last night. "We live as we dream – alone." This has never felt truer to me as I sit here, returning to a place where only ghosts and the corrupt know my name. When I read I'm not alone anymore; there are no such things as countries or borders or prisons; with a book I'm holding proof that there are other people out there in the Real World that have felt the same things I do. I'm a small man in a big world. But isn't it a big world to everyone – whether you're Korean, American, British or African? If I can just get close to one other person, to really know what's inside them, to feel what they feel, and see what they see, I'll know that I'm not so alone, and maybe then I can finally start living.*'

Han closed the notebook abruptly, as if he had been too honest with himself and had to shut his thoughts down, the way he did when he sometimes stumbled upon a sad memory he didn't want to visualise all the way through to its end. This was the problem with the past's infinite refrain: it's always inside you, and can never be let go. Such melancholy had been threatening since leaving Pyonganbuk province, lurking in the backseat among the other luggage. Now the loneliness had properly arrived and could be denied no longer, it hung around Han's shoulders, gathering him up in the kind of embrace only mothers are capable of. He shuffled the notebook back inside *A Great Mind* and drove off again.

The city unravelled before him in a series of gradually familiar columns, from the harmonicas – the lowly, identical bungalows attached wall to wall at the city's less privileged outer edge – to the charcoal high-rises and smoky-white apartment blocks clustered around the centre, with their balconies big enough to fit only one person.

A tar-yellow dawn sunlight blushed across the empty plazas, breaking through the legs of the street sweepers hunched over their brooms, their shadows stretching far along the gutters. There was only dust to sweep. Monuments of Kim Il-sung, Eternal President of the Democratic People's Republic of North Korea (the ultimate in tenure – one of the few men to see in life how they would be worshipped in death) stood imperious over the squares like sleeping gods. The city was still largely asleep, about to be woken by morning announcements from the street-side loudspeakers. Little boxed islands of grass, and birch trees that seemed to grow straight out the concrete, dotted the pedestrian precincts like metre^2 oases. Clouds flew past oppressively low, the way cigarette smoke haunts a windowless room. And the birds sang.

By the side of the road, running congruent to the Taedong River, a young girl foraged at the bases of willow trees and bushes for stray seedlings or forgotten scraps of rice, which she collected in a hand-woven pocket. The girl's tiny mouth formed an em-dash, thin lips pursed together in concentration as hunger throbbed through her body. This was hunger's paradox: how the body – and mind – can make the absence of something feel like a presence. Above, dwarfing her doubled-over figure, a mural of the Dear Leader took up the whole side of an apartment block, the words

"WE ARE THE HAPPIEST PEOPLE IN THE WORLD!"

written below his victorious, beneficent smile, pearly teeth a kind of white not to be found anywhere else in North Korea. His eyes peered straight out like a Western billboard ad, following you no matter where you stood.

Traffic wardens pivoted in quarter turns inside white circles painted at the centre of crossroads and interchanges, waving their arms around at sharp angles, directing non-existent vehicles, dancing to some silent militant disco. No matter how empty the road was they kept up their performance: they were always keen to impress a passing Party member walking to the nearby Ministries, or a Party-sanctioned tour bus of foreign tourists – the kind Han would be guiding around the capital. Han once heard from a colleague in the Ministry of Communications about a warden spotted in a dozing posture with his arms hanging forlornly at his sides. The Party reassigned him to a remote outpost in a dead wheat field along the DMZ, looking out for imperial invaders from the South, stuck up a checkpoint tower there wasn't even room to sit down in, and banished his family from the capital. It would be three generations before anyone bearing his name would be allowed to work in Pyongyang again, let alone tend traffic. The Party's Three Generation Rule was seen as crucial for wiping out all trace elements of disloyalty, or as Han's father once wrote in one of his many editorials for State newspaper *Rodong Sinmun*, 'behaviour contrary to the goal of Socialist victory'. Since the death of his parents ten years previous the rule wasn't something that concerned Han anymore. This freedom from familial reprisals was seen as something of a rare liberty by Han's colleagues in Pyonganbuk province. 'What do you have to lose now?' they would say to him, thinking all Han might have in mind was a little extra trading in American cigarettes

10

and the occasional bottle of whisky. It wasn't long after that he started collecting illegal Western literature.

Han checked the time on his battered dashboard, the plastic cover cracked through the three and the nine, dividing the face in two. He rapped on the clock with his knuckles trying to awaken the mechanism inside, as if time had stopped altogether, his country stuck in a permanent past, and was now drifting through a cold stasis.

He fumbled with a new pack of cigarettes, wedging it between his thighs, cursing, '*Eminai*,' ('bitch') trying to tear open the rubbery outer packaging with one hand. They were designed to look like Marlboros with their red banding across the front, except the brand name was spelt in Russian Cyrillic. Commie Marlboros, Han called them. Though never in public.

He turned on the radio to the *Korean Central Broadcasting Network* – one of only two available stations across the whole AM bandwidth – to find the announcer in a state of some concern: '... of anti-government graffiti found in the east bank of Pyongyang have been confirmed by the Ministry of Communications as a false alarm. Messages seen on a wall were in fact extolling the many virtues of our Socialist cause and the Great Leader's *Juche* ideology, which has led us to be the most prosperous nation on Earth...' Then amid brassy trumpets in the background at the report's end, the announcer proclaimed, 'Long live the Dear Leader comrade Kim Jong-il!'

Han, concentrating on the cigarette packet, repeated under his breath, 'Long live Kim Jong-il!' He was barely aware of having done it, the words falling out his mouth as thoughtlessly as a cough.

As he managed to wrench a dented cigarette free from the pack, he noticed a man on a far street corner wearing white overalls, frantically painting over the last remains of graffiti on a wall with an extendable paintbrush. Two policemen kept lookout, swaggering off the kerb, trying with great alarm to assure people hanging out their windows across the street that nothing was going on, their panic barely contained. They growled to the man in the overalls for him to hurry up.

Han rolled his window down, the cigarette between his lips

dipping as he opened his mouth. Between the policemen he could make out the line:

'김정일 독재 타도하자!'

('LET'S BRING DOWN KIM JONG-IL!')

One of the policemen awkwardly tried to smile. 'It's OK,' he explained to Han, 'just keep moving, comrade.' His hands were trembling.

Han floored the accelerator. He had never seen anti-government graffiti before. In a country with, apparently, no dissent or opposition, he knew when the perpetrators were caught they would find themselves facing down the multiple barrels of a firing squad.

A traffic warden suddenly pirouetted into view at an interchange ahead, thrusting out a white-gloved hand at Han's overheating car. His head still spinning from what he had seen, Han slammed on the brakes, his skinny, balding tyres skidding across the loose road surface, sending his luggage piled up behind hurtling into the back of his seat. Han stayed leaning over the steering wheel, his cigarette still dangling from his lips, then let out a relieved laugh to himself. His photographic travel permit – Han Jun-an, 28 years old, Senior Officer for Communications (Pyongyang) – allowing him access to the city swung back and forth from the rear view mirror. His cheekbones were prominent in his photograph like he had been cut out the rock of Mount Paektu itself. Lack of food through his teens had kept him baby-faced, giving him a vulnerable look around the eyes, which – despite being framed by sharp, long eyelashes – were dim and deflated, hinting at some kind of well-like sadness that had been trapped deep inside him for a while, and would remain there long after the camera shutter had snapped; the kind of sadness that packs a bag for you and throws it onto your shoulders, and tells you it's going to be your only company for a very long time.

The warden stared Han down, mirrored sunglasses hiding her eyes. The warden looked left, then right. There wasn't a vehicle in sight.

Han was too busy pushing the fallen boxes off the back of his seat and around his headrest at first to notice how pretty she was. Then a little whirlwind whipped up inside his chest, something that always happened to him when he met someone he thought was much more attractive than he was. Han reckoned himself a six out of ten most days, maybe a seven. But when sixes and sevens try talking to nines and tens like the warden was, basic competence of communication seem disconcertingly elusive. Han hung out his window, letting out a heavy cloud of smoke which he tried to bat away. After a few false starts at a sentence, finding only a string of prepositions, he managed a 'Good morning, comrade,' breaking away to splutter a cough into his lap. The whirlwind inside him grew swiftly to gale force. He held his cigarette up disappointedly, hoping she would find the habit charming. 'Damn Russians know how to make a good smoke.'

The warden saluted as firmly as she could. 'Good morning, comrade Han!' She stared sternly over the car roof at the sun coming up out of the mist ahead, just a dull yellow button reflected on her sunglasses.

It was the first time since his promotion that Han had been saluted by someone younger than he was.

'How are you this morning, officer?' Han asked gently, trying to defuse the notion the warden would be intimidated by his rank, and she might be inclined to talk to him like an equal. His nervy, slanting smile reflecting back in her sunglasses made him desperately want to see her eyes. Without them, he felt locked out by her.

The warden bellowed back, 'All glory and long health to our Dear Leader comrade Kim Jong-il!' Her clothes hung loose, the shoulder pads in her white, military-style jacket jutting out sharply, her shoulders a few inches inside them, her blue skirt, cut exactly below the downward slope of her kneecaps, clinging against sparrow-like shins.

'Are you having a nice morning?' Han asked more insistently, trying to let her know she didn't have to impress him with Party loyalty. But it was useless.

The warden rattled off recent traffic statistics and the success of her station ('no accidents in three months at my interchange,' she stated proudly). Han's gaze drifted vacantly away to the ground at the pretence they had to play out. He knew nothing he said or did could get him close to her. Han often wondered what it was like being someone else, feeling out the topography of someone else's head; did thoughts *feel* the same travelling through her body as they did in his? Was there underneath her regimented exterior some order of desire? Han was reminded of what he had written in the margins of his Conrad the night before: '*We are not just bodies; we are machines made of feelings.*'

The radio in Han's car was reporting on illicit literature smuggled over the border that had been captured by the police, repeating warnings of vigilance and urging citizens to report on anyone they suspected of being involved. Han quickly twisted the volume dial down.

The warden took a step closer, still standing at attention. 'I've been expecting you all morning, comrade Han.'

Trying to be light-hearted, Han asked, 'Do you know the name of every senior officer that passes through here?'

The warden didn't know how to respond. If she said yes, she would be implying Han wasn't special, and if she said no, it would look like she was only performing her duties well because she knew Han was coming.

'Sorry, I was only joking. Did you see what's going on back there?'

The warden paused. 'They're cleaning the wall, comrade.'

'Could you make out any of the graffiti?'

'The radio said it was a false alarm, comrade.'

'The radio says a lot of things,' Han said dismissively.

She dropped her poise for a moment, letting slip, 'There seem to have been a lot of false alarms lately.'

'There have been others like this? I've heard rumours.'

She paused. 'Is this a test, comrade?'

'A test?'

'You are in the Ministry of Communications, are you not?'

'Yes, but... we're just talking.'

The way the warden's forehead creased and mouth turned down suggested this was impossible. 'I'm a loyal Party member, comrade. You have nothing to worry about with me.'

Han felt a sudden desire to take hold of the warden's hand and squeeze it gently, to tell her how pretty he thought she was and though he was a six, a seven at best, and she was so clearly a nine, hell even a ten, that maybe some time they could possibly... he started saying it: 'I've just got back to the city after a long time away, I was wondering...' He noticed her raise a heel, about to step back. He imagined her eyes narrowing with discomfort. 'No... of course. How silly... forget I mentioned it...'

The warden looked over his car, seeing another approaching in the distance. 'I'm sorry, comrade, I have to get back to work,' then shouted over the car roof, 'All glory and long health to the Dear Leader Kim Jong-il!'

Han drew the cigarette up to his mouth again and drove away. Beauty like hers had a way of quietly crushing him, the way certain piano keys or violin strings played together can bewilderingly, and instantly, drain your heart.

The warden saluted him until she was a tiny figure in Han's rear view mirror.

Sunan Airport, fifteen miles outside Pyongyang, 15th December Juche 99 (2011)

They were somewhere over the countryside surrounding Kanggye, when Englishman Ben Campbell turned to his American cameraman Hal Huckley, and said, 'Six months of visa debates with the consulate, two years badgering the network, and what gets us into the hermit kingdom? A fifty-dollar bribe to a Chinese customs officer round the back of Shenyang McDonald's.'

'I'm lovin' it,' Hal sang sarcastically.

'This is not a serious world we live in.'

Hal momentarily raised his sunglasses onto his forehead, looking out his tiny porthole window, picking out through light, sporadic clouds that seemed more atmospheric than meteorological, smatterings of black figures working the land lightly powdered with snow below. 'Tell that to them down there,' he said, then flicked his sunglasses back down.

Ben replied, 'You hear writers and philosophers talk about how we're all alone in the world. They've no idea.'

They had been able to talk relatively freely to one another throughout the flight, ten rows in each direction from them empty. There was no in-flight movie. At the front of the plane two flight attendants – not exactly glamorous, but cute in a country-girl-just-left-home kind of way – were dealing with a party of bald Chinese businessmen complaining about the quality of the on-board whisky.

Ben leaned over to get a look at the farmers. 'What do you think it's like down there, seeing planes flying overhead from places they'll never see so much as a picture of? We're as close as they'll ever get to the outside world.'

Hal, hungover, shrugged, making a whirlpool in the dregs of his beer. 'Probably.' He hung a hand out to an attendant. 'Hey, can I get another beer? A big one?'

Ben pulled back from the window. 'You could at least show a little enthusiasm.'

'You're the one who wanted to come here, Campbell. If a celebration of humanity's what you're after then you should have picked a different travel agent.' Hal dragged himself up in his seat and ruffled his straggly beard, flecked with grey, rubbing the six am rise from his face. 'Christ, what the hell are we doing here, man...'

Ben flicked his elbow at Hal, teasing him to lighten his dire mood. 'You scared?'

Hal took his beer from the attendant's hand before she could put it down, then waited for her to get a safe distance away. 'I don't know. We've gone to the most reclusive, secretive country in the world, to make a documentary under the guise of being tourists.' Hal turned to face him. 'I'm fuckin' A.'

During their eight-year partnership Ben and Hal had made their name with the American digital upstarts *REBEL News*. Backed by a dotcom billionaire, *REBEL*'s format of anarchic, Gonzo-style documentaries had been eaten up by a generation that consumed most of its news from YouTube, and had tired of endless reporting from Iraq. *REBEL*'s channel had over a million subscribers, with gritty videos on Kazakh anti-capitalists, Yemeni jihadists, Congolese environmentalists... wherever there was a conflict *REBEL* had someone there. And it was usually Ben and Hal. The only people with comparable passport stamps were arms dealers. They hadn't had a Christmas at home (Ben: London; Hal: New York) for the last five years, and were about to make it six. A week after leaving Sudan their producer insisted the pair get themselves 'out the shit for a while and just do a human interest story.' *REBEL* was surely the only news network in the world that considered shooting an undercover documentary in North Korea a holiday.

Gazing out the window at the mysterious country below, Ben was still thinking of his (now ex-) girlfriend Sabrina back home in London, packing up the last of her things. The demise of their relationship had seemed sudden to Ben. Not so Sabrina, whose manifold reasons they simply *had* to split up could best be summarised as, 'You're never here. And when you are you never let me in.'

Ben had tried to explain to her that after documenting genocide first-hand in Sudan, going Christmas shopping on Oxford Street and trying to act and talk like a normal couple seemed somehow hollow and unimportant in the circumstances. Sabrina would look at his sunburnt face and realise he was still there in the shit, and not there with her.

Hal gently kicked Ben's ankle. 'You OK? You kinda spaced out there.'

'Yeah. Fine,' Ben replied. 'You?'

Even by Hal and *REBEL*'s cavalier standards, Sudan had gotten out of hand on the human level. One evening Ben and Hal left their hotel to shoot some B roll. It should have taken ten minutes. What they ended up capturing was a man being set upon by a mob of nearly fifty on the edge of Khartoum. Charges that the man was homosexual and an apostate quickly rang round in some fatal game

17

of telephone. The mob beat the man to death with fists, feet and sticks, as Hal recorded from across the street. *REBEL* uploaded the raw footage online, including Hal audibly holding back Ben from intervening. Hal's seemingly cold and impotent plea of 'What can we do?' became the title of a million-plus hit on YouTube, shared to death by horrified liberals around Facebook and Twitter under the hash tag: #whatcouldwedo?.

Hal had been obsessively watching the clip on repeat on his laptop in their hotel room in Shenyang, refreshing the page every few minutes to see another few hundred views, and the Dislike bar – in Hal's mind, essentially a graphic barometer of his lack of empathy – rapidly filling with red. Hal quickly closed the video page when he realised Ben was standing there watching him.

Hal had rationalised the event post-mortem by telling himself they could never have defended the man from such a mob in a hostile theocracy; they had themselves barely escaped afterwards, and, like the naturalist who refuses to help a wounded animal for fear of interfering with the natural order, resolved that it was the world itself which had caused such barbarity. But that hadn't stopped the man's screams and pleadings for that most basic of human privileges – to be alive, and remain so for as long as possible – from waking him each night for the last week.

'Yeah, fine,' Hal replied blankly.

And so the pair sat there, nursing their own private horrors, and two flat North Korean beers in plastic cups.

There was no cheering in the Western celebratory tradition when the Air Koryo flight from Shenyang touched down on Sunan Airport's only operating runway. A seemingly random picture of an old man's face, like someone's rather senile grandfather who can't stop smiling, was perched on a grey pedestal on the terminal roof. Further along was a sign of 'PYONGYANG' in red capital letters, under which hung a mural of a snow-covered mountain scene surrounding a crystal-blue lake, where a smattering of pink and yellow flowers sprang miraculously through the snow. Four Air Koryo planes sat in a row at empty gates, as if forgotten about, the airport foreground deserted: Ben and Hal's flight was the only arrival all day.

The passengers, mostly Chinese businessmen with small briefcases who had made the journey dozens of times, and foreign tourists dressed like bourgeois extras from *Doctor Zhivago*, were dealt with methodically and with prejudice at customs. The officers sat in raised platforms, dispensing with the Chinese as a matter of routine, but fiercely questioning the Western tourists, of which they were only five. Ben exchanged muted waves with them at the luggage carousel. Much like a solitary driver spotting another vehicle on a lonely country road in the dead of night, Ben wondered what they could be doing there a week before Christmas.

Ben and Hal clutched their single rucksacks and passports, along with signed waivers they had filled out during the flight, saying they were bringing in no

– weapons, ammunition, explosives or killing devices
– drugs, exciter, hallucinogens, poisons
– GPS or navigator
– hand phone, cell phone or other communication device
– historical and cultural wealth, artistic works
– publishing of all kinds

The bottom of the form warned that 'answers known to be false will be dealt with in the severest terms.' Ben had spent much of the flight speculating on what those terms might be. Hal seemed positively nonchalant about the whole thing. 'They can't even keep the lights on in Pyongyang, you think they have electronic sweepers waiting for us at the terminal? These guys are lightweights.'

'Well I don't want this documentary to have any unplanned chapters set in a concentration camp.' Ben knew he was up to something.

Ben and Hal had some experience of authoritarian hospitality over the years: a night in a Bolivian jail after Hal was accused of dealing cocaine (he wasn't dealing, he was buying. Luckily he had stayed under the legal limit of fifty grams); and kidnapped in Barranquilla where the Colombian Caracol cartel kept the pair in a damp basement for ten days until *REBEL* wired a ransom of US$50,000.

'Stop smiling,' Ben said, looking straight ahead at the customs booth. 'And take your sunglasses off. You look like a fucking American.'

Hal ruffled his shaggy blonde hair and put his sunglasses up in it. 'I am a fucking American.'

Ben couldn't have looked more English: short, side-parted hair, his face all polite geniality, wearing sensible cargo pants with multipockets, hiking trainers, and a utilitarian Berghaus jacket. His soft, large eyes and gentle voice had been instrumental in making him so successful a journalist for his age: he made you want to tell him things.

A little girl standing by her father, getting her first look at a rugged American male (Hal was what the Marlboro man would have looked like if he smoked weed rather than tobacco) attempted to point in glazed wonder at Hal, but the father batted her arm down as if she had hung it recklessly out a train window. 'What gives, man?' Hal wondered aloud.

Ben informed him, 'They need special permission to interact with foreigners.'

The walls of the airport were covered in more landscape murals of snowy mountain ranges, with blood-red skies, lakes a sort of blue found nowhere in nature, and portraits of victorious North Koreans dressed in military regalia, looking out over some vast indomitable land. Swivel-less plastic chairs bolted to the floor like a school canteen's filled the centre of the hangar-like terminal. Most of the terminal was in darkness thanks to a power cut. The flicking plastic digits on the Departure board said the next flight didn't leave for another two hours. Only two destinations: Beijing or Shenyang.

The customs officer collected the Chinese waivers like they were nothing more than cinema tickets, eyeing Ben and Hal further down the queue.

Ben looked down at the ground, blinking heavily. 'I have a confession,' he said suddenly.

Hal snorted with knowing laughter. 'I knew it. You brought it in, didn't you?'

Ben's voice went up an octave. 'How did you...'

'Eight years, you think I don't know when you're hiding something? No publishing of any kind, it says. You're such a cliché, man. Where did you put it?'

'Tucked down my UNICEF t-shirt. They won't body search us, will they?'

Hal paused and gave a definitive shake of his head. 'It's no big deal. They turn a blind eye to that sort of thing. Like journalists posing as tourists. They just don't want you flaunting it. As long as they don't catch you reading it in public or anything you'll be fine...'

Ben gave him his best suspicious-older-brother glare. 'You packed your bag on your own last night. We never do that. That's our thing. Our only superstition. It's what those CNN guys laugh at us for.'

Hal wore a fixed smile.

'What did you bring, Hal?'

He paused guiltily, clearing his throat.

'I won't be mad,' Ben lied. 'Don't lean in, don't whisper it. Just say it quietly.'

Hal unwrapped a stick of gum, then spoke whilst his hand was at his mouth. 'Laptop.'

Ben smiled warmly, looking down at the waiver. 'Did you even read the waiver? Were you confused by the wording? Or did you think communication device just meant semaphore flags or a ham radio?' He nodded calmly to himself, noting how close they were getting to inspection. 'Where did you put it?'

'I hid it under the extra camera batteries.'

'Not bad, Hal. Not bad at all. If it's not smuggling marijuana into Syria, or pornography into Iraq... I mean what are you, the bloody Santa Claus of the Axis of Evil, the fucking benevolent bloody of... whatever?'

Hal popped his gum, unmoved. 'I hate seeing a reporter get inarticulate, Campbell. It'll be fine.' He folded his sunglasses into his coat's top pocket. 'We're up.'

Things didn't start well: while American customs officers are inclined to hide animosity towards travellers with questions like 'What's the purpose of your visit?', the North Koreans gave a whole new definition to bluntness.

'What do you want?' the officer snapped, relieving the pair of their passports with a Venus Flytrap hand reaching out from the gloom.

The pair gave their prepared answer:

'Holiday.'

'Vacation.'

The officer scrambled out his perch with the speed of a Wimbledon umpire, his lips pushed together like the dot on an exclamation point. He opened their luggage in turn, taking out the basic point-and-shoot video camera from Hal's bag, the only kind allowed in the North.

The customs officer presumed, 'And no telephoto lens?'

Hal shook his head as gravely as the question had been asked. 'No telephoto lens.'

'No lens more hundred fifty millimetre.'

'No telephoto lens,' Hal repeated.

The officer started disassembling all the removable parts of the camera. 'How big memory?', he asked, taking the SD card out.

Hal bobbed his head from side to side, 'Ten, eleven gigs. I think.'

The officer stared back at him, giving Hal a chance to change his mind. 'You think you are smart American and I am stupid North Korean, don't know technology?' He inspected the memory card, and saw that it was indeed ten gigabytes. He handed the camera back. 'Underneath?' He reached for the camera batteries.

Ben couldn't even look.

Hal stonefaced the officer, chewing his gum a little more aggressively. 'Just batteries.'

'Just batteries?' the officer wondered aloud.

'Just batteries.'

Ben couldn't take it any longer and interrupted, coming between the two. 'Is there a problem?'

'Ah, you English.' The officer smiled, somehow, impossibly.

'I am, yes.'

'Ah. I like English. I like the cricket. A stupid sport, but I like. English is good.' He looked at Hal, voice dropping. 'American not so good.' The officer took his hand off the batteries and zipped up the bag. He looked around the deserted terminal, then asked out a tiny conspiratorial slit in his mouth, 'You have any American cigarette?'

Ben, although not a smoker, had a pack of Red Marlboros ready in his pocket. 'Here you are.'

The officer pocketed the cigarettes and his whole demeanour changed. 'Enjoy most glorious country of Democratic People's Republic of Korea!' Then the officer closed up his booth and disappeared into the gloom, satisfied with his contraband.

Hal picked up his bag then patted Ben, slouched in relief, on the back. 'See. Told you it would be fine. Now where's this Mr Han guy?'

Chollima Street, Pyongyang

The apartment the Party arranged for Han had only been described in terms of its proximity to the so-called Forbidden City, the Central Party Offices, where Han would conduct the operations of the Propaganda and Agitation Department (its public euphemism: the Ministry of Communications). In the middle of a forest of concrete columns in varying levels of disrepair, Han's building was distinguished by being one of the newer ones. So new, in fact, they appeared to still be building it. A large skeletal grid of scaffolding was attached all the way up the east side. It was unclear whether the builders had forgotten to take it down or had simply abandoned it.

Han pulled into the car park, where three men dressed in the same brown military uniforms as Han's were waiting. They compared their watches in disappointment. Wide panels of crass, oversized medals on their lapels shimmered in the sun aching up between the high-rises across the road.

Han recognised the men: the Propaganda and Agitation Department's top brass. And he'd obviously kept them waiting – men who are never waited on.

He stabbed his cigarette out in the ashtray and hurriedly smoothed back his jet black hair, smoke still exhaling from his mouth and nose as he urged himself, 'Relax relax relax...' Then he remembered the box of books sitting in the backseat. He arranged a two-deep pile of Kim Il-sung titles over the top of his Western ones, then rushed across the lot with his hand out to the men from several strides away. He shook each of their hands in turn. 'Comrade Secretary Sun, comrade Yong, comrade Li, I didn't expect to receive such a distinguished welcoming party.'

Secretary Sun stood back slightly from the others, hands petulantly stuffed in his deep mohair-coat pockets. As a small boy Han had sat at the dinner table listening to his father complain to his mother about whatever politically underhanded affair Comrade Officer Sun (as he was known then) had been up to that week to further his career. To the young Han Sun seemed a monstrous figure, almost pathologically apathetic to anything outside himself. Han had imagined him sitting on the sofa in his penthouse with his shirt open, hands perched on his belly after a large meal, burping brazenly – regardless of whether he was in company or not – and scratching places that should only ever be touched in the shower, sprawled in the glow of his television, as if scandalized by his own vulgarity. A nickname had once done the rounds at the Ministry, calling him 'The Only One', such was his solipsism. And now he was Han's boss.

Li presented himself as something of the group's spokesman, a smile on his face he seemed uncomfortable wearing. 'Comrade Han, on behalf of my superior officers from the Propaganda and Agitation Department...' Li corrected himself, 'Sorry, the Ministry of Communications...'

The men chuckled among themselves.

'...we welcome you back to Pyongyang. And indeed,' he pointed upwards, 'to your glorious new home.'

Han looked up at the exterior, the pockets of exposed brickwork like the vicarious smatterings of a teen's acne, clear tarpaulin blowing out the window frames up top where the glazing was still to be installed. It looked like it could never be warm inside.

Li whispered by way of apology, 'I'm afraid my secretary took me a little too literally when I told her to put you in the newest building we had.'

Han put his hand on Li's chest to reassure him. 'It will do perfectly, comrade. I'm honoured the Party took the trouble to assign me to Pyongyang at all.' He turned to address the others. 'I am so sorry for keeping you gentlemen waiting on such a cold morning. If only I'd known I could have prepared.' He glanced back at his car.

Mr Yong, Chief Officer for Tourism – one of the few government departments unburdened by high targets – stepped forward. 'You know, comrade, I met your father, Song-man, when he was a journalist at *Rodong Sinmun*. I'm sure today would be a day of great pride for him to see you appointed Senior Officer for Communications in Pyongyang, carrying on the illustrious Han family name. It is a great responsibility.'

Han parroted back, 'It is a great responsibility. But I think not of the spirit of my father, but of our Eternal President, Kim Il-sung, watching over me today. Even in death he shows me the way.'

Yong clapped his hands at Li. 'Haha, you see! That's the sort of rhetoric we need around here.'

The miserable-looking Sun kept checking back at his Mercedes, longing for its warm interior. He had had sex that morning with someone who wasn't his wife and was keen to get back to his office and shower. He still felt his legs aching dully from the effort to orgasm as quickly as possible. His Mercedes' engine was still running, pumping out exhaust-fog into the air: Sun wanted the others to know he didn't plan on staying long.

Yong had a little routine planned: 'As the senior guide for tourists and foreign journalists in the area, you must come to think of yourself as the face and voice of the Party,' his arm stretched out and arced through one hundred and eighty degrees, 'of all Korea. And what a voice it is! So proud, so respectful, so patriotic. And what a face. Handsome bastard...'

Han had never thought of himself as handsome. To the Party dinosaurs he might have seemed handsome, but only in the sense they

25

hoped their daughters would end up with someone like him, someone who would never complain or cause any trouble.

Yong continued, 'With your help, we can demonstrate the full glory of the Korean people, and we'll show those imperialist bastards, those long-nose Yankee devils nothing they can do will ever bring down the nation the Great Leader Kim Il-sung so bravely fought for!' Yong thrust his arms triumphantly up in the air as if addressing hundreds of people, 'We will never be defeated!'

Through the others' applause Sun finally spoke, his bass voice quivering with solemnity. 'To the Great Leader Kim Il-sung!'

Li was nearly on the verge of tears, sensing – wrongly – that he was impressing Sun. 'May we endeavour to be even half the patriot he was!'

Before the men all saluted, Han added at the last moment, 'May he be flown by winged angels in the heavens!'

Sun waited for the euphoria to die down, the men parting for him. 'It must feel strange to be back in the city after so long, Han.'

Han felt the mood had suddenly turned. 'Yes, comrade Secretary.'

'What are your thoughts?'

Han hesitated. 'On my role in the Party?'

Sun gave a rapid tremble of his head. 'What else?'

'Well... the Party, my job, is everything to me. That I have nothing else is one of my strongest assets. If we all gave as much to the country as we could, we could be even greater. We must all give a little pain for the greater good.'

'You don't mind pain?'

'I don't believe in it, comrade Secretary. Pain is just weakness leaving the body.' The phrase wasn't Han's.

Sun pulled out a file from inside his coat, finding a timeline tracking where Han's family had lived through the years. Official Party membership headshots of his father lay loose between the papers. 'Your file shows you were raised here in the city, along with your younger sister.'

'That's right, comrade Secretary.'

'Until the death of your parents.'

'That's accurate. In *Juche* eighty-nine, I believe. A tragic car accident.'

'Ten years. Good. You will have adequately dealt with that by now then. And your sister, she's dead as well.'

Li and Yong shared a look of shock at the Secretary's wanton bluntness.

Han found himself gripping his jacket sleeves. 'Yes, sir. Of starv—'

Sun's eyes narrowed accusingly.

'—of natural causes in *Juche* eighty-two. We were living in Kangwon province then. I was eighteen when my parents died, then I started working in Communications in Pyonganbuk province.'

'That's exactly what I have here. I often say the Party actually knows us better than we know ourselves.' Sun stuffed the file back in his coat and stepped close enough for Han to smell the punchier aroma of American tobacco on him. His pupils were deep black and dead, giving nothing away of what was going through his mind. 'We must be on our toes at all times. Showing our appreciation for what the Party has given us, with our loyalty. And love.'

'Love, comrade Secretary?'

'Yes, Han. The only kind that matters! Love for our country, the mother homeland.' On cue, having been monitoring the time carefully, Sun's driver parped the horn, and Sun stepped back. 'I'm afraid I have a meeting to get to. Everyone's going berserk over this graffiti they found yesterday.' He flicked his chin up at Han. 'What do you make of it?'

Han paused. 'Whoever's doing it is quite bold. And clever too.'

'Clever?'

'Painting slogans on walls and roads is hard to keep quiet. Too many people see it. They tell their neighbours, who tell other people at the market. Rumour becomes fact very quickly.'

'And what about our facts?'

Han tried to smile, but felt it turning into a smirk, the kind he had seen senior officers make over the years. 'Our facts are better, comrade Secretary.' He let the smirk drift from his face: he was surprised how easy it was to look and sound like them. 'Perhaps it would be a good idea to put up some pro-Party graffiti, on a busier street, so the radio reports appear more genuine. Offset the more damaging stuff. Change the story.' Han thought it best to leave out that he had heard the phrase from an American diplomat.

Li scribbled a note of it. 'A fine idea, comrade.'

Sun waited at his door and smiled, showing the same pearly teeth as the Dear Leader's on the billboards. 'I look forward to working with you over the coming decades.'

Han swallowed hard at the intimidating timeframe.

Sun's Mercedes whipped violently out of the car park and rushed him back to the Ministry.

Li signalled to a small windowless campervan near Han's car, where a side door flew open, and several skinny soldiers all as short as each other came charging out, forming a line of frightening conviction. 'We arranged some help for your moving day, comrade.' Li pointed the men to Han's car, who rushed over as one and started untying the sofa and table from the roof, throwing the two doors and boot open. All of Han's possessions were stripped from the car and taken upstairs in one brief flurry. 'OK, boys,' Li said as they charged inside, 'floor eighteen, apartment C. As much as you can carry.'

Remembering the box of books in the backseat, Han protested, 'R-really, comrade, as grateful as I am, this isn't necessary...'

Yong opened a black leather briefcase, cradled underarm (always a sure sign of something illicit), revealing a bottle of Whyte and Mackay whisky. 'I've got ten-year-old nectar of the gods here that says you're about to be even more grateful.'

Han said as plainly as he could, 'It's nine o'clock in the morning.'

Yong broke out into a beaming smile and smacked Han hard on the back, pushing him into the lobby. 'Exactly, my boy. Imagine if we were alcoholics. We'd all be drunk already! Come on, the bozos can take the stairs.'

Han watched a soldier carrying the box of books disappear into the stairwell. All it would take was one little look inside, and Han's career, probably his life, would be over a lot sooner than anticipated.

The elevator jerked and spluttered the whole way up to the eighteenth floor, a motor no bigger than a lawnmower's powering a pulley system that was keeping them from going into freefall.

Li's shoulders kept bouncing up and down in exaggerated thrusts at Yong's unfunny jokes. Han stood at the back watching the floors slowly tick by, each number bringing him closer to possible disaster. He found himself thinking about his family. It was often the case that in the middle of some important event their memory would revisit him. Grief was like that: it had a habit of kicking in your door at unexpected hours of the day. Grief was a full-time occupation. It rang inside him like tinnitus.

The elevator doors opened and they exited into the dark hallway, their footsteps brisk and harsh on the concrete floor.

Han looked around, wondering why the building was silent. 'How many people live here?'

'You're the first one, comrade,' Yong answered chirpily over his shoulder. 'So you won't be troubled by noise.' He produced a key from his coat pocket, his fist already curled around the door handle.

'You have a spare key,' Han said, eyeing it nervously.

'The Ministry has keys for all our officers' apartments. For security.'

'Of course.'

Yong unlocked the door, which had no spy hole. With each knock on the door he would have to prepare for the worst. Living in such a building was going to be tiring. Han waited for some sort of olfactory sense of home, but nothing came. It was the smell of vacancy, of absence. To Han, something about the apartment made it feel like he was still outside.

Yong toured the rooms, hmmming and ahhhing, trying to rationalise everything that was dismal about the place: 'Big windows with views will only distract you... it's better to have somewhere with less space instead of too much... it won't take as long to heat up...' His stumbling footsteps made more sense when Han spotted the third of whisky already missing from the bottle, sampled earlier that morning in Yong's office.

A stripped bed sat in the middle of the bedroom, a slight depression still in the centre of the mattress from the previous user. Nothing was said about where it came from.

The view from the bedroom window was the brick wall of the neighbouring block, that if the window was open Han could reach out and touch. But he was pleased. He would at least be able to read in peace.

The daylight was already weak and spent by the time it reached the hallway where the soldiers were bringing in their loads, quickly filling up the tiny corridor with boxes of Han's paperwork. One of them flicked a light switch back and forth: another power cut.

Yong collapsed into the sofa before it had even been fully set down, his weight snatching it out of the soldier's hands. 'Ah, this is the life.'

They started leaving the boxes in the living room in front of Yong and Li, including the suspect box Han had been waiting on. He stood helplessly in the middle of them all.

'Do you keep *all* your paperwork?' Yong asked, chuckling at the files overflowing on to the floor.

'Files on the foreigners I've acted as minder for,' answered Han. 'They interest me.'

'Interest you?'

'I find it helpful if I get to know them.'

'My god, man, what can you know about someone from a piece of paper? Those are just words. No, you want to feel the grip of someone's hand, look into their eyes to really know them.'

'Dangerous and deceitful things, eyes. A man once said, "The world is all that is the case." And words are my world, comrade.' *No use mentioning Wittgenstein*, Han thought. They would never have heard of him.

Yong poured measures for Li and Han into plastic water dispenser cups from the Ministry. 'This,' he explained, 'I don't need to tell you, is rare around here.' Yong held the bottle out, hovered over where the coffee table should be, glaring expectantly at a soldier who rushed the table into position then bowed as he backed away.

Han squeezed onto the sofa with the other two, and they all gently charged their fragile cups. The men knocked back their drinks, Han recoiled from the unfamiliar sharpness of strong liquor.

'I know I said my secretary found this building for you,' began Yong, landing a weighty palm on Han's thigh, 'but it was actually Secretary Sun who arranged it. I'm not sure he wanted you knowing, but I couldn't let his gesture go unnoticed.'

Han grimaced in acknowledgement. 'He's very generous.' He couldn't help sitting forward, taking anxious gulps from his cup every few moments, like a nervous man at a bar with nothing else to do with his hands. He threw his right leg over his left knee, foot rocking urgently in the air.

Yong was still talking, '...and just look at all the wonderful amenities you have here.'

There was silence as the men surveyed the desolate room, which, with its conspicuously blank walls, resembled an interrogation cell at *Inmin Boanseong*, the Department of Popular Security in Pyonganbuk province where Han had once witnessed an 'interview' of a man suspected of smuggling Western literature out from the Grand People's Study House in the national library and sharing it around friends. It was only after the interview that Han found out the book was *One Hundred Years of Solitude* by Gabriel García Márquez, a book that Han had read only a month before with permission as one of Pyongyang University's students. He went to bed that night toiling with the idea: what were the Party so scared people might find out if they were allowed to read what he was? And why did they trust him not to let subversive ideas corrupt him, but not the public? Why was it a perk of the job for a Party member, but a crime for another? Han had never found a reasonable answer to this.

'And you have some wonderful bars around here at the centre of town.' Yong reached over Li to tap Han on the leg. 'The women, comrade, you should see the women that go to the karaoke bars downtown.'

Han tried to hide his discomfort at Yong's ribald ways. 'I just want a quiet life, comrade. I find romance to be a distraction most of the time.'

'What do you mean?'

'Don't you find you end up performing – trying to appear intelligent and attractive – rather than being yourself. Sure, you might have a good time for a few nights, you can talk and eat together and share jokes, and maybe become intimate, but there's always this distance between you. Like a bridge you can never reach the other side of. Don't you find? And no matter how often it goes wrong, we keep trying. Isn't that strange? Like going back time and again to an empty well hoping this time, finally, there will be water.'

Yong laughed haughtily to let Han know how mistaken he was. 'Let me tell you, after these women are done screwing your brains out, and they light a cigarette for you and rub your belly, you won't be worrying about empty wells.'

Yong went into a lengthy waffling anecdote about the one time he met Kim Il-sung. To him, all other occasions of his life – the births of his children, his wedding, and numerous deaths of family members and spouses – were relegated to minor events in comparison to the few seconds he'd spent shaking hands and staring into Kim Il-sung's eyes, behind which lay The Greatest Thinker And General The World Had Ever Known. Li sat captivated, edged forward in his seat, as if some great answer were about to be relayed to him.

'The Great Leader told me a story from when he was a young soldier,' Yong said, getting to his feet for effect, swaying slightly as if he were standing on the deck of a slowly pitching ship. His speech was already starting to slur.

Han couldn't help but notice how close he was getting to the box of books.

'What was I saying? Oh yes, the Great Leader, he was once presented by a comrade with a book of such powerful ideas, it was said the author possessed a kind of genius never heard of before. Do you know what the Great Leader said? He said... comrade, authors are not possessed of genius. The author is merely a vessel inspired by the power of the people's ideas. So does the book not prove the Korean people to be a people made up entirely of geniuses?' Yong paused, waiting for the inevitable profundity of the Great Leader's words to sink in. He saw the Great Leader's face looking up at him from Han's box. He reached for the book on top. 'Speaking of genius: *A Great Mind*, a fine book indeed. A rare glimpse into another man's soul. I felt like I really knew him after reading this...'

Han rose up, knowing if Yong opened it it would reveal the book's false centre. In desperation Han sprang up out the sofa. 'You cretin!' he bellowed at a soldier laying down the last box at the living room door behind Yong. 'How dare you!'

The soldier froze, bent over the box, wondering what he had done.

'My god, man, what's going on?' Yong asked.

'My beloved portraits of the Great Leader and the Dear Leader are inside this box and this soldier is throwing it around like a dog's plaything.' Han loomed over the stricken soldier who cowered back into the hall. 'Forgive me, Chief Officer,' Han said, casually closing the lid on the box of books on his way past, leading the soldier out the room.

'I've completely forgotten what I was saying...' Yong complained, draining his whisky.

Han closed the living room door over and offered the soldier a carton of Commie Marlboros, whispering, 'Here, take these and we'll forget about the whole thing.'

The soldier, still dazed, pocketed them, his colleagues forming a terrified queue out in the hall wondering what had happened. Han caught the front door before it closed and waited until the men's footsteps had disappeared far down the corridor. He spied through a gap in the living room door's frame, seeing Yong collapsing back into the sofa, pouring Li more whisky though he still wasn't done with the last one.

Han sensed an opportunity to score some free points, yelling to the empty hallway, 'I don't care, Sergeant! Have you any idea the distress you have caused me? Those are the most precious things the Party has given me. The Party has seen fit to give you your job and this is how you treat their sacred property?' Han could see through the gap in the door how his speech was impressing the two men. 'It was reckless, *reckless*, I tell you. Get out of here. We have Party business to discuss.' He waved his arm up in disgust towards the front door, gently opening it, then slammed it shut as hard as he could. He walked back into the living room, head bowed in contrition, a blizzard of panic still swirling inside his chest. 'I'm sorry about that, Chief Officer. But I can hardly think of a worse start to my first day than finding some ignorant upstart breaking my beloved portraits. I'm particularly precious about them. The Party is everything to me. You understand, of course.'

Yong deferred. 'Of course. I rarely see such passion in young officers. You were right to give him a hiding.' Yong peered down into the bottom of his cup. He turned to Li and started to weep, the whisky having softened his faculties. 'It really... really was, the greatest moment of my life meeting him. I doubt I will have the privilege to feel such joy ever again in my life. Some nights my wife and I will sit and look at photos taken of the event, and we just hold each other, overcome with emotion like I am right now... and we are so happy, because we will always have that moment with the Great Leader.'

Li wiped his eyes – which were dry – as if he were crying too.

Yong hastily refilled all their cups, holding his out at the two men, getting back to his feet (stumbling as he did so), his body stiff with pride. 'To Kim Il-sung our Eternal President, and may he grant long life and superior knowledge to his fine son, the Dear Leader, General Secretary Kim Jong-il. May he lead us proudly and confidently into battle against the American imperial bastards and those that seek to destroy our wonderful country!'

Li got to his feet as well, raising his cup. 'To the everlasting glory of Korea!'

Han charged his cup with them, quieter than the other two. 'To a great mind.'

Yong lost his balance as he reached out for Han, grabbing the armrest to steady himself. 'Damn Scots,' he laughed, 'don't know how they get any work done...'

Li made as if he were feeling the effects too, pretending to stumble slightly. 'Yes, comrade, we should probably be on our way. I'm sure you have plenty to attend to for your first day.'

'Very well,' Yong drawled. 'Got to keep our discipline. It's the only thing between us and the graffiti-spraying troublemakers. I tell you, they're going to ruin it for everyone.'

Han nodded. 'I can't tell you how grateful I am for this welcoming party.'

Yong held out his hand, more for balance than anything else. 'You're going to make a fine ambassador, comrade.' He turned to leave, then twisted back to refill his cup one last time, taking it with him. He pointed at the bottle of Whyte and Mackay on the table. 'You can keep that.' Yong started singing the "Ode to General Kim Il-sung" as Li helped him to the elevator:

#'So dear to all our hearts, is our General's glorious name,
our own beloved Kim Il-sung of undying fame...'#

When the front door closed behind them, Han leaned his forehead against it and closed his eyes, listening for the elevator doors closing. Yong was starting another story. 'Li, did I ever tell you...' he exclaimed, giving the sentence several more syllables than it required, 'did I ever tell you about the General Party Conference of seventy-six? That was a great conference. The Great Leader was there and—'

Han went back to the living room, picking up the box of books to hide in the bedroom, revealing, underneath, a leather photograph album, and various framed photographs wrapped in old copies of *Rodong Sinmun*. He took one of them out, seeing his family standing in front of their old house, from Han's childhood, still vacant somewhere across the city. His mother and father had their arms around the teenage Han, who was dressed in his Young Socialist League military uniform, including hat, like a miniature General. His sister, Cho-hee, wore a dress that swamped her skinny body, the possibility of a smile rinsed from her face before the shutter could capture it. Cho-hee: it meant beauty and joy.

Han often thought about the importance of photographs. Behind each one he saw not only a memory – an image that captures Time, immovable, invincible and intensely pure – but also a meaning. The meaning in the photograph he was holding was nothing less than: *all of these people, whom I loved so deeply, are now dead.* These tools of memory – photographs, possessions of theirs; things irrevocably *connected* to them – were all he had to try and bring them back to life. The photograph was simply a means of missing their totality. He would close his eyes and conjure his family in his mind, trying to rebuild them, but some other memory or thought would always get in the way, and he would have to rebuild them all over again. He found, even with much time to himself and total concentration, he could never complete this task; nothing could make them live the way they used to all those years ago, watching them move and hearing them speak. He envied those Western families with their family video footage documented so extensively (and flippantly) on their phones and computers. Perhaps, he thought, that would have gotten him a little closer to them. Photographs were all he had.

He took the box of books into the bedroom where there was a single wardrobe cut into the wall, and no other cupboards. If someone from the Ministry or police came it would be the first place they checked. Walking back across the room, a floorboard underneath gave an upward creak, sounding like a question. He rocked back and forth over it, toe-to-heel, then noticed the carpet hadn't been fixed between the wall and skirting board. It curled up round the edges like the cover flap of a well-read book. He peeled the carpet back and found he could finger the creaking floorboard up, revealing a perfect hiding spot, dry and deep.

He opened the box and started filing away his Dickens, Austen, Kafka, Shakespeare and the rest, keeping the books by Kim Il-sung and Kim Jong-il on top.

'I thought we weren't going to make it there,' he said to them, before fitting the floorboard back in place. There wasn't time to unpack anything else: he knew an Englishman, Ben Campbell, and an American, Hal Huckley, would be arriving at the airport in only an hour.

He gathered up the dossiers he had assembled on them – notes scribbled liberally in the margins – putting them inside a briefcase that looked much too small for him when he carried it, along with his copy of *A Great Mind*. He knew what was waiting for him: as always, he had done his research.

'An Invisible Cage; A Man Of The World; A Disappointing Time For Humanity'

Sunan Airport Terminal, 15ᵗʰ December

Han sat in the back seat of a six-seater minibus outside the terminal building, the driver, Mr So, gripping the steering wheel as if still driving. Han was consulting the itinerary in his lap, circling on a map places of particular Party interest, trying to blink away Yong's morning whisky, and the ordeal with the books.

His deputy, Mr Ryong, as the visitors would call him, sat up front, watching the foreign tourists be quickly hustled on to a bus bound for Yanggakdo Hotel, their faces aglow at this strange new land.

'I don't know why we let them in at all,' Ryong growled. 'It used to be the Westerners would come grovelling about the sorry state of their leaders' views on Korea. They used to thank me for showing them the truth. Not anymore. Always with their damn questions...'

Outsiders often made the mistake of calling North Korea 'Stalinist' or 'Maoist'. But the Party P&A Dept. had been clever not to try and convince the people of things they knew to be demonstrably false (viz. "We have had the biggest ever corn crop this year!", as farmers surveyed ruined, blackened fields like in the Soviet Union's most famished days). The Party were wise to the fact such lies only breed contempt, and stoke discontent. Instead, the Party couched their language, using phrases like "economic difficulties" instead of "famine." Anything that couldn't be proven by witnesses (that when Kim Jong-il was born the birds had sang in Korean), that was when the outlandish, CS Lewis-esque imaginations of the P&A Dept. really kicked in. Sometimes the only thing fact and fiction have in common is suspension of disbelief.

Ryong was still venting: '...and they never speak the language.'

Han was too involved with the itinerary to look up. 'As someone with a translator's degree, I would have thought that last one would please you.'

'Please me? They come here to laugh at us. We don't need them, these foreign bastards.'

'Would you calm down? They told me at the Ministry you were a professional.'

'I *am* a professional,' Ryong sulked.

'We're guides, with a task of presenting our great country in order to further ties with the outside. It's not our job to air petty grievances.'

'Why do they even come here?'

'I suppose they want a glimpse of what few get to see.'

Ryong looked at Han with hopeful eyes. 'The most glorious socialist regime left on the planet? The full majesty of the Great Leader Kim Il-sung's socialist project?'

So peered back at them in the rear view mirror.

'Of course,' Han said. 'The most glorious regime on the planet.' He felt So's steady glare strip-mining him. There was always someone watching or listening. 'We should stand outside,' Han told Ryong. 'They'll be here soon.'

Ryong made a fuss of rushing round to open then close the door for Han, making a sweeping gesture of his hand directing him out.

With mild embarrassment Han rubbed where he had shaved earlier (only required above his top lip and the point of his chin). 'Thank you, Ryong, but you don't need to keep doing that. You're five years older than me.' Han forgot that, in Pyongyang, elders took a back seat to Party ranking.

Ryong stood slightly behind Han, arms behind his back, trying to look tough. 'I must follow the rules, comrade.' He thought of himself as one of the old guard, those grumpy bastards in brown military uniforms whose sole currency was how many times they had witnessed one of the Great Leader's 'on-the-spot' guidance sessions, where he bestowed apparently profound advice (normally suggested to him beforehand by experts in the field) to workers and farmers. Ryong wasn't interested in power, he just wanted to hang on as best he could to its slipstream, before his unremarkable career fizzled out. He envied those intelligence officials in smart suits and ties, with their solid postures and disarming smiles. People like Han.

Ryong practiced his stance in front of a mirror in his ramshackle apartment, but he could never exert their authority or menace, no matter how many different tie-and-jacket combinations he tried. This was primarily because of his large ears, big enough to catch a tailwind, and how he stooped when walking: tall, but with no power in the torso. He had the receding hairline of a tax accountant who dreamt all day of retirement. Ryong was under no illusions he would never be taken seriously in the Party. People like him had nothing else to help ascend the ladder, than total, unquestioning loyalty.

Han spoke like a father does to a delicate child. 'Speaking of rules, Mr Ryong, if anything... uncomfortable comes up, just talk to me calmly. In Korean. And don't let them know there's a disagreement or disturbance. If they ask anything rude, say the question cannot be rendered into Korean. Then take a note of which one said it. I'll need it for my report.'

'Yes, Mr Han.'

'I'll be doing most of the talking in English, but if something comes up then don't be afraid to speak. I'm not a dictatorial boss.'

'I'll keep a close eye on the Yank, comrade.'

Han tilted his head to the side, faking weighing up his elder's approach. 'In my experience, comrade, it's better to treat visitors from the West like friends, they're more agreeable than if you pick arguments. If they are nice, we'll show them more.'

'Very well. I'm sorry I missed your welcoming party this morning, Mr Han. I only found out about it afterwards. Nobody tells me anything around here!'

'You didn't miss anything.'

'Is it true Chief Officer Yong got drunk? I overheard the secretaries say he came back to the Ministry stinking of whisky.'

Han lit a Commie Marlboro, lingering on the first drag. *This is going to be a long week*, he thought. 'An impertinent suggestion. Chief Officer Yong is a respected Party official. What secretaries said that? What are their names?'

Ryong thought better of it. 'Forget I mentioned it. I must be mistaken.'

Ben and Hal came out the terminal exit, struggling with the sticky, manual front doors. Coming out of the dark terminal, Ben had to shield his eyes from the sudden burst of light. Hal had on his sunglasses, and was holding his camera, ready to get to work.

Ben presented himself first, bowing politely, trying to appear as deferential as possible. 'It's so nice to meet you, Mr Han. I'm Ben Campbell. This is Hal Huckley.'

Hal shook hands whilst pointing the camera at Han.

'Hello, I'm Mr Han. Welcome to Democratic People's Republic of Korea! We also have Mr Ryong with us, for extra assistance. For translations. Language can be sometimes tricky.'

Ryong was surprised, and impressed, at how easily Han morphed into his Official persona.

Ben was taken aback at how pleasant Han was, the charming kind smile of a next-door neighbour, rather than some brutish instrument of the State.

Still smiling, Han said, 'Thank you. I will take your passports now.'

Ben and Hal exchanged looks; this hadn't been discussed. Ben was first to make tentative enquiries. 'Our passports? Is our paperwork not in order?'

'Is just procedure,' Ryong chimed in, arm extended, palm up.

Hal tried to make Han feel at ease, wrapping a stocky, tanned arm (the hairs still bleached from Sudan) around his tiny neck. 'No problem, Mr Han.' Hal turned to Ben and shrugged, handing his passport to Ryong. 'The man says it's just procedure.'

Ben gave Ryong his passport too, who forwarded them to Han.

Ryong mumbled to Han in Korean, looking Hal up and down, *'He looks like a Jew.'*

Han stuck to his plan, giving no hint of discontent as he spoke. *'I don't want to hear any of that talk, comrade. Now get in the van and be quiet.'*

'Yes, Mr Han, sorry, Mr Han,' Ryong said, bowing.

'Will we go to the hotel first?' Ben asked, getting into the van after Hal.

'Soon,' Han said cryptically. 'Our itinerary will arrive us there. First, we stop off somewhere special on the way. It is most special place for all Koreans, we must go there first for great honour.'

When their door was slid closed, Hal gently tried the handle – just to check. It was locked.

They were now officially guests in the hermit kingdom.

So rallied around the streets of Pyongyang, muttering insults about his countrymen's driving after each sudden swerve and toot of the horn. The wardens were mere white blurs at the interchanges. Ben and Hal grabbed at their seatbelts, their buttocks tensing at each crossroad, awaiting an imminent collision.

Han, sitting up front with Ryong, the engine covering their voices, said to him, *'I'll bet you all the coal in Chongjin they're not tourists.'*

'How can you tell?' Ryong looked back at them.

'Don't turn round!' Han said, kicking Ryong's foot, unseen. *'They're not sharing the camera for one thing. Tourists always take turns. And only journalists can pack so economically for a week-long trip. Tourists, they fill their suitcases with extra clothes, cosmetics, luxuries.'*

Ryong was practically spinning in his seat. *'We must report this to the Ministry at once! This is an outrage! The foreign swine...!'*

'Calm down, comrade, this is how it works. It happened all the time in Pyonganbuk province. We give them a little of what they want, and in return we get what we want. Which is exactly what we're doing right now.'

The few Pyongyang buildings that had been constructed in the past quarter century seemed based on blueprints and designs circa the Iron Curtain's height. The citizens walked around oblivious to any sense that time had stopped moving forward. Not so much the bird that has come to love its cage, but rather the bird that isn't aware it's in a cage at all.

Ben became aware of a weird dynamic playing out up front in the minibus, with Mr Han and Mr Ryong trying to outdo each other in some game of who loved the country and honoured its history more, but the pair of them seemed to be performing more for Mr So's benefit, as if he were simultaneously the least and most important member of the entourage. He kept clocking Ben and Hal in the rear view mirror, giving them scary Socialist eyes.

Ben shouted forward to Han. 'Have you been doing this long, Mr Han? You're very young.'

Han, not wearing his seatbelt, spun around in his seat, unperturbed by the NASCAR manner in which So accelerated through tiny gaps in the morning traffic. 'I been working outside the city for some years. Show tourists round our factories, collectivised farms. I been to sites we will visit in your stay many times.'

'What about here in Pyongyang?'

He turned back around, as if embarrassed. 'First time for me showing tourist staying in Pyongyang.'

'And you live here?'

Han confirmed with a sharp nod then remembered to smile again. His smiles seemed confined to the area immediately around his mouth; his eyes never lit up, like his heart played no part in the action. 'Yes, I live here. But please, is not about me. We will be arriving at first destination shortly, very exciting. Please note the picture ahead of our Great Leader Comrade Kim Il-sung. The slogan read,' Han swung his fist enthusiastically, '"We will unite Korea through hard work!" For 'zample, in nineteen seventy-eight, or as we name it here the year of *Juche* sixty-seven, the Great Leader started a fine revolution in our mining industry through a series of genius methods...'

Han talked without stopping for the next five minutes, on the strength of the Workers' Party, the vagaries of history that had constantly conspired against the Korean people, the corruption in the United Nations and its persecution of the DPRK.

Hal whispered, 'Why are we going so fast?'

Ben's head flicked from left to right – not wanting to miss a thing – transfixed by what might be going through the mind of everyday North Koreans. Were they really as clueless about the outside world as he had been told? Did they really believe the great evil South was home to wild dogs rampaging through desolate streets, hunting orphans for food? The reason for So's terrifying speed quickly became apparent. Ben tried to provide commentary to Hal's video that sounded like casual conversation, using euphemisms. 'Oh look at the little children, Hal.'

Hal zoomed in on them as they zipped past the shoeless wraiths, crouching down in the grass, picking through it for something edible.

Ryong was clearly agitated. *'We shouldn't have come this way.'*

Han was more stoic. *'There's nothing we can do. We can't exactly put blinds over the windows.'*

'It's not the worst idea in the world.'

Hal pointed to the other side of the road, towards the Taedong River that ploughed through the capital – the widest river Hal had ever seen in a major city, though there was nothing travelling up or down it, no boats docked or even in sight. Old men sat on the dockside, their legs dangling over the edge, lines twitchless, nets empty.

Han spoke to So without looking at him. *'Take us to the Arch of Triumph. I want them to see all the great monuments.'*

'Yes, Mr Han,' So replied, swinging a left.

'No, no, right,' sighed Han, the minibus now stuck on a long avenue he hadn't included in his route. *'There's graffiti down here! You told me you read the manifest!'*

'But you said they can't read Korean, Mr Han,' So protested.

Hal pointed the camera at the passing alleyways and dark lanes.

Han relaxed in his seat as he saw the wall had been painted over, a long white rectangle on the brickwork where the slogan had been.

Before the end of the street they reached another monument: one of a group of soldiers thrusting their weapons over their heads, grenades hanging from their mouths, determined expressions on their faces. Behind the soldiers were farmers holding pitchforks, factory workers with hammers and wrenches, all huddled around a North Korean flag that swept like the tail of a dragon, rippled in the wind as the people charged forward. To where was unclear. Victory hadn't been represented.

'I think Mr Han's directing the driver,' Ben told Hal. 'Must be taking us the scenic route to try and impress us.'

So made a right onto an empty boulevard – the correct one this time – where a huge roundabout encircled what looked like the Arc de Triomphe on growth hormones. Ryong waved his hand excitedly at them. 'Gentlemen, please, much excitement, please!'

'The Arch of Triumph,' announced Han, pointing at the monument ahead. 'Famous landmark in Pyongyang, to celebrate Korea fighting off the Japanese oppressors.' Though Han's English was very good by most international standards, he had a habit of stressing irregular parts of English words – op*press*ors became *op*pressors – giving his commentary the occasional feel of an early Mac computer program that could technically read out single words at a time, but whose rhythms became stressed by complete sentences. 'It is a place of great pride for us,' then Han hurriedly suggested, 'please do take many pictures, fine structure.'

Ben agreed dryly, 'It's very beautiful, Mr Han.'

The arch was surrounded by pristine marzipan-like gardens, and hedgerows that looked like they had been trimmed with nose-hair clippers by an expert in topiary. There wasn't a single piece of litter in sight.

They took in mural after mural of Kim Il-sung giving speeches to swarms of loving Korean children waving flags (his mouth always hanging open as if in mid-song), Kim Il-sung applauding a crowd of coal miners, Kim Il-sung handing out flowers with soldiers gritting their teeth in the background... all in the brightest Powell and Pressburger technicolour (reds and blues seemed much deeper than other colours). Ben couldn't help but notice the dullness of everything else around these murals. The rest of the city had the colour and contrast turned all the way down like a malfunctioning TV. Everything a kind of matted grey and dull gloomy green, the colour of dampness.

'We've been down this street already,' Ben said, sitting back now, getting restless and bored at Han's already repetitive rhetoric.

Hal recognised the old men fishing. 'We passed those guys ten minutes ago. Still haven't caught jack.'

So kept swinging lefts and rights, until they had taken in each major landmark Pyongyang had to offer, except the biggest one of them all.

As soon as Ben and Hal had taken their first tentative steps out the minibus, Ryong pounced on Hal who had his camera at the ready.

He pointed accusingly at Hal's face. 'You cannot take picture of the Great Leader Kim Il-sung until we say so, understand! You wait until we get to top of stairs and we will instruct you.' He then shunted into Korean, '*This is the most sacred place for Koreans, you long-nose, you swine…*'

Hal put his hands up in surrender. 'What did I do, Mr Han?'

Ben pushed down Hal's arm holding the camera. 'He's saying don't point it at the statue yet, Hal.'

'I'm not! I'm not!' he protested.

Han rushed around to pull Ryong back. '*That's it, I've had it with you, you crazy fool. Wait in the car.*' Han turned as if to take Ben and Hal off up the towering staircase himself, only for Ryong to reach out to stop him.

'*Please, Mr Han, you're not allowed.*'

Han spoke without aggression. '*How dare you question me, a senior officer. Do you think your anger is impressing me?*'

'*Forgive me, Mr Han. But I have orders.*'

'*Orders for me?*'

Ryong didn't seem sure in his own mind who to be loyal to first, so he did what all good Party members did in such a dilemma: he repeated what he had been told, quoting official department memoranda. '"*Two minders must be present with tourists at all times.*"'

'*Am I not to be trusted with the foreigners? Is this how it works in Pyongyang?*'

'*Yes, sir.*'

'*Who gave you these orders?*'

'*Direct from comrade Secretary Sun.*'

'*He thinks I will tell lies about our great country, is that it? Or accept bribes?*'

Ryong stared at the ground. '*You do not know this?*' It wasn't normal for Party officials to acknowledge openly, as Han had, the levels of subterfuge suspected among close colleagues on a daily basis. '*It is to ensure security*.'

Han snorted with derisive laughter. He knew the line was straight from Sun's mouth.

Hal lowered the still-recording camera away from the guides, he and Ben acting like they had no interest in what the argument was about. 'Mr Ben and Mr Hal,' Han called out, 'we will now climb the stairs with Mr Ryong to the Mansudae Grand Monument.'

So remained in the minibus, talking on a mobile phone, reporting back to Secretary Sun (as instructed) on everyone's behaviour. To So's surprise Sun was more interested in Han than the tourists.

As the four men climbed the stairs the top of a bronze statue came into view, then an outstretched hand, then a torso, then legs the size of Redwood trees. By these giant feet that could have trampled a VW Beetle a crouching brigade of tiny women brushed the immaculate concrete paving slabs with brooms, some down on their knees, making sure the square surrounding the statue was clear of anything resembling so much as a grain of dirt. They worked tirelessly, egged on by the enthusiasm of the woman next to them, and the woman next to them, and so on; the group sweating from pressure to be seen working hard by each other. The arrival of Han's tour group did little to relieve their largely imaginary load.

Han had practiced his lines faithfully, confident he could perform them casually, like a tragic actor doing comedy. 'This statue was built in honour of the Great Leader Comrade Kim Il-sung's sixtieth birthday in nineteen seventy-two. He is our Eternal President. He work always for the people, and when he die...' Han pumped his fist in a downward stabbing motion, 'great tragedy!'

Ryong trailed close behind, always within earshot of Han.

Ben tried his best not to sound abrasive, or make Han sound absurd. 'Mr Han, do you think it's strange having a President who is dead?' Ben made the mistake of thinking that simply saying such a thing out loud would render the insanity of the idea obvious.

Han gave his best a-smile-but-not-a-smile. 'When the Great

Leader Kim Il-sung died, the Great Marshal of Korean people, thousands of cranes came down from heaven to lift his body up. But the cries of millions of Korean stop them, and they leave his body with us forever.'

'So he's a god?'

'Not really a god. Just... a Great One. He have a mind that no one else can be capable of.'

Ben looked up the length of the statue, as God-like as he had ever seen. The cleaners never raised their heads from their work, everyone in the surrounding area all dutiful reverence. And like God, the Party would claim generosity on your behalf, as long as you bowed and prayed, night and day. 'You mentioned the *Juche* calendar earlier. That's his own calendar, isn't it?'

'Is true. We calculate *Juche* Year from when the Great Leader was born in nineteen twelve. So we are now in *Juche* Year...' Han paused to allow Ben to work it out.

'Ninety-nine.'

'Is right. We do this to honour his memory.'

'And what about Kim Jong-il, the current President? There seems to be less about him, and more for his father.'

'The Great Leader gave birth to our great country. So when he die, we mourn for three years before the Dear Leader Kim Jong-il take over. Because it was so sad for us. We love the Dear Leader just as much, and if Kim Jong-il die...' Han broke off, as if the possibility were too tragic to contemplate, sensing Ryong close behind. 'It would be terrible for us. In time there will be as many statue for Kim Jong-il as his father. But we not like to think of losing the Dear Leader so soon.'

Han led them over to a flower stall where it was "suggested" they might purchase flowers to leave at the feet of the statue, as a mark of respect. Ben and Hal picked out their flowers and handed over their dollars, the first time they had been alone together since leaving the airport.

Hal let out an hour's build-up of absurdity, whispering, 'Goddamn, man, this place is fucking crazy!'

The flower seller – dressed in a fluorescent yellow robe – made no eye contact as she handed them their flowers. She was humble and melancholy as if the Great Leader had only recently died. There were no options as far as flowers went: all the bunches were cut exactly the same length, five flowers in each.

'The little one, Mr Ryong, he doesn't like me,' Hal said. 'He had his finger all up in my face.'

Ben deflected. 'Don't worry about it. It's just because you're American. Come on, you Yankee bastard. Let's go worship a dead guy.'

Han and Ryong consulted one another while Ben and Hal bought their flowers. *'What do you think they're saying over there?'* asked Ryong.

'That we disagree on how to proceed. That one of us is behaving like a child. That one of us is confusing anger with patriotism.'

'Mr Han, I...' He broke off. *'I've been unprofessional, comrade, I apologise. I just wanted to show you how much I love my country.'*

'I know you think my promotion should have been yours.' He put his hands up to halt Ryong's protestations. *'It's alright, comrade. I know you've been a loyal and dedicated Party member for many years. And I hope to write up many appraisals of your work in the next few months. My modest success doesn't have to mean your suffering. I hope we can be not only close colleagues, but friends too.'*

Ryong smiled, beating his hand comfortingly over his heart. *'I would like this very much, comrade.'*

Han suddenly found himself feeling like the subordinate. Loneliness had a habit of making this so. *'I don't know anyone else in Pyongyang, you see.'*

'No one, comrade? You are a senior Party member. Don't you have a girl at home?'

Mildly embarrassed, Han considered lying. Seeing as he spent much of his time at night in bed imagining a great beauty lying next to him, it didn't seem like much of a leap. But he thought better of it. Having to talk about a girl he didn't have would only make him feel worse. *'No. I don't need anyone,'* he replied bluntly.

'A man of the world,' Ryong said. *'Me? I need a girl around. My last girlfriend, I swear she knew me better than I knew myself.'*

Han wasn't ready to get into such talk. It would only depress him. '*We must really get back*,' he said, setting off for Ben and Hal. 'Gentlemen!... Now we must pay our respects to the Great Leader, is very important.'

Ben and Hal noted what had at first been a suggestion was now an obligation. They walked to the foot of the statue, where Han pointed carefully where to stand, and exactly where to leave their flowers – placing them on top of a pile three rows deep and four layers thick. The men stepped back and Ben bowed with Han. Ben cursed himself inside as he rose. It was only for Han's benefit that he went through with it, not wanting to embarrass him or get him in trouble.

Hal was still standing upright.

Han mimicked to him what to do. 'Please, Mr Hal, you must bow too.'

'I'd rather not, Mr Han,' Hal said simply.

'Hal...' Ben warned him.

Han felt his face burning, sensing the cold stares from military officials at the top steps. They could see something was going wrong. 'Mr Hal, everyone must bow. Is crucial.'

In the background Ryong muttered under his breath. '*I'll throw you out the country for this, Yankee.*' Then he set off after him, swearing loudly at Hal: '*Jongganna saekki*!'

'Just do it, Hal,' Ben pleaded quietly to him.

'Sorry, Mr Han, Mr Ryong,' Hal said, pointing to his ear. 'I misheard. I thought we were to bow one at a time.'

'No,' Ryong snapped. 'Together.'

'I'll bow, I'll bow.' He bowed slowly and deeply.

Han noticed, with some relief, the military officials walking back down the stairs. 'Mr Ben. Mr Hal. We can now take you to your hotel.' He turned to make his way back to the minibus, not realising Ryong was standing saluting the statue, thinking the military officials were watching him. Ben and Hal were momentarily alone.

'Not exactly the time to make an ideological stand, Hal,' said Ben. 'You can't do that. You're gonna get Mr Han in trouble.'

Hal was unperturbed. 'Relax, Campbell. I was just testing their boundaries. It's handy to know.'

'Mr Ryong threatened to throw you out the country. Do you know what he called you?'

'What?'

'It basically means child of a female slave.'

This seemed to entertain Hal immensely. 'I've been called worse. Did you make out what that argument back at the bus was about?'

'Something about security. Can you play it back for me?' Ben was struggling with the more jagged, aggressive brand of Korean they spoke in the North. He had learned the language from an ex-girlfriend whilst a junior correspondent on the Seoul desk at *BBC World Service*. In the end he had become particularly adept at the Korean for 'When are you coming home?', 'This isn't working anymore' and 'When are you moving out?' To Western ears there was a kind of anger in how North Koreans spoke, as if perpetually offended or put out.

Hal inserted some earphones into the camera socket. As he searched back through a twitching still of the pavement during Han and Ryong's argument on the viewfinder, he wondered aloud, 'It doesn't look like they were arranging after-hour drinks.'

'It must be something to do with Mr Han.' Ben played the section back, pressing the earphones hard against his ear to cover the military music that had suddenly started up over the loudspeaker system.

Han, at the top of the staircase, now realising he had left the men alone, came rushing back. 'Mr Ben, Mr Hal, is your camera broke?'

Hal smiled, trying to wave him away. 'Fine, Mr Han, thank you. Just checking audio levels.'

Audio levels, thought Han with a smirk. Definitely journalists.

'What are they saying?' asked Hal.

Ben squinted. 'Something about Mr Ryong. He's here to watch Mr Han...'

'Why would they do that?'

Ben sighed and closed his eyes. 'So we can't bribe him. That's what Mr Han says, anyway. Party loyalty's like a currency at their level.'

As Han descended the stairs, afternoon smog smothered the sad, empty buildings, all of Pyongyang stretched out before him. As thick snowflakes started to fall, he turned his collar up, his shoulders hunched, head hanging low against the wind. Already he didn't want to be in Pyongyang anymore. It felt like he had made a grave mistake coming back.

Hal said, 'I wonder what he's going home to.'

Ben unplugged the earphones, the military music building to a crescendo. 'There's no way these guys can really believe all this, can they?'

The men surveyed the square from the top of the staircase, seeing Ryong corralling the cleaning ladies into saluting the statue of the dead Eternal President.

Koryo Hotel, Pyongyang

The last stop of Ben and Hal's whirlwind opening day was the forty-five-storey Koryo Hotel, where they would be staying the rest of the week. Most of the money spent on the Koryo had clearly gone into the marble-laden lobby, tasteful spotlights shining on yet more mountain-range murals.

'Oil painter must be a popular profession,' Hal noted.

The Koryo had only four other guests, part of a Norwegian tour group dressed in red puffy jackets with 'NORGE' written in white under the back collars like a visiting Winter Olympic team. They huddled in the marble lobby, lamenting the fact that three of their party had been booked into the Yanggakdo Hotel across town, situated on an Alcatraz-like island. There were no problems with tourists wandering away without their guides there. The Koryo Norwegians had been placed on forty-four with Ben and Hal. Every other floor was vacant.

Ben and Hal checked in, with a little language-barrier assistance from Han, who received a series of borderline-sycophantic bows from the receptionists. The presence of three security officers taking it in turns to strut unsubtly past Ben and Hal like they were likely shoplifter-teens at a mall wasn't helping Ben and Hal's queasy paranoia. After each officer made a pass, they reconvened at the lobby doors and put together their pieces of the conversational jigsaw. Their conclusion being: there's no way those guys are just tourists; they need monitoring. Hal's loud Boston accent did little to dampen their prejudices.

'You like your camera,' Ryong said to Hal, while Ben signed some check-in paperwork.

'Sure do, my friend,' Hal replied.

'Most tourists I see don't use camera as much as you. You hold it well. Like professional.' Ryong stared him down, waiting for him to blink. 'You go on many holidays together?'

'Not very often,' Ben answered. 'We're both busy working most of the time.'

Ryong tilted his head. 'Ah yes? What is your jobs?'

After a pause, Hal said, 'Public relations.'

'Very good,' said Ryong, pretending to know what it meant.

Ben was troubled by the small print of the paperwork. 'What does this mean?' he asked Han, pointing to a paragraph written in Chosongul.

'Is just reminder you not allowed to leave hotel grounds without a guide,' Han said.

'*Mr Han, we have adequate security,*' the receptionist said, gesturing to the Mall Cops prowling around outside with radios on their hips.

'*Last month there were six reported incidents of wandering tourists without their guides. They don't cross that door without me. Understand?*'

'Is everything OK?' Ben asked.

Han gave a firm shake of his head and passed Ben their room key. 'Is all in order.'

Hal was busy taking a light off one of the Mall Cops, enjoying the relaxed smoking laws.

'See you tomorrow morning, Mr Hal,' Han called to him.

'Bright and early, please,' added Ryong, pointing to his wrist where a watch would have been.

'Thank you, Mr Han, Mr Ryong,' said an exhausted Ben. As they trumped wearily to the elevators, Ben told Hal, 'He gave the hotel our passports.'

Hal didn't care anymore. 'What does it matter. I need a drink.'

Then a boy of around nineteen, a porter, came running after them, shouting, 'Mizzer Cambo, Mizzer Hucklee!'

'Oh Christ,' Hal sighed, 'what now?'

The porter relieved the pair of their rucksacks as Ben said, 'Thank you, but you really don't need to.'

The porter insisted. 'Is necessary.'

The elevator had piped-in military music, what Ben recognised as the national anthem, 'The Patriotic Song', all tinny brass that sounded like it was recorded on a small Casio keyboard, gruff vocals triumphant and unwavering. The elevator vibrated mercilessly all the way up to forty-four, as if all of Pyongyang was being sucked dry just to keep it going. Hal pictured the lights in the lobby dimming as they went up. The porter had also made the curious decision to stand and face the men rather than the elevator door – part of some obscure Koryo-porter protocol. Apparently guests couldn't even be trusted to stand in an elevator without supervision. Each time Ben or Hal made fleeting eye contact the boy renewed his smile and gave a nod, as if he had answered some hotel-logistical question. Forty-four floors had never felt so high.

A camera much too large for such an elevator hung from a top corner, leaving no blind spots.

Ben wondered if there was an unseen microphone next to the lens. He couldn't really be sure. Anything felt possible.

Apropos of nothing, the porter asked Hal, 'America?'

'Yep, America,' Hal answered.

The boy smiled and gave an enthusiastic thumbs-up. 'Cool, man.'

Hal couldn't help thinking how odd it was for a country to have such reverence and hatred for America at the same time. The porter looked at him like he was a celebrity. Or an alien.

*

The room they would be sharing, room 442, was stoically adequate in an East German kind of way. The room almost shrugged at them as if to say, I'm a bedroom with two beds, a bathroom, a television, and a window, what more do you want? An overpowering smell of bleach emanated from the bathroom. The carpets had a sickly floral pattern on them, as if someone had gotten the carpet and wallpaper orders mixed up. The porter overcame his tentative English by walking round the double bedroom, pointing at appliances and switches, dismissing the failing light switches with a desultory wave.

Ben's attempts to tip the boy US$10 were rebuffed with near-violent refusals – until Hal intervened, snatching the bill out Ben's hand and shoving it into the boy's top pocket, then made a 'Shhh' gesture.

The boy said, 'I cannot accept thank you,' then bowed at Ben and Hal in turn before closing the door behind him.

'Nice kid,' Hal said, then noticed the bill being slid back under the door, and the boy's muffled repetition of, 'I cannot accept thank you!'

Hal went to the window and started shooting – their first unmonitored view of North Korea: a largely still frontier, building cranes in suspended animation across the city, where construction had been temporarily abandoned, pillars of smoke churning out of towering chimneys. Hal whispered, 'He thinks we're journalists. Mr Ryong. I can tell.'

'It was always going to be at the back of their minds,' Ben said with resignation, switching on the television out of habit. He flicked through the five available channels, finding only one picture, nothing but static on the rest. He sat transfixed by the State television, filling the room with military cries and trebly voiceovers of glorious Korean victories in World War Two. Every day was Korean History Day on state TV. Huge columns of soldiers goose-stepped together through Pyongyang Square, lorries of missiles ambling behind them, the weapons angled as if they might be fired at any moment, cut together poorly with shots of citizens applying gas masks, multi-coloured slogans flashing on the screen, saying

당의 령도따라 내 나라 위해 힘차게 일해나가자

('LET'S DO AS THE PARTY TELLS US')

and

최후의 승리를 위하여 한목숨 바치자

('LET ME SACRIFICE MY LIFE FOR THE FINAL
VICTORY')

Ben looked out the window next to Hal, an industrial smog lowering on the city. 'So what do you make of the argument with the guides?' Hal asked.

'Mr Han seems nice. A little guarded. It's going to be tough to get him to open up. Keeping Mr Ryong out the way's going to be harder.'

'Ryong's probably got where he is with brute loyalty. Always trying to be the one who shouts loudest at parades, that sort of thing.'

'I bet he's done his fair share of denouncing over the years. It was the same in East Germany with the Stasi. I read about a woman there, she was so notorious for denouncing friends and neighbours of hers in order to fast-track herself up the Party system, when she showed up for dances or drinks the room would empty. They're trained from the youngest age to spy on people. It's a good way of social climbing. I don't know, maybe Mr Ryong has his eye on Mr Han's job. He's getting on a bit to still be someone's assistant.'

Down below, tiny figures crouched in the long grass beside the Taedong River, along with dozens of people fishing.

Hal opened the window and stuck his head out as far as he could. 'It's so quiet. I mean listen to it. It's five o'clock in the middle of the week, and how many cars do you see? There's just nothing going on out there.'

He turned the camera round on Ben, who set about inspecting the room for bugging devices, checking behind the large mirror on the wall, opening drawers, flipping the mattress, tapping light bulb sockets for hollow points, anything he could think of. After finding nothing he started unpacking, only taking out anything he needed for the next twelve hours. Spending years in seedy hotels in war zones meant that if he needed to, he could walk into his room, zip up his bag and leave immediately. The routine had once saved his life in Haiti, after local elections went sour and the people turned on foreign press they were told were responsible for the corrupt result. Ben and Hal hightailed it from their hotel and were on a plane within thirteen minutes. Hal had counted every one of them.

'So Mr Ben, what did you bring into North Korea...' Hal corrected himself. 'Sorry – the DPRK?'

Ben reached into the waistband of his trousers, pulling out a copy of *Nineteen Eighty-four* from under his t-shirt. 'Just a little tourist guide. It's quite old, but most of the information is still correct.' He lay down on the bed, propping his head up on the backboard with thin pillows. He mouthed almost silently, 'Where should I leave it when we're gone during the day?'

'Put it in the bag. With the camera batteries.'

'We'd better take the bag with us. God knows what'll go on in here while we're gone.'

'Good call.' Hal lowered the camera a shade. 'You want to try a piece?'

Ben and Hal's *REBEL*-routine was well engrained by now, with Ben speaking to Hal as if the camera wasn't there. He preferred his words to come over as casual observations from a softly-spoken, impartial friend, free of the official correspondent's theatrical gravitas he had come to despise when reporting from Afghanistan and Iraq in the early frenzy of the War on Terror; those wannabe warriors-with-microphones in their helmets and battle fatigues embedded with the coalition troops.

'You hear so much about what it's like, but until you get here you can't fathom how controlled it all is. The drive from the airport to our hotel had obviously been arranged by our guide, Mr Han. You're in charge of nothing: you've got no say in where you go, what you do, what you photograph... Everything is controlled. We knew it was going to be like this though. We think our minders know we're journalists, but we were told before we came that they're used to it. That if we follow their rules, they'll give us a little more freedom as the week goes on. We'll need to see how that works out. Mr Han is in charge with his deputy Mr Ryong, but they don't know that I understand Korean, and they've been having conversations in front of us about how to handle the tour, and what they should tell us. Which is really weird for me. Like having people talk about you while you're in the same room. Normally we'd have to wait and get back home for a translator to look over our B roll, so it feels like we have the upper hand on our minders. For now anyway.'

Hal held up his hand for a pause and lowered the camera. 'Don't you find it a bit hokey reading that here?'

Ben sat on the end of the bed and signalled for him to keep filming. 'I swore I wouldn't bring this up on camera, but I was reading this back in Shenyang,' he held the book up, 'and came across this passage. I know it's a cliché to talk about Orwell in North Korea, but they make it impossible not to.' Ben opened to his marked page and started reading. '"Always the eyes watching you and the voice enveloping you. Asleep or awake, working or eating, indoors or out of doors, in the bath or in bed — no escape. Nothing was your own except the few cubic centimetres inside your skull." He was a great journalist Orwell, people don't remember that enough. And the reason we've come here is to question what's really going on, what *has* gone on; to question what the Party and our minders want outsiders like us to see. That's why they're letting more tourists in these days: isolation hasn't worked. The people near the borders have radios that can illegally pick up South Korean frequencies, and what the Party tells them about the world is starting to clash heavily with what they actually experience. So North Korea wants to engage with people like us now, that's why our minders are so important to the Party. And we've got to make sure we keep asking them difficult questions.'

Hal didn't give his regular 'OK' sign, turning to start filming out the window again.

'Was that OK?' Ben asked.

'Fine,' Hal said distantly, with his back to him.

Ben flicked the pages of his book back and forth before tossing it down beside him. 'You know... we're only going to scratch the surface of what life is really like here.'

Hal swooped his head back in from outside and switched the camera off. 'Don't.' He tousled his hair in agitation.

'What?'

'I've seen that look on your face before.'

'What face?'

'The same face when you said we should get out the Green Zone and into downtown Baghdad. We're in North Korea and we haven't even broken out of a whisper in our hotel room, and already you're starting—'

'Starting what?'

Hal put his camera down and knelt on the floor beside his rucksack, emptying its contents in a distracted, haphazard way just so he had something to use to punctuate his sentences. 'You want to do your heal the world act again. Can we just get through this fucking week quietly, without any...' He threw a shirt on the floor then sat back on his heels.

Ben was a little rocked. He'd never seen Hal so shaken up. 'Is this about Khartoum?'

Hal tossed the rucksack aside then sat back against the dresser the TV was on. 'It's...' He rested his head against the dresser and closed his eyes. 'I think when this is done we should take a break.'

'Look, man. I saw you watching that video on your computer in Shenyang. At least talk to me about it.'

Hal stared at the foot of the bed. 'There's nothing to talk about. I filmed a guy being killed. And all those keyboard warriors on YouTube think they hate me, but what they actually hate is the idea that they live in a world where things like that happen every day. And we film it. Because that's all we can do.'

'Well I'm getting a bit tired of what we do. I'm tired of the desert, I'm tired of wars, rendition flights and torture, and I'm tired of saying, "This is Ben Campbell from yet another hopeless situation at a largely disappointing time for humanity." This is just a puff piece to *REBEL*: the ironic Western reporter goes to North Korea and points out how absurd everything is. Don't you want to do something that actually makes a difference?'

Hal exhaled, and finally made eye contact with Ben. 'I don't even know what that means anymore. Nothing you or I do is going to change a thing for Mr Han, Mr Ryong, those little specks down by the river – none of them.'

Ben clasped his hands together, as if invoking a prayer. He wasn't used to quarrelling with Hal. 'It's this Mr Han, I'm telling you. He says all the right things to us, but...'

'But what?'

Ben threw his legs off the side of the bed and turned the volume up on the TV. 'That fight we recorded at Mansu Hill. Mr Ryong said he was ordered by "comrade Secretary Sun" not to leave Mr Han alone with us.'

'You know who Secretary Sun is?'

'About three months ago – no one knows for sure – he was made Secretary of the Propaganda and Agitation Department. Before we left Shenyang I saw reports on a dissident North Korean news website that the previous Secretary had been purged. And that Sun wants his Department to reclaim its old position as leaders of the Party, like they were in the seventies.'

'What happened in the seventies?'

'Kim Jong-il was put in charge of the Guidance Department, a very similar and competing department to Propaganda and Agitation. He has someone else running it now of course, but they're saying Sun is starting a power grab. Sun's predecessor hasn't been seen at public ceremonies for months now. The man is ruthless. Now why would someone like that be involved if he didn't trust Mr Han? He said himself, this is his first tour in Pyongyang. And you don't get to Pyongyang unless your family and political background is impeccable. *Perfect*.'

'So why would he even get this job if he can't be trusted?'

Ben swung his feet back up on the bed, and opened his book

again. 'That's the question now, isn't it. Maybe Mr Han's past isn't as impeccable as everyone else thinks.'

Hal lit a cigarette. 'I'm telling you. I've got a bad feeling about this whole week.' He reached up in annoyance to the shrill TV, and switched it off.

'Sadness Makes Very Little Noise; A Moment's Surrender

Chollima Street, Pyongyang

Before he did anything else, Han knew he had to hang the portraits of the Great Leader and Dear Leader. Inspections of new occupant's apartments were almost always carried out in the first week, and having made such a scene earlier with Yong and Li about them, it wouldn't do to have someone from the Ministry find him complacent about hanging them.

Every citizen had the same portraits hanging on their walls, as well as in government buildings, classrooms, subway cars, and military complexes. In Han's line of work, those two faces followed him everywhere he went, invading his every moment.

Following his promotion, Han was issued with a third portrait – that of Kim Jong-suk, Kim Jong-il's dead mother – to signal his new, higher social standing, but all three looked as new as the day they were issued to him. Han placed a small box that held a special white cleaning cloth on the floor under where the pictures would hang. The cloth would be used for nothing else other than dusting them.

The living room walls were flaking and psoriatic where the builders had scrimped on plaster, using too much water to pad out the mixture, but he managed to bang three nails wonkily in and hung the pictures side by side. With Kim Il-sung in the centre, Han appraised their straightness from several angles, distances and trajectories.

Comforted that the apartment was now legally satisfactory in the eyes of the Party, he poured himself a glass of whisky from Yong's bottle still sitting out on the coffee table. He drank slowly and methodically at the kitchen counter as he fixed himself *kim'chi* and boiled rice. He sat in silence with his dinner on his lap, trying not to eat the gummy, slushy meal too quickly, although he could have devoured it three times over. During the famine of the nineties, the public infomercials declaring 'LET'S ALL EAT TWO MEALS A

DAY' explained that eating your food slowly filled you up for longer, as food is digested slower. Two meals a day. Han could still taste that hunger. It never leaves you.

After washing his plate immediately after he was done, Han started unpacking the rest of his belongings. He kept Ben and Hal's visa applications out on the coffee table, finding himself returning to them every few minutes for another look at their pictures, imagined histories of theirs flooding his brain. He wondered what their homes looked like; did they have families? Could they see their breath in their living rooms like he could? If they really were journalists, what were they saying about him, and his country, back at their hotel, safe in the knowledge that it wouldn't be long before they returned to their inevitably happy partners and made love in loving beds. Such a cruelly ironic twist of loneliness: one becomes certain of everyone else's unbridled happiness, and that no one can possibly be as lonely as they are, when the opposite is so often the case. All these lonely people in the world, going about their day, oblivious that everyone else had just as much longing making the weary journey around their heads.

He sorted out stacks of stiff shirts with wide collars like pyjamas, all in different shades of brown, with trousers to match, and a pair of shoes he kept for meetings with superiors at the Ministry, highly polished, and one size too big for him. When he was twelve he had found them by the side of a dirt road outside Yodok, that led to one of the concentration camps, Camp 15 as it was known to the locals. They were just lying there, side by side, box-fresh, as if waiting for someone to try them on. He would wander around holding the shoes, speculating on many possible scenarios for them having arrived in his life. It was nineteen ninety-five, the height of the famine, or the Arduous March as they were encouraged to call it, a time when neighbours of Han's slowly stopped coming out of their houses, collapsing instead on their beds, starving to exhaustion, where even sitting up was too much of a burden. Han could feel death rotting through the ground in Yodok. He pictured it leaping from tree to tree, and floating down the brown, reed-lined rivers and streams overflowing from the flooding rice fields. And now Han had been given these shoes: a miracle. Each night, for

63

months, he praised the recently departed Great Leader, interpreting the shoes as a parting gift from the afterlife. On the morning of each birthday, the first thing Han did was try the shoes to see if they were closer to fitting him. He packed them to the toes with newspaper, and slid hay under the inner soles. After ten long years they finally fit him. And as he walked into important meetings across polished parquet floors in ostentatious wood-panelled rooms with huge pictures of the Dear Leader Kim Jong-il, he couldn't help but wonder if every day he was walking around in a dead man's shoes, or a political criminal's, right under the noses of the Party.

Then there were boxes of his father's newspaper archive ('WORKERS UNITE TO BUILD HYDROELECTRIC DAM AHEAD OF SCHEDULE!' screamed the top page); his grandfather's Korean War medals, last polished the morning he died; an old red Corona typewriter; a box of candles; shoeboxes of photographs of his family: shots of his father shaking hands with Kim Il-sung, notepad in hand; Han as a boy holding Cho-hee on his knee... it all felt so long ago.

He hadn't really believed Yong's line earlier about his father being proud of him. Han knew for a fact his father would have been dismayed at what he was doing. Not the man the Party knew. The man only Han knew.

Next to his bed, candlelight generously filled the room, making it feel like the room was slowly expanding. He took through the boxes of dossiers and files he had accrued over his years in P&A in Pyonganbuk province, where he had cut his teeth translating for mid-level diplomats and foreign dignitaries, the kind the Party mistakenly believed would be interested in touring factories and industrial warehousing, cherry-picked for their high-output and cleanliness. Sometimes when the bosses went off to get drunk on *cheongju* in the offices, Han would be left with the Westerners' translators. They would sit on cardboard boxes outside in the summer sun, and forget where they were, drifting comfortably from English to Korean and back again, like they were all the same. Han lived for those moments, when the foreigners brought the outside world a little closer to him. Then they got into their diplomatic jeeps and sped off back to Pyongyang, the cars leaving dust-trails behind on the road, so all Han could see in front of him was a dirty haze. And he was alone again.

With all the profiles and application forms laid out on his bed, he cut out the passport photos in the top corner, arranging the faces in the order in which he met them. He started with Assistant Trade Secretary Mr Leung from Taiwan, who wanted to sell cars to the DPRK. Mr Leung had a warm smile, an upturned chin and downturned nose, as if the two were trying to meet each other.

Han contemplated the photo. 'He likes how deep the water feels when swimming in the ocean, as if it never really ends below him, and if he had enough air he could keep going down forever.' He placed the photo next to him on the bed, then picked up the next photo. Phillipe Cardier from the French embassy, who had come to inspect several rubbish dumps few people knew the French government had operated on North Korean soil for the past twenty-five years. Han recalled Cardier's cruel sneer, and the way he would pompously and untrustingly raise his eyebrows whenever Han translated his words. 'Doesn't give money to homeless people even when his pockets are filled with money. He has a driver take him everywhere so he doesn't have to walk the streets. He has a mistress and has an inherent distrust of anyone willing to sleep with him.' He dropped Cardier's photo on the floor, and moved on to the next, holding it closer to the candle. With each face he remembered their characters perfectly, how they moved, how they spoke, and with all these together, he started forming a picture of their interior lives.

'Ho Chow-sun: hates wearing ties, but he has to. Every day. Wanted to tell me news from the rest of Asia but never got a chance. Loves his children more than anything.' Han placed the photo beside him. 'Arthur Boyumunga: has only ever seen snow twice in his life. Both times here in Korea. It's still one of his fondest memories. Even now, when sitting at the dinner table all these years later, he recalls to his children about Mr Han, the translator he met in the DPRK, and the time we walked through the snow. He often wonders what's become of me.' He placed the photo beside him. 'Li Juntao: likes to weep while listening to Chopin through headphones in a dark room. Sometimes he wishes I was there listening with him so I knew what it sounded like.'

By the time he had gone through all the files he had an arc of passport photos surrounding him on the bed, like a halo; the pile on the floor only a handful. Han always had tried to see the best in people, but the problem, he realised, was that all these wonderful qualities were simply what he imagined. There was nothing else to go on. Taking a mirror off the bedroom wall, he stuck the photos to the back of it with tape, forming an atlas of kindness, their gentle smiles overlapping. He placed the mirror back to front on the wall so the photos faced him, and he sat in front of it on the edge of his bed with a whisky. 'Where are you all now?' he wondered. Now, more than ever, Han felt that loneliness was not a question of human proximity.

His evening read had to be taken in bed due to the draft from the loose living room window seals. After rummaging around under the creaking floorboard, dismissing various titles on impulse, he settled on *The Sorrows of Young Werther*. Something about the title, and the forlornness of the man's face on the front cover, spoke deeply to him. The man looked like a Germanic version of Han: eyes that looked sad no matter how they were used.

He got into bed with a puff of warm air into his fists, and wheeled his gas heater a little closer. As soon as he read the first line he knew he had made the right choice: "How happy I am to be away! My dear friend, what a thing is the heart of Man! To leave you, whom I love so, from whom I was inseparable, and to be happy!" Those three exclamations in a row! The honest joy of the man's realisation! And to speak of happiness when clearly he had been suffering! This was why he read. Werther's happiness and suffering somehow infused with his own, and Han felt himself to be in the novel, feeling what Werther was. Han wanted Werther to instruct him how to feel. They had much in common, except the most vital element Han craved: freedom.

After an hour, Han realised he wasn't monitoring how many pages were going by, or comparing the thin slither of read-to-unread pages, as he so often did when plots tired, or characters stopped speaking to him. He knew *Werther* wasn't a novel he could skip a few lines of here and there, or skim just for dialogue as he had when he was younger. It now felt to Han that the only satisfying explanation of what a novel is about was every word of the novel itself.

Once, when he was a small boy, his father had happened on an illicit recording of Schumann's "Träumerei", and whilst listening to it his father had left the room. When he returned, he was distraught to find Han hadn't lifted the needle to pause the music. He re-placed the needle, and Han heard a combination of piano keys that made him forget to breathe. When the passage ended, his father opened his eyes and explained to Han: 'That is why I never skip a note of music. You never know what you might miss.'

Han stopped reading when his eyes merely drifted over the words – scanning rather than reading – and he realised he hadn't actually taken in anything that had been said the last three pages. The cold still got in under the blankets no matter how tightly he tried to seal up every leak. His feet felt like they were glowing with cold under his socks.

He slid his bookmark into the page and left the book on his bedside cabinet where a candle had been slithering down, an oily lagoon of wax shimmering below the flame. He thought of Ryong asking him whether he had a girl at home, and Han found himself picturing the traffic warden he had met that morning. Fantasising about strangers was the closest Han could get to relieving loneliness. In fantasies, strangers could love and desire him as fully and intensely as his imagination could summon. In what few short-lived relationships he had had, Han found that no matter what declarations were made (physical or verbal) between two people, there was something about the Self that the other person would never have access to, like a wall too high to ever climb over. And as long as Han felt trapped on the other side of that wall, love would always be somehow incomplete. What he liked so much about reading was it broke the illusion that one person's interior life was any less complex than another's, regardless of how unaware they were of it, or failed to articulate it. But in real life, all Han's partners' feelings and emotions – which were incredibly deep and intricate and complex and seemed to beg for explanation every single moment of the day – could never hope to be understood the same way Han understood his own interior life. He was forever locked out of anyone else, and forever locked in himself. With a fantasy, Han built the other person's Self for them – like a novelist does – and in a weird paradox made the imagined love feel somehow more real and tangible than actual love.

His cold hands felt unmysterious and clumsy travelling down his stomach towards his erection. Sexual inexperience made his body feel under-used, and torpid. Over time, he tried to convince himself that masturbation was a perfectly adequate replacement for sex, that the ultimate feeling – his own sensory, neurological and ontological pleasure – was ultimately the same. Particularly the ontological part, because nothing is as unique-like-a-snowflake yours as an orgasm. But it was a lie. Masturbation was a lie, a lie that said it was a fraud that another person could make you more supremely yourself: it was a failure on a human level. Sex is to masturbation as what comedy is to telling a joke to an empty room. Because to Han half the pleasure of sex was derived from making someone else feel ecstasy, their foreign hands becoming warm and familiar, gently figuring out where to touch, in search of the kind of orgasm that makes your IQ disappear. With masturbation, as soon as the orgasm was over, whatever fantasy he had conjured, no matter how elaborate and vivid it seemed just a few seconds ago, quickly vanished. This was where it became complicated for Han. The only cure (it was really more of a treatment than a cure) for loneliness was the exact thing that made him lonely in the first place: he simply couldn't connect in any real meaningful way with another person. The harder he tried to imagine the traffic warden's touch the more alone he felt.

Then he heard something that didn't make sense: a scraping and shuffling sound coming from the apartment below. He stopped, then pulled the covers up over his exposed body, waiting for the sound to return. Then, slowly, familiar vibrations crept up through the floor, a gentle seesawing noise, much like the lowly tuning of a cello. Bass softly throbbed up through the thin carpet, between sturdy sweeps of the strings, like tiny helicopters being released upwards.

Han slid back into his trousers and crept around the apartment trying to find where the sound was loudest. He slipped on his shoes barefoot in the hall, pulling on his officer's jacket to keep the cold out. Poking his head out the doorway into the corridor, he called out, 'Hello?... hello?' His breath turned to steam. He crept towards the stairwell, where the music became clearer, fuller.

The darkness of the stairwell heightened his sensitivity, identifying the low-end sweep of a cello, he was positive now, something slow and mournful.

He came out on the floor below his, as the cello broke into some frantic passage. At the end of the corridor was a woman sitting on a stool with her back to him. Unobstructed moonlight came from the window in front of her, lighting the outline of her almost embracing the cello, her legs splayed around it as if giving birth. She was wearing trousers but no shirt, just a bra, her hand chugging the bow as if trying to keep an engine turning over.

Han hugged the wall, creeping down towards her. He had never heard music like it, music that tried to sound the way a person feels. It didn't tell him what to feel, just that he ought to. There were no vocal proclamations of sovereignty or leadership or victory on battlefields long-forgotten; no military trumpets or brass. Her cello sounded to him like a musical expression of what it felt like sitting upstairs on his own, yearning for someone, anyone, to relieve his sadness. A voice inside Han told him the music was foreign, and she shouldn't have been playing it, but he couldn't bring himself to tell her to stop.

She built to an attacked-by-bees flurry of an ending, a long drawn-out note low on the fingerboard as if she were touching a live wire and couldn't release her hand to break the circuit. Then she dropped her head, and let her arms fall limp by her side.

Han, who had hung back farther down the corridor, broke the silence with gentle applause, not wanting to startle her. The woman screamed as she whipped around, dropping her cello. The vibration of the wood against the floor sent a chorus of mixed notes into the air at once.

Han called out, 'I'm sorry, I...'

'What are you doing creeping up on someone like that?' she yelled, trying to simultaneously cover her top half with her arms and grab her shirt lying on the floor.

Han rushed towards her, pulling the cello up whilst looking away. 'I was upstairs, I heard you playing...' When he saw her face, a line of poetry came to him, but he couldn't place where from. She had a mole above her left cheekbone, which she thought made her look ugly, but Han thought made her beautiful.

With her back to him, the woman wrestled into her shirt, her hand caught in the sleeve. 'Why do clothes never respond to panic?'

'You must be freezing.'

She tried to explain as quickly as possible, like a soldier asked to explain themselves, 'I'm a cellist with the National Orchestra, you see, and I was practicing. The acoustics for the cello are better out here, and I had my shirt off because I like my arms free when I play.'

'It's good wholesome Korean music your orchestra plays. I haven't heard what you just played before.'

'I thought I was alone.' She glanced at Han's lapel, noticing his Propaganda and Agitation Department pin. She bowed her head repeatedly to him, joining her hands. 'Oh, I'm sorry, comrade. Please don't report me, I was just practising, I didn't mean any harm, I'm a good citizen, if I don't play difficult pieces I—'

Han carefully spun the cello by its rubber endpin so the strings faced her. 'You should be more careful. What was that you were playing?'

She paused, wondering if he was about to arrest her. 'Dvořák. Concerto in B minor.' Her head slowly tilted up to face him, taking the cello from him and placing it against the stool. 'You like classical music?'

'I don't get to hear much outside the Ministry. My father, he had this gramophone, sometimes he would sneak records home from his office. I've never heard the cello like that though.'

'Am I in trouble, is that why you're here?'

If Han wasn't clear he was angry she had broken the law she might grow suspicious of him. 'Yes, well... playing illicit music detrimental to the State can be, of course, a serious matter.' He went to check his watch then realised he wasn't wearing one. 'And it is long past curfew... but I suppose this time we can forget about it.'

She took a half-step towards him. 'Thank you, comrade, that's most understanding of you. I have a concert tomorrow night. It helps me prepare. And I thought I was the only person in the building.'

'I moved in today.' He pointed above his head. 'I'm right up there.'

She walked to the nearest doors and pushed them open one by one. 'These don't even have locks on them yet.' A gusting wind buffeted the door of the apartment next to hers, let in through an empty living-room window frame. She held her arms up, the wind tousling her shirt, and her hair leaped around her face.

Han waited by the door, calling out to her, 'Why have they put us so high up?'

'They can't get the water to run downstairs. And the wiring is no good. All the good electricians and builders are working on other buildings. It's strange but you get used to it.'

Despite the walls and ceiling, it felt like he was standing outside.

'My name is Han, by the way. Han Jun-an. But they call me Mr Han.'

'Who calls you Mr Han?'

'At work. I'm a Ministry guide to foreigners. That's what they call me.'

She brushed past him in the doorway. 'You can call me Mae.' She shut the apartment door and it was silent again. 'I'm very sorry for keeping you up, comrade.'

'It's quite alright. You have a way of moving when you play...' Han shook his head.

'I can't play like that with the orchestra. It's so rigid. I don't look like how I feel inside.'

'What do you feel when you play?'

She reached for her cello and plucked a random string. 'What I

71

hope the composer felt when he wrote it. Whether he was happy or in love, lonely or suffering.'

'I do that reading books,' Han said, drumming his fingers in folded arms, the way jumpy nervous people trying to look calm do. 'I wonder if the writer actually wants people to know how they feel, or if it's more of a warning.'

Mae's hand crept around the outside of her door. 'Perhaps, one night, you can come here and I can play something for you. No surprises this time.' Just as she dragged her cello around the door, a low buzz crept through exposed wiring lining the ceiling, and the lights suddenly came on across the street and in Mae's hallway, illuminating a large pile of books on the floor in front of an open closet. A few of the titles Han knew: he had the same ones upstairs under his floorboards.

In an instant, Mae was a different person to him. Knowing she had spent six or some hours reading the same book he had – that the same author's thoughts had passed through her mind too – changed how he was looking at her. She felt somehow closer to him now.

Han looked quickly away down the corridor, but they both knew what he had seen. 'Y-yes, I'd like that,' he began.

The books on the floor had never looked so exposed. Mae quickly shut off the hall light and narrowed the door, her voice a few decibels higher. 'I'm sorry, comrade, I should really be getting to bed.'

'Be careful in the future, Mae. You never know who may end up at your door.'

'Goodnight, comrade.' She shut the door and pressed her back up against it, waiting to hear Han walking away.

'Goodnight, Miss Mae,' he said, turning away. As he reached his front door, the line of poetry he had tried to place came to him. It was TS Eliot's, from *The Waste Land*: "Blood shaking my heart, the awful daring of a moment's surrender."

'Kevin Carter; The Demilitarized Zone; Hiding The Axe'

Banquet Hall 2, Koryo Hotel, 16th December

Ben and Hal sat yawning at their breakfast, dozens of little silver bowls and plates with steel lids. They had been woken at seven by a maid leaving fresh towels and bottled water, and who switched the radio on beside Ben's bed, playing the same military-style brass band music as the loudspeakers outside the hotel.

While Ben took a shower, Hal stayed in bed, watching the Khartoum video on his laptop with headphones on. He kept thinking about Kevin Carter. Carter was the reason Hal wanted to be a press cameraman, after seeing the photo that won Carter the Pulitzer Prize in 1994. It was of a starving Sudanese toddler, hunched over with hunger – what most people imagine starving to death looks like – while a vulture stalked the background like some angel of death, seemingly waiting for the inevitable. Laden with debt, guilt and nightmares of atrocities, Carter killed himself three months after winning the Pulitzer.

When Ben (already dressed) opened the bathroom door, Hal closed the laptop. Ben didn't need to ask.

Ben and Hal were making their way across the huge open-plan lobby to breakfast, when they saw a short uniformed man with a broom, and a pan that made a clumping sound like someone hopping in a clog each time the pan hit the marble floor. The cleaner seemed oblivious to the racket he was making. He swept up thin air for fear of not looking busy. Hal gave him a waist-high wave and his best Bostonian, 'How ah ya.'

The cleaner couldn't understand Hal's changing of Rs into AHs. He took a guess, giving a bow. 'Good morning, sir.'

Without Han, hotel customer service was a bit of a high-wire act, embarrassingly deferential and sedulous in body language and tone, but with semi-creepy smiles that suggested a semi-sinister adversarial intent. No, they couldn't take a short walk around the hotel grounds. They should make their way to Banquet Hall 2 so they are ready for Mr Han's arrival, and another fine day learning about Korea.

Waitresses in fluorescent green gowns – giggling at something unknown to the men – showed them to their table, at the centre of a deserted restaurant. The Norwegians had already eaten and left for the day. The men faced a mural of the Kumgangsan mountain range – of which every meticulous waterfall and crevice would have stood up to photographic comparison – that took up the full length of the wall. Menus were placed in front of them, bearing gaudy passport-sized photos of the food next to the blurbs, like a Texas waffle house, except none of the dishes existed. No orders were taken; the waitresses wheeled out tray after tray of food on hostess trolleys to the other thirty empty tables. The same had happened the night before at dinner.

A waitress put down nearly a dozen little bowls in front of them. The language barrier limited her to simple nouns, and conversation was impossible. Ben had to bite his tongue to not ask her questions (he didn't want word spreading to the other staff that he knew Korean). There was a human being in front of him with an entire history – a database of experiences and memories all jostling and competing interiorly in what could sometimes feel like the darkness and vastness of deep space shrunk to the size of pinhead, or other times like watching a play performed by ghosts – and Ben would know none of it. All Ben knew for sure was there was duck and there was pork.

Hal closed his eyes and silently said Grace to himself. Ben never knew what to do while Hal prayed. In the past he had tried eating through it, but that felt like he was actively trying to disrupt the ritual. So he sat back, arms on the arm rests, his brain switching to auto in the downtime. It was absurd to him that people still prayed. When he watched Hal do it, Hal seemed farther away somehow, like clouds at different altitudes, both looking down, only one seeing the other.

Hal crossed himself, then poked his fork around his bowls. 'Is this duck or pork, you think?' He picked up something deep-fried and crescent-shaped, shrugged at it, then took a bite. Several seconds later he was still unable to either describe or identify what he had eaten. It was the sort of bad that robs you of adjectives. 'There's sure as hell no meat here.'

Ben tried something from a similar bowl. 'We'll insult them if we don't eat *some* of it. This is probably more food than they see in a week.'

The men ate silently, until Ben pointed out, 'Your cross is still hanging out.'

Hal looked down at his chest. 'So what?'

Ben continued eating. 'They're not great fans of Christianity here, Hal. I'm not saying take it off, just—'

Hal slid the cross back under his loose-yarn, fisherman's sweater. The sweater reminded him of home. 'How many days we got left?'

'Six.'

Hal hung his arms down between his legs like he was already done.

There was no music in the hall, just the occasional wood-on-linoleum screech of Ben or Hal adjusting their chairs, or the tiniest chink of Ben's cutlery carrying to the other side of the room. Three male waiters stood by the kitchen door, all the tables now served.

Hal looked around at all the uneaten food. 'They have food shortages but they waste all this every day?'

Ben put his fork down in exhaustion. He couldn't take another bite. 'Do they really think we'll leave here thinking all this is normal?'

As they left, Ben hung back at the door to see the waitresses picking up all the bowls and putting them back on the trolleys, in a laconic but kind of dutiful way. None of them spoke. And they all looked sad but in different ways.

Han flashed a badge at one of the Mall Cops guarding the lobby door.

'The Americans are finishing their breakfast, Mr Han,' the Mall Cop said.

'Very good.' Han touched his stomach as he crossed the lobby, humming something perky to himself.

Ryong and So were out by the minibus, sharing a cigarette. So was enjoying the silence until Ryong suddenly took up the line of dialogue So thought he'd heard the last of twenty minutes ago, about various *Hannah and her Sisters*-like love triangles going on back at the Ministry. Then Ryong would forget someone's name and break off, and just as So thought the silence was going to sustain Ryong suddenly raised both hands up, as if he were lifting a toddler, and announced the forgotten name with a relieved exhalation.

When Han saw Ben and Hal in the lobby he exclaimed, 'Gentlemen! Such a good morning!'

'Good morning, Mr Han,' they replied. When Ben offered Han a handshake, Hal followed suit. He just wanted an easy day, not upset anyone, and get one day closer to home. He felt like the guy on court who doesn't want the ball.

'We have a big day ahead of us,' Han said. 'Much travelling, so we now go.' He made the last four words sound like one.

In the drive out the city, Han used the hum of the engine to cover his humming Dvořák.

The two and a half hour drive from Pyongyang to the Demilitarized Zone that marked the jagged border between North and South Korea was quiet and fast. The six-lane highway outside the city had more livestock on it than cars. Pedestrians ambled slowly alongside the safety lane as if unconvinced of the day's purpose. The sky's colour was a single shade of shale.

'Are we late?' asked Ben, raising his voice so Han and Ryong could hear him up front. So was intermittently hitting the car horn for no clear reason.

'No, no, we travel speedily as it is best,' came Han's vague reply, watching Hal shoot video out the side window as the bus passed a group of women selling vegetables off the backs of their rusty bicycles at a layby.

'Mr Han,' Ben said, slipping into journalist mode, 'I thought there were no private food sellers allowed.' He was interested to see how Han would respond to visible proof of private enterprise, and that the government's food rationing programme wasn't working.

'No, no,' Han replied, using the same excuse he used in his old job, 'these women are the government. This show the Party plan is working.'

In the northern countryside the fields were covered in snow a kind of crystal white that no mural could ever capture. Farmers batted along their solitary skeletal cows whose eyes had the deadened dull glow of bureaucrats'.

Ryong, getting restless at the roadside distractions, instructed So on his right to speed up.

'*Mr Han is in charge of this tour,*' So fired back.

Han wasn't paying attention to any of it, his eyes glassy from concentrating on the Dvořák in his head. His elbow perched on the curved edge that joined the door and the window, an edge slightly too thin to be comfortable.

Ryong mumbled at Han, '*He should go faster, shouldn't he?*'

'*What, do you want me to teleport them there like Star Wars or something?*'

'*Star Trek!*' Ryong replied in sync to shoving his fists down angrily. He knew So had said it on purpose, but he couldn't let it go.

Han put his arm out like a music conductor saying stop. He found himself coming over all liberal-parent. '*Can we, please, not argue for just a few minutes.*'

In the backseat Ben didn't feel like adding words to what Hal was shooting: the bleakest, most desolate countryside they had ever seen, like some rural dystopia. The air looked sick, the colour of flu, and the bare trees trembled feverishly. Han told them the deserted fields full of knee-high brown weeds and clotted black soil were 'collectivised farms'.

'Where are the workers, Mr Han?' Ben asked, trying to be delicate.

Han heard the Dvořák swell in his head as he stared hard out his window at the fields. For once, he wanted to just tell the truth. That they weren't collectivised farms at all, that most of what he said this week would be lies, that he read books he shouldn't, and all kinds of personal things like feeling alone in crowded rooms, and that the concept of infinity scared him more than death. Han replied with a deliberate non sequitur, 'We will take you to a very excellent collectivised farm. You will see what is good there.'

Ben spoke to the camera, adopting a slightly lower tone than he used with Han. 'Our guide says these are collectivised farms, but we won't stop at any of them. We have planned visits later in the week, to farms that have been checked and vetted.'

They all turned comfortably silent the way only groups of men can, as the countryside became more overgrown and heavily forested – the outskirts of the most surreal tourist spot, and least-aptly-named place in the world: the Demilitarized Zone.

The minibus was halted at the DMZ's entrance at Panmunjeom by a DPRK soldier swaggering coolly out of his watch hut, finishing a butter sandwich.

Han leaned out the window to show the soldier his considerable credentials. The soldier was jovial in a way that made no sense to Ben and Hal given the surroundings. The soldier and Han seemed to be previously acquainted.

'*So good to see you again, Mr Kang*,' Han said. '*It's been a long time*!'

'*You too, comrade.*' Kang took one last bite of his sandwich before tossing his crusts to the side of the road. Sparrows descended from the trees like spitfires and pecked the bread gone in seconds. '*What do we have today, Americans?*' Kang leaned down to look in the back window, seeing Ben hugging the backpack sitting on his knees, and Hal purse his lips as if having heard something second-hand and sad.

Han said, '*The short-haired one is British. The other one is American, but he's okay.*'

Ben smiled to himself.

'What is it?' Hal whispered.

'Mr Han likes you.'

Kang suddenly lurched his head in through Han's window, waving hello. 'I Mr Kang. You Mr Campbell? And Mr Huckley. Hello!'

Ben gave a wave of his itinerary leaflet. 'Hello, Mr Kang.'

Hal's wave was like a golfer accepting consolatory applause after a missed putt.

Kang pulled back but remained close enough to appear conspiratorial.

Han said, '*If we can keep the focus on reunification, Mr Kang. Those are my instructions from Pyongyang.*'

'*Certainly. I do it every day with the Chinese and Japanese.*' He gave Han's door an assertive thump with his fist, then said, '*I'll go ahead, you follow me through.*' He climbed into the roofless Jeep in front and lit a cigarette, spreading his arms across both the back of his and his driver's seats, puffing smoke up into the air with his head back. Ben had never seen a man happier in his work.

They passed dozens of anti-tank cement blocks perched on the tops of walls the height of the minibus, raised over the road by little bridges vectored every fifty metres, ready for detonation come an invasion.

'Soon we will be in Joint Security Area,' Han said. 'Is where North and South Koreans patrol their sides of the borderline together.'

There was something exhausting about listening to him. It was conversation-as-series-of-announcements.

While Hal filmed him, Ben called forward to Han, 'We saw a film once called *JSA* that was set here.'

'Is South Korean film,' Han replied dismissively.

'Is it very realistic to how it is here?'

'I not seen it. I hear it very biased against DPRK. I not interested in Western propaganda.'

So announced cheerfully, '*I saw it last year.*'

'*On that DVD you bought at the market?*' Ryong grinned.

So batted him on the arm, abandoning an attempt at '*Shut up*' before he'd really started.

The harshest reprimand Han felt like giving was, '*You really shouldn't be buying South Korean films, Mr So. Not in your position.*' Selling foreign DVDs was commonplace where So lived on the edge of the city, but Han's colleagues would have been surprised if he'd let it pass without comment.

'*It's pretty good actually. There's this really cool bit in the minefield in no-man's land—*'

'*Mr So, please...*'

Ben took his first pass at diplomacy. 'There's a bit where one of the South's soldiers accidentally wanders into the DPRK after a training exercise, and ends up playing cards and talking to an enemy soldier. I thought it was quite hopeful.'

'I not seen it,' Han repeated.

'*How do you and Mr JSA know each other?*' Ryong asked.

'*We started out at the Party Academy together,*' Han answered.

'*I bet he gets four meals a day here.*'

'*Don't believe everything you've heard about the JSA, Ryong.*'

'*They're all here because they had relatives that died in the war. Like it's my fault the Japanese and Americans didn't kill any of my family. Like I'm less loyal because of what someone else didn't do. I've given everything for the Party.*'

'*Loyalty isn't everything, Ryong. You have to be smart too.*'

So braked as Kang's Jeep slowed up ahead.

Han turned round to Ben and Hal. '*This is JSA, gentlemen.*'

Ben didn't understand how they could make it so quickly. When Ben and Hal had visited the South Korean DMZ five days earlier, they were shown around by American G.I. Westwood, whose whole tour was punctuated with checkpoint after checkpoint, passport inspections and pat-downs, and dire warnings of geopolitical chaos if they didn't follow his instructions 'To. The. Letter.' In a conference room a team of United Nations officials briefed the tour group on conduct within the complex, to not point or wave at the North Koreans, as any hint of communication could potentially be photographed and used in propaganda. Westwood assured them it had happened before. And they weren't to call out anything even if it was something praising North Korea and the Dear Leader. All communication had to be rigorously policed and predictable. Waivers were to be signed, saying visitors understood '[t]he visit to the Joint Security Area at Panmunjom will entail entry into a hostile area and possibility of injury or death as a direct result of enemy action.' They were handed UNCMAC (United Nations Command Military Armistice Commission) passes which had to be visible round their necks, Westwood emphasised, 'at all times.'

They were driven around on a bus more suited to theme park rides than touring a military standoff, passing Freedom Bridge (the 'Bridge of No Return') that crossed the DMZ demarcation line, where North and South prisoners had been exchanged at the end of the Korean War. Past the overgrown plantation, just visible above the tree-line in the North was a propaganda sign in large white letters

우리 장군님이 제일이야

which Westwood said translated loosely as 'Our General is the best General'. To its left was another sign

양키 고 홈

which said, 'Yankee Go Home.'

The South's side was run like a corporate theme park. They charged US$75 for entry, and had gift shops where you could buy Military Police shoulder patches, and toy soldiers dressed in South Korean Army uniforms. There were swivelling coin-operated PPV binoculars embedded in concrete columns on the roof of the South's HQ. Far off in the distance, near the city of Kaesong, North Korea's southernmost city, was an enormous radio tower used to block radio and television transmissions coming from outside the hermit kingdom. Through the telescope Ben could see north to the village of Kijong-dong, the buildings empty shells, windowless. The North Koreans ran vast quantities of electricity through Kijong-dong, lights on in every room, trying to look attractive to the South at night. Sometimes after a shift, Westwood went up on the roof for a look. The sight of an entire village with no sign of life in it was creepy in a way he had no comparison to.

*

As soon as the back door was slid open, Hal started recording and didn't stop until they were back on the bus nearly two hours later, made possible by the weirdly relaxed atmosphere on the North's side, like they had the upper hand in some way. Where the South marched, the North prowled; where the South sneered, the North laughed.

Kang walked in an exaggerated heel-to-toe motion. Nobody was in any rush. Entry was only $20. If the DMZ was a theme park, the North had the rides with no age or height restrictions. Chinese tourists laughed and joked with the North Korean soldiers, photographing anything they wanted; they could point at American soldiers across the DMZ, they could wave: the only rule seemed to be don't walk towards the border.

Kang led Ben and Hal past a group of mostly aged Chinese war veterans with tripod walking sticks, into the Panmumgak building, leaving Han to fall back into a translator's role. Ben and Hal looked down at the JSA from the roof (the North's telescopes were free), a row of three UN-blue huts straddling the border marked by a concrete strip along the ground. The South Korean guards stood half in profile, peeking out from behind their end of the huts, to make a smaller target for any North Korean soldier stupid enough to take a shot. Their legs were wide apart, hands fixed in fists as if they would sooner resort to hand-to-hand combat than reach for a gun. Like the guys in bar fights who don't want to just win the fight, they want to hurt the other guy. The North Koreans were a good six inches shorter, a result of stunted growth during the Arduous March. To rub it in, the South Koreans put their tallest, strongest men at the border – the kind who took protein shakes with breakfast.

After a few minutes inside one of the lecture rooms in Panmungak, the North's agenda of reunification was all Kang, the other military officials and Han could talk about.

Han translated a lengthy diatribe from a captain about the Armistice and the end of the Korean War: the reason the DMZ existed. The captain – with more medals on his lapel than could comfortably fit – shuffled tanks and infantry brigades around on a detailed miniature model of the border region laid out on a table, explaining how the Americans were 'whipped back' and 'pummelled' here, and 'heavily defeated' and 'blasted away' there. He reached with his pointing stick to 'an American atrocity' behind one little hill, and the 'relentless bombing of innocent Korean civilians' over at the rocks. He relayed stories of pregnant women with their bellies slit open by the evil Americans; beheadings, rape and pillaging. The crimes were extraordinary. Barely human. Ben told Hal that Han was greatly strengthening the captain's already hyperbolic language.

When the captain was finished, Kang lobbied Han, '*You should tell them about my family. Tell them what the Americans did. They should know the truth about their country. You know all about it, comrade.*'

Ryong, hands in pockets, trailing subordinately behind Han, spoke to Ben and Hal. 'Mr Kang had ten member of his family killed in Korean War. By the Americans. Massacred.'

Kang took up the story, adding extra details and colour.

Han translated, 'He say only his father survived, and now all his relatives serve in the military. If American try to invade again they will be crushed, like bugs.' Han ground his fist into his palm.

Kang broke into what little English he knew. 'Korean people want peace. Reunification.' He formed his hands like two halves coming together.

Ben said, 'I read that one in every ten males in the DPRK is in uniform. Why is military membership so high?'

Han made a slight move toward Kang, who was about to answer. 'The Korean people very loyal to the country. We proud to fight for our country, to defend our country from the imperialists.' If Kang and Ryong weren't there, Han would have told them the truth: the army was the only place you were guaranteed three squares a day.

Hal circled round behind Ben to get a shot of Kang so he wasn't backlit: the lights in the room had gone off.

'*Ah, sorry,*' said Kang, consulting with a junior colleague flicking helplessly at the light switches. '*I was worried that might happen.*'

Han translated several minutes of rote history and Ministry-approved rhetoric, polishing Kang's language on his feet with some heavier adjectives: '...and after these massive defeats and heavy losses for the Americans, the resilience of Korean people is proven without shadow on doubt, and the Americans suggest Armistice talks in June fifty-one. In fifty-three they sign the Armistice to prevent further massive defeats and heavy losses.'

Ben asked, as much for the camera as anything else, 'But technically both sides are still at war. It is simply a truce on paper?'

'This right,' said Han. 'No peace treaty signed. Both sides set up conference halls on border, the three blue buildings. We use these to discuss reunification and talks, and since then we try to reunify this country—'

'Reunify,' nodded Kang, like a cuckoo clock going off at one.

'—this right, yes, and when we reunify we will shown the American imperialists their war is over.'

Satisfied Han had hit all the necessary points, Kang led them out onto the balcony of Panmungak. Hal zoomed in on the bigger, taller, more modern American building, Freedom House, like a corporation HQ with stylish roof curves and abundant glass. Walking down the front steps of Freedom House, accompanying South Korean and American tourists, was Westwood, prompting derisive jeers from Kang to the Chinese war vets: '*Look. An American.*' The Chinese rallied behind Kang. Each one of them wished their granddaughters would bring someone like Kang home someday. He was the young man they wished they had been.

Panmungak looked like a Soviet relic, the high windows on the top floor like an air traffic control tower. Westwood had speculated to Ben (off the record), that the United Nations weren't convinced the North Koreans had the electricity to operate what few security cameras they had twenty-four hours a day. The North looked like they'd been on duty for decades longer than the South. Their uniforms were the frumpy, too-long, too-brown of seventies Communism, while the South's chiselled frontier were bursting out their shirts. A South Korean guard could leave work and comfortably sit in a nice restaurant with only the removal of tin helmet to make good with the dress code. Not so the NKs.

As Kang went off with the Chinese and Hal and Ryong, Ben and Han stood leaning over the balcony together in silence, taking in the bizarre scene before them. The afternoon sun hung low in the sky, appearing brighter as it fell, like it had misjudged its axis. A high-pressure front had moved in, raising the sparse clouds as high as clouds could possibly go.

'It's like a movie, yes?' Han said, grinning in a glazed way at the sun.

'A movie?' Ben asked.

'At the end of the cowboy movie. There always one who doesn't make it. I don't like the cowboy movie.'

'I never cared for them, either,' Ben said.

Han, disarmingly comfortable in the surroundings, hummed peacefully to himself.

'What is that, Mr Han?'

Han suddenly realised what he had been doing. 'What?'

Ben imitated a bar of melody. 'You've been humming it all day.'

Kang and Ryong were farther down the balcony, standing with Hal who was corralling the Chinese war vets into a group shot, communicating mostly in upped thumbs.

'Is some music I hear last night,' Han said, his smile coming and going in waves.

'Korean music?' Ben asked.

'Western music is not allowed. All foreign music, the government call it "jazz". They say it stink of capitalism. Is decadent.'

'Have you heard much Western music?'

'My father, sometime he had this music. He worked for *Rodong Sinmun*.'

'The newspaper?'

'A very important newspaper to the Party. It was hard for my father, growing up in a family with no one who fought in the war. It takes longer to move up.'

'Do you have any brothers or sisters?'

'I had a sister, but she die in nineteen ninety-three.' The height of the Great Famine. 'My father very well-respected journalist. He die ten years ago in a car crash with my mother.' Han looked down at the transversal lines across his palms, intersecting like motorway flyovers.

'I'm sorry.'

'Is your father proud of you, Mr Ben?'

'I don't know... maybe. He was a journalist too.' For safety, Ben added, 'Like your father, I mean.'

'What was he like?'

'He was very powerful, a long time ago. A very influential journalist in Britain. For a while, at least.'

'What happened?'

Paring the story down to basic English made it easier for Ben to get it out – if he could have resorted to just nouns and verbs, he would have. 'When I was eleven my mother died of cancer. After that, dad started drinking more, working less. He became an alcoholic, and died in a hospital.'

Assuming this was all long ago, Han asked, 'When did he die?'

'Six months ago.'

'So is still recent.'

'I don't know. I try not to think about it too much.'

As if on autopilot, Han drifted back to proselytising. 'This where the Great Leader's teachings on *Juche* ideology are very important.'

'What exactly is *Juche*?'

Despite having read the numerous books on *Juche*, Han was (as most who read books on *Juche*) still unclear of its vague definition. 'Is very complex... it mostly mean to be strong. The self does not exist; you are not alone, you are part of a people. And if your mind is strong, it can take the weight of the world. I learn this every day. I take words that make no sense to one person, and make them have sense. This is what I love about language. It bring us together. Without it we can never know each other. And we are stuck in our own heads.'

'We have a word for that, Mr Han. Do you know this word: solipsism?'

Han motioned to his ear to indicate he didn't understand.

'It means, um... out of all that exists, the whole world, the only thing you can know is yourself.'

Han nodded, as if he were kick-starting the smile that followed. 'This is strange conversation to have here.' When he smiled it was like sunlight suddenly breaking out from behind a cloud. 'I'm standing here, and the whole world is just over there.' He didn't point, but it was clear he meant the South. 'Is so close but I can't reach.' He grimaced at how inadequate the description was to the complexity of the idea in his head. Han's dilemma wasn't temporal or ontological, it was linguistic. And without the right words to describe his loneliness to Ben, Han felt the entire external world fall apart. Translation was essentially mimetic to Han, and like the inarticulate novelist, if he couldn't form the same picture in Ben's head that was in his, he had failed. He and Ben would forever be apart, and there was no way around it. He didn't have the words. For many years he had tried to put a name to what he felt. But without the Western word 'depression' for Han to self-apply, it was as if the feeling didn't exist. 'Sadness' was the closest he could get to it, and he had felt it for so long the sadness came to be normal to him. But over time it had changed: at first a feeling of sadness directed inwardly, for being shy and awkward and unattractive, but since the death of his parents it had become a sadness that reached outwards; sadness that the rest of the world was lost to him, and there was something more out of control, something deeper about this kind of sadness, the kind that felt like it might never end, no matter where he happened to be in the world. It wasn't he, it was the world that was broken. 'I can't explain this...' Han said. 'What I feel.' He shook his head terribly. In order to explain, Han turned to a source that took Ben by surprise. 'Shakespeare, he write once, "All the world's a stage". Only, some people play the parts, some sit in the audience. And other people stand outside the theatre, they see nothing. The only thing they hear is the applause at the end.'

'We have this funny problem in the West, Mr Han,' Ben said. 'The more ways we invent to communicate, we think we're getting closer to each other, when we're actually getting further away. You might see a news report from Sudan, and for ninety seconds a reporter brings the story into your life. In those ninety seconds have to be the most important things you say all day. My dad told me that once. He said the reporter's job was to make people forget you were on the other side of the world.'

Han suspected Ben was talking about himself. He liked to think he was, anyway. 'There are all these rules in language, sometime I don't know which to follow. Then I am stuck on the other side of this language. When there is something I don't know how to translate, like just now, it kills me...' Han laughed in a rather anguished way, laying a lazy hand on Ben's shoulder just as Ryong looked back at them. Han took his hand away, and told Ben, 'We had a saying at language school: "We don't need more rules; we need more words."'

Kang was back in charge for the group visit to the blue conference huts on the borderline. The only person on the South's side was a military policeman in a tin hat and sunglasses, standing at the halfway point of the negotiation table in front of a triumvirate of flags: the United Nations, South Korea, and the United States. The snug way the tin hat encased the MP's head made it seem it was designed to stop thoughts escaping from underneath it. Or any others getting in.

As Kang discussed minutiae on the Korean War with the Chinese war vets (the Chinese largely satisfied with Kang's summation of events), Ben whispered to Hal, 'See that South Korean there,' he motioned at the military policeman. 'He's guarding the flags. Some DPRK soldiers defaced them one day when the room was empty.'

The image of North Korean soldiers huddled over some tabletop flags with markers in their hands, one less-popular soldier keeping lookout, like schoolboys stealing sweets from an unattended shop, made Hal smile for the first time that day.

When Ben and Hal had visited the conference huts the week before, they were given explicit warnings not to photograph or film the soldiers standing outside on the North's side. But Kang was letting the Chinese war vets photograph whatever they wanted.

'Is that okay, Mr Han,' Hal asked, reluctant to raise his camera.

'It's okay to film and point?'

Han deferred to Kang.

'Of course,' Kang said gleefully, 'we can do whatever we want on our side. They can't stop us. I had some beers in here with a captain once. And nobody going to war over a few beers.'

Hal took a shot of the two North Koreans standing at the border. Ben, trying to edit on his feet, followed him over. 'Why do the DPRK soldiers face each other in pairs, Mr Han?'

'Is just extra security,' Han replied.

Westwood had told them the real reason: 'One is there to watch the other. So they can't make a run for it and defect.'

The North may have acted like they had the upper hand, but the South at least knew their soldiers were in no danger of crossing over. When a South soldier entered the blue conference huts to inspect the locks on the inside of the North's door, he had a compatriot clutching his arm to stop from being pulled into the North. The South feared a comrade's capture; the North feared a comrade's escape.

Some late-arriving Japanese tourists joined Kang's group in the middle of his speech about guilt, a speech he greatly enjoyed making nearly every day for six years. No matter what was said, the South Korean MP watching the flags didn't waver or look over at the North's side. Han translated for Kang in a proud, almost breathless voice.

Kang's body language was all openness in arms and transparency in eyes when he spoke. *We have lived here peacefully on the Korean peninsula for thousands of years until the Yankees came along and split our beloved country in half. It's been fifty-eight years now. We have a saying here: that committing a crime is bad. But if you're not feeling guilty, that's even worse. You have to take responsibility.*

The Japanese tourists suddenly broke into spontaneous applause. Ben noticed Hal glance at the floor when Han translated the word "guilty", his eyes flicking to Ben at "responsibility".

Han had a quiet word in Kang's ear, then Kang announced, 'You want to see axe that kill Americans?'

'The one from seventy-six?' Ben asked.

'*Ah*,' Kang said, turning disappointedly to Han. '*The Americans already told them.'*

Kang took them to the North Korea Peace Museum, nothing more than a series of dim, dingy rooms, with framed pictures hanging on the walls, mostly of American soldiers with their hands over their heads, surrendering as prisoners of war. The lights were off again.

Ben whispered to Hal, 'Can you film in this light?'

'Yeah, it's on night-mode.'

Kang strode ahead towards the axe display, talking over his shoulder to Han and Ryong: *'Another damn power cut. Just tell them we're fixing it.'*

Ben gestured at his ear. 'What did he say, Mr Han?'

Han made little of it. 'Is not a problem. He said they are fixing the lights.'

Kang gestured at the pictures on the wall, getting Ryong to direct Hal. *'Make sure he doesn't skip any shots of the Americans with their hands up. He has to give us some of what we want too.'* Kang stopped at a glass case sitting on the floor, almost hidden away in a dark corner of the back room. The axe sat on a red velvet bed inside the case. 'This is it,' Kang said.

Han translated Kang's version of the story: 'This is what the Americans used to provoke the incident. They sent out their men to chop down a tree on our land that blocked their view. We stopped them and kill one American with his axe. They provoked us so they would have excuse to stay in South Korea. We give back the body; we keep the axe.'

Kang marched them off towards the Armistice Agreement before Han had finished the translation.

With Ryong safely ahead with Kang and the Chinese and Japanese, Han tacked on his own thoughts, 'He also said, we hide axe back here because there should be no pride in killing a man.'

'Really,' Ben said, knowing the words were Han's alone. 'That's surprising to hear from a soldier.'

As Han turned around he happened to look straight into Hal's lens. 'There all sorts of people with surprising things to say, Mr Ben.'

'The Debriefing; What The Real World Looks Like'

Central Party Offices, aka The Forbidden City, Pyongyang, 16th **December**

Secretary Sun sat behind a large oak desk (at least three trees' worth), thumbing through the remaining files he had pulled on "Han Jun-an". The simplifying of the guides' names for foreigners had been an idea of Sun's predecessor, the now disappeared Hwang, who had once written in a memo:

'...we must make it easier for tourists to warm to their minders, making them more approachable by Westernizing the minders' names. Minders should be seen less as official apparatuses of the State, and more as genial, impartial Korean friends.'

Plates of *pulgogi* (beef) and *kalgi* (pork) sat out in front of Sun, along with a steel dish piled high with cold buckwheat noodles. The air was lurid with grease and had the stodgy smell of overcooked carbs. He tucked a white napkin into his collar, to cover his brown Party blazer.

A cockatoo he kept in a cage by the window chirped for attention, hopping along its perch, calling out more to itself than anything outside the cage. Sun got up angrily and went over to enquire what the fuss was, his looming shadow sparking increasingly frenetic flapping of the bird's wings. Sun took a black sheet from the window sill and threw it over the cage, the bird chirping in a mournful descending scale as its view of the outside world was taken away.

There was a tentative knock on his door, barely audible from across the room. Sun called out, 'Come!' and returned to his desk.

His secretary, wearing full Party regalia, rushed over holding a document, her tiny feet clacking rapid footsteps across the polished wooden floor. 'Here is the finished paper, comrade Secretary. "Directives Against Anti-Socialist Phenomena."' She had no room to place it down on his desk for all the food. It never occurred to him to offer her so much as a bowl of soup, rationalising that the Dear Leader admired a 'free spirit' in his senior officers.

He took the document, then sat back in his chair and smirked. 'We are damn good at naming things aren't we, Miss Lee?'

'Yes, comrade Secretary.' She didn't smile. 'Comrade Han is ready outside.'

'Send him in.'

She lingered by the food for just a second before returning to her post, trying to take the earthy smell of *pulgogi* and potatoes with her.

Han whispered, 'Thank you, Miss Lee,' as he past her wearing a stranger's shoes. He stood in front of Sun's desk at full attention, hands behind his back, staring over the top of Sun's head at the portraits of Kim Il-sung and Kim Jong-il behind him. Han wondered, were they really "up there" somewhere, looking down on all his crimes and deceptions? What if he had gotten it all terribly wrong, that there was indeed a good side and a bad side? It wasn't like in cowboy movies where the bad guys almost seem to know, and enjoy, they're the bad guys. In North Korea, no one thinks they're on the bad side. 'Good evening, comrade Secretary Sun.'

Sun didn't acknowledge him, flicking through the DAA-SP document. '"We must pull out the roots of individualism and selfishness, and firmly arm ourselves with group awareness."' He paused.

Han wondered whether he was supposed to comment.

'"We must battle fiercely against the invasion of imperialist ideology and culture." Would you agree with these statements, Han?'

Couching his terms, Han said, 'They are essential doctrines of the Party, sir.'

Sun seemed irked by Han's answer. 'But do you agree?'

There was nowhere in language left for him to go. 'Of course, sir.'

'And how are things with the Westerners?'

'Very well, comrade Secretary Sun—'

Sun raised his hand. 'Spare the formalities or we'll be here all bloody night.'

'Very well, sir. I took them straight from the airport to the Mansudae Grand Monument, which impressed them greatly, I think.'

'And they both laid flowers at the Great Leader's feet? They were respectful?'

Han was a picture of mock outrage. 'Of course, sir. I demanded it! Then I took them to the hotel, reminding the receptionist of reports on tourists wandering out of hotel grounds unaccompanied.'

'I'm glad to see you've been reading the Department of Tourism's memos. Research is important in our line of work.'

'I'm spending the rest of tonight in the library doing just that, sir.'

'Good. You're in a department full of strangers. It always helps to have a fresh pair of eyes go over everyone once in a while. So what was it today?'

'We visited the DMZ this afternoon, escorted by Mr Kang. We placed specific emphasis on reunification, as my guidelines dictate. Mr Kang was eager to show them the axe in the Peace Museum.'

Sun's head dropped. 'Right.'

'I explained to the Americans how we had been deliberately provoked, and they shouldn't believe their Western propaganda.'

'Had the Yank and the Brit been on the other side?' Sun swiped his head left.

'It's likely, sir.'

Sun turned a page on Han's file as if he were just discovering its data. 'I see you have a commendation from the Secretary of the Guidance Department. You were escorting a delegation from the Chinese Foreign Ministry around a munitions factory in Chongjin. During trade negotiations one of the Chinese Minister's aides denied having held rival talks with the Russian Commerce Secretary in Beijing the week before. You pulled out a photo from the Reuters News agency, of the aide shaking hands with him. The Chinese signed the deal with us the next day. Do you know how much money that deal was worth?'

Han shook his head humbly. 'I wasn't party to those discussions, sir.'

Sun arched an eyebrow. 'It was a *lot*, Han. The Guidance

Department took all the credit from the Party, and they fobbed you off with this,' he held the commendation up between his fingers, like it was soiled, 'this certificate. My question is: when are you going to pull a coup like that for this Department?'

'I'll do my best.' Han corrected himself. 'Soon, comrade.'

Sun drummed a finger on his desk. 'It is the Dear Leader's birthday after the new year, and I want the Department to give him something substantial. It's time we reasserted our authority.'

'I agree, sir.'

Sun feebly looked for a file – not lifting anything, simply touching what was already visible. 'What's this I'm reading about Mr So?'

'Sir?'

Sun gave up looking. 'He's been buying foreign movies at the market.'

'Yes, sir. That did come up today.'

'We're going to have to start clamping down on these private enterprises. Sure, one day it's movies, the next it's distributing propaganda and denouncing the Party.'

'It's a slippery slope, sir,' Han added seamlessly.

'And Ryong, you are satisfied with him?'

Han hesitated, shifting weight from foot to foot. 'I would prefer he soften his approach to the Westerners.'

'Soften?'

'Yes, sir. He sees the tourists as adversaries. To be frank, sir, he is of the old isolationist mentality, and that is contrary to our assignment, as I understand it.'

Sun rose from behind his desk and opened a filing cabinet against the wall, pulling out records with the name "Ryong Jang-ung" on the front. 'Ryong's committed to the socialist cause. He's loyal. He'd do anything the Party asked him.'

'Of that I have no doubt.'

'Traitors do not lurk in the shadows here; they work alongside you, and applaud loudly at Party meetings. And like my predecessor, sometimes operate at the highest levels of government. Hwang,' he shook his head. 'You think you know someone... Anyway, Ryong is still older than you, and you could learn a thing or two from him.' Sun stood in front of his window overlooking Pyongyang Square, where hundreds of children were finishing another long day's preparation for the upcoming Mass Games, synchronizing marches and dances in the dusk, holding up colour-coded cards which formed elaborate pictures and slogans of North Korean prosperity and happiness. 'Don't think because I went to school with your father that you have nothing to prove to me here.'

'Of course, sir.'

Sun turned to the birdcage, nudging it into a gentle swing (to the bird's audible annoyance). 'I suppose your father will have talked about me.'

'About what, sir?'

'Old Party matters. You know how it can be. Sometimes old allegiances can get confused over time. Your father and I didn't always see eye to eye about the future of the Party.'

'I don't recall him saying anything like that, sir. My father wasn't one for talking about Party matters to me.'

Sun left the cage alone. 'It's important to talk about Party matters to people. It tells you so much about a person.'

Han needed to swallow, but he was afraid Sun would be able to hear it across the room.

Sun produced another file from his cabinet. 'Miss Mae Soon-li. One floor down,' he said, striding back to his desk.

Han was interested to see where Sun was going to go with it. 'I just found out last night that she lives below me.'

'She's a cellist in the National Orchestra at Mansudae Theatre. We've been watching her for a while. I was hoping you might pay her closer attention. Ask her about Party matters. I'm pushing for a home search, you see.'

Han nodded diligently. 'You can never be too careful with artists, comrade.'

'She is due at Festival rehearsals tomorrow morning. We'll send in a team once she's left the apartment.'

Han got a flash of the books sitting in Mae's hallway. 'You're sure that's necessary, sir? I must say, I didn't get the impression from her she was the sort.'

'Han. You barely know her. She's hardly going to confess to being anti-Party to a complete stranger. That's why they call them secrets.'

'Actually, sir,' Han said. 'I was thinking... it's a quiet street. A team arriving at a new building during the day might create a scene. I have easy access to the apartment. Maybe I could—'

'The plans have been made. The men have instructions to make it look like no one has been there. If she suspects she's being monitored she might alter her behaviour.'

Miss Lee buzzed the intercom. 'Your next appointment, Secretary Sun.'

'Talk to her, Han,' Sun urged him.

Han saluted him, then turned to leave, walking towards the door he came in by.

'No, Han. Out *that* door if you don't mind.' Sun pointed to a smaller door beside his drinks cabinet, leading to an anteroom.

Strange, thought Han. *Who doesn't he want me seeing come in*? He held back in the anteroom, his ear against the inside of the door to hear who it was.

Sun buzzed Miss Lee, who brought in Ryong, checking over his shoulder, turning his hat nervously in his hands. He stood in front of Sun's desk. 'Thank you for inviting me, comrade Secretary,' he said, flushed.

Sun gestured for him to sit down. 'Make yourself comfortable.'

Ryong was about to put his hat on Sun's desk, then quickly retracted it, sitting it in his lap instead.

Sun leaned forward, clasping his hands together over Han's file. 'So tell me...' A grin stretched across Sun's face like an earthquake. 'What do you make of comrade Han?'

Han's chest dropped as he exhaled. *Of course*, Han thought. *Loyalty is everything.*

Banquet Hall 1, Koryo Hotel

The service at dinner felt like the entire hotel staff had descended on Banquet Hall 1 (meals continued to rotate between BH1 and BH2; you never ate in the same BH two meals in a row). Ben and Hal were attended to by an incessant stream of fluorescent-robed dish-servers, bow-tied floor sweepers and tray-clearers, while stern-suited ambience-monitors stood in the wings. The Norwegians two tables away were on their third round of on-the-house beers.

Ben ate most of his dinner without looking at his fork. 'Did you get anything good on the balcony with the Chinese?'

Hal moved a lot of food around in the bowls, but ate hardly anything. He was withdrawn, and unusually pale. He only spoke to answer direct questions. 'Mr Ryong was trying to piss me off by teaching them how to say "American imperialists" in English.'

'Mr Han was telling me about his family. His parents died in a car crash in two thousand one.'

'Seems the only way out of this goddamn prison for a North Korean.'

'It wasn't suicide, Hal.'

'Then they got lucky.' Hal drank half his bottle of beer in one go, then saw how uncomfortable Ben was. 'I'm sorry, I wasn't trying to be... you know. Morose or whatever.'

Ben tried to change the subject, hoping work would take Hal's mind off whatever it was on. 'It's funny,' Ben said, with a brief laugh. 'Mr Han said the strangest thing. Or actually the most inaccurate thing.'

'Whadd he say?'

'When Mr Kang was speaking in Korean about the axe incident, saying the Americans provoked it and they keep the axe out so they can tell people about it. But Mr Han translated him as saying North Korea wasn't proud of killing soldiers over such a small offence as cutting a tree down.'

'He couldn't have just made a mistake?'

'There's no way. He wasn't translating Mr Kang, he was just talking to me.'

'Why would he do that?'

'There's two reasons: on a superficial level, he doesn't know I understand Korean. And the second is the more interesting one: on a political level... he obviously doesn't blindly approve of everything the Party does.'

Hal had known Ben long enough to know what was coming.

Ben dragged his chair closer to Hal's. 'I really think we can get him on the record.'

Hal shook his head despondently. 'It'll never happen—'

'If we obscured his face?'

'What if he panics and throws us in jail for plotting—'

'Plotting what?'

Hal struggled to keep his voice down. 'I don't know, Ben, whatever the hell he feels like! Have you forgotten where we are?'

Ben stretched his legs out, stabbing the table from a distance with his finger. 'This isn't as big a deal as it sounds...'

'You're talking about asking our official government minder if he'll go on record that his Party and its authority is a sham, and no one really believes the propaganda they have to say day after day.'

Ben stared back, his shoulders held in a shrug. 'Why not?'

Hal covered his face and laughed behind his hands. 'This place is getting to you. Have you forgotten Iran already? Locked up in an interrogation room, swinging light bulb and all, and threatened with execution for spying. All for trying to get someone to go on record about the regime.'

'This is different.'

'How?'

'We won't get caught this time!'

Hal threw his hands up in exasperation, a madman in his midst.

'This is what we're *supposed* to do, Hal.'

'It's not realistic. No one expects us to get anyone, let alone an official, on record against the regime.'

'My father would have tried.'

'Not today, not under these circumstances. The story was getting in here at all.'

'*CNN, BBC World Affairs*, these people got in, they spoke to defectors in the South. We've got to get something they didn't. And that means a little calculated risk.'

'Oh my god, you're like the guy who puts his hood up to walk through a puddle. Your feet are still going to get wet. Is this all because your dad died when we were in Iran?' Hal shook his head. 'Don't try to keep ghosts in a cage, Campbell. They'll always get out.'

Ben didn't respond.

Hal was taken by the sound of two waitresses singing a traditional Korean song to the Norwegians. The four Norwegians clapped along at four different speeds, and on the second beat instead of the fourth. Hal didn't know a thing about any of the Norwegians. Yet in that moment he would have gladly swapped lives with any of them. He didn't understand where this thing came from: assuming everyone else must be happier than him. He asked with a frown, still watching the waitresses' song, 'Do you think you're a good person?'

Ben was glad of a reason to stop eating. 'Why are you asking that?'

'What about me? Would you describe me as a good person?'

'Of course.'

'What about after you showed them the Khartoum video?'

Ben leaned back, then sprang forward to intercept a waitress trying to replace the half-eaten bowls with new ones, despite there still being a dozen other bowls that hadn't even been started. 'No, thank you. Really. Thank you.'

Hal took out a cigarette and showed it to the waitress, as if for permission. 'Is this okay?' he asked.

The waitress nodded vigorously. 'Yes, smoke is okay.'

Hal raised a fist in celebration, then the Norwegians, seeing Hal light up and Hal's encouraging them to follow, started lighting up and cheering too, sparking a tennis rally of back-and-forth cheers.

Ben wasn't sure how he felt about being the only sober Westerner in Banquet Hall 1. Ben stared at Hal, his good cheer with the Norwegians transparent to him. 'Is something on your mind, Hal?' Ben asked.

Hal took a drag, then withered back in his chair like a balloon deflating. 'Those that speak do not know; those that know do not speak.'

Ben put down his cutlery. 'Do you think if you keep watching the video, replaying your protestations in your head that it will stop hurting? You didn't do anything wrong, there was—'

'Nothing I could have done, yes, I know. Apparently the rest of the world thinks differently. What do I always tell you about God?'

'That he cares what you do, not what you say.'

'So what do you think God makes of what I've done?'

'But is that the only reason to be good? That's the only reason people here are good. Because they're scared someone's watching them, and there'll be reprisals.'

'You're talking about judgement.'

'I am absolutely talking about judgement.'

'Then we're having two different conversations, because I'm talking about forgiveness. I'm talking about redemption.'

'Maybe what you should be talking about is why is God so hard on people who do nothing but try and please him? Because it's actually pretty goddamn hard to be a good person. You smile at strangers who will never spend a second wondering about you as a person, you hold doors and get no thanks, you work harder than your colleagues but you get paid the same, and you start to wonder who you're doing all this extra shit for. Now, *you*,' Ben motioned to Hal, 'feel better because you think God has seen what you've done. But I think it's because you already know what good is.'

'What about the tweets? The YouTube comments? Do those people not know what good is?'

'Not off the back of a thirty-second morally grey event. You can only judge a man once all the facts are in.'

'They beat him to death, and I was thinking "this can't be happening, I wish this wasn't happening," at the same time checking my focus was right.'

'And more people are talking about Sudan now because of it.'

Hal wasn't convinced. 'I just keep thinking about Kevin Carter.

Maybe people kill themselves when they think they're no longer good people. Maybe just wanting to be good isn't enough.'

'Hey.' Ben eyes were bulging, now he knew the seriousness of what Hal was talking about, even if Hal didn't directly realise it. 'You're a good person. I know you. Do you understand?'

Hal raised his beer to the departing Norwegians, and finished the dregs. 'Don't you just feel sometimes like you're *carrying* all this *stuff* around all the time?'

Ben couldn't think of any other ways to comfort him. The Norwegians were gone. The other tables' food was being cleared back onto trays. Trolley-pushers made a soporific journey through the maze of BH1's tables and chairs, that if watched in its entirety, from table to kitchen, was unbearably sad.

Hal sat on the end of his bed with the lights out, smoking a cigarette in the glow of State TV. Evening broadcasting was wrapping up with a series of VHS-quality slow-zoom-in shots of Mount Paektu, scored by what sounded like a choral group recorded in a small bathroom.

Ben sat on the edge of the bath with the shower running, towel around his waist. He stared into his hands, wondering if this was what his dad had felt like. How sad did you have to be to want to drink every day? Through his father's illness – cirrhosis being a long drawn-out affair – friends kept telling him to make the most of every hospital visit, to be sure he was leaving his father (in a way it felt more like he was leaving his father, rather than the other way around) on good terms. But every time he got to his bedside, he couldn't find the depth of words he thought his father needed to hear, or that Ben needed to hear himself say. That there were times Ben hated him, and had made Ben feel more alone than he had ever thought possible, but now it was coming down to it, all he felt was regret, and all he wanted was his love, and for him not to die. That he wasn't ready to see him leave before he had done anything substantial and proven his worth to his father. But he never told him any of that, and he died with Ben still believing himself to be a professional failure. And now that his father was dead, Ben felt like he suddenly had so much to tell him. He felt like calling him all the time, and often saw his face in strangers'. All Ben knew for sure was that his dad knew none of the above. The dead know nothing.

In the bedroom, Hal pulled his laptop over, waking up the screen with a sweep across the mouse pad. He highlighted the Khartoum video file on the desktop, then dragged it to the Recycle Bin and deleted it before he could change his mind. Something about getting rid of the video made him want to pray. He got down on his knees by his bedside, forearms resting on the duvet. Just as he was about to close his eyes, Ben opened the bathroom door. As ever, already dressed for bed in loose boxers that gave nothing away, and his UNICEF t-shirt. 'Sorry,' Ben said, stepping carefully over Hal's legs to get to his bed.

After sitting for a moment watching Hal pray, Ben felt the compulsion to kneel beside him.

Hal opened his eyes after he felt the slight depression of Ben's arms on the mattress to his right. Ben's eyes were closed, but he couldn't bring himself to pray. The few times as a boy he had tried it, he never felt his prayers *go* anywhere. They were just words he said to himself. But in that moment he didn't care, and so he asked his father for forgiveness. Beside him, Hal was also asking for forgiveness, but his prayers were interrupted by the sound of Ben crying. As Hal opened his eyes, Ben had covered his face with his hands. 'My dad's dead,' Ben said, crying with his eyes shut. Hal hugged him; he didn't need to say anything.

On the TV, on mute, Mount Paektu fade-cut to the final close-up image of a waving DPRK flag.

Central Party Offices, P&A Dept. Library

The junior officer at the library reception had on a set of seventies noise-isolating headphones, learning advanced English from an audiobook. Seeing Han approach his desk, he slid the headphones off round his neck. In the silence of the library Han could hear the

English voice from the tape saying: '*I will do as the Party tells me...*'

After Han signed the logbook, the junior officer said, 'Thank you, comrade,' then moved as if to put his headphones back on.

Han stayed looming over the desk. 'Are you going to check my ID? Or can anyone just walk in off the streets and be given access to classified materials?' Han could see the panic in the junior officer's face.

'I just assumed that downstairs had already—'

Han placed his ID down on the logbook. 'Han Jun-an, Senior Communications Officer, Pyongyang.'

He made a frantic note in the logbook beside Han's name. 'I'm sorry, comrade. I'll be more diligent in future.'

'Do you know the English word *trust*, comrade?'

'Yes, sir.'

Han picked up his ID. 'Never trust a stranger.'

The P&A Dept. library housed the Party's collection of foreign, otherwise banned, books. Only the most trusted senior Party members like Han had access to such material, benign as they were – there was nothing as incendiary as the books hidden under Han's creaky bedroom floorboard.

The bookcases were in an unlit back corner, no more than one hundred titles. Desks with cassette tape decks were laid out like a foreign language classroom, with banks of computers lining the far walls, separated by cubicle dividers, but low enough to see your neighbour's screen. The computers were the only ones in the country open to the Internet – monitored, but uncensored. In Pyongyang University where Han had studied, computers had only the most basic of intranet systems, where all access could be rigidly controlled, and sites outside of Korea could blocked.

Han's only company was a junior administrator who looked fresh out the university, dressed in official Party garb, his hat too large for his head. He sat at a desk with all eight volumes of Kim Il-sung's *Reminiscences with the Century* piled in front of him. Not that he could ever read so much in one sitting. He just thought his library record would look good if it showed him checking them out, particularly late at night. Eager to be noticed for his endeavour, the administrator said, in a voice too loud for the room's atmosphere, 'Good evening, comrade.'

'Comrade,' Han replied without looking up, picking a computer whose screen faced away from the administrator. Younger Party members who didn't have Internet clearance were always trying to catch a glimpse of what the Real World looked like, pretending to shelve books as they peered over senior members' shoulders, awestruck as a foreign news webpage opened up. Even Han still felt like he was committing a crime accessing the Internet uncensored. It was like running red lights with the police behind, but never pulling you over.

Han logged on, going first to Google, typing in "Ben Campbell". After the first entries of senior professors at Ivy League universities in America, professional-model photographers, and unrelated YouTube videos of someone called Ben Campbell playing acoustic covers of Radiohead songs on his webcam, Han scrolled down to "Images for Ben Campbell". There he was: pictures of his tourist sitting on a rock somewhere in what looked like the Middle East, dressed in khaki combat trousers, and a sky-blue t-shirt that read in bold letters 'PRESS'. He clicked through the links to find the webpage they were taken from: *REBEL News*, dispatches from Afghanistan the year before. His heart sank before he even reached the byline: "Ben Campbell reports" with "Photographs by Hal Huckley (AP)" underneath. He clicked links to *REBEL* videos, finding a video clip of Ben talking to Iraqi market stall owners in the aftermath of a car bomb. The camera was shaky, the video grainy, from a handheld. 'Is that you behind there, Mr Hal?' he wondered quietly to himself. Seeing Ben *out there*, outside Korea, in far-off places Han would never see in his lifetime, he remembered how quickly they would be disappearing back into that world after the week was through.

It had taken hundreds of hours for Han to understand the language of the Internet. There were opinions everywhere on every possible topic. People abused and swore at perfect strangers in comment sections for no reason other than they didn't see the world in the same way. Was this what was going on in people's heads in the Real World?

Were they all really this mean and bitter and angry and selfish and devoted purely to their own pleasure? Han couldn't understand it: they had so much freedom, so why were they so unhappy?

He typed in his favourite URL: facebook.com. Some profiles had political images with ironic slogans underneath, protesting Wall Street bailouts (Han had been following the Western financial crisis closely through the *New York Times*, one of his bookmarked websites), or showing solidarity with the Arab uprisings. It never failed to surprise him how free they were to say what they wanted. All those foreign, white faces in their profile pictures, wearing baseball caps of local sports teams – all those Tigers, Bulls, Yankees, Giants, Lakers – huddled with their friends on drunken nights out, all laughing, holding up drinks to the camera, or wedding photos, graduations, in shopping malls, restaurants, theme parks... And for a little while, because Han could see updates on what they had been doing, he could pretend he was part of their lives. But the more deeply he tried to immerse himself in them, the further away he felt – like a bird flapping its wings in a headwind, going nowhere.

Ben's was the first profile returned in the search window. He had thousands of followers, his Wall filled with congratulatory posts from all over the world. His photos had been set to Private, but there were still a number of public ones: always Ben by himself in a different country. There was no family or girlfriends, not even any actual friends. There he was in Paris, Berlin, Rome, Tokyo, Cairo, but with no one else. And no matter how much Ben smiled in the photos, it couldn't cover up what seemed obvious to Han: he was just as alone as he was.

Then he found a single picture of Ben with his arm around an older man, who, under the ravages of cirrhosis, would once have been handsome. The description below said 'Me and dad'. Han closed Facebook and went back to the *REBEL News* homepage, clicking on Ben's bio. It described Ben as being a television and print reporter. Thirty-five, born in Edinburgh (Han knew this already from his passport and visa documents) but raised in London, and best known for his "gritty, undercover exposé style on secretive foreign regimes like Syria and Iran." Han took a long intake of breath and pushed himself back in his seat. He scrolled down the page, wondering how things could get any worse. And when he reached a summary of Ben's talents, they did.

As Han held his hands in a prayer pose over his mouth, the junior administrator looked over, trying to get a sense of what Han had seen. What had happened in the Real World? What was the news? Han's eyes met the administrator's, and he lowered his hands. Han felt a terrible urge to pace. Ben's bio listed him as being fluent in English, French, Arabic, and there it was: Korean. Han drummed his leg fitfully up and down under the table, cursing himself. *How could I be so stupid*? he thought. Then he caught himself in a difficult truth: *maybe I didn't check because I didn't care*? He printed out screengrabs from the pages he'd looked at, stuffing the printouts into his bag as soon as they rolled into the printer tray. He logged off the computer and hurried past the administrator who bid him a hearty 'Goodnight, comrade.'

Han said nothing, rushing out through the swing doors, straight into Ryong.

They both looked as distressed as each other.

Han struggled to hide the tension in his voice. 'Comrade. What are you doing here so late?'

In the panic of the moment, Ryong managed to blurt out a lie. 'I was just meeting Chief Officer Yong about next week's visits.'

'Is that so.' Han's heart sank a little, knowing Ryong was lying. 'We should probably be getting home. We have an early rise tomorrow.'

'Would you like a lift home, comrade?' Ryong asked, his eyes travelling down to the printouts sticking out the top of Han's bag.

Han zipped it up. 'No, thank you. I'm in the mood for walking tonight.' Telling Ryong what he had found wasn't an option. If only he knew about it, he could control the situation.

'Well, I'll see you tomorrow morning then, sir.'

'Goodnight, comrade,' Han said. He pitied Ryong, that there were so many things he had never considered about life and the world outside Korea. That when he said how grateful he was to the Party for all they'd done for him, he couldn't picture a single thing – like food or housing or safety – that shouldn't already be afforded to him by the pure, unspoken laws of humanity. Ryong had no access to all the secretive yet obvious things books had told Han over the years: how the consolations of loneliness can be almost exactly equal to the consolations of joy; how sometimes you can feel a person's presence in a room when they're not there, and this absence is still somehow comforting; how if you sat in a room for long enough and just thought about how insane and absurd it is to be alive, you would find it very difficult to think a sane thought ever again.

Han spent most of the walk home through the deserted pre-curfew streets imagining people all over the world watching him in Ben's future report, and it struck him that his assignment had radically changed; he now had not only a profound responsibility, but an opportunity: to portray his country the way he always wanted the outside world to see it.

'Only The Dead Don't Starve'

Han family residence, the outskirts of Pyongyang, 7ᵗʰ July Juche 82 (1994)

Jun-an sat at the dinner table, his legs alternately swinging underneath, feet unable to reach the floor, his stomach rumbling as if his insides were rearranging themselves. The second his mother, Ji-won, turned her back in the kitchen Jun-an started playing with his *sujeo* spoon and chopsticks.

'Put them down,' she called through to him.

He didn't understand how she could know. 'But I wasn't—'

'Yes, you were.'

There was little smell in the kitchen from the night's soup, just heat and steam.

Jun-an's father, Song-man, walked in, preceded by the smell of an American cigarette – Jun-an could always tell the difference. None of his friends' fathers had American cigarettes.

Song-man stood in front of the table and stared at the place settings. 'You've done it again,' he said sadly.

Ji-won came over to see what he was talking about.

He picked up the extra *sujeo* and table mat beside Han, exhaling irritably in the kitchen as he brushed past Ji-won.

'I'm sorry,' she croaked, still facing the other room.

Song-man banged the drawer as he put the cutlery away. 'You couldn't have reminded your mother?'

Jun-an's legs were no longer swinging. 'I thought mother wanted us to pretend.'

'Pretend?'

'Like Cho-hee was still here. I thought it would be nice.'

Ji-won brought in the pot of soup, explaining, 'Now remember, boys, this is for two nights.'

Jun-an's spoon barely dragged in the bowl as the soup was mostly clear liquid. It only took one nod from Song-man in Jun-an's direction

108

to make him start eating. He knew his father was telling him not to complain, that it was still better than the other houses around them were having. Sometimes Jun-an and Song-man could hold whole conversations in silence. A simple expression from his father could add up to more than a hundred words. Jun-an would copy how his father held his *sujeo*, unbuttoning the top button of his Young Socialist League shirt like his father undid his Party shirt.

'Sun called me today,' Song-man said, recoiling from the harsh seasoning used to give the soup some semblance of taste.

Ji-won replied, 'What did he want?'

'Just to tell me he's a big shot in Communications now.'

'He's moving up pretty quickly.'

'I'm not surprised. He's had three superiors arrested in the last six months. Hard to believe we started out in the same classroom. I told him about my new position but he didn't care. He kept going on about how he was finally going to clean up the Department.'

Ji-won stopped eating. 'You got a promotion? That's wonderful news, darling.'

'It means I'll have more work for the same pay.'

'You won't get a bigger ration?'

'I'm still at *Rodong Sinmun*, but I'll be able to travel around more. Maybe I'll be able to trade some more of these American cigarettes at the markets. Seems like Sun's being groomed for a top position at the Ministry by Secretary Hwang. If I can stay in with those people... things might get easier.'

'It's all about his *songbun*. From the day he was born he's never had to worry about obtaining a high-ranking position, and all because his grandparents fought in the war.'

Everyone was finished with their soup in a few minutes, even lingering on each spoonful it never seemed to last long.

'Dad,' Jun-an started. 'The boys at school make fun of me because I always want to be an American imperialist bastard when we're playing war. It's not fair.'

'They don't take it in turns?'

'No.'

'That doesn't seem very socialist does it.' Song-man sniggered.

Ji-won put her finger to her lips and thumbed at the living room wall. She knew their neighbours could spend long evenings with their ears pressed up against the walls, hoping to overhear some counter-revolutionary discussion they could feed to the local *inminban* – the Party-assigned community group who kept tabs on the other residents – at the next meeting in the hope of receiving some kudos from the local Party chair. There was always the chance of some extra rations as a reward.

'Dad,' Jun-an started again.

'Yes, son.'

'What does imperialist bastard mean?'

'Reductio Ad Absurdum; What Fear Denies, What Hope Asserts'

Chollima Street, Pyongyang, 16th December 2011

Across the city Mae was playing music that she felt nothing for, unaware plans were already in motion to search her apartment the next morning. There was nothing Han could do about Sun's suspicions of her. The Party hadn't gotten unshakeable power and control by bowing to simple cries of innocence. Once you were a suspect, you were a suspect for life. It wasn't that you might be innocent, the charges against you just hadn't been proven yet. It was their unbeatable argument, *reductio ad absurdum*: evidence of no crime only proved the further crime of concealment. Presence proved absence, and absence proved presence. To the Party, exceptions always proved rules.

Han sat in bed writing by candlelight, *A Great Mind* sitting open beside him where he hid his notebook.

'I can't shake the belief that if only Mae knew I was also a reader, wouldn't she feel the same as I do about her? That's making an assumption, of course: that because she reads the same books I do, that she feels the same way about them. What if she has taken completely different meanings from passages I think of as unshakeably unambiguous? What if the things that move me in a book, do nothing for her? There are no guarantees about any of it.' He resolved that the knowledge that any kind of feelings – he was thinking mostly of empathy at this point – close to his were travelling through Mae's mind, was reason enough not to feel so alone. He drew a line under the last section and started a new paragraph.

'I keep replaying all the conversations I've had with Ryong in front of Mr Ben and Mr Hal, and all the other things they will have on camera that they can listen back to. They crash over me all at once like the torrent of a broken dam: the argument at the Grand Mansudae Monument, whatever has been overheard in the bus, mistranslating Mr Kang at the

DMZ, the lie about why the axe was hidden away. They don't know much, but they know enough to know I am not everything I pretend to be. And I'm not. I smile when I'm sad. I'm lonely beyond measure, yet the more I need love, I make it impossible for someone to love me.'

He heard the metallic feet of Mae's cello case being put down outside his front door, followed by tentative tap ta-ta tap knocks. He slipped his notebook back into *A Great Mind* and slid it under the bed. Each step towards the door brought a vacant rush through his head, as if it were trailing several inches behind his body.

Mae was still wearing the elegant black gown she had performed in, a silk shawl draped over her shoulders. 'Good evening, comrade,' she said as he opened the door. 'I hope I haven't disturbed you.'

'No, not at all. I was just reading.'

'Oh yes?'

'Yes.' He stammered for a title to say. '*A Great Mind*. Do you know it?'

'I've heard of it,' she said ambiguously. 'It's been recommended to me a number of times.'

Like the books on *Juche*, there were more people who claimed to have read all the books available on the Great Leader than there were copies in print.

'You look very beautiful, Miss Mae. Was the concert a success?'

While sliding her hair back behind her ear, her shawl slid off her shoulder, revealing a slither of skin dotted with pale freckles like stars in a misty sky. 'Everyone stood and applauded at the end. They always do, but the Chairman of the Presidium was there. The music was very primitive tonight, no nuance or dynamics. We were accompanying a choir singing about the new legislature building in the Forbidden City. We might as well have been beating rocks on our strings.'

'That sounds...' He searched for something positive and flattering to say, but descended into a laugh. 'Dreadful.'

When Mae laughed she tried to swat him playfully on the shoulder, but Han was slightly too far away, and the half-step she took forward felt like a mile to Han.

'I need to play something,' Mae said, 'but I realise it's late now and didn't want to waken you by playing downstairs again. So I thought I might come to you instead, in case you wanted to listen.'

'That would be lovely, Miss Mae. Come in, come in.' He showed her into the living room and apologised about the mess, referring to a single bowl sitting on the coffee table.

Mae put down her cello and opened up the case. She looked around then said, 'Oh. You don't have a chair I can sit on.'

Han did a three-sixty of the room. 'No, it appears not.'

'The sofa will be fine.'

'Would you like a drink?' Han asked, breaking off to the kitchen counter for the last of Yong's whisky.

Mae looked up from her cello, settling into a spot on the sofa, setting the endpin down on the carpet. 'I'd better not. I need my coordination.'

'No, of course.' Han was relieved. He only had one glass. To go with his one bowl, and one plate. As he fixed a drink, he wanted to move conversation to literature. 'I think it was in Macbeth Shakespeare said alcohol is good for the desire but not the performance.'

'A smart man.' The body of Mae's cello still bore watermarks where her sweat had flown off her forehead earlier. 'I've come straight from the theatre, so I need to tune up a little.'

Han sipped his whisky at the kitchen counter, watching her delicately adjust the tuning pegs, holding her ear close to the strings as she plucked them, ascending then descending.

'Come and sit next to me,' she said, patting the cushion with her bow hand. 'Nothing else sounds like a cello up close.'

He took a galvanizing drink and sat down, trying to think how to raise Party talk like Sun wanted. He was thankful for the glass to stop from fidgeting. It was like he was sitting beside two different people: Mae the Beautiful Neighbour, and Mae the Criminal. And while his eyes concentrated on the former, his brain concentrated on the latter.

'I'm sorry if this is not good. I'm quite tired. This is Shostakovich, Cello Concerto number two.' She didn't use sheet music, not that she could have read it in the darkness of the room. The candlelight from Han's bedroom didn't make it far past the hallway. Her poise changed as soon as she pulled the bow back for the first long mournful notes. She didn't look at the strings when she played, picking out a spot somewhere on the floor ahead, peering with intensity. The opening bars were ominously dark, the bow sliding back and forth ever more slowly, like a person's chest rising and falling in their last breaths. She shook notes out with her left hand with a power and strength that seemed impossible with her thin fingers, which were remarkably even in their length, giving her the ability to make much smoother transitions between the strings than other cellists. A fact that her early tutors had pointed out, insisting to her parents that her hands were made to play the cello.

Mae's fingers had grown accustomed to the tiny room for error that cello strings have compared to thick piano keys. She liked to think of it as the difference between walking along a narrow wall and walking a tightrope. She never over-pressured the strings on the fingerboard as so many cellists did, playing like the instrument was something needing to be throttled into submission. When Mae played, the dynamic between player and instrument seemed to be somehow reversed, the cello playing her. Han had often thought of books in the same way: the reader makes the book, not the author.

When the notes became louder and heavier, Han couldn't take his eyes off how rapidly Mae's arms and shoulders shifted position approaching the climax, her bowing-hand chopping and diving up and over and across the bridge. The melodies were overwhelming, but never repeated like modern Western pop music. There was no work to do with such music – it wanted to satiate your every base wish. With Shostakovich – the way Mae played him – you had to keep up. It made demands of you, and if you did, the rewards were huge. Out of nowhere, emerging from a delirious passage that saw Mae's hand flying up and down the fingerboard, came a kind of miracle: a double-stop, playing two strings at the same time, slashing violently at the strings with the bow right on top of the bridge, a final high note that seemed to blow the roof off the world. Mae brought her face close to the strings and opened her eyes.

Han hadn't moved in the several minutes the movement had

taken, his drink now warm in his hand.

She didn't have to say anything. It was all perfectly clear: this is what I have inside me, this is what I'm capable of, this is how much love I have to give. She straightened the cello upright, away from her body and released herself.

Han emptied his glass in one gulp and lit a Commie Marlboro, scratching his head with the cigarette in his hand.

Any thoughts about questioning Mae had long disappeared. 'I could listen to you play all day, Miss Mae. The perfect end to a very strange day.' Their eyes met, and Han wondered if she could tell he wanted to kiss her.

'It's getting late,' she said, getting up abruptly. 'Thank you for letting me play for you.'

Sensing the moment had passed, Han said, 'Hold on.' He got up to go to the bedroom, and returned with his notebook. 'There's something I'd like you to have. Something to read when you get the chance.' Maybe it was that Mae had shared so much of herself that made him do it, but he wanted her to have something of his, something no one else had ever seen.

Mae put her cello in her case, her cheeks flushed from exertion. She met Han in the hallway and took the notebook from him. 'What is it?'

'We seem to be sharing things tonight. It seemed appropriate.' He opened the door for her, turning slightly so she could manoeuvre past. She seemed to linger in front of him, and he leaned in and kissed her cheek, keeping his lips on her skin as if it were her lips. Her skin was hot. 'Goodnight, Miss Mae.'

'Goodnight, Mr Han.'

'Miss Mae,' he said, leaning out the door.

'Yes?'

'Don't show it to anyone else.'

He sat on the edge of his bed watching the morning light slowly change outside, checking the clock on his bedside table every fifteen minutes. When it came to seven AM and the nationalist music from the loudspeakers spread throughout the city – cleaners making one last scrub of the streets – he heard Mae shutting her door downstairs. He went to the window on the landing, and watched her rushing out onto the street as if she were late (he liked to think she had been up all night reading his notebook). Her cello case was strapped over her shoulder, and she looked different with her hair tied back – more conservative, not the intense, passionate musician he had watched the night before, when her hair had fallen around her face and her skin looked hot. She disappeared into a crowd of people dressed in brown and blue uniforms, everyone thin, and walking slowly.

Han bounded down the hallway into the stairwell, not waiting for the elevator to make its tiresome journey up from the ground floor where Mae left it. Secretary Sun's men would be coming at any moment, and he knew if he got just one thing wrong, neither he nor Mae would live to see Christmas.

When he was at Pyongyang University, learning Russian as was the fashion among the young students, Han had shared a room with a young Party member, Lu-ran. Much like himself, Lu-ran was terribly serious, always debating the ills of Western capitalism and the triumphs of Eastern Communism in the canteen standing on a chair to a rapturous crowd – like Emma Goldman addressing anarchists in 1930s Union Square – urging the others to follow Kim Il-sung's ideological invention. Swept up in *Juche* fervour one morning, Lu-ran left a sign on their dorm door saying, 'We don't believe in property; our door is always open.' Han returned from his day's classes to find their television and radio gone, stolen by a fellow student. Han and Lu-ran learned a valuable lesson about ideology that day. Lu-ran was arrested two years later, trying to cross the border into China. Han never heard from him again.

When Han picked the lock on Mae's door and got inside, the hallway looked different, less cluttered. The books he remembered seeing there had been moved – as soon as she closed the door on him that night, he suspected. There was still a smell of breakfast cabbage soup, the remnants left in a small pot on the kitchen worktop for dinner, still steaming slightly in the cold air. He sat down on the living room couch and scanned the room, deducing any possible hiding spots, imagining the way she would move around the room gracefully and elegantly, perhaps humming Shostakovich to herself.

He stood in front of the portraits of Kim Il-sung and Kim Jong-il, the latter hanging slightly at an angle on the wall, with fingerprints marking the glass. She had gotten sloppy living in the building by herself. Such lax standards would be unthinkable anywhere else, where there was always the possibility of neighbours suddenly stopping by for a gossip, or worse yet, the leader of the *inminban*. He picked up the dirty white cloth sitting in a crumpled mess on the table below, and was about to breathe on the glass to aid cleaning it, when he noticed unframed photographs sitting in a loose pile on the sofa. The first was of her standing next to her mother and father outside Mansudae Theatre. Were they dead, and the memory of them seeing her perform was on her mind after last night's concert? he wondered. The others were of Mae performing with the National Orchestra, taken from the cheap seats way back in the auditorium; Mae as a little girl playing cello, her tiny fingers struggling to reach across the strings; Mae in her Junior Socialist League Party uniform, holding up a certificate for musical achievement; the last a more recent one of her standing in front of the theatre alone, two cello cases by her side. He made sure the photos were in the same order, ruffling them into a consciously uneven manner as he had found them.

He went to the bedroom and put his hand over the mattress where the duvet had been thrown back. It was still warm. A different cello to the one Mae had played the night before stood against the wall beside the window, where she had a similarly miserable view of the brick wall of the building next door. The dress she had worn lay in a heap on the floor under the window along with a pile of other laundry, salt-white Rorschach blots of dried sweat marks on t-shirts from rehearsals. There was so little furniture in the rest of the room he started wondering whether she had lifted up floorboards as he had, but he didn't have time for that. The *Inmin Boanseong* could come at any moment, and So would be arriving soon to collect him.

Then he looked again at the cello, and remembered the two cases from the picture. He picked the clothes up from the floor, revealing another case underneath. When he dragged it away from the wall and put it up on the bed, he felt something loose inside tumble down from the neck to the bottom. She must have left in such a hurry that she had thrown the clothes over it in a futile attempt to hide it. Either she was reckless beyond any kind of common sense, or she had no fear of having her apartment searched.

The case was lined with purple velvet, the shape of the cello moulded into a concavity inside. A pile of dog-eared books with deep cracks lining the spine, like the years of a tree, lay scattered around inside, the Korean-translated covers seeming to glow in a semi-mystical way. Han had searched fruitlessly for such titles over the years: *Jane Eyre, Lolita, Crime and Punishment, A Day in the Life of Ivan Denisovich, Wild Swans, The Beautiful and the Damned, Waiting for Godot*; poetry by EE Cummings; Proust, Flaubert, Graham Greene, Thomas Mann, John Cheever, Hemingway... not a single book on the Great- or Dear Leader. He opened up the EE Cummings, fascinated by the strange, childlike construction of the poems, all written in lowercase like the author's name on the front, capricious punctuation throughout the stanzas. He opened to a poem called "true lovers in each happening of their hearts". He read it slowly to himself. "'true lovers in each happening of their hearts, live longer than all which, and every who; despite what fear denies, what hope asserts, what falsest both disprove by proving true.'"

The more he read it back, the better it sounded. He had been taught at University to make sure all public poetry expressed your love for the Party and the Dear Leader, not your love for an individual. Mae would get twenty years for possessing such material.

He put the Cummings back, and opened the copyright page of one of the silver Penguin Modern Classics. 'Published in the United Kingdom. James Joyce. *Ulysses.*' His hands trembled as he lifted one in particular. He had read so much about it he felt like he knew it already. 'George Orwell. *Nineteen Eighty-four.*' Ever since he started acquiring banned books, it had been the one book he kept asking sellers for. Each occasion brought the same heavy shake of the seller's head. From the blurb alone Han could see why the Party didn't want people reading it. It all sounded uncomfortably familiar, speed-reading it: "'Winston Smith works for the Ministry of Truth... the ruling Party uncover every act of betrayal... they watch him wherever he goes... frustrated by their authority... when Winston falls in love with Julia he begins to question the Party...'"

Then outside in the car park he heard a vehicle pulling in. Han ran to the living room window, and saw five officers from the P&A Dept. filing out the side door of an unmarked van with members of the *Inmin Boanseong*. Han's insides jolted as he saw the last man emerge from the back of the van. It was Ryong, and he was ordering the men inside the building.

Han cursed, '*Eminai*,' and ducked back away from the window. He grabbed the cello case off the bed and bolted for the door. Adrenaline rushed through his hungry body, his vision turning white as if he had stared at the sun. His hands shook as he tried to pick the door locked again, his eyes hunting down the corridor, awaiting the gentle rumble of the elevator doors opening, blindly stabbing at the lock. He finally got the pin in and turned the lock, but as he sprinted down the corridor, holding the cello case under his arm, the books rattling around inside, he heard the ping of the elevator and saw the awful glow of the red light above it. He was out of time.

He started back in the opposite direction but realised there was no stairway there, nowhere else to go. As Ryong barked out the room number to the men, Han remembered the unlocked door next to Mae's, closing it as quickly and gently as he could. The men came stomping past and Han held his breath, the cello case clutched at his chest. He didn't so much as shift his weight for fear of upsetting a noisy floorboard.

There was no crash of Mae's door being booted in: Ryong had the lock picked as he was instructed, leaning down to inspect the slight scratch marks Han had left around the keyhole in his haste. Han put his ear up against the wall, following the men from room to room. On the wall backing onto Mae's bedroom he could feel the men just inches away on the other side. The wind blew through the apartment the same way it had a few nights before, but for some reason Han didn't feel like he was outside this time; he felt both outside and inside at the same time.

There was scraping on the bare floor as the men pulled out furniture, clothes hangers being swept aside as they rustled through the wardrobe.

After ten more minutes of searching, the room fell silent, some muted discussion taking place in the living room that Han couldn't hear. He replayed his movements there, trying to remember if he had missed or forgotten something.

Ryong suddenly ordered the men out, and they stomped back towards the elevator. And with another ping of the doors closing, they were gone. But Han knew it wasn't over yet.

He bounded down the corridor, taking the stairs two at a time, sometimes trying three, causing him to stumble. The cello case broke open, spilling books all over the stairs. When he got back upstairs he filed the case away under his bed, placing pillows and a blanket in front of it, checking it couldn't be seen from the bedroom doorway.

Gathering his thoughts and telling himself – in a frantic fashion that could only have the opposite effect – to calm down, he sat on the end of his bed with his head in his hands. 'Well,' he said. 'You're in it now.'

Ten minutes later, So had picked up Han and they were on their way to meet Ryong at the Ministry, who was looking pleased with himself. 'Mr Han, Mr So, what is it today?' he asked climbing in behind Han.

'The Pueblo,' Han answered, holding off quizzing Ryong on the morning's events. Ryong wouldn't be able to keep any success a secret for long.

They weren't even halfway to the hotel before Ryong crowed, 'I caught one this morning.'

Han tried not to react. 'Caught what?' he asked.

'I bagged one for Secretary Sun.'

'What are you talking about?'

'A woman Secretary Sun has suspicions about. I'm sorry I couldn't mention it last night, but he said he had informed you. Well I went with a team to her apartment this morning.' He couldn't hide his delight. 'He gave me a team!'

Han couldn't bear to look at him. There couldn't possibly have been another stash of books there, he thought. He tried to ask casually, 'What did you find? She seemed like a good citizen to me. My instincts are normally pretty sound when it comes to this sort of thing.'

Ryong flicked his head to one side. 'Perhaps you need to sharpen those instincts, comrade.'

'And why is that?'

'The musician obviously hasn't been paying much attention to protocol seventeen B.'

It was just like Ryong to know the protocols by heart. 'What did you find?' Han asked.

Ryong grinned. 'You should have seen it. Her portraits. They were filthy. Fingerprints all over the glass on the Dear Leader. I've never seen such flagrant disregard! She hasn't cleaned it in weeks. I'll be honest, I was hoping for something a little juicier, maybe a few illegal DVDs, eh, Mr So.' Ryong prodded him playfully.

So laughed along. 'I'm sure I've no idea what you mean, Mr Ryong. I'm a loyal and abiding Party member, don't you know.'

Han instinctively put his hand to his head in despair, then managed to change seamlessly into pretending he had an itch. He'd forgotten to clean the portraits for her. Given the context, anything other than hearty congratulations would arouse suspicion. 'Well done, Ryong,' he forced out. 'I'm sure Secretary Sun is most pleased. You never know, one day it's neglecting the Dear Leader's portraits, the next it's distributing propaganda and denouncing the Party. It's a slippery slope.'

Ryong replied, 'That's what I say. I wish you'd been there, comrade.'

Downtown Pyongyang, later that day

The USS Pueblo was only a short drive from the hotel across the city, which meant So had to take them through downtown Pyongyang.

The traffic was mostly buses – the people packed like livestock inside – and trucks carrying nothing. Men carried copies of *Rodong Sinmun* under their arms, one of which sat under the windscreen on the dashboard of the minibus.

'What's the headline this morning, Mr Han?' Ben asked.

Han pulled the paper down and ran his finger along the script, showing it to Hal who was filming in the backseat. 'DPRK Agricultural Workers Vow to Accomplish Revolutionary Cause of *Juche*.'

'It's quite a small newspaper, isn't it.'

'Six pages is standard.'

'Really, that's all?'

'Yes, but remember there's a new edition every day.'

Hal gave Ben what the pair had come to call his OINK expression (Only In North Korea), a mixture of futile exasperation and disbelief.

Armed with his new intelligence on Ben's linguistic talents, Han raised his voice to So, loud enough to be heard in back: '*Can you speed up a bit, we're approaching Sadong-guyok ward and I don't want them to see the new graffiti. Secretary Sun said this morning it's even worse than the last lot.*'

Ben nudged Hal, directing him towards the back window as if suddenly interested by a passing bus. With their heads turned, Ben whispered, 'He says there's graffiti on a wall coming up. Don't miss it.'

'*It's alright Mr Han, Mr Ryong has already informed me.*' So slowed down as children up ahead in immaculate uniforms were about to cross in small columns, led over the interchanges by crossing guards.

'We haven't seen many old people on the streets of Pyongyang, Mr Han,' Ben said.

'Is right,' Han replied.

'Is it true the authorities, the Party, don't like old people to be seen outside? Or the handicapped? That they tell them to stay at home because they don't fit in with the image of a strong Korea?'

Han leaned round to face Ben, his eyes a little wider than usual. '*That's propaganda, Mr Ben.*'

Ben tried to pretend like he didn't understand. He looked at Hal. 'Um...'

'*Mr Han,*' Ryong said, frowning slightly. '*You're speaking to him in Korean.*'

His gaze at Ben still unbroken, assessing his reaction, Han said, 'Sorry, Mr Ben. I said, this is propaganda.'

Ben could tell something was going on. 'I see.'

Han was now looking at them with different eyes. The true, dark heart of North Korea was now at the autopsy stage: its chest cut open, exposed. They were listening.

'*I think it's coming up soon,*' Ryong said, keeping an eye out for the graffiti.

Han peered ahead. '*Damn. They're still cleaning it.*'

So smiled mischievously. '*They probably ran out of paint again.*'

'*Did you hear what they wrote last time?*' Han didn't wait for Ryong to answer. '"*Let's Bring Down Kim Jong-il." Can you believe that?*'

Hal turned the camera to Ben, who winked at him on the minders' blindside, letting him know he was ready. Ben's mood had changed since the night before, like he had been unburdened of some heavy weight. He sat closer to Hal.

Ryong shifted uncomfortably in his seat between Han and So. '*We shouldn't be repeating things like that, Mr Han. It's bad for morale.*'

Han saw police cars down the road. '*Look, here it is coming up on the right, where the women in the yellow overalls and scrubbing brushes are.*'

So said a little brusquely, '*I know, I know! Do you think I'm blind?*'

Ben tried to look casually out the window, as if he didn't know what they were approaching.

The women had their hands up in defeat and pointed at the wall they had been scrubbing since first light, telling the police and officials from the Guidance Department that the graffiti wasn't coming off. A small crowd of onlookers stood on the other side of the street, pointing and whispering amongst each other.

Ryong, flush with confidence since his morning search, leaned back, trying to explain the crowd away. 'We try keep the city very clean.' Then he actually saw what had been written. Bubbles from the women's soapy water and cleaning chemicals dripped down the slogan: in thick black lettering, it was unmissable on the otherwise blank street:

'김정일 동지여, 굶어죽는 백만 인민을 보라'

('DEAR KIM JONG-IL, LOOK AT 1,000,000 STARVING TO DEATH')

Ryong gasped, '*Jongganna saekki*,' then slammed his hand over his mouth.

Ben asked, 'What does that say on the wall, Mr Ryong?'

Ryong couldn't think of an explanation.

Han intervened. 'Is praising an old economic policy widely rejected by the Party.'

'What does it really say?' Hal whispered to Ben, while Ryong hollered about traitors and sons of bitches.

'I can't read Chosongul script, but it must be pretty bad. Ryong said the same thing he called you at Mansu Hill.'

Hal grinned. 'Jeez, something he hates more than me.'

So stared at the wall as they went racing past, but when he brought his eyes back to the road, a small boy came bolting out from under a tree. On the run like a baseball fielder, the boy picked up a rotten apple sitting in the middle of the road. So swerved out the way and blasted the horn, sending Ben and Hal scooting along the vinyl seats, squashed up against the window.

'*Slow down, Mr So!*' Han demanded, grabbing on to the seatbelt round his waist.

Ryong was still raging about the graffiti. '*Why would someone write that about the Dear Leader?*' He was trembling.

'*You're upsetting the tourists, comrade.*' Han looked back at Ben and Hal, still untangling themselves. 'Are you alright back there? A pedestrian run out into the road. Mr So apologises.'

'Still in one piece, Mr Han,' Ben groaned.

Hal casually saluted Han while lying on his side. 'No fear, Mr Han.'

'*Mr Han, their camera. What if they got a picture of it?*' Ryong asked.

Han gave his best impression of disgust, speaking as slow as possible so Hal's camera mic would pick him up. '*Imagine writing for the Dear Leader to look at one million people starving to death!*'

Hal whispered to Ben. 'Did you hear that?'

Ben winked.

Ryong now had his hands over his ears. '*No, please, comrade, don't say it! Pretend it never happened!*'

But Han was almost serene. '*Calm down. It's not like they can understand.*'

The USS Pueblo was docked on the Taedong River in downtown Pyongyang harbour, at the bottom of a long staircase – 'North Koreans love long staircases, don't they,' Hal puffed – coming down from the Victorious Liberation Fatherland War Museum, and a street of residential high-rises, with little to explain the boat's presence. It was like leaving a tank on display in Times Square. Everyone in Pyongyang knew all about the Pueblo. The Party had made sure of it, and Ben and Hal were about to find out why.

Han and Ryong escorted them to the dockside, where they were met by a female military officer in her sixties, in full uniform of brown shirt, tie, and a jacket with gold epaulettes. Han handed over proceedings without introducing her. She had the expression you would expect of someone that had performed the same thirty-minute tour every day, several times a day, for nearly a decade. There was a saying among old Party members: Once you prove yourself capable of performing a task in North Korea, be prepared to do it for the rest of your life.

'She very experienced,' Han told the men on the way down. 'She been here since before Kim Il-sung died.'

'She looks like she was here when Noah was building the ark,' Hal mumbled.

Before either Ben or Hal could say hello, she started into soporific, prepared words, in excellent English, but with the same difficulty Han had with vowels preceding Rs, as if her tongue was trying to go in opposite directions. 'This is the Pueblo, which was captured by our navy in nineteen sixty-eight. The American imperialists had disguised it as a civil foreign research ship,' she pointed accusingly at the unassuming grey boat, 'before they intruded into our territorial waters. It is the only American naval ship currently in captivity, and is moored permanently here, for all of history to see over the coming centuries the extent of the American imperialists' crimes.' She then turned her back and walked onboard, as if that were the end of the matter.

Hal mumbled behind the camera to Ben as they followed her over the gangway, 'She knows imperialist doesn't have to come after every time she says America, right?'

They were taken to a tiny bunkroom with a flatscreen television attached to the wall, where Ben's questions about what all the red circles on the inside of the hull were, and how many Americans had died, were put off with a curt, 'Will be answered in the video.'

Ben and Hal sat down to watch it, while Han and Ryong stayed up on the deck, talking to some members of the public who were intrigued about the Westerners' presence.

The officer started the video and stood in a doorway behind the men, where she was supposed to be making sure they were paying sufficient attention. She stood holding the remote, staring down vaguely at the ground. She heard the video's narration in her sleep most nights.

The video was more of a slideshow of still shots cobbled together from American stock footage, showing apparently incriminating shots: Lyndon Johnson wasn't just talking with his generals, he was conspiring; then cut to sticks being pointed ominously at maps of Korea; then the Statue of Liberty, as the narration informed the audience that 'The US imperialists had long been eyeing a chance for a pre-emptive strike against the Democratic People's Republic of Korea, resorting to acts of espionage on the land [cut to shots of American tanks], on the sky [cut to American fighter planes], and in the sea [cut to an American aircraft carrier].'

It took a moment for Ben to notice there were no subtitles. 'They actually keep a dubbed version in English for Westerners.' He turned to ask the officer about it, but she was already gone. The narrator (a proud job for someone in the P&A Dept.) had problems getting his tongue around many of the words, a consequence of learning his spoken English from films like *The Sound of Music*, as was common practice in Pyongyang University.

The video moved to grainy archive footage of the crewmen holding their hands up in darkness on deck, lights shone in their faces so only two or three of their faces were visible at a time. Looking at the crew, it had obviously been staged after the fact. '...these are the crewmen of the Pueblo. They were eighty-three, including six officers but one of them was killed at the time of capture as they attempted to resist.'

'This is horseshit, right?' muttered Hal, opening his eyes.

Ben leaned forward, deconstructing all the edits. 'I love how they found an American ship in their territorial waters and just happened to have a film crew onboard. Finding this boat is the best PR exercise that ever fell into their lap. They used to set up fake press conferences with the crew that had been rehearsed for weeks before. They'd get the crew to write letters home saying they were enjoying their stay, but the letters would mention events in America that had never occurred, like, "it reminds me of that time President Kennedy played for the Boston Celtics."'

'I don't get it,' Hal said blankly.

'So the US authorities would know the letters were all bullshit. When they got hauled out for photos some of them held their middle finger up while pretending to touch their face, or when their hands were clasped together in group photos. Eventually the North Koreans started getting suspicious and asked what it meant. The crew told them it was a "special Hawaiian good luck sign".'

Hal struggled to stop his laughter being heard outside. 'Did they believe it?'

'Yeah. Until *Time* magazine ran an article about it later that year. The DPRK military got hold of a copy and they went ballistic, I mean totally bananas. It started something they called Hell Week. They took one crewman at a time and tortured them for seven days straight. Belts, whips, chains, chairs, you name it.'

'I'd like to have sat in on that editorial meeting. Yeah, that was a killer edition last week guys. The North Koreans loved it.'

The rest of the video was mercifully short; the Party wanted the officer present to explain the grizzlier details.

Right on cue, she suddenly reappeared with her eyes watering, and for a moment Ben and Hal thought she had been crying, when she had in fact been yawning. 'I must show you around the rest of the boat.'

Hal shot out of the bench, adding, 'The US imperialists' boat, you mean.'

She smiled for the first time. 'He's been paying attention to the film,' she said to Ben.

'I've seen it before actually,' Ben said.

She stopped in the passageway, stepping aside for the Pyongyang residents making their way in to watch the Korean narration of the video. 'Where have you seen this?'

Ben had to hide his pleasure in telling her, 'It's on YouTube. It's been watched thousands of times.'

She didn't understand.

'On the Internet. Anyone in the world can look it up and watch it. The description said it's available for sale in Pyongyang. Can we buy one?'

'This shouldn't have been taken out the country.'

'I guess someone forgot to tell them that.'

As the officer took them from floor to floor, Ben could now see what the red circles dotted all over the inside of the hull were: bullet and shell splinters from the Korean ship that had been tracking the Pueblo. They had circled each one like some crime scene investigator with ADHD. The circles were everywhere, on nearly every wall. It had been quite the shootout.

Her face lit up taking them down a dim corridor, saying, 'The Yankee, he reached for a gun sitting in this compartment, but the splinters finished him off in seconds, coming through the hull here.'

Ben put his finger through the little craters. 'My god, he must have been in bits.'

'Oh yes, many bits,' she replied cheerfully.

Up on the captain's deck – the only part of the tour she enjoyed – she acted out how the American captain ducked to avoid Korean fire as the search team boarded. A galaxy of red circles littered the wall behind the ship's wheel and on the cracked window in front. 'A movement an inch or two either way and he would have been killed,' she said. That he hadn't been seemed to disappoint her greatly.

While Ben and Hal were taken to watch the "history" video, Han stood up on deck with Ryong who was holding one of the artillery guns, pointing it out to sea, pretending to shoot, shouting gleefully, 'Die, Yankee sons of bastards!'

The civilians on deck laughed along, mimicking with imaginary machine guns.

'Really, Mr Ryong,' Han said. 'You're meant to be representing the Department.'

He let go of the gun and leaned on the deck railing like a scolded child. 'I'm sorry about the graffiti earlier, Mr Han. I couldn't think what to tell them. I've been doing this ten years,' he shook his head in shame. 'I don't know how you are able to think up lies so quickly.'

'They aren't lies, Mr Ryong. Everything the Party says is the truth. And I'm the voice of the Party to them.' Han stood next to him, looking out over the river which now had the vaporous quality of cigarette smoke, starting to drift south at a child's walking pace. 'About the woman from my building.' He had waited as long as he could to ask.

'Miss Mae.'

Han pretended to suddenly remember. 'Oh, is that her name? See,

I'm not familiar with the procedure. What will her punishment be?'

'That depends. The duty officer might keep her for questioning, hoping a relative comes by with a bribe.'

'Worst case scenario?'

'In Pyongyang? Labour camps. You never know. She might get lucky.'

'For a dirty portrait of the Dear Leader?' His incredulity took Ryong by surprise.

'You sound positively defensive of this woman, comrade. A crime has been committed!'

The officer greeted Han as she took Ben and Hal out on deck.

Ben was in the middle of another question, delicately trying to make his point. '...and isn't this boat docked in the same place as the General Sherman incident?'

The officer wearily directed Han to take over, saying to him, '*You've put up with this guy all week?*'

Ryong stepped forward in front of Han. '*I know, comrade. He's a pain in the neck, but what can we do.* Mr Ben, General Sherman was long time ago.'

'I know,' he said, 'but considering that was about a Korean attack on an American merchant ship hundreds of years ago, do you think some people might find it a little... provocative to keep this boat in the same place?'

Ryong thought about it for a moment. 'Is coincidence. We go next door now, because we have arranged for you to meet a captain who was part of the team that captured Pueblo. Very exciting, no?'

Han's mind seemed elsewhere and he was about to be left behind when Ryong shouted after him.

'*Mr Han, aren't you coming?*'

All he could think about was where Mae was, and worse yet, what had she done with his notebook?

They led Ben and Hal (still filming) into a small room, where a man in a pristine white uniform bedecked in an array of medals and wearing his captain's hat, sat back on a bench with his legs crossed, smoking a cigar.

The officer introduced him. 'This is Captain Choi.'

'Does he still serve?' Ben asked.

'He's retired now.'

'He still wears his full uniform?'

'For special occasions.'

His skin was thick and leathery, the sort of man that had been fed and laid a thousand times over by the P&A Dept. for one night's work seventy years ago. Gravy trains didn't come any bigger in Pyongyang.

Captain Choi held his hand out to shake whilst still sitting back, *ex officio*. It had been a while since he had had to rise for anyone. '*They're American?*' he asked.

'*Just the big one,*' Ryong replied. '*The other one's English.*'

The captain shrugged. '*English are alright. Don't like Americans though.*'

'Nice to meet you, Captain Choi,' Ben said.

The captain's smile disappeared when he shook Hal's hand.

'So you were part of the original crew that took the Pueblo?' Ben asked.

Ryong translated for Choi. 'This right. We find the US imperialists in our waters, so we board this boat and we take it—'

Captain Choi clicked his fingers.

'—like this. We arrest eighty-six of American villains, we so sick of their war mongering, and determination to destroy Korean people...'

The Captain got to his feet, growing more and more animated. He was directing his speech towards Hal, performing for the camera, and Han: the old man knew he still had to keep up appearances.

'...and I tell you, if imperialist ever try anything like it again...'

Captain Choi made a fist and mashed it into his palm, his voice still rising.

'...we will chase them to ends of the earth, and bomb them relentlessly; reduce their cities to smouldering ash...'

Ben loved that Ryong couldn't follow English tenses, but was quite at home with phrases like 'smouldering ash'.

Choi looked upwards and pulled his hand up to a salute.

'...and with the Eternal President, comrade Kim Il-sung as my witness, I will be on first boat that leads the invasion—'

Feeling conversation drifting away from where he wanted it, Han stepped in before Choi could get anymore carried away. '*Thank you, Captain, we all admire your sentiments. I'm afraid we must be making our way upstairs now to the Liberation Museum.*' He held his hand out to say farewell, but Ryong interrupted.

'*Mr Han, they haven't signed the book yet.*'

Captain Choi opened up a leather book on a table by the exit door and held out a pen towards Ben. 'You sign the book?' the Captain asked, the only English he ever had to use.

Han said, 'Of course. Mr Ben, Mr Hal, please to sign the visitor's book. A gesture for our hospitality.'

Ben knew what Han was getting at by the English comments others had left already, praising "the strength of the Korean people" and to "never surrender to the imperialists." Ben took the pen and after a brief pause started writing. Captain Choi, the officer, and Ryong, looked eagerly over his shoulder. 'No pressure,' Ben mumbled to Hal, still filming. He wrote: 'Thank you to our guide for the video, and Captain Choi for his memories of the capture of the Pueblo. Maybe one day I can come back and North Korea and America will no longer see each other as enemies, but as friends. Who wish only to live in peace.' Ben put down the pen, satisfied with his diplomatic best.

The others leaned closer to read it back.

Captain Choi asked, '*Did he praise the Koreans? Did he stick it to the Yankee bastards?*'

Han said, '*He wrote that he was very grateful for your time, Captain.*' He shook the Captain's hand.

Ryong was still reading Ben's words back to himself. 'Maybe if you put something about your hope for reunification. Or your surprise at proof of American war crimes?'

'No,' Han said, urging him on. 'We must be going.'

The Victorious Liberation Fatherland War Museum at the top of the stairs was like most State buildings in Pyongyang, flat-roofed, utilitarian, symmetrical. It was also incredibly long but shallow, a common ploy in DPRK architecture that made buildings seem much more impressive when standing in front of them. The entrance was decorated with rows of tiny green conifers, the only colour other than grey in sight.

A female junior corporal holding a long pointing stick welcomed the men and brought them inside. There was undoubtedly plenty to point at in the Victorious Liberation Fatherland War Museum.

The corporal looked at the floor, as if she were picking a very particular spot to stand in the expanse of marble, then got out her big stick and thrust it at the mural that ran several long strides of the wall. 'So we are happy to welcome you to Victorious Liberation Fatherland War Museum. This mural show comrade father, Kim Il-sung, leading the people, and you can see the people very happy.' Her face was so pale, Ben asked Han if she was feeling alright.

'She fine. Is just the light.'

Ben held his arms out and realised what Han meant. The square lights set into the ceiling tiles were so far apart, depending on where you stood you could be in an ethereal ghostly light, or in shadow.

The corporal proceeded to examine each facet of the mural in a fashion that seemed designed to induce comatose. The idea seemed to be that naturalistic mountain ranges with waterfalls were not just about the beauty of nature, but of the purity and rugged strength inherent in the Korean people. Ben and Hal kept looking off in other directions, dulled by the banality of it all. After ten minutes on the mural alone even Han and Ryong were shuffling their feet. It was with some relief that she took them off to the actual exhibits. 'Now we will show you the military hardware of the American imperialists.'

Ryong walked ahead with her, his arm flapping around, gushing about the clean state of the museum.

As they trailed behind, Ben asked Han, 'Why does she say "we"?'

'Maybe she means her and her stick,' Hal suggested.

Han whispered back, 'The guides here speak on the Party's behalf.'

The corridors and halls reminded Ben and Hal of public museums built in the early seventies their schools would take them to: the staircases lined with cheap wooden-panelled banisters, tinny brass music and shrill operatic female voices coming out of tiny speakers that had the treble set too high.

The corporal took them into a room filled with recovered American service vehicles, tanks, a torpedo boat, even a complete MiG-15 fighter plane. Ryong shadowed her, finishing her sentences to prove how much he knew about Korean history, trying to out-muscle her talk of US imperialists and aggression. Ben was growing frustrated with the corporal's evasion of his questions ('If it was America that invaded first, why did Kim Il-sung ask the Russians for permission to invade the South beforehand?' 'How did the North advance so quickly and far into the South if the North had been invaded first?'). Everything would always be 'explained later', that if he just waited until they got into the next room that evidence of the American aggressors' guilt would be revealed. But only more obfuscation came ('We don't have time to explain this today'), and mind-numbing repetition of interchangeable words ('American', 'imperialists' and 'aggressors').

The corporal wrapped up their tour early to take care of a busload of Westerners huddled by the front doors, flanked by their minders. Ryong went with the corporal to talk to his colleagues from the Department to show off his seniority to her, leaving Han wandering aimlessly, staring into glass cabinets of random equipment – helmets, handguns, tattered American flags – thinking about how it had been someone's job to pick up all this abandoned bric-a-brac on battlefields at the end of hostilities.

'Look at them,' Ben said to Hal, motioning at the group of Westerners. 'All with the same glassy expressions, like it's all just a big joke.' He slid down the pillar he was standing against and sat on the ground.

'That graffiti didn't look like much of a joke. What did Mr Han say it was?'

Ben snorted in disbelief. 'It was directed at Kim Jong-il, and how many people had starved because of him. I'm telling you, there's something serious going on in this town.'

Hal sat next to him, rewinding that day's action on the camera. 'Looks like we timed our visit pretty good.'

Ben made a tent with his fingers, staring through it at Han. 'I really thought when I got here they'd all say their piece, then I'd tell them how absurd everything they were showing us was. All the lies, all the propaganda... but it's not the way you imagine it. You look into their eyes, and you feel this... weight, of everything they've seen growing up here, what they've had to put up with from the Party. The corporal, she's young, she probably doesn't know any better. But Mr Han, he's seen what the outside world is like, he must have in his position. How does he keep up the pretence?'

Han wandered towards them, clocking how Ryong had drifted out of sight of them with the corporal, swaggering around, pigeon-footed.

'It's fear isn't it,' Hal said. 'What other option does he have but to stick to the line.'

'But he's not, is he.' Ben unclasped his fingers. 'Time after time, he's showing us, telling us, exactly what a guide shouldn't.' He shook his head. 'It's weird.'

'What is?'

'When we passed the graffiti, and he repeated to Mr Ryong what it said. It was like he was telling *us*.'

Han waved to them as he approached, checking no one was in hearing distance. '*Enjoying the trip?*' he asked Ben in Korean.

He didn't know what to do. 'I don't understand, Mr Han.'

'*I'm sorry. I thought you understood, Mr Ben. Your* REBEL News *webpage said you know the language.*'

Hal knew something was wrong. 'What's he saying, Ben?'

Ben smiled at him, butting his tongue into his cheek. '*How long have you known?*'

Han sat down next to them against the wall, taking a deck of cards out from his top pocket. '*Since last night.*'

Ben said to Hal, 'He knows I speak Korean. He's been researching us on the Internet.'

Hal put the camera down. 'Oh, Christ.'

'Does Mr Ryong know, Mr Han?' Ben asked.

Han could see him still cavorting with the corporal, showing off in front of the more junior minders. Han tossed cards across the floor to Ben and Hal. 'Is okay. We just sitting here playing cards, is fine. Only I know about it, Mr Ben. I could be in trouble if anyone knows I haven't reported it.' There was a slight tranquillity in him now that the pretence could be dropped between them, a truth finally revealed. 'So you know about my argument with Mr Ryong at the Grand Monument.'

Ben picked up his cards. 'And when you lied about what Mr Kang said about the axe at the Peace Museum.'

Han lifted his head back. 'Ah, of course.'

'And you know we're reporters?' Hal asked, pretending to thumb through his hand.

'Is right.'

Hal knocked his head back against the wall.

'Who are you reporting for here? *BBC*? *Channel Four News*? Or American?'

'I have a producer for *REBEL* back in London waiting on us.'

'So it will be seen by many people, yes? Some of your videos have millions of views.'

'We hope millions of people see this.' Ben threw down his hand on the floor. 'Is there something you want to say to us, Mr Han?'

'That depends. I don't know what you're holding yet.'

'If you found out last night, then you knew I would understand what you said about the graffiti this morning. This is a country with no opposition. No dissent. What's going on?'

'It's just a few corrupted minds.'

'The Party must be worried though. Those were officials there this morning, not just police. Were they from the Guidance Department?' Ben couldn't stop himself now. All the questions he had wanted to ask came flooding out. 'I've read reports about Secretary Sun, that he wants the Propaganda Department back at the head of the Party. Is he the one who got rid of Secretary Hwang?'

'I don't know any of this.' Han threw his cards down, then gathered up the rest, dealing them back out again. 'But you should know, you're not the first journalists I've met trying to be tourists.'

Hal covertly hit the record button on the camera which was lying on its side. The rapidly-blinking bars on the viewfinder told him the microphone was picking up Han's voice.

'What are you wanting to do here?' Han asked.

Ben threw a card down with a shake of his head. 'I just want people to know the truth.'

'You don't do this already?'

'Maybe. I'm not sure anymore.'

Han nodded like he understood. 'Tell me, Mr Ben, do you know Robinson Crusoe?'

'Sure. I read it when I was a boy.'

'There a passage in it, when Robinson write about how much he loves the island. That it is all he has and does not care for the outside world anymore. He say, "I look'd upon the world as a thing remote." I think I understand this like him: The world is nothing to do with me. Robinson was stuck on that island twenty-eight years. Did you know this? That's how long I've been in North Korea, Mr Ben.' Han turned his head up toward the front doors of the museum. 'The Real World out there somewhere. What good am I to you?'

'You're always in the world, Mr Han. It's not a choice. Because you're always inside your head.'

'I don't think he's going to understand that, Campbell,' Hal said, eyeing Ryong's progress back towards them.

'No, I think I understand,' Han said. 'I read once, if your prison has no walls is it still prison? Is this what you mean?'

'Head, prison, same difference.' Hal threw his cards down. 'Whatever we're playing, I'm bust.'

'You read a lot, Mr Han?' Ben asked.

Han grew evasive. 'A little.'

'Don't you want to get out of here, Mr Han? Where you can read what you like?'

'Leave North Korea? Impossible.'

'It's not impossible.'

Han corrected himself. 'Not impossible. But difficult. You must have right contacts, but it's very dangerous.'

'We met people in the South, defectors, who did it.'

'For a prisoner, it is the only way out of his cell: escape or die. For me, I can only go deeper inside myself. Is the only place they can't get me.' Peering over the cards, Han noticed Ryong coming back with the corporal. '*Game's over*,' he said switching to Korean, and started gathering up the cards.

Ben stayed sitting down. 'Mr Han,' he said urgently. 'We need to talk more. Alone.'

Han dusted his trousers off as he got to his feet. 'What fear denies, hope asserts.'

'The Secret Reader; Talking Heads'

Chollima Street, 17th December

Han pulled the cello case out from under his bed, getting the same rush of excitement he had felt when he first opened it in Mae's apartment. He wondered if the previous owners of *Nineteen Eighty-four* could have ever imagined it finding its way into North Korea, where its presence would be an on-going matter of life and death. The book had found a way to come alive, to prove itself.

He sat on the end of his bed and read the first line quietly, as if someone else were in the room who he couldn't disturb: "'It was a bright cold day in April, and the clocks were striking thirteen.'" He held the book in a tight grip – the blood draining from the tops of his fingernails – scared that if he let go for even a second the spell he was caught in would break.

As the pages passed, he listened out for some sound of Mae coming home, but he found himself lost in the figure of Winston and his silent suffering in his lonely Ministry of Truth office. The pitiless way Winston looked at his fellow citizens, helpless to do anything for them except grieve the sad passing of time. Han dragged *A Great Mind* across the bedspread, now realising how long he had been sitting in what he thought would be a temporary position at the end of his bed, and took the pencil out of the book's hollow centre. He lit a Commie Marlboro, letting his thoughts crystallize in the pause required to drag on it, then turned to the book's empty back pages to write:

'I have discovered the tourists and they have discovered me. There is nowhere left to hide now and we are getting to know each other.

'There is still no sign of Mae downstairs, and now I realise how Werther felt. You see, I didn't have anyone before she came along, and now I'm in love. There are limits to how long you should go without love, or at least desiring someone. Humans' longing for connection requires a target, otherwise you're throwing darts in the ocean as a means of fishing.

You are just slowly decaying, by yourself, the sky's invisible cage descending on you. I don't know what kind of love would be good enough for me. How much love could I take? Is it possible to want someone too much? If I was with Mae would I not be like a young man having a whole bottle of whisky for his first drink? I'm not sure I could take it. Maybe my body isn't built to withstand such love. Listen to me: I don't even know her, yet I talk of loving her. How can I miss someone I don't even know? Because when love appears inside you, you realise it's what you've been waiting on all those other times you've been suffering. The Inmin Boanseong *might take Mae away from me, they might even take me away, but locking someone up for what's inside them, for what they think and feel, is so futile. As long as we have bodies, we're already prisoners.'*

There was a subdued knock on his front door, the kind of knock when a part of you hopes there isn't an answer. Han stabbed his cigarette out and closed *A Great Mind*. His cigarette smoke tumbled over his shoulder on the way to the hall.

His shoulders visibly dropped in relief as he opened the door. 'Miss Mae, I'm so glad you're alright,' he said.

She looked naked without her cello case. 'I think you might have something that belongs to me,' she said.

In the half-light of the corridor, Han could see she was dishevelled and nervous, holding one hand in the other. He let her inside and fetched his blanket from his bed. 'Here,' he said, 'put this around you.'

She wrapped the blanket around herself and sat on the sofa. 'Thank you.' She fidgeted with her fingers, her eyes drawn to Han's portraits of the Two Leaders up on the wall. 'Your pictures look remarkably clean, comrade.'

'Miss Mae...' Han began, standing at the living room doorway holding the cello case he had taken from her apartment that morning. 'What happened?'

'I was walking to the theatre this morning, when a police car pulled next to me and asked to see my papers. They said an inspection had taken place and they had found discrepancies in my apartment.'

'Your portraits were dirty.'

'Funny. That's exactly what they said.'

140

He put the cigarette in his mouth and carried the cello case to the coffee table underhand, like a body. He didn't open it. 'You know how much trouble you would be in right now if they had found this.'

Before he could sit down she threw her arms around him, pushing him back against the armrest. 'I don't know how to thank you, Mr Han.' She kissed his forehead, then, worried she had gone too far, ran her thumb over it, as if she were trying to take it back or erase it.

All Han could think to say was, 'Please, call me Jun-an.' He had never been held like that before. Like he was important to someone.

'I knew you had seen the books the other night. At first I thought it was you that had told the *Inmin Boanseong*. But all they asked me about was a dirty portrait of the Dear Leader. And when I got back and couldn't find my other cello case I realised someone must have taken it before they got there. You were the only one it could have been. I've gotten so sloppy living here myself, and when you showed up the other night, I didn't have time to hide them.'

'I'm afraid I owe you an apology, Miss Mae.'

She reached for his cigarette, index- and middle fingers separated in anticipation. 'May I?'

Han passed it to her.

After a brief, joint-like drag to calm her nerves, she passed it back. 'Soon-li,' she said, through an exhalation. 'My given name is Soon-li.'

'I owe you an apology, Soon-li. My superior, Secretary Sun, informed me the night before that your apartment was to be searched. I knew they would find the cello case and its... contents. When I went to your apartment I saw the dirty portrait but I forgot to clean it before I left. I could have saved you a lot of distress today.'

'I would be in a lot more distress if you hadn't taken the case.'

Now that she was there with him again, Han couldn't keep track of all the levels on which he was having to operate on. Was this not still the person he suspected of having being sent there to entrap him? In which case, what was Sun doing ordering raids on her apartment? Why did she only keep incriminating herself further the more they talked? Was Sun setting him up by having him question Mae, and if he didn't would she report him?

He moved to the edge of the coffee table, leaning on his knees as he smoked: he wanted to face her. 'When I met you the first time that night, when the lights came on I saw the books sitting in your hallway. I knew as soon as I saw them what they were. I, too, live a quiet life.'

'It is always wise to live loudly on the inside, and quietly on the outside, Jun-an.'

Both of them stared at the closed cello case, neither knowing what to do next. Han's act of hiding it for Mae brazenly stated he not only approved of her criminality, but actively wanted to help cover it up. 'You haven't read my notebook yet, have you?' Han asked.

'I haven't had the chance. It's your journal isn't it? I couldn't think why you would trust to give me something as personal as that.'

If he were being set up he knew he was already far beyond deniability. He knew it was time. He went to his bedroom and opened up the creaking floorboard, taking out a bundle of books and carrying them to the living room.

'There,' he said, dropping them down next to her. 'I seem to have put myself in an impossible position, but I'm not afraid anymore.'

She inspected the books one at a time. 'Why are you showing me these?'

'Because I've got nothing left to lose. And I suspect you might feel the same.'

She sprang up from the sofa, pacing back and forth in the dark. She reached for the pin holding her hair back and shook it loose. 'You don't even know me. Why would you trust me?' She seemed angry.

'The only thing I know for sure is there's something alive inside you I've never felt before. And I know this sounds crazy, but seeing those books in your case makes me feel like I know you.'

She couldn't look him in the eye when she asked, 'How do I know you're not setting me up?'

He hadn't considered the prospect from her point of view. But now he heard it, it made sense. 'What? Why would I do that?'

'You work for Secretary Sun, don't you? The one who purged Hwang, and probably a dozen others the last few months?'

'You know about that?'

'I might be a cellist, Jun-an, but I do hear things beyond the brass section of the National Orchestra, you know.'

He took a final drag on his cigarette then stubbed it out in the ashtray on the kitchen counter. 'You can disavow me, you can inform on me, you can choose not to trust me, but you can't stop me loving you.' He swiped his hand through the air with finality. 'It is *impossible*.' He paused as she stepped towards him. 'My father was in a similar line of work to me. He once told me there were two things that were impossible in North Korea: proving your innocence.'

She tilted her head towards his, her lips opening slightly. 'What was the second?'

'Never trust a stranger.'

Mae put her hands on his hips and pulled him closer. Nothing had felt so alien to him as the seconds preceding their kiss, then so instantly familiar once it began. He had spent so long thinking about what kissing her would be like, once it happened it was like being given the answer to a riddle.

She pulled back first, whispering to him: 'I want to take you someplace. But you're going to have to break that second rule. You'll need to bring a jacket with your Ministry badge on.'

Han did as she asked. He would have gone anywhere with her in that moment.

Mae took him out into the unlit streets, carrying a shoe in each hand. Clouds rushed past a *Wuthering Heights*-type moon, its light forming vectors of shadow they tried to follow under the trees. Han had taken his shoes off as well – his idea – to navigate the night streets unheard. Ringing footsteps after the ten o'clock electricity curfew would only draw attention from people at their windows with nothing else to do except keep lookout for suspect behaviour. A solitary car could be heard several blocks away, the engine bumbling away in the opposite direction, echoing up the slumbering apartment blocks.

'Where are we going?' Han whispered, unaccustomed to being out at such an hour.

'I want you to meet some people. Friends of mine.'

He slowed his pace until she noticed him falling behind. 'I can't do this,' he said. 'What if someone catches us?'

She put both shoes in one hand, pulling him on. 'No one's going to stop someone with a senior member of the Ministry of Communications.'

He reluctantly staggered on, the freezing cold concrete reaching up through the soles of his feet into his legs.

When they heard a bus driving towards them from an indeterminate direction, buzzing unseen like a fly in a bedroom at night, Mae grabbed Han's hand and pulled him out of sight into an alleyway, waiting for the bus to pass. They pressed their backs up against the wall, both holding their breath as if it would help conceal them.

Han had to stay in profile to stay in the shadows. He whispered, 'I'm sorry I said that I love you. Just so you know, you shouldn't feel indebted to me about the cello case if that's what this is about.'

'You saved my life. What more do you want to do for me?' She kissed Han hard enough for him to drop his shoes, taking it in turns to be the aggressor, rolling each other down the wall.

The bus came puttering past on the road adjacent. It was the Western tourists from the Liberation War Museum earlier, their minders rewarding their good behaviour and profound lack of questions with a night out at the karaoke in downtown Pyongyang. Through an open window, Han could make out the sound of them singing Frank Sinatra's "My Way" with one of the minders. Nights out with tourists were rare, and it only took a few beers and a glass or two of *cheongju* to get them drunk. Drunk was one of the few universals left, the great equilibrium, where everyone was equally, mercifully, mindless. The guides and translators could often be found slouched at the bar near closing time, chugging coarse Russian cigarettes their fragile lungs pained to absorb.

The bus had long since passed before they stopped kissing.

After a twenty-block dash in and out of darkness to the left bank of Taedonggang-guyok, Mae took them up a narrow lane lined with dumpsters where a fire escape ladder had been lowered to the pavement, leading up to a first-floor balcony of a minor-slum building off the main street, safe from prying eyes.

Mae whispered in Han's ear, 'Don't trip, it'll wake the neighbours.'

Han stuffed their shoes down his jacket as Mae climbed the ladder first. Halfway up, Han stumbled with a clatter into the ladder, making a metallic clang that glued his feet to the grilled step. Mae froze, waiting like Han for some motion from a window across the street, but none came. When he made it to the top, Mae tapped with her fingertips on the balcony window then waved. 'I've brought someone with me.'

The window opened enough for Mae to crawl through, a woman inside saying, 'Are you crazy?'

Han, waiting for permission to come inside, gathered his bearings by catching sight of the *Juche* Tower illuminated (as always, no matter what the power shortage might be) farther down the east bank of the Tacdong River. Not far from the graffiti in Sadong-guyok.

After a brief discussion, Mae leaned out the window and beckoned Han inside. In the middle of a small living room, four people sat lotus around a candle on a table, shoeless, each with a different book in their lap, their faces tight with worry.

Mae closed the window behind Han, then introduced him. 'Everyone, this is... Mr Han.'

'Hello,' he said, placing their shoes beside a row of other shoes underneath the window.

A woman, Oh-ran, whose apartment it was, came into the room holding a candlestick, her face a warm orange glow, and heavily lined like a dry river bed. 'It's alright. My neighbours are all old and deaf, and the walls are thick. One of the few advantages of living in the old ward: no plasterboard, so you don't have to listen to your neighbour clipping their toenails, or singing songs to the Dear Leader at the top of their voice, like you're meant to be impressed and tell everyone how dedicated you are.'

The group smiled knowingly at each other: the safety of collaboration.

'We were wondering where you had got to,' Oh-ran said, placing

145

her candlestick down on top of the television. 'Cutting it a little close to the hour rule.' She knelt in front of the television, taking a screwdriver to the wood panel around the screen, which came away in her hands, revealing a hollowed-out hiding hole where the cathode ray tube should have been.

'What's the hour rule?' Han asked Mae, still whispering.

'If someone doesn't make it here within an hour of the arranged time, we all leave.'

'Why?'

'We have to assume they've been caught on the way here, and if interrogated might feel obliged to give us up. So we need to be ready.'

One of the women on the floor said, 'Oh-ran, is it wise to let the stranger see where you keep them?'

Oh-ran reached inside the television and took out three paperback novels, putting them on the table. 'If Mae brought him then I trust him.'

Han was relieved to see he wasn't the only one breaking his father's second rule.

A young man at the table noticed the light catch Han's lapel, under his Kim Il-sung badge. 'That's a Ministry badge.'

Han looked down at it as if in shame. 'It is.'

'What branch?'

'Communications,' he said softly.

The man, who was wearing a Party uniform, laughed in disbelief as he stood up. 'I don't know how you all could be so foolish. Everybody knows Communications is just a soft name for the Propaganda and Agitation Department. Have you any idea what they would give to infiltrate a group like ours?'

Han had to step aside to let him past. Oh-ran was the only one who tried to stop him, but he was already opening the window. He paused, one leg out on the balcony. 'Remember the day you let him come in here. It'll be the first day of the end of your lives.'

A man at the table smoking a cigarette said, 'Well that's one down.' He was wearing the tuxedo of an orchestra member, his bowtie undone around his neck as if he had come straight from a performance. He put his hand out to Han. 'I'm Kim-cheol.' He had the ease of someone that had been coming there a long time.

'Look, I don't really know what's going on,' Han pleaded, not knowing whether to stay standing or not, 'but I came with Soon-li. I promise I won't be any trouble.'

Oh-ran sat on the floor with the others and motioned for Han to sit next to her. They were all broadly middle-aged, except for one old man, sitting on a chair at the edge of the group, his hands hanging limply over the handle of his wooden cane.

'Is this...' Han started, peering through the dim light at the books in the others' laps. Korean translations, smuggled in from the South and sold on the black market.

'This is our book group,' Oh-ran said, patting him on the leg. 'So, what has everyone been reading this week?'

Mae sat across from Han, the candle-lit table between them. She took out a book from her coat's inside pocket. 'I brought *Collected Poems* by EE Cummings.'

They went round the circle:

'*Lord of the Flies.*'

'*Pride and Prejudice.*'

'*Great Expectations.*'

Kim-cheol said, 'Wasn't that a headline in *Rodong Sinmun* yesterday?'

The room filled with laughter.

The Dickens reader, the old man, added, 'He also wrote *Harsh Times* and *Bleak House.*'

'My god, was he North Korean?' the *Pride and Prejudice* reader joked.

Everyone laughed again, revelling in being able to openly mock the State. It was the happiness of letting their true selves be known.

Oh-ran said, 'Mine is *Empire of the Sun.*' She turned to the blurb on the back. 'It's about an English boy called Jim, who's obsessed with aeroplanes and flight. He lives in Shanghai, you see, and it's the Second World War, so when the Japanese—'

It felt strange to Han to not hear "Imperialist bastards" follow the word Japanese.

'—take over, he loses his parents and ends up in an internment camp. Jim has to fight to survive in the camp, finding food however he can. But mostly he thinks about the Japanese pilots. He has this idea that if God is in the sky, then if he flies he can get closer to him.'

There wasn't much talk of God in the DPRK. According to Kim Il-sung North Koreans didn't need religion or God, not when they had the Korean Workers' Party. God was a decadent illusion that distracted people from socialist-revolutionary thought. It had, of course, crossed Han's mind from time to time, but when he asked his father he said to him, 'God? Look around you and tell me where he is.'

'Imagine being able to get in a plane and fly anywhere,' the woman with *Lord of the Flies* said. The way she said it suggested she had spent a great deal of time thinking about such a thing.

Han couldn't help but be intensely aware that sitting there they were six distinctly different people, but regardless of the limits of what they would ever know about each other, the one thing they did know was that they weren't alone. And somehow that seemed enough. He imagined being tasked with describing everything in the room, from the shape of every object, their textures, the colours, the smells, the dimensions of everything, and then there were the people, what they looked like, what they said and how they talked, how they moved or didn't... there would never be enough time in the universe, let alone a human life, to convey the complexities of everything there, because there would always be something further that could be said: like fragments of time that could always be halved into infinitely tinier amounts. But when they talked about their books and quoted passages from them, Han was able to see through the invisible barriers between them in a way he never could if he were sitting on a bus with them, or at a Party meeting, or bowing next to them on Mansu Hill. From the lines they read and talked about with admiration, it seemed they appreciated, and were scared about, their place in the world the same way Han was. Only books could provide such empathy.

He sat there, staring at the candlelight on the table, thinking about what Secretary Sun would do to him if he found out he was there. His whole life he had done the smart thing when in public: stayed out the way of people with dangerous ideas and big mouths; sang at least as loud as the person next to him; saluted as rigidly as everyone else; kept his portraits of the Two Leaders spotless; praised the military for everything good; blamed the American imperialists for everything bad; pretended like everyone else to have read all of *Juche* ideology; and now, after everything he had been through, everything he had seen and tried to forget in his short life, he was risking everything he had tried to protect – his ability to keep living – and for what: a woman? Love?

'What do you think, Mr Han?' Oh-ran asked.

Han realised he hadn't been listening. 'Me? Oh, I haven't read it.'

'That's OK, neither has anyone else. It's hard enough finding one book let alone five copies. So what do you think?'

He repeated, 'What do I think.' It didn't sound like the same question the way he said it.

'About the book,' Oh-ran said.

He couldn't remember ever being asked his opinion on something other than the Party, or his department. 'I'm just a government minder, I don't know anything about all this. I'm not supposed to read books, I recommend which ones should be banned; I don't think for myself, I tell others what to think; I spend all day talking about foreign crimes, and ignore our own; I watched my sister starve to death, while my bosses at the Ministry grew fat; I'm so insignificant, sometimes when I get up in the morning and look in the mirror I don't expect to see myself there; the only people who really know me have forgotten about me by the time their aeroplanes cross over the Chinese border. I'm just a government minder. But I like the sound of flying away.'

The old man, comfortable in a paternal role, asked, 'Well? What do you read, Mr Han?'

He looked up hopefully at Mae and cleared his throat. 'I started a book tonight, as it happens. *Nineteen Eighty-four*.'

Han's admission united the room in coy grins.

'Good choice,' the old man mumbled, nodding away. Unlike Han, who was brought into the DPRK's Orwellian world when it was already fully formed, the old man had seen it grow, and had lived it all, page by page, chapter by chapter, horror piling upon horror as the Party's stranglehold became absolute. He pitied his own older generation who at least had some memory of relative freedom when they were children.

Oh-ran said, 'So tell us about it, Mr Han.' Her patience reminded him of his mother, the gentle way she had of encouraging him as a boy. Strange, he thought, how you can feel closer to a stranger by seeing other people in them.

The *Pride and Prejudice* reader said meekly, 'I don't actually know much about it.'

Galvanised by this admission, the *Lord of the Flies* reader said, 'Me too.'

'I'm not long into it,' Han said, 'But so far... I can see why the Party banned it.' He smiled at this, and the whole room responded, chuckling with him. He finally looked them in the eyes, one by one. He couldn't tell what rank they were, or what job they did. Sitting there in the dark with their books, they were all the same. 'The main character, Winston, works in a government Ministry that rewrites history, changing or ignoring anything that doesn't fit with their apparently socialist ideology, even though the way they rule isn't fair. It's a terrible country he lives in, where everything you do is monitored by the Thought Police, and everyone has to proclaim their loyalty to the Party at all times. Despite all this, Winston has a kind of fascination with the truth, and he starts keeping a diary, which is against the Party rules, and the more he writes the more he realises he actually hates the Party, and wants to escape it. Which terrifies him, mostly. He lives in a place where no one speaks out and everyone is a potential spy – even little children denounce their parents because they've been so indoctrinated from a young age. He lives on his own, and has done for quite a long time it seems. Then he meets this woman, Julia,' he looked into Mae's eyes and held contact with them until he finished speaking, 'who he falls in love with, even though he doesn't really know her. They start an affair, and he knows the longer it goes on the more likely it will be they get caught. He doesn't even know for sure she's not just trying to trap him and get him arrested. The whole time he worries about getting caught. All the same, he feels her love changing him, and that he doesn't want to live his life the way he has for so long.' He stopped to light a Commie Marlboro. 'That's as far as I've got.'

Mae was enjoying being able to just sit and watch him. He had the kind of face where it was clear precisely what he was feeling, wondering how it could turn melancholy so quickly, lost in his thoughts, his eyes searching around him as if each second of his life was spent assessing the world and everything in it; how someone so kind and gentle could be so tortured by all around him. It didn't seem fair to her. She could feel him taking up more and more of her brain, like an autumn sun burning away a morning fog. He just seemed so hurt all the time, with a child's perpetual sense of amazement – how incredible and ridiculous it is to be alive! – and an old man's hardened acceptance that being alive is all there is.

Oh-ran turned to Mae. 'Mae?'

She finally drew her eyes away from Han, and took out a crumpled piece of paper from her pocket. 'I know we're supposed to talk about the book we've read this week, but I've found myself writing more than reading. It's inspired by the EE Cummings, though. I find you learn so much about a poet from a poem. But when you read or hear a poem that you love, you learn so much about yourself.' She coughed nervously. 'The thing is I've never read this one to anyone before, so be kind.' Her hands were unsure around the paper which she held close to her face. The woman to her left passed the candle nearer.

Han thought about how in control she was with her cello, but sitting with her poem she seemed vulnerable and exposed.

'This is called "Your"' She paused. '"Your legs wrapped around me; your lips telling me I'm beautiful; your smile when I tell you how beautiful you are; your body turning into mine in the middle of the night, and me instinctively reaching out to kiss your forehead; your sighing when I kiss your back; your eyes watching my eyes and not having to say anything; your arm around me on the Metro; your morning kisses; your desire not to hurt me; your heart; my tiny hands in yours; my breasts touching your chest; your fingers tracing my scars; your neck could be kissed forever; your skin is like an ocean I can't find the edge of. Your.'"

Han knew he heard different things in Mae's poem than any of the others had – no one else having kissed Mae that night, or saved her life – and now he had her words, a dark, unknown mind now opened up in front of him, shining brighter than the *Juche* Tower. He was the last of the group to applaud, still taking the words in. Poetry always lets you see exactly who someone is. There is nowhere to hide with a poem.

Han chain-smoked through the others' discussion, preferring to listen. They talked, not so much about the books themselves, but the act of reading, rejoicing about how they would reread passages they found moving or funny or profound, and each time they read them back they just got better and better; and how once the words were *in there*, inside them, they could access them whenever they wanted, drip-feeding into the everyday; how in a book you were never stuck in time, because it was impossible for two sentences to exist in exactly the same time and place. The books that moved them most were about places and times they would never otherwise know. Like they were building houses they could never live in. Whether it came from a recognition that their experience of being alive was the same, or from something unfamiliar that the author made appear miraculously familiar, the thoughts had always been with them, and as readers all they required was someone to access it in their heads on their behalf and show it to them. And their experiences weren't unique: they all recognised the same things in themselves in different books. It made Han wonder, if books were really a solitary device as he believed, then why didn't the people he was sitting with now shake their heads in mystification when someone explained what was beautiful and true and recognisable in a book? A million people could look at a beautiful sunset and describe it in a million different ways, but the conclusion they could all come to would still be the same: That Is A Beautiful Sunset.

Oh-ran checked the time on a clock on her mantelpiece. 'We should probably finish up. That's after half eleven already. Mr Han, I'm glad you could join us tonight. I assume it goes without saying to keep our little group to ourselves.'

Han puffed out his cheeks. 'Believe me, if anyone knew I was here, I'd be in as much trouble as the rest of you.'

The others started filing silently out the window, one by one, back into the night – into their heads – fanning out to their different parts of Pyongyang, the rest of the city oblivious to what had taken place in a single tiny room: The Pyongyang Book Club.

Back down on the street, Han and Mae walked much slower home: there was too much to discuss.

'Did you enjoy that?' Mae asked him.

Han exhaled in confusion and threw his head back. She felt miles away when they weren't holding hands. 'It was... interesting.'

'That must be a euphemism.'

'I don't know...' As he searched for the right words his eyes darted around, seeming to change direction with each new rapid thought: Mae could see he was back in his head again, instead of there with her. 'Books have always been between me and the author. They were more of a confession than a mass. I've always read with the author in mind, not other readers.'

'You would rather be alone than share?'

Sensing her question had a dual purpose, Han tried to explain. 'I guess it's a little like language. When I started reading I used to think of the scenes as little pictures in my head, mimetic. When you think of language like that it cuts off the outside world: all you have are these pictures in your head and you can never really *get* at anything else outside them. But when I started translating – I mean with foreigners in the field, people from the Real World – I realised that was wrong: language is impossible if it's not shared between people. Like how you can gain an understanding of something through someone else's *mis*understanding. And that sounds a lot nicer at first, but all it really means is that instead of me being in *here*, and everyone else out *there*, it's really *all* of us in here, and nobody can get out.'

'Which makes us what? Prisoners?'

He considered this. 'Maybe the kind that have come to know their cage so well they can no longer see the bars.'

She tried to be playful, quickly grabbing his hand and laughing. 'So you *didn't* enjoy yourself?'

He looked down at their hands intertwined, clenched so hard together that if it weren't an act of love or tenderness you would complain that it hurt. It was the meaning behind the act that made it feel fine. 'I'm sorry, I haven't even thanked you for bringing me.'

She swung their hands up in the air to chest-height. 'You're the one who broke the second rule.'

Han's eyes lit up and he didn't look so lost in his own thoughts anymore. Mae wished he could look like that all the time. He asked, 'How have you all gotten away with it for so long? How did it start? How do you go from one person telling another they're a criminal, to a group of people sitting in a room sharing books?'

'The same way we have. At a certain point you take a risk and let someone in. I bought a book from Oh-ran in the market one day. She took me to her house where she said she had more foreign ones, and Kim-cheol was there, buying books as well. Eventually we all ended up there at the same time. It made sense for us all to share it together.' She stopped walking and swung his hand behind her back.

They both dropped their shoes on the ground with a quiet thud.

Sudden kisses when you want them the most – when you *need* them the most – have an ability to make you disappear. The kiss is all there is – time stops – and you're sure the kiss is all there will ever be. Like the start of the universe when nothing was all there was, and out of nowhere, out of nothing, everything exploded, and it was all fire and light and unbearable heat. Han felt her body insistent against his, mysterious and familiar, like a book that, page after page, keeps surprising you, leaving you so breathless you have to put it down to gather yourself. *Make no mistake*, he thought: *falling in love is a decision; just don't go fooling yourself it's yours to make.*

Ben slammed the door shut. 'Look, we knew this might happen. There's no reason to panic.'

'I'm not panicking!' Hal snapped back, 'I'm freaking out!' He put his camera down by the television and paced around the room.

Ben sat calmly on his bed, legs crossed. 'I don't see what the problem is, frankly.'

'How do we know he's not trying to set us up, a minder like him at his age would love a foreign spy-catch on their record. What if they take the camera off us and see what we've been talking about up here? That conversation in the museum, he has total deniability. He goes to his boss, that—'

'Sun.'

'Right, Sun, who even *you* know is a little Macbeth-in-waiting. I'm telling you, I don't buy this graffiti story.'

'You don't trust him?'

'Why should I? Listen to yourself, Ben! Have you forgotten where we are?'

He knew Hal was serious when he used his first name. 'You know when we went to the old East Bloc, there was always a little joke told in a quiet corner of a bar, or a dirty message directed at the President or the Party in the men's toilets, something that really cut through all the official Party lines and air of obedience. They don't have that here. There must be chaos in the Ministry of Communications.'

Sensing he wasn't getting through to him, Hal asked almost reluctantly, 'D'you want to do a talking head for today?'

'Alright then.'

Hal started rolling, and without any preparation, Ben turned to face the camera, the Pyongyang skyline bathed in a cool blue light behind him. He discussed the events of the day, the video, the musty museum and regimented corporal tour guide. 'One of the things we – Hal my cameraman, and I – have found in all the totalitarian regimes we've visited, is the kind of crushing boredom of it all. No one has anything to say except praise the government or the Party, or whoever.

There's this torpid fear on their face, begging you to just play along and not make life difficult. Which is hard for me, because I'm supposed to be here asking difficult questions.' He paused, looking down and away from the camera. He started thinking about what might happen to Han after they were gone. Hal moved away from the viewfinder to see what was going on. 'But when they're there in front of you and it hits you: they have to live in this... this unremitting misery, this slave, slash, worship state. And all you want to do is leave them alone. You already know the truth of what's going on, any tourist can. But you do wish there was something more you could do other than try and share the odd joke with them. Some journalist friends of mine that have been here warned me: don't get too attached. I can't help it though. This minder of ours, Mr Han, he's killing me.' Ben made a 'cut' gesture by swiping his hand across the front of his neck, then got quickly out of frame.

Hal closed the viewfinder, and said, 'That was good.'

They both sat on their beds, facing the wall in silence. After a long pause, Hal said, in a tone meant to induce admiration, 'I deleted the Khartoum video on my laptop.' Ben thought it would have been cause for celebration, that Hal was on the road to recovery.

Hal's posture slowly curved forward, putting his head in his hands, driving the pits of his palms into his eyes. 'I don't want to live like this anymore, Ben.' His voice croaked with the beginnings of tears. 'I'm so tired all the time. I've been running on sheer bravado the last ten years. I'm tired of being alone. Everywhere I go. I'd never really thought about it until recently: I don't really know myself. I don't want to lose myself, Ben. You don't want to know what I've been thinking of doing.'

Ben reached across to him and put his hand on his shoulder. 'I have a fair idea.' He moved over next to him, patting his back reassuringly as Hal started to cry.

'I thought if I got far enough away from home, I...' He broke off. He sat up straight, groaning the way masculine men do when they're trying not to cry.

Ben had never seen Hal cry before, or heard him talk like this.

He spoke softly. 'I used to think I could change the world, you know. Doing this. That if people knew what was going on, it would somehow make a difference. And that was fine for a while. You know you can't stop wars, but...'

Hal looked up suddenly and nodded. 'Praying for forgiveness is one thing. But I don't think that's enough.'

'What do you want to do?'

'Mr Han. I don't want to leave Mr Han here.'

'Happy Birthday, Choi-kuang!'

Central Party Offices, The Forbidden City, 18ᵗʰ December

When Han arrived at the Ministry that morning, he was met with a scene of panic. This-will-only-get-worse, Archduke-Franz-Ferdinand-has-been-shot-type panic. Secretaries clacked across the marble lobby in low heels, and assistants with terse expressions crisscrossed past each other, clinging on to documents flaking off the tops of their piles, all the myriad sub-departments and -divisions of Communications trying to contact one another with conflicting evidence and hearsay: more graffiti had shown up overnight, only it wasn't confined to just a suburban wall this time.

Han stood in the middle of the crowded lobby holding his briefcase, waiting for someone he recognised. He put his arm out in a semi-clothesline at Jang-ung, a junior researcher from the Residential Communications sector, his head buried in a list of names on a spreadsheet.

'Mr Han,' Jang-ung said in relief. 'I thought you were Secretary Sun for a second.'

'What's going on, comrade?' Han asked.

'Haven't you heard?' He moved in closer, lowering his voice. 'Dawn patrol radioed in this morning that another slogan had been found.'

'Dawn patrol where?'

Jang-ung bumped his glasses up the bridge of his nose – the lenses as small and perfectly round as coins – his lists held tight against his chest. 'Kim Il-sung stadium.'

'On a wall?'

'On the *pitch*. They wrote it in petrol and set it alight.'

'But the Mass Games, the Arirang Festival is only—'

'Precisely. And a whole stream of new slogans down the outer walls of the Forbidden City.'

'*Here*?'

'On the east side.'

Han worked out the geography: close to Sadong-guyok where the first graffiti appeared. 'They must have hit that on the way back. They'll be concentrating on the east bank of the river. You don't run from one side of the city to the other to do this. Didn't they get anyone on camera?'

'It was after ten, sir.'

'So?'

'The power was out. They're re-laying the pitch right now. The bosses are going nuts. I could hear Sun, sorry, comrade Secretary Sun screaming in his office from the second floor.' He moved Han slightly away from a group of conferring secretaries. 'You know what they're saying, right?'

Han flicked his head up to indicate 'What?'

'About the Dear Leader. That he's had another stroke.'

'They've said that before. There's no point speculating.'

'No, sir, of course not.'

'So what are you doing?'

Jang-ung shrugged. 'Rounding up the usual suspects.'

'You've been watching *Casablanca* in the film library again, haven't you. You know you're not meant to be in there.'

'Yes, comrade.' He smiled bashfully. 'You seem pretty chipper this morning, if you don't mind me saying. Pyongyang's working out well for you?'

Han slipped into the best American accent he could manage. '"*Of all the gin joints, in all the towns, in all the world, she walks into mine.*"' Han laid a hand on Jang-ung's shoulder, then disappeared back into the throng upstairs.

Upstairs, Sun was leaning back against his desk, giving dictation to Miss Lee. He was wearing sockless loafers, as if he had left his house in a hurry. As Han approached Sun's wide-open door he made out the words, '...in the harshest possible terms.' Sun looked towards his door seeing Han skulking around outside. He bellowed Han's name, sending his cockatoo shrouded under its black cage-veil into a chirping frenzy.

159

Sun's breakfast was untouched, so Han knew it must be serious. He kept his distance, saying, 'Good morning, comrade Secretary, I've just heard the news.'

Sun handed Miss Lee the rest of his correspondence, and she hotfooted it back to her post. 'We'll need to keep this brief today,' Sun said. 'I've got the Ministers and the Vice Premier in fifteen minutes.'

'I understand, sir.'

'I need – why are you grinning, Han?'

Han straightened his face immediately. 'Sorry, comrade Secretary, I didn't realise I was.'

'You were. Anyway, I need you to get the foreigners out the city for the day. There's too much going on for them to be around the Metro stations and,' he perused his copy of their itinerary, 'the Memorial Palace. Where can you take them?'

'Well, sir, perhaps a visit to the collectivised farms out in Kosong in Kangwon province. We can show them the dedicated work overseen by the Ministry of Agriculture. I spent some parts of my childhood there, and there are plenty of stops we can make on the way.'

Sun's eyes were slits from lack of sleep. 'Very well. But it will only be you and Mr So. I need Ryong to follow up some leads in the city.'

'As you wish, comrade Secretary.'

'Good work on that Mae woman. Ryong brought her in on misconduct charges. Something about unclean portraits of the Dear Leader. Only a warning this time, but still.'

Han was suspicious at mention of her name so close to Ryong's task for the day. 'She isn't still under surveillance is she, sir?'

Sun ignored the question, twisting into his military jacket. 'Miss Lee!' he shouted, gathering up his paperwork for the Ministers. 'I'm leaving in ten seconds. Have the car ready.' He rushed past Han. 'That will be all.'

Han was left alone, drawn to Sun's cockatoo still chirping in its cage. He looked back at Miss Lee's desk, seeing her swamped with work, the phone clamped between her shoulder and cheek. He went over to the cage and delicately lifted the bottom of the veil, raising it just high enough for the bird to see daylight. It chirped in a softer fashion. Han put his finger through the cage and the cockatoo hopped along its perch to sniff him. 'You'll get out there, one day,' Han said. 'I promise.'

Miss Lee suddenly appeared in the doorway. 'Mr Han...'

Han's heart leaped. 'Sorry, Miss Lee. I was just going.' He spoke quietly to the bird, 'But not today,' then lowered the veil again.

There were no duplicitous diversions that morning; Han wanted to get as far away from Pyongyang as possible. The streets were crawling with police, civilians hounding their cars, eager to appear helpful even when they had nothing useful to say.

Ben and Hal's hair was still bed-shaped when they came stumbling into the minibus two hours earlier than planned. Their mood significantly lightened, especially Hal's, when they clocked Ryong's absence:

'Mr Ryong has been called away on other Ministry business,' Han explained, a spring in his step. 'Is only us today.'

'Mr So doesn't speak English, does he?' Ben asked.

'Only me.' Han couldn't resist giving them a wink after he told them this. 'Today we will see the real North Korea.' He said to Hal, 'I hope your batteries are full. I have plenty to show you.'

Kosong, Kangwon province

Kangwon province was the most mountainous the men had seen so far. This was the near-mythic DPRK, the cerulean sky full of angelic birds, and snow-topped mountains just like the murals of the Koryo Hotel's BH 1.

So blasted his horn at anything vaguely close to them on the pavement as they raced out of Pyongyang, rallying through the quiet municipal roads into the countryside, where he finally slowed down. The motorway stretched out plum-straight for miles at a time in front of them in slow rises and falls, the only other traffic convoys of military trucks packed with materiel and open-top personnel carriers all going back in the direction of Pyongyang.

Han had climbed into the backseats with Ben and Hal, *'for monitoring purposes,'* he told So, and in the two-hour drive to Kangwon province they enjoyed their longest, unbroken conversation.

Hal had to put the camera down, his eyes hurting from the sky's incessant blue. A nice kind of hurt. Like feeling too hot on a summer's day.

'Where did you grow up, Mr Han?' Ben asked, luxuriating in his newfound freedom.

'I was born in Pyongyang. With my father's job he travel around a lot.'

'The journalist?'

Han laughed ironically. 'We don't have journalist like you in Korea, Mr Ben. He work for State newspaper.'

'*Rodong Sinmun*?'

'Is right. He used to tell us as children: I'm not a journalist, I'm a, you say ventriloquist? A ventriloquist, operating the dummy, making other people's words come out.'

'How did he die? If you don't mind me asking.'

Han looked absent-mindedly out the window. 'They say he was on a dispatch to Chongjin, we call it a *kauboi*...'

Ben translated for Hal. 'Cowboy.'

'Yes, cowboy town, lot of prostitutes, lot of begging, people trying to get money to be smuggled into China. Chongjin is wild. My mother was with him, she had got work in munitions factory. They said their car crashed off the road when it was raining.'

'Who is "they"?'

'The Ministry. Communications. The Propaganda and Agitation Department. They were his bosses.'

'You didn't believe them?'

'I still don't.' Han lit a Commie Marlboro – giving one to Hal also – and cracked the window down. 'I think they might have tried to get across the border to China. I heard them talk about it after Kim Il-sung died. Anyway Mr Ben, it is smart not to believe everything you are told here. All my father's records are with Secretary Sun's office. I'll never know.' Han faced out the window when So adjusted the rear view mirror to see what was happening. 'If the sky is falling down, Mr Ben, where do you hide?'

'*We'll be there soon*,' So told them.

'*Fine*,' Han replied blankly, much too quietly for So to hear him, still looking out the window.

The mural-beauty of the countryside was now long gone. They were deep in the backwoods of the DPRK, the fields strewn with weeds and tiny empty cages used for baiting rabbits. The farms were in disarray, cropless, dotted with abandoned tractors without wheels that had been rusting for years with their hoods up, ready for maintenance that never came. These were the collectivised farms Ben had seen on his friends' documentaries, their driver racing at breakneck speeds past them, but they were so vast no speed could get them past unseen. The odd body stooped over some patches of seeds, their fingers red raw from the December cold, the ground beneath their feet frozen to marble.

Han was taking them to one of the few farms that was still in some kind of working order. Calls had been made ahead of time, and everyone was well briefed.

A welcoming commission from the farm collective met them at the front gates, ready to greet the foreign guests with flowers. Pictures of armed soldiers holding bayonets surrounded the farm entrance, proclaiming: "THROUGH HARD WORK WE WILL DEFEAT THE CAPITALIST ENEMY!" and "A STEADY FOOD SUPPLY WILL KEEP OUR COUNTRY THE STRONGEST IN THE WORLD". An old man sat on a stoop, puffing on a pipe, seemingly oblivious to the slogans behind him. An official quickly shooed him away from the scene as So pulled the bus in and the three men stepped off. Flowers were thrust in their faces like they were about to deliver sacks of food aid.

'So is this the real North Korea, Mr Han?' Ben asked, accepting the flowers from little children, their faces gaunt with hunger.

'Not quite,' Han replied.

The farm's Party delegation took them straight to the home of an older farmer, who waited with his entire family on the front steps like Ben and Hal had been lost at sea for years and had finally come home. The farmer was dressed in a smart black uniform – not military – with medals over his heart next to his Kim Il-sung lapel pin.

Han spoke to Ben and Hal on the way. 'His name is Choi-kuang.'

Choi-kuang looked scared to death.

Hal kept accepting flowers from the children, his arms so full they started falling into the dirt. 'Mr Han, could you please tell them I'm not Bono.'

A tiny administrator for the farm, dressed like something from Siberia in a long coat and fur hat that reached down to his eyebrows, came running up alongside Han, begging his attention. He was in a state of some distress. '*Mr Han, we didn't have much time to prepare, you understand.*'

'*That's fine,*' he replied, not looking at him.

Hal pretended to be filming a panorama of the surrounding countryside, staying close enough behind to pick up the conversation.

'*I got him to wear his medals and Party uniform. He's a little old, but he's the best I could find. I sent out for food this morning after the Ministry called.*'

'*You don't want to check first that the people standing next to me can't speak Korean?*' Han stopped outside the farmer's garden and glared at the man. '*Before you go spouting off in front of them.*'

'*I'm... sorry, sir, I assumed...*' He nudged his fur hat up which fell immediately back down again. He looked with terror at Ben and Hal. '*Can they speak Korean?*'

Han paused. '*You got lucky this time. But what will the reason be?*'

'*Sir?*'

'*What will the reason be for him wearing his medals and uniform? They might be Westerners but they're not idiots.*'

The man didn't know what to say.

'*You mean to tell me you got this man dressed up, in what are obviously not his everyday clothes, sent out for food everyone knows they don't usually have, and leave me to explain how this is all just another regular day?*'

The man stared at the ground, his will shattered.

Han sighed, feeling sorry for him. *'Look, you did your best on short notice. I'll commend you in my report to the Ministry if you do one thing for me.'*

He straightened to attention, nudging his hat up again. *'Yes, comrade!'*

'Go tell those people in the field over there to stop smoking and do some work. Or send a tractor out there or something. I don't care how little work gets done around here, just not today. Not while I'm here.' He signalled towards the bus. *'My driver is sitting there wondering whether he should tell my boss about the state of this place, but assumes it's so bad that I will. I don't want to have to do that. Fix it, please.'*

'Yes, sir,' the man barked back, and went tearing off towards the work shed where everyone had huddled around a fire to keep warm.

The farmer was well past retirement age, but maintained he was only sixty. He showed Han, Ben and Hal inside, followed by a posse of junior Party members from the surrounding area, all looking to get some face-time with Han, *'the big man from the City'* as they called him.

No one else spoke English apart from Han. He explained to Ben, 'So they're saying this is regular farmer's house, but there is no way. In fact, this probably not even his house; probably local Party delegate that place him here for the afternoon.'

Ben said, 'Does he always wear his medals?'

Han asked, *'He wants to know if you wear your medals every day?'*

Choi-kuang looked, bewildered, to the delegates for direction. *'Why am I wearing my medals today?'*

A discussion broke out amongst them: *'Because you're a proud Korean War veteran!' 'That's not what he's asking stupid, he's asking why is he wearing them today? He's not supposed to know the Americans were coming here—' 'They're not both Americans, the younger one is English, I think.' 'Choi-kuang, tell him that... tell him—'*

Han kicked at a loose pebble. *'It's his birthday.'* The room fell silent. *'If you guys want to make it to Pyongyang, lie better. And faster. I'll them it's his birthday.'* Everyone suddenly became fascinated with their shoes, taking their telling off.

'They speak too fast for me,' Ben said to Han. 'What's happening?'

Han said, 'They not thought up a reason. Someone had idea his medals would impress you, so I tell them to say it's his birthday.'

'Ah, *saeng-il chugha*!' Ben bowed towards the baffled Choi-kuang, who seemed unfamiliar with the geography of the house.

Everyone smiled and cheered, joining in in the imaginary birthday wishes.

Han said, 'You misunderstand, Mr Ben. Is not really his birthday. That's explanation for all food and party atmosphere.'

A delegate put his arm around Choi-kuang, explaining to him, '*Happy birthday, comrade! Put your arms up like you're happy it's your birthday.*' He turned to the other delegates. '*Quick, someone get a birthday hat. And get a cake...*'

'*Where the hell am I going to get a birthday cake, you bloody moron?*' another delegate volleyed back.

Choi-kuang put his arms half-heartedly in the air, wondering what on earth was going on.

On a low table on the living room floor was a flamboyant spread of week-old beef cuts, and chicken, surrounded by dozens and dozens of tiny vegetable dishes to give a false impression of abundance. They had managed to find a few bunches of bananas.

'They're very rare around here, are they not, Mr Han?' Ben asked.

'Very,' he said grimly. 'Someone will get a commendation for finding those.'

The tour went out into the fields, where they had managed to coax some people out of the work shed. They had no tools, not even spades or hoes or pitchforks. They just picked away with their hands, or kicked at the frozen ground with their heels, like a football punter about to kick a field goal. The farm had found a spokesman from the local delegation to accompany them, someone familiar with the lines about farming in regard to socialism. The man was well versed.

Han translated with as little enthusiasm as he could get away with.

'Is it alright to ask about the Arduous March?' Ben enquired.

'Not directly, no. Let me phrase this for you. *Comrade, he asks, haven't there been many food shortages, especially in the early nineties?'*

The man was mildly shocked at the question. *'Really, they can ask that sort of thing?'*

'Haven't you done this before, comrade?' Han asked, knowing full well the man hadn't, that even talking to Han was a major coup for him. Han particularly enjoyed throwing in the 'comrade' at the end, just to throw him off.

Predictably, the man gave the same line the Party had given to the people throughout the period, one that many still believed.

Han translated, prefacing it by saying: 'You should know what I'm about to say is *shit...*'

Ben turned to the camera and saw Hal's shoulders bouncing.

'...The food shortages were because of American and Western sanctions. They cannot defeat us fairly, so they try punish us, and it is the Korean people who suffer most...'

In the middle of Han's translation, a tractor came puttering past yards away, a clearly-visible Chinese flag-sticker attached to the bonnet, saying 'DONATED BY THE PEOPLE'S REPUBLIC OF CHINA'. The tractor was making such a racket, Han had to stop what he was saying.

'Mr Han, can you ask him why, if the DPRK is so self-sufficient, they have to use Chinese tractors?' Ben stepped aside for Hal to get a clear shot of the flag.

A delegate walked between the men and the offending tractor, trying to look casual.

Han translated Ben's question.

The Party man was getting tired of this now. *'Why are you letting them film this, tell them to stop!'* He stepped in front of the offending flag and put his arm out, first towards the camera, then Hal.

Han knew the man's anger could be deflated easily. *'How dare you tell me what my guests can or cannot film! I have permission from—'*

The man put his arm down and tried to apologise.

'No, don't interrupt me. I'm from the Ministry of Communications. I decide what they can film.'

'I'm sorry, comrade. I don't know what to say.'

'Never mind. I'll handle it. He doesn't have an answer, he doesn't know anything. The truth is, without foreign aid we be even deader than we are already. The aid that get in is stolen and sold by our military near the border, sometime back to the Chinese.'

Ben tried to work it out. 'So you have North Korean soldiers selling American aid to the Chinese?'

Han said simply, 'Yes.'

The Party man asked, *'What did you tell him? It might be helpful if I have to answer such a question again.'*

Without hesitating, Han said, *'I told him that as a favour to the Chinese, we take some products from them. But once we get real, true socialism instilled in the minds of the people, such acts won't be required any longer.'*

Impressed at Han's flawless performance, he held his hand out for him to shake as they made their way out the field. *'It's been such an honour listening to you speak, comrade. Tell me, I don't suppose there's any chance of a commendation. I've been trying to get into Pyongyang for two years now, and I'll be thirty next month. My wife won't stop—'*

Han laid his hand on the man's chest, as if assessing his heartbeat. *'Leave it to me. I think you would fit in just fine at the Ministry.'*

'Savour this,' Ben told Hal as they trailed behind. 'No one has ever had access like this before: we're getting a live North Korean-guide commentary on what is actually going on in front of us.'

Hal seemed sceptical. 'I just wonder... what's going to happen to Han.'

'What do you mean?'

'When this airs. What's going to happen to Han when they see what he's been doing?'

Ben got a lump in his throat. 'I hadn't thought about that yet.'

As they left the farm, Han saw Choi-kuang being ushered out the house, the food from the living room boxed up, being put into a car. Straight to the local head of the Party.

Choi-kuang's birthday was over.

*

So had barely said a word since leaving Pyongyang, feeling left out of the English conversation. His window was open just enough to let in a steady stream of cold air which knifed through the warm air from the car's interior heaters, mixed with the deep-tar smell of Russian cigarette smoke which first jettisoned back towards the others before whirling back out the window. Turning off another empty road into yet more miles of dying farmland, conversation in the backseats had stopped.

'*Should we really be going off-map like this?*' So asked tentatively, his arms shaking on the steering wheel from the vibrations from the treacherous side road Han had pointed him down.

Han replied, '*I know this place. I spent some of my childhood here.*'

'*I think there might be some farms down here the men shouldn't see. They haven't been certified by the Party.*'

'*It's OK.*'

So reluctantly drove on, continuing his quiet complaints.

'When did you live around here, Mr Han?' Ben asked, waving at a famished boy no taller than three feet standing in the middle of a field, as if he had fallen out of the sky. The boy turned in profile and almost disappeared completely.

'I live here for most of ninety-five,' Han said. 'Middle of the Arduous March.'

'Kim Il-sung had died the year before, it must have been a very confusing time.'

'It was the countryside that fall apart first. Pyongyang have too many other ways of finding food, too many people to bribe, smuggle in rice, trade rations. Out here, no one have anything.'

'Why were you living out here?'

'My father was given a job to report on the crop, to write is not as bad as people think, that things will get better soon. One day I ask him what he did. He tell me he wrote lies. And if anyone asked, I was to say he was reporting good news.'

Children were running around in trousers torn at the shins, and sandals without socks, kicking around a dead corn shrub as a football. They abandoned their game as soon as they saw the bus, running alongside it as So navigated the rocky back-road, the children slapping the chassis and shouting hello. So leaned out his window, a cigarette dangling from his mouth, waving them away. '*Keep your hands off my bus!*' Then the front nearside wheel hit a pothole, and So's head clattered against the window frame. The children all cheered and laughed, egged on by Ben and Hal wincing at the impact. '*Damn little monkeys*,' So muttered as he rubbed his head.

Han put a commiserating hand on his shoulder. '*Are you alright, Mr So?*' he asked through stifled laughter.

So groaned. '*This is your fault, Mr Han. We shouldn't even be on this road. I'm turning round.*' He scouted for a place to turn. '*I'll bet Secretary Sun might be interested in hearing about this little excursion.*'

Han leaned over the front passenger seat. '*Mr So, do you still keep your South Korean DVDs under your mattress or in your wife's underwear drawer?*'

So didn't reply.

'*I thought so. Keep driving, we're almost there.*'

"There" was an inlet at the bottom of a bare brown hill scorched by summer sun, at the foot of which sat rows of harmonicas – dozens, all attached to each other by paper thin walls. Old men sitting on the front steps disappeared inside when they saw Ben and Hal getting off the minibus and Han's Party uniform.

'What happens around here? There's no one out in the fields.' Ben gestured at the mile upon mile of empty land, a few cattle-drawn scythes sitting abandoned. Not even weeds could find the energy to break through the soil.

Han said, 'Nothing. Production has shut down. Is no cattle to pull the equipment.'

'No equipment,' Hal added, panning across the apocalyptic vista.

So stayed back at the minibus, sulkily smoking his Commie Marlboros, checking his head for a bump in the side mirror.

'I lived in that one, over there.' Han stopped walking and pointed to the harmonica at the end. 'My sister, she die over there.' He pointed to a lone tree beside the field.

'I'm sorry,' Ben said, spinning his hand round to tell Hal behind to keep filming. 'How old were you?'

Han looked at the sky for a moment. 'I was ten. I didn't know anyone here. My father was always out on assignment. The people here were scared of us, saying we come from the city to spy on them. Everyone hate us.'

Han hadn't started talking until he was four. Song-man's colleagues kept imploring him to make sure Jun-an's first words were 'Dear Leader', just like all their children apparently had. His father had told him it was as if he was so overwhelmed with the world he couldn't bring himself to verbalise his thoughts about it.

When they got closer to the tree, Ben squinted, noticing old ripped sections on the trunk that hadn't grown back.

'I walked into town a few mile down the road, over hill there, to find some rice or vegetable to steal. The other people here already picked the last seeds out of the field. I came back in evening, and she was sitting up against the tree. She was holding tree bark in her hand. She look like she was sleeping.'

Hal moved his head away from the mic, asking Ben quietly, 'What was she doing with the tree bark?'

Ben rubbed his forehead in despair. 'She was eating it.'

Han explained, 'When we very hungry, sometime we do this. Boil it in a pot. People say is good for you, but I find out later it was useless.'

'What will Mr So think of you showing us this? Won't you get in trouble?'

Han crouched down by the base of the tree, picking up a strip of bark on the ground. Was it the same strip Cho-hee had held? he wondered. 'I have no family. I have already lost everything.' He tossed the bark aside.

'One Plus One Equals One; Only The Dead Don't Starve'

Downtown Pyongyang, 9th July Juche 82 (1994)

Each morning Jun-an left for school he was joined by fewer and fewer of his classmates. 'What's the point,' they would say. 'The teachers are too hungry and exhausted to teach, and we're too hungry and exhausted to listen.' Jun-an would mock their weak-willed nature, telling them it was all the American's fault and he knows all about it because his father wrote about it in the newspaper. 'You're the reason the country is suffering,' he told them.

One morning he was the only child walking around, looking up at the balconies in the surrounding apartment blocks for signs of life. When he got out his neighbourhood, any people he saw were standing still, leaning against walls, gathering their breath at the exertion of simply standing up. Even at ten, you can tell when a city, a country, is falling apart.

At half past seven there was already a long line of pupils outside the headmaster's office – Young Socialist League members waiting for their turn to denounce their teachers in the hope of some reward. It had gotten so bad most of the teachers had stopped showing up.

Jun-an hated roll call the most. The children stood behind their desks, looking around at who was missing, wondering if their parents had stopped making them go, or if they had died in the middle of the night. That was when most of them went. How close sleeping is to dying.

'Choi-kol?' the teacher, Miss Yong, called out pessimistically, her eyes searching the room.

Silence.

She put a line through his name on the register. 'Hyok-li?'

Silence.

She scored out his name too. 'Lee-som?'

One of the children said, 'I saw her mother this morning. She was crying and said something about Lee-som passing into the yellow springs. What does that mean?'

Miss Yong knew the phrase from old oriental folklore. She scored out Lee-som's name. 'Lee-som won't be coming back.'

Her register was now mostly scored-out names, question marks next to the ones who were simply missing, presuming they were being kept at home. She tried not to linger on the sorry silence after some names were called out. The first act of the day to establish who was still alive required a degree of dissociation not taught in teaching college. Slowly she let standards slip in the classroom: the board on the wall showing how well the pupils were behaving, their enthusiasm towards *Juche* ideals, and commitment to informing on fellow pupils was forgotten about (the parents had little left to bribe the teachers with to give their child better marks). Most of their time was taken up with spurious writing exercises like copying out reports from Party newsletters, and memorising long passages from Kim Il-sung's memoirs, repetitive lessons about the uniqueness of the Great Leader's brain at their age. Miss Yong painted a picture of a natural genius from birth. 'When sitting in a mathematics class, the young Kim Il-sung had been told that one plus one equals two. He shot to his feet, indignant, taking a lump of plasticine from his desk, separating them in two, then joining them back together. "See," he said. "One plus one actually equals one." And his teacher and all the other pupils realised they were in the presence of greatness; that young comrade Kim was destined to prove the impossible to us.'

A boy at the front raised his hand. 'Miss Yong, is it true the Great Leader would go climbing on Mount Paektu and catch rainbows?'

'Yes, of course,' she replied.

The pupils whispered in awe to each other. Jun-an, troubled by the one-plus-one story, couldn't help but put up his hand.

'Yes, Jun-an.'

'But Miss Yong, all the Great Leader proved with the plasticine was that two halves make a whole, not one plus one equals one. He took one of something and halved it, so it wasn't one to begin with.'

'Are you questioning the Great Leader comrade Kim Il-sung's genius, Jun-an? Do you actually think your intellect is equal to his?'

Jun-an felt the whole class staring contemptuously at him. 'One plus one equals two.'

Miss Yong stood up behind her desk. 'Jun-an, take that back. Apologise for your insolence immediately!'

He stood up also, and repeated, 'One plus one equals two, Miss Yong!' He spent the rest of the class facing the back wall, his legs trembling weakly.

'OK, more mathematics,' Miss Yong continued. 'Write this down... if the Korean army slaughters twenty-seven Western long-noses with guns, and fifteen Japanese imperialists with bayonets, how many corrupt foreign bastards have they killed altogether...?'

Lunch came soon after, the noun long since disassociated from its meaning.

The boys sat together in the middle of the playground, each examining their aching joints like old men. Han sat quietly after his rebuke for contradicting the Great Leader.

A boy with skin flaking off his face from malnourishment and lack of vitamins was talking. '...I have a cousin out in Ryanggang province. It's got so bad out there a friend of his was left in his house alone. His parents just took off and didn't come back. When he ran out of things to make soup with he started eating rocks and stones.'

'It could be worse,' another boy said. 'My dad took me to a Party meeting last night and they all said not to worry. That the people in the South are even worse off because capitalism has failed so badly. The children have to shine people's shoes all day and only get cigarettes instead of food. They get chased by wild dogs through the streets and people are murdered all the time for talking about socialism.'

As much as Jun-an believed in *Juche* ideals, even this seemed a little far-fetched. 'Do you believe that?' he asked.

Nobody replied.

*

That night, Han Song-man sat in his chair, a notepad on his lap – his typewriter was liable to draw complaints with its clacking at such an hour. Jun-an always asked what he was doing, but his father was evasive, calling it simply 'work.'

'How was school, my boy?' he asked.

Jun-an never lied to his father. 'I got in trouble today. Miss Yong was telling us a story about the Great Leader and how he told his teachers that one plus one equals one.'

'I know the story.'

'I said the Great Leader was mistaken in his mathematics.'

Song-man put down his pen and removed his glasses. 'You have to be careful, Jun-an. It's alright for us to talk like that sometimes in the house. But when you're on the outside and there are strangers around it's best to pretend you agree; it's easier that way.' Jun-an tried to interrupt but his father put his hand up to stop him. 'Now I know that doesn't seem right, but when you're older you'll understand: no good can come of it. There are too many people who are waiting for an excuse to denounce someone. The most important thing is to never get arrested. What are the two things that are impossible?'

Jun-an closed his eyes, straining with concentration. 'Proving your innocence... and trusting a stranger.'

'Right. As soon as you forget those, you're in trouble.'

When Song-man was done for the night and he was a little drunk from too much *cheongju*, he left the pad under the chair, the pages loose. Jun-an snuck out of bed later on and took some of the pages to read in bed by candlelight. The first was a draft of a report for the newspaper:

"The Ministry of Procurement and Food Distribution has issued a statement today relating to the on-going Arduous March, saying that the people's commitment to *Juche* ideals of self-sufficiency must be the cornerstone of working through the current struggle. It also reminded us of the chaos caused by countries abandoning socialism for capitalism. If we give up now our society will collapse as badly as

175

theirs have. Now is not the time to abandon our superior ideals – in fact it is the time to become stronger than ever as only the Korean people can. Pain is just weakness leaving the body."

The next piece of paper had no title:

"I was called to the *Inmin Boanseong* this morning to cover a constable's promotion who had helped shut down a private market in the city. The story itself was routine and, bored, I found myself talking to one of his colleagues at the booking-in desk. He told me a story about an interrogation he had been sitting in on that afternoon. A distressed man came in first thing, saying he had a crime to report, that he not only suspected his girlfriend of conversing about the Party in derogatory terms, he had proof. He then produced a cassette tape from a Dictaphone and put it out on the desk. They took him for an interview, where he systematically detailed his girlfriend's daily routine of badmouthing the Party, being 'loudly spiteful about the lack of food in the city' as he put it, whilst breaking into long speeches about how fortunate he was to even live in Pyongyang, and that he simply couldn't take it any longer knowing she was being so 'criminal'. In between all these pronouncements he kept asking whether his statement would be handed up to a Party official or mentioned in *Rodong Sinmun*. What he didn't know was that his girlfriend was sitting in an interview room next door saying exactly the same thing about him. And that his Dictaphone was South Korean, bought at an illegal market. So they were both arrested and got quite a surprise when they met each other at the holding cells. 'You said you were going to visit your mother!' the girl screamed at him. 'Me?' he shouted back, 'What the hell are *you* doing here?' They were still sitting on the benches arguing when the constable finished his shift. He thinks they'll both get five years at the *rodong danryeondae* (re-education through labour). Is this really what we have come to? Two lovers leaving their bed with kisses in the morning, only to denounce each other in the afternoon?"

10th July Juche 82 (1994)

Months before that summer, the food situation had been rapidly declining. Song-man found a carton of cigarettes didn't buy him as much as it used to; people took to growing vegetables in balcony baskets, which itself threw up a night-time raid-epidemic of people scarpering up ladders and picking what they could from the balconies. Private enterprise like growing food only for your family – despite the Party's official denunciation of such practices – became essential. Day after day, officials told Song-man (off-the-record, of course) if it wasn't for the markets Pyongyang would have totally collapsed. Not that he could ever print such sentiments in *Rodong Sinmun*. It became a trading game in itself: news of what was actually going on behind the scenes at Party headquarters for flattering mentions in the newspaper – 'soft news' – which was vital for a journalist like Song-man in keeping in the loop. Neighbours were always offering favours so they could find out from him if there was any talk of food crops on the way, or upping the rations for the city dwellers. There was simply no network for telling people what was going on other than word of mouth. And as Ji-won told Jun-an, when stomachs are hungry, mouths flap.

She was spending greater amounts of time indoors, and took against opening curtains wherever possible. Glasses of *cheongju* were being poured closer to morning than evening once Song-man had left for the day. 'Why are you drinking?' Jun-an asked her.

'Because I'm sad.'

'Maybe you wouldn't be sad if you didn't drink.'

'But if I didn't drink I would be sad.'

'I don't want you to be sad.'

Ji-won knew she should be stronger, but as a mother it was too much to take that the one child they still had only had maize porridge to eat. When Ji-won drank, grief and sadness followed her into every room.

That day, Song-man was home by early afternoon, tossing his briefcase down beside his chair.

'You're back so soon?' said Ji-won, who had just poured herself more *cheongju*. 'You're drinking so soon?' Song-man retorted.

Too drunk to restrain herself, she exclaimed a little too loudly, 'What else is there to do in this godforsaken country?'

Song-man urgently put his hand up for silence, listening to the rustling noise coming from the neighbours' wall next door.

Ji-won and Song-man's eyes shot over towards the noise. Song-man crept across and put his ear against the wall, putting his finger to his lips at Jun-an who had just walked in.

'Did someone hear?' Ji-won whispered.

'Everyone's home early today.' Song-man switched on the TV, then sat in his chair and explained the situation to his family. 'They've suspended the mail service. You can't post anything abroad now.'

'Why would they do that?'

'They don't want word of what's happening getting to the Real World.'

Jun-an looked up at his father, magisterial in his chair, smoking proudly. 'Why are you home so early?'

Song-man pointed at the TV with his cigarette. 'There was noise in the office from the boys that the Central News Agency is making some announcement at noon. I think it might be big. They want us all to come back into the office later tonight. That normally means a one-story front page.'

The last such special report had been to tell the people North Korea was pulling out of talks with the International Atomic Energy Agency, so Song-man thought there was a chance they had launched a nuke, possibly at the South, maybe even China or America. With all the obscene expenditure on armaments over the past decade no one really knew what existed in a bunker somewhere. Talk of nuclear weapons had dominated the news since Bill Clinton had encouraged the United Nations to take a harder line with them. Would they be tuning in to see pictures of a razed America? Had the world ended and they didn't know?

They sat there quietly until a news reporter appeared, dressed in black and already on the verge of tears, her voice trembling. Jun-an stood next to his mother at the kitchen door.

The reporter started talking, 'The General Committee of the Workers' Party of Korea, the Central Military Commission of the party, the National Defence Commission, the Central People's Committee...'

'We're going to be here all day,' Song-man complained.

'...report to the entire people of the country with deepest grief that—'

'He's dead. He must be dead!'

'—the Great Leader Comrade Kim Il-sung, passed away from a sudden attack of illness at two AM.'

The family said nothing.

Uncontrollable wails of anguish sprung up from all around the neighbouring walls, cries of 'No! Please say it's not true.' 'Great Marshall, how can you leave us now?' There sounded like pounding fists on the floor from the apartment above.

Song-man stubbed out his cigarette and started crying out as well: 'Comrade leader, our Great Marshall. Whatever will we do now?' He encouraged Ji-won and Jun-an to play along too, moving closer to the walls to make sure the neighbours could hear.

Ji-won ladled out more watery soup for dinner, a few vegetable leaves floating around at the bottom of the pot.

'Oh well, it could be worse for the son of a bitch,' she said. 'At least the dead don't starve.'

After dinner, Jun-an was sent to his room to read, but he couldn't concentrate with all that had happened in the last few hours. Neighbours were still crying and wailing. He climbed out of bed and tiptoed to his door, listening in to what his mother and father were discussing.

Song-man sat close to Ji-won on the couch holding her hands. 'What if we could get out, you and Han and I?'

She wept, but not for the Great Leader. 'What about Jun-an? I'd rather die than see him in the *kwan-li-so*.'

'Can't you see, my darling, things are only going to get worse now.

179

There's going to be all sorts of turmoil in the Party as they prepare the new leadership, and I want to get out this country while we still have one of our children alive.'

'The Village Below; All Desperate Desire Now and So Much Want; Living is What We Do'

Kasong, Kangwon province

Han and the others got up from around the tree, their legs and backsides freezing from sitting on the ground for so long. Hal checked the battery on the screen: he had been filming Han for so long that the camera was running low.

'We're going to need a longer broadcast time for all this,' Hal told Ben.

A pile of cigarette butts sat at So's feet by the minibus, sitting side-on in the driver's seat with his legs hanging out. '*We're late,*' he said bitterly, as the others returned.

Han turned back to the harmonicas, seeing a little boy and girl the same age as he and his sister were when she died, come running out the front door of his old house. They were laughing and chasing each other around the tree, oblivious to the horrors it had been witness to.

Now he was so much older, everything looked much smaller than he remembered. He hadn't really started to grow until he got the Communications job at Pyonganbuk province and the Ministry was able to feed him two meals a day. Now he was seeing the old village from a greater height. It reminded him of an old phrase the Party had for South Korea. They called it the 'village below'. He always thought it was a more appropriate name for his own village: a forgotten place at the end of the earth. He didn't ever want to come back.

Rain streamed down the minibus windows all the way back to Pyongyang, little being said by anyone. Han sat in the back with Ben and Hal again, smoking Commie Marlboros one after the other. Hal, always uncomfortable with silence, suggested, 'Maybe we could go out for a drink tonight, Mr Han. It's been a long day. How about we buy you a couple of beers?'

'Is very kind, Mr Hal,' he replied, 'but I have to get you back to the hotel. There is curfew tonight.'

'Why is there a curfew?' Ben asked.

'I'm sorry. It is my orders from the Ministry.' Han laughed exhaustedly. 'I don't think you see the danger I in now. I could be shot for telling you what I have. Because Mr So doesn't know what we are saying does not mean I am safe. Secretary Sun would arrest me if he only have half the chance.'

'Why?'

'He didn't like my father. He used to tell me about Sun when they were growing up. They were working in the field at school one day, my father say to him he didn't believe the propaganda they were taught during lessons. That he had seen a South Korean newspaper and all they been told about them being poor and living miserable lives was lies. He had seen pictures of how well they doing.'

'Was he arrested?'

'Nothing. Sun never told anyone. But from this day, no matter what my father do, he always know, deep down,' he signalled to his heart, 'my father not really loyal to the Party. He was willing to lie, to pretend, to have easier life.'

'Does Secretary Sun trust you?'

'I think Sun want me in a high position. He can catch me for a bigger crime that way. Like conspiring with foreigners, or...'

'Or what?'

Han tossed his cigarette out the window. 'Nothing.'

Downtown Pyonyang

So's speedy return to the city got the men dropped at the hotel before the soldiers appeared on the streets, guns wrapped across their chests.

'Somewhere there's a military compound missing a lot of soldiers tonight,' Han said to So, watching military trucks unloading soldiers on every other street.

'They're not messing around,' So said direly.

It was the first they had said to each other since leaving Kangwon province, and the air had been strained since dropping off Ben and Hal.

They pulled up outside Han's building, and as Han reached for the door handle, So lunged across him and held the door closed. 'Mr Han,' he began. 'You weren't being serious before about reporting me over the DVDs were you?'

Han sighed, letting go of the door handle. 'I don't like being threatened, Mr So.'

'Neither do I.' He flashed him a look of concern. 'I don't know what you're telling the foreigners—'

Han turned his head quickly towards the window, away from him.

'—and to be honest, I really don't care. I just drive the bus around here. But look around you. Clearly something big is going on, and I don't know if you're on the inside or not...' He gently slapped Han's cheek and turned his face towards him. '...but you need to be careful. Maybe now isn't the best time to be reckless around those you haven't worked with for long.'

'Are you talking about yourself?'

'I'm talking about Ryong. Maybe you should be asking why he hasn't been with us today. Are you sure he has nothing on you?'

Han took the elevator up to the eighteenth floor, looking away from the bank of floor-buttons lighting up as it went past seventeen. He had never talked to anyone for so long about his family. And as the floors ticked by, all he could think was: everyone I've ever loved always leaves.

After fixing some watery vegetable and maize broth, he took out *Nineteen Eighty-four* from under the pillow on his bed, hoping it would take his mind off his hunger. He lay there reading, not noticing the dimming sunlight outside as the hours passed and the pages turned. All of a sudden it had seemed to turn from light to darkness, like a switch had been flicked.

As Han suspected, Winston was caught by the Party's secret police, as was Julia his lover, like Winston had repeatedly predicted. Han couldn't help but will him to escape, but he knew, as Winston did, that there was nowhere to hide. When Winston was informed of Julia's betrayal, Han found himself crying out, 'No!' in disgust, and turned the book over on the bed, unable to take it – that two lovers could do such a thing when all they really had was each other.

By the end Han's spirit was drained, as Winston resigned himself to the power of the Party. He slapped the book shut and moved to the living room, needing to inhabit a different space. As he cried, thinking about his family, his grief turned to annoyance as the portraits of the Great- and Dear Leaders stared at him everywhere he paced around the room. It was their fault he was so alone, he told himself, and he didn't want their lying eyes staring at him anymore. Taking the portraits down off the wall, one in each hand, he raised them up over his head, his arms trembling with anger and tension at what he was about to do, then he threw them down on the floor as hard as he could. The thin glass covering them shattered everywhere, shards of pinewood and glass scattered at his feet. The faces of the Two Leaders were torn apart, their ever-present smiles finally gone. He closed his eyes in relief.

Taking *Nineteen Eighty-four* with him, Han took the stairs down to Mae's apartment, and knocked frantically on her door until she opened it. He fell into her arms, dropping the book on her hallway floor. All the longing he had stored up since last he saw her drained out his body through his lips as he kissed her, the force of it knocking her back a step. She countered his strength, kissing him so hard they stepped back into the hallway, pushing him against the wall. That was what he wanted: her, and only her, all of the time, reading EE Cummings to him, her body precious and glorious against him, golden fingertips running through his hair and touching his face all desperate desire now and so much want, like he had forgotten what it was to feel, all made of light now with him, and the way she smelled and the sound of her sighing with his sigh and kissed with his kiss tongue hands gripping strongly hers and never wanting to let go and it was true and he never wanted it to stop and they couldn't control it anymore it was love it was love it was love and all perfect in harmony together and he wasn't thinking anymore, and he wasn't worried as long as he had her.

She finally pulled back, and as his lips brushed against her ear, he whispered, 'Don't ever leave me.'

They lay spooning in Mae's bed, facing the brick wall-view outside her window. Han gently brushed her hair, clearing the nape of her neck to kiss it.

'I was telling the Westerners about my family today.'

'Where did you go?'

'Kangwon province. Where my sister died.'

'How did she die?'

Han held her a little tighter. 'Starvation.'

'What about your parents?'

'They died in a car crash in Chongjin. What about your family?'

'My mother and father were imprisoned two years ago. A neighbour found a Bible in their house.'

'Why did they have a Bible?'

'They're Christians. They used to read it together at night in their bedroom and pray together. I begged them to be careful, but...'

'You can never be careful enough.'

'Right.'

'It was one of the first books I read. The first places I read about that weren't in Korea. I don't know if I'll ever see them again.' She reached for her watch on the nightstand.

'Do you need to leave for the theatre soon?'

'I'm afraid so,' she said, getting out of bed.

'What is it tonight?'

'Some opera about the Ministry of Land and Marine Transportation.'

'Sounds like a riot.'

'I hear your boss is going to be there.'

'Sun? He'll be bored out his mind.'

'Everyone will, then they'll all clap wildly at the end. They always do.'

Han sat up as she stood in front of her wardrobe, delicate and slender. He imagined her disappearing in her sleep and being made new each morning. Her cello case sat on the ground under her clothes. 'They betrayed each other, you know,' he said.

'Who?'

'Winston and Julia. In the book.'

'I know.'

'My father heard of a couple like them. They denounced each other to the *Inmin Boanseong*.'

Noticing the change in his voice and his darting eyes again, she crawled over the bed to him, raising his chin so he looked into her eyes. 'We're not the same as them. Or Winston and Julia. That's just a book. It doesn't have to be like that for us.'

'I've been thinking about that today.'

'What have you been thinking?'

'Don't you wonder what the point is, of being alive in a place like this? What if the best thing that could happen to you would be to stop existing?'

She slowly shook her head in confusion, watching his little mind working.

'There's something beautiful about dying. The past and future get severed equally. We're destroyed on either side and left as the person we were last.'

She moved back onto her knees. 'You shouldn't say things like that.'

'I don't know how we manage to keep going.'

She grabbed hold of him. 'Because living is what we do. We carry on, no matter the hunger, the grief, the loneliness. We keep living, because it *is* something, and dying is nothing. Death is a negative; the absence of life, of joy, of love. That's why I read; that's why I sneak out in the middle of the night to talk to other people who read; that's why I play Shostakovich; that's why I love you. Because living is what we do.'

Han paused. 'You say Sun will be there tonight?'

186

'I saw him on the guest list. He'll be there until ten o'clock.'

He got up and dressed with her. *Living is what we do*, he thought – a plan forming in his mind.

'How To Die Twice; Karaoke'

Room 442, Koryo Hotel, 18th December

From Hal's vantage point at the hotel room window, the military, and officers from the *Kukga Bowibu* (Department of National Security) he was filming looked tiny and insectile. Once they took to the streets there didn't seem to be any plan other than to be highly visible and threatening.

Ben lay on the bed, reading through webpages he had archived on Hal's laptop when they were in China – hundreds of reports from *Naenara News* (the DPRK's official news page for foreigners), and dissident-run insider news sources like *Chosun Ilbo* and *NK News* – searching for mentions of Secretary Sun.

'It's like *Empire of the Sun* out there,' Hal said, pulling back from the window.

Ben replied with a distant, 'Hmmm.'

'Not so mad I brought my laptop now, are you.'

'I'll be happier if I find something. It might take a while, though.'

'How much you got on there?'

'I archived everything on senior officials in the past three years. About two gigs.'

'Can you keyword search through them?'

'It doesn't help much. Sun is mentioned in nearly every major dispatch in *Naenara*. If there was any kind of meeting of senior officials, or a ceremony for unveiling another Kim statue, or welcoming a foreign dignitary, he's in it.' He clicked through the reports he had found on former Secretary Hwang. 'It's strange, though. Hwang just disappears from the official DPRK news after a while, like he's fallen off a cliff.'

Hal grimaced at the camera battery dying, turning it off. 'Or defected?'

Ben pursed his lips. 'Doubt it. He would have shown up in Seoul or Washington by now. This one from *Chosun Ilbo* from January this year says that the Party has been grooming Kim Jong-un, Kim Jong-il's son, for the leadership of the Party.'

'Didn't they make him a four-star general last year?'

'And vice-chair of the Central Military Commission. It says the State Security Department had purged about two hundred senior Party members, either detained or executed, to ensure Kim Jong-un's ascendancy was unobstructed. They raided their homes, finding stashes of cash, up to a million dollars in some of them.'

Having run out of things to film, Hal took to playing with settings on the camera. 'That's how these guys roll.'

Ben turned the screen towards Hal. 'Says here Sun ordered the arrest of Hwang.'

Hal rushed over to see the report, crouching beside the bed. 'Was he executed?'

Ben snorted derisively. 'He killed himself. Jumped out a window while they were interrogating him at his home. *That* is how these guys roll.'

'So what does that mean?'

'The Party's in a lot more confusion than most people realise. We might be seeing an off-shoot of that power struggle outside right now. We already know Sun's trying to reclaim the dominance of the Propaganda Department. Maybe all this anti-Kim graffiti that Mr Han has been told to keep us away from is coming from within the Party.'

Hal put his fingers on his temples, eyes closed. 'Right, but where does that leave us? We've only got a couple days left.'

'We've got Mr Han on record about what really went on during the famine.'

'Which we still need to talk to him about. If we use that footage he could end up in a lot of trouble.'

Ben slapped the laptop closed, then paced the room. 'I know.' He put a hand on either side of the window frame, head hanging down, trying to think what to do.

'Unless we can get him out of here,' Hal said unexpectedly.

'And how you do propose to do that?'

There was a knock on the door, followed by a sharp demand of, 'Mr Campbell, Mr Huckley, you are wanted downstairs.'

Ben shot around, looking at Hal, then the computer, then the copy of *Nineteen Eighty-four* sitting on his pillow. 'Just a minute,' he called out towards the door, trying to sound unpanicked. He threw the book into his rucksack, while Hal hid the computer in the camera bag.

'Now's the time to get worried, right?' Hal whispered.

The Forbidden City

After dropping Mae at the Mansudae Theatre, Han drove to the Ministry, his travel permit checked three times in the space of a few miles by the many humourless soldiers on patrol. Each time when they realised he was a senior Party member, the soldier apologised profusely.

'You think someone is coming into the city from outside to write the slogans?' Han asked.

'I'm afraid I can't discuss that, comrade,' the soldier replied, before waving him on.

The military and the *Kukga Bowibu* were everywhere. There would surely be no one crazy enough to attempt any more vandalism that night, Han figured.

Two guards stood outside the entrance of the Ministry of Communications, one of them saying, 'Good evening, Mr Han,' as he opened the door for him. The cleaners mopping the marble-floored lobby suddenly found a spring in their step when Han appeared. The woman up a set of ladders cleaning the enormous portrait of Kim Il-sung hanging over the staircase started polishing like she was trying to make a spark to start a fire. They had expected an easy night with the various department heads at the opera with Secretary Sun.

Han went past the Propaganda Department library, where the young assistant he had seen before had his head now buried in volume two of Kim Il-sung's *Reminiscences with the Century*, his face hardened with concentration. Han was confident he wasn't going anywhere.

The corridor outside Sun's office was in such total darkness Han didn't realise he was at Sun's door until he felt the wall making way for the doorframe. He still found himself knocking quietly on the door, some last-second terror kicking in that for some reason Sun might still be there, or Miss Lee. He gently opened the door, turning the knob fully so as to make no noise, and found the office empty as expected. Floodlights from the square outside the window, where rehearsals for the Mass Games had spilled over into nighttime, bathed Sun's bird cage in a soft white light.

The filing cabinets were laid out simply: current employees at the top, previous employees near the bottom, their family names in alphabetical order. Han took out his cigarette lighter to see, not realizing how fear-of-God nervous he was until he noticed the flame trembling in his hand. There was no excuse he could premeditate to explain what he could be doing in such a position at such a time of the evening.

He skipped to the *H*'s and found his father's file along with his security pass and travel permit photo on the front: Han Song-man. Song-man's face was so blank and unassuming like the other photos filed away, it was hard to remember he was not the Party faithful everyone thought he was. But then Han had come to appreciate in his years with the Ministry in Pyonganbuk province that no one *looks* like a dissenter.

The file covered his father's life, from birth to death and everything in between, detailing back six generations of his family and their positions and Party membership that made up his *songbun*, which in turn affected Han's social ranking. There was too much in the file to go through in such a dangerous position. He gathered up the file, stuffing it inside his jacket. No one would be looking for the ten-year-old file of a dead journalist any time soon. As he was about to close the cabinet drawer, he couldn't resist a quick look through the *M*'s. Not that he wanted to find anything there, but he needed to know once and for all. The confirmation Winston could never get with Julia. He held the lighter into the drawer as he jogged his fingers to Mae's records, her eyes on the front picture colder and sterner, like someone had asked her not to look her usual self. When he saw the heading on the inside page, he closed his eyes tightly, his face in a kind of heartbroken rictus. He wanted to swear loudly, and throw something across the room.

"Mae Soon-li" the file said. Her role was listed as "Agent of the Propaganda and Agitation Department/Informant." He didn't want to read any more but he knew he had to.

Mae's record stretched back two years from when she was recruited a few months after joining the National Orchestra. There were no details of information she had passed on to the Department, or arrests arising from her activity, but it listed her parents as interned in a political prisoner concentration camp, Kaechon, otherwise known as Camp 14, on 5th August *Juche* 97, for "cultural crimes." *Was that you who told on them?* he wondered. He looked further down the page. They were recorded as being executed six weeks later. 'She thinks they're still alive...' he whispered.

A light suddenly came on, glowing under the doorframe. Han's first guess was a cleaner, but he didn't plan on hanging around to find out. If Mae was currently active, he couldn't bring her file with him, so he put it back in order, and made a quick exit through the anteroom, sneaking out a back staircase.

He drove to a secluded alleyway a few streets away, where he could have some privacy to look through his father's file in more detail, but all he could think about was Winston and Julia. The inside of his head felt hot from what he had just discovered.

After all the hard copies of Song-man's articles and opinion columns from *Rodong Sinmun*, was a Secret Police report with his father's name on it under a heading "Suspect". His car hadn't crashed in Chongjin with Ji-won. He had been arrested, on suspicion of people smuggling. Han turned the page over, and when he saw the signature at the bottom, he beat his fist on the steering wheel. 'Bastard!' he shouted. Below the signature was the printed name: "Assistant Secretary of the Interior Sun." There was something galling about how shabbily Sun had signed it. Like it was an afterthought, signing for inconsequential mail.

The next pages detailed the holding stations his father had been taken around for processing to Hoeryong, the notorious Camp 22 near the border with China, for political prisoners like Mae's parents in Camp 14. The final sheet in the file had a small mug shot of his father, his hair mussed up, his face grey and gaunt from weeks of starvation and forced labour. It ended with, "Date of Execution: 1st September *Juche* 89."

Han covered his face in despair. Images of his father standing in front of a firing squad flooded his mind and he couldn't shake them, no matter how hard he closed his eyes. He swatted helplessly at the steering wheel, scrunching up the sheet of paper from the prison administrative office, throwing the file against the windscreen. But out of the despair, he realised: if his father hadn't died in a car crash, that there had never been a car crash, then what happened to his mother? If she had been arrested, she would have been listed alongside Song-man. Han grabbed the files off the dashboard, frantically shuffling through them for the arrest report. He flattened it out on his leg and angled it towards the light above the rear view mirror.

Under "Offence(s)" the police had written, "Charged with aiding and abetting the illegal crossing into China of a single, unknown female."

'It can't be...' he said.

Stapled to the back of the arrest report was an internal memo from Sun, instructing, "...the wife of the accused was identified with him at the scene and shall be declared dead."

Surely the border guards would have shot her, he thought. They didn't take the trouble of running after defectors with a pair of handcuffs. But where was the report?

He stared at the street ahead, wondering what to do. They could have arrested him by now given what Mae knew about him, so why hadn't they? His *songbun* had been irreparably tainted by his father's crime, so why had Sun specifically allowed him to come into Pyongyang? It was only a matter of time before they got to him. Mae would be home in a few hours: just enough time to start making preparations.

Koryo Hotel lobby

Ben and Hal were escorted in the elevator to reception by a man dressed in plain clothes but said he worked for the hotel. He held his arms in a V-shape, hands in front of crotch, the practiced pose of a security guard. They stood in silence the whole way down, Ben and Hal with their hands behind their backs, already half-resigned to arrest on whatever numerous charges the police could land on them. Illegal filming, use of a laptop, smuggling in banned literature, political conspiracy: there were plenty of options.

The Norwegians were at reception, being checked out by their minders. They looked so unburdened and free, freedom that until precisely three minutes ago Ben and Hal had taken so massively for granted.

Ben scanned the lobby for police or any sign of officials. 'Is something the matter? Who wants to see us?' Ben asked. The escort showed them towards reception, and would only say, 'Please, this way, please.'

The Norwegians' minder barracked them out of reception, waving goodbye to Ben and Hal, revealing Han standing signing a register. Han looked up as they approached, showing no sign of the traumatic news he had discovered only an hour before, but he was speaking quicker, his overly exuberant exterior disarming Ben and Hal. 'Mr Ben, Mr Hal, thank you for coming down! A little later than planned, but I made it. I must sign you out.' He quickly put his arms around them and walked them to the main doors.

'Where are we going, Mr Han?' Ben asked, not sure if it was too early to relax.

'Remember I said we go to karaoke tonight,' he replied boisterously, loud enough for the security guards outside the entrance to hear as they passed. 'Is best thing to do at night in Pyongyang.'

'We're not using the bus, Mr Han?' Hal asked, looking at the rusty BMW in front of them.

'This not official visit,' he said quietly in Hal's ear as he opened the backdoor.

As they left the hotel grounds, Ben slumped in relief in the front passenger seat, confessing, 'We thought we were under arrest.'

Han peered into the rear view mirror to check they weren't being tailed. 'I'm sorry for confusion. I could not wait until tomorrow.'

'What's happening tomorrow, Mr Han?' Hal asked.

'Tomorrow is last day of tour.'

Ben checked with Hal, turning his head slightly. 'We still have two days left, Mr Han.'

'Not anymore,' he mumbled. 'Did you know,' Han pointed to the steering wheel, 'when I was growing up they tell us BMW built in North Korea.'

'Did you believe them?' Ben asked.

'At the start you believe everything, Mr Ben.'

Ben was calm now. He had lived through more hostile situations in his career, but none quite as surreal.

Han drove them to the city centre, the full extent of the troop deployment becoming clear to the men.

'What is going on, Mr Han?' Hal asked, more annoyed he didn't have his camera with him. 'Why is the tour ending tomorrow? Has someone found out something?'

'I find some documents I think you want to take home.'

'What kind of documents?'

'*Mingamhan.*'

Hal held himself forward on the back of Ben's seat. 'What did he say?'

Ben said, 'Sensitive.'

'Yes,' Han nodded, scanning the rear view mirror with every flash of headlights behind. 'Important.'

Up ahead, a soldier waved the car down. He hadn't seen a car pass for the last hour.

Hal sat back in his seat, asking Ben, 'Are we okay?'

'I don't know,' he answered.

'Is not a problem, gentlemen,' Han said, rolling the window down.

The soldier leaned in to the car, his eyes narrowing at Ben and Hal. *'Permit and ID, please.'*

Han handed him his papers and explained, *'They're diplomatic aids. They want a night out on the town. Honestly, these Westerners and their drinking.'*

He examined Han's travel permit and credentials. *'Very good, comrade. Do look out for any suspicious persons.'*

As they drove away, Han angled the rear view mirror to see if the soldier made any calls on his radio. He didn't.

'Is alright. I tell him you diplomatic aids.'

Ben sneaked a look back. 'Is that really necessary?'

'It is tonight, yes, Mr Ben. No tourists allowed out hotels tonight.'

Han took them to a karaoke bar he knew would be quiet and had little chance of meeting anyone he knew there. Two women in fluorescent pink gowns stood in front of a television screen with a photoshopped still-picture of Mount Paektu – the sky in the background a hellish red – singing traditional Korean songs through a tiny PA system cranked with reverb, giving their voices an angelic quality.

Until the men arrived, the women had been singing to no one.

Ben and Hal sat in a cramped booth in a corner of the room, under two portraits of the Two Leaders.

'So this has gotten a little strange,' Hal suggested.

Ben could only laugh, rubbing the tiredness from his face.

Han signalled to a waitress for three beers which she ran over with in tiny steps, her legs inhibited by her tight dress.

Hal read the label on his bottle, which had also been Romanized. 'Taedonggang.'

'Is made by the State brewery company,' Han said.

Hal cut his first swig short. 'The Government makes beer?'

'Is not so strange. The White House makes its own beer.'

'No way,' Hal said, chuckling to Ben.

'Is true. I saw it on the Internet.'

The karaoke girls got their game faces on now they had company, singing with arm movements like they were swans very very slowly flapping their wings, their faces strained in such fake smiles it looked like parody. The volume of the Casio keyboard-like instrumentation they were singing along to easily covered the men's conversation.

'I think we should talk, Mr Han,' Ben began. 'We should talk about what we're going to put into our final documentary.'

Han stared downheartedly at his bottle, twirling it slowly between his fingers. His happy act long gone. 'It does not matter.'

'You should know, there's a good chance someone here might see it.'

'It does not matter, Mr Ben. The worst they could do is threaten my family, and I don't have any.'

'What about your girlfriend?'

'You didn't tell me he had a girlfriend,' Hal complained to Ben, giving Ben's arm a backhanded slap.

'We not together anymore,' Han said, releasing his bottle.

'I'm sorry to hear that,' Ben said, but he wanted to get straight to business. He wasn't sure how much longer they had alone. 'About what you've said on camera, Mr Han. Hal and I need to make sure that we're not putting you in any danger by doing this. We can obscure your face, change your voice, but we can't hide ourselves from the tape. I think you know someone in the Ministry will be able to work out who you are.'

Han had lost all interest in his beer, casting it aside. 'Is not concern for me.'

'What's happened?' asked Ben, leaning in closer to him. 'Is it to do with your girlfriend?'

Han checked no one was looking, then took out his father's file from inside his jacket. 'I find this tonight in the Ministry.'

'What is it?' Ben asked, unable to read the Chosongul script.

'This record say my father was not killed in a car crash with my mother. He was arrested in Chongjin.'

'Arrested? For what?'

'Helping someone who sounds like my mother escape into China.

They arrested him, then killed him. All ordered by Secretary Sun.'

Hal, noticing one of the karaoke girls holding the mic up in their direction and about to come over, waved his hand to say 'No.'

Ben exhaled heavily. 'I'm sorry, Mr Han.'

Han checked over his shoulder again. 'I going to run away to China. Try to get to the South.'

Ben pulled back from the table with a low sigh. 'Mr Han. I don't know if that's a good idea—'

Han interrupted, 'You not understand, Mr Ben. My girlfriend... she had books. Books you are not allowed to have here in North Korea. She take me to an apartment with other people that read these books, they talk about them and...'

Hal pumped his head forward in amazement, remembering to keep his voice down. 'A book group? In North Korea?'

'She knows I have books as well. Foreign ones. Illegal ones. I am in serious trouble.'

Ben rested his hands on top of Han's. 'She's been informing to the police?'

'I find her file at the Ministry with my father's.'

'What have you been saying to her?'

'The most dangerous thing: the truth. What I really think about the country, the Party.' He shook his head, gutted at how reckless he had been.

'How long would they put you in jail for?' Hal asked.

Ben and Han stared back at him.

'What?'

Ben answered for Han. 'They won't put him in jail. They'll execute him.'

Han moved on quickly. 'So tomorrow, we have our final day together, and my final day in North Korea. I have to try. They will kill me anyway. What I want to bring you here to say is, on your film, don't cover my face, or change my voice. Tell them my name. Han Jun-an. Tell them my name.'

The singing girls, wondering why the men didn't want to sing, put on a song for them. 'We try "Old Blue Eyes", ' one of them said in English, giggling in her hand. A toybox piano version of Frank Sinatra's "My Way" started up, the girls valiantly struggling with the English words.

'An entire man's life,' Ben said, sliding Song-man's file over, looking into the terrified eyes staring back from the mug shot. 'He would have known what was going to happen to him when they took this.'

As the men sat and listened to the song, Han pulled his beer closer and took a long drink. 'Do you miss your father, Mr Ben?'

'I miss him, Mr Han. Every single day. And now it's like...' He laughed ironically, hoping he wouldn't cry. 'I'm sorry he never got to see me do something important.'

'You report the news, Mr Ben. Real news. If it not for people like you writing on the Internet, I never know about the Real World. I can't think of something more important.'

Hal reached across the table, tapping his hand in front of Han. 'We were talking in the hotel room. We want to help you get out of here.'

'That's not good idea, Mr Hal. Too dangerous. I have to leave myself.'

Ben kept turning his bottle around slowly, like it were a globe. 'You said you have books, Mr Han.'

'Many.'

'Have you ever heard of a writer called John Cheever?'

'I don't know this one.'

'I was on an overnight train travelling through Spain once. I was sitting up in bed reading Cheever with the window open, the train vibrating against my back. I read this sentence of his: "I've been homesick for countries I've never seen, and longed to be where I couldn't be."'

The girls were nearing the song's climax.

Ben appealed to him, 'Let us help you.'

'We can do it,' Hal added, nodding vigorously. 'We've talked to people who've done it.'

Han looked down at both their hands holding his outstretched arms.

'Do you have a plan?' Ben asked.

'Is very dangerous, Mr Ben,' Han warned him. 'We must cross Tumen River into China, and after that...' He broke off. 'I don't know yet.'

'We have money,' Ben said. 'It could help you get to Thailand, maybe Vietnam, then you could have a try at the South Korean embassy there where they're not so strict. The Chinese embassies won't touch you.'

'I know. But I can't take your money, it's not—'

Ben interrupted, 'You're taking our money, and you're taking us.' He turned to Hal. 'Right, Hal?'

Hal grinned ruefully and shrugged. 'What the hell, man.'

'It's perfect. Documentaries have caught up with people that have escaped, but they've never actually followed someone through all the way. It'll be the first of its kind.'

Han was choked. 'If you are sure, Mr Ben and Mr Hal. I would owe you my... my...'

Ben raised his bottle and handed Han his, just as the girls reached the song's crescendo. 'A toast: To our fathers. Wherever they may be.'

Hal raised his bottle. 'Our fathers.'

Han raised his too. 'Our fathers.'

As they chimed bottles, the girls took a bow in front of the television screen showing a picture of Sinatra's face. The men stood and applauded.

After signing Ben and Hal back into the hotel, Han made his way across the city, a trickle of traffic coming from the direction of the Mansudae Theatre: Mae would be back soon. He took an indirect route home, holding his hand out the window, feeling the stale, thick air rushing through his fingers as he turned onto the left bank of Taedonggang-guyok running alongside the Taedong River.

Washed linen hung from some of the balconies to dry overnight, the white shapes like ghosts suspended in mid-air. The river seemed to have stopped moving, its gentle eddies silent and unseen in the moonless night.

Han parked in the alleyway Mae had led him down two nights before, looking up to see if there was any movement behind Oh-ran's window, but there wasn't. He took his shoes off and climbed the metal staircase, wondering how he was going to tell her what he had found. When he reached her landing he took a quick look inside before knocking on the glass: he didn't want to frighten her, and from the darkness inside she appeared to already be in bed. The closer he looked, cupping his hands around his eyes, he could see furniture had been upended, and the television sat on its back, facing the ceiling, its false front taken off. After knocking a few times on the glass, he shunted the window up.

He whispered, 'Oh-ran?' as he crawled through into the living room. He could tell it was already too late. Pictures and family heirlooms littered the living room floor, china and pottery were smashed in the kitchen, the cupboard doors hanging open, clothes strewn across the bedroom, the mattress flipped on its side. It was the sort of thorough search that only happens off the back of solid evidence.

The television set on the living room floor was empty, all Oh-ran's books gone. Han flicked his cigarette lighter on to see in the kitchen. Sitting in one of the open cupboards under the sink were three tins of white paint and a near-empty can of petrol. 'Oh-ran,' he sighed. Apparently her hobbies extended far beyond a weekly book group. The geography of all the graffiti sightings, and their walkable distance to the left bank of the river, made sense to him now.

Then from somewhere behind in the hallway, he heard a door creak open. An old woman in a nightgown stood at the front doorstep holding a candle without a candlestick.

'What do you want?' she snapped.

'It's alright,' Han replied, extending his ID towards her. 'I'm with the Party.'

She squinted harshly at Han's badge. 'They took her already.'

'Who did?'

'Them. The police.'

'What kind?'

'*Kukga Bowibu.* They had dogs and everything. They started shouting at us, how couldn't we know what she was up to, and the rest. I said I was the reason they were there at all.'

'You told the police on her?'

'Of course. The country's in a sorry enough state without letting these nihilists run amok.' She was still muttering when she closed her door behind her, 'They bring it on themselves. I'm not going down with them. I've made it this far...'

Han returned to the kitchen, taking one of the paintbrushes and tins from the cupboard. 'If the sky is falling down, where do you hide?' he said to no one.

He wondered how many others from the group had been rounded up in the middle of the night, perhaps as part of some coordinated raid on addresses across the city. It seemed that Mae had started naming names.

'Winston And Julia'

Chollima Street

The elevator had been out of order – Mae's doing, to slow him down? he wondered – and Han's heartbeat rolled like a timpani drum as he dashed up the eighteen flights of stairs. He rushed around his apartment, throwing his warmest civilian clothes into a rucksack on top of his bed like they were laundry. Clothes he could change into later the next day when they were safely out of the city – he wouldn't be needing his Party uniform after that. He packed up his family pictures from the living room, removing their frames to take up less room in his bag. He shuttled back and forth to the window, expecting to see an *Inmin Boanseong* van arriving outside, its side door sliding open and a squad of soldiers hurrying out to take him away. Mae had told him not to wait up, that one of the violinists would drive her home. That was fine with him. He didn't plan on saying goodbye anyway.

He opened up the loose floorboard in the bedroom and held his hand over his books, as if checking them for heat. Caught in some *Sophie's Choice*-dilemma, he knew if he took one he'd have to take them all. All he'd risked to get them in the first place, the life they had given him, and now he had to say goodbye. Although he cried as he replaced the floorboard – the gentle silent kind of tears you cry when moved by a piece of music – it was out of hope for what the future might hold. Whatever happened in the next twenty-four hours, he wasn't going to be a prisoner anymore. As he stood up, he caught his reflection in the bedroom mirror. He turned the mirror around, taking one last look at the pictures of Ho Chow-sun, Arthur Boyumunga and Li Juntao et al, then left it hanging with the pictures facing the room. 'Thank you for your company, gentlemen,' he said, wiping his tears away.

There didn't seem much point in arranging things into neat piles, or tidying away the shattered remains of the pictures of the

Two Leaders. His crimes were far beyond that now. He lifted his suitcase off the bed, then froze as he heard his front door creaking open. He knew it couldn't be the police. The *Inmin Boanseong* didn't do restraint.

He carried his bag into the living room, where Mae stood with her back to him, surveying the smashed portraits and Oh-ran's tin of paint on the floor with a hand at her mouth. She turned around, too horror-struck to immediately notice the bag in his hand. 'What have you done?' she asked.

'I could ask you the same question,' Han said.

Her cello case sat on its side in the front doorway. 'You left your door open, so I...' She glanced at his bag. 'I thought I'd surprise you. Where are you going?'

'I was just leaving.' He regripped the bag's top handle, his hand clammy with nerves. 'How was the opera? Any intimate conversations with Secretary Sun?'

Something about his demeanour made her keep her distance. 'The senior Party members left early actually. All of them. I think something must be going on. There's talk of some kind of announcement tomorrow on the television. It must be something big. The last time there was a special announcement it was to say that—'

'That Kim Il-sung was dead. I remember.'

She stood in the middle of the room, hugging herself from the cold. She was only wearing her performance-dress. 'Jun-an, what's going on?'

Han walked to the coffee table, picking up his father's Party file with his free hand. He didn't speak to her like they were lovers anymore. 'This is the part of the book where the Thought Police come swooping into the apartment and take me away, and we denounce each other.'

She tried to come closer but he stepped back from her. 'I don't understand.'

'You said that was just a book, that we weren't like them. Now look at us.' He handed her his father's file. 'There are some good stories in here too.'

She looked through the pages. 'Han Song-man. This is your father... He didn't die in a car crash.'

'He was arrested then executed.'

'Where did you get this?'

'In Secretary Sun's filing cabinet. Along with yours and all his other Department informers.'

Her legs buckled and she fell back onto the sofa. 'Wait. You don't understand... I know what this looks like—'

He was more distraught than angry. 'What does it look like? Huh? That you've been lying to me from the start. This whole thing, us, has just been a set-up.' He made for the door. 'I don't know how I could have been so stupid.'

Mae grabbed him from behind, pulling his arm back. 'Please, Jun-an, it's not what you think... I was going to tell you tonight, that's why I came here.'

'What was the plan? Lure me downstairs, then Sun shows up in the middle of the night to take me away? Is that it?'

'There's nobody coming! It was my parents. Sun organised this, you're right: me living here, meeting you, it was all arranged. When my parents were caught with their Bible, they were going to execute them, and they would send me to prison for life as well. Sun said he would spare them and reduce their sentences if I helped the Department. He told me about an *inminban* leader on the east bank who suspected some residents of meeting illegally after curfew, so he got me to infiltrate the group. I had to!'

'Oh-ran and the others?'

'Yes. In the beginning I thought I was really going to have to name names. After a few weeks I realised, all I had to do was tell them what people were saying, when and how often they were meeting and if they were planning anything. I never mentioned the books – Sun had no idea. He thought they were meeting to listen to South Korean radio stations. If he knew what had really being going on he would never have let it go as long as it has.'

'Like the graffiti, and the burning slogan on the stadium pitch.'

She didn't respond, wondering how he knew.

'I went to Oh-ran's tonight. I found the paint. And the petrol too. The police had trashed the whole place. They've arrested her.'

'I know. After the opera, Sun told me they were bringing Oh-ran in. Kim-cheol from the orchestra took me to hers afterwards, but it was too late. It all happened so quickly. The group would go out without me. They never told me what they were doing, but when I saw where the slogans were showing up, I knew Oh-ran had to be behind it. But I never told Sun any of that. All I had to do was keep the details vague, that no one would tell me their names, that I never found out where they lived, that everyone swore themselves to secrecy, and he believed me. I swear! I never gave anyone up.'

'Why would he trust you if you never gave anyone up?'

'Oh-ran's brother-in-law works at the *Inmin Boanseong*, he would drop me names of people they planned on arresting, people they already had evidence against. When I gave them to Sun he trusted me. Then he told me about you, how he knew your father, and that he wanted you moved here where he could keep an eye on you. He set me up downstairs and told me to wait, that eventually we would meet, and I could... but I fell in love with you. I still love you.' She implored him, 'Don't you believe me?'

Mae's grip on him felt insistent, and real. 'Why has Sun not arrested me already?'

'Because I've been holding him off. Wait another week, I told him, maybe a month. He wants something he could put you away for for a long time. Maybe worse. I've only been trying to protect you! He said my loyalty to the Party had spared my parents, so I thought I could protect you too.'

Han had forgotten about her parents. 'Soon-li...' he began. As soon as he put his bag down, Mae smothered him like she'd never let go, her arms round his neck, plunging her head against his chest.

'I'm sorry, Jun-an. I'm so sorry.'

Han tried to gently pull her arms off him. 'Soon-li. Your parents were in your file as well. Their prison records.'

She let him go. 'What?'

'Sun lied to you about them. Like he lied to me about my father.'

'Like your father?' she repeated feebly. 'They're dead aren't they.' She retreated to the sofa, sitting on the near armrest. Song-man's file fell out her hands, the pages ducking apart on their way down.

The few metres between them felt like miles as he explained. 'The file said he had them executed six weeks after they were arrested.'

Mae's head was dipped, and when she raised it her eyes were full of tears. 'This whole time... how could I believe him?'

Han went to her, taking her hand which she didn't seem to notice. He suddenly felt fortunate that his father had been dead as long as he had been. At least his mourning wasn't entirely new.

'Then this has all been for nothing,' Mae said, now gripping his hand.

'No,' he begged her, crouching down so their eyes were parallel, 'not nothing. We still have each other.'

She kissed him, feeling her tears running over her lips. 'I never meant for any of this to happen. You've got to believe me.'

'I believe you. And I love you. But we can't stay here. What if Oh-ran tells the police our names? She could be doing it right now. There's no time.'

She stood up and paced the living room, in denial about the severity of their situation. 'No, Oh-ran would never do that.'

'They'll start by telling her they'll be lenient if she gives them some accomplices. I've seen it before. She already knows my name and that I work in the Department, and she already knows you. They could be on their way here right now!'

'So what should we do?'

'Leave with me. Run away with me. Tomorrow's my last day with my tourists. They're going to help me get across the border. There's nothing left for us here.'

'What if we don't make it? What about the *kwan-li-so*, Camp 22? Aren't you afraid?'

Han could see she thought he was crazy. 'Not anymore. I don't want us to end up like our parents.'

She gathered up the pages of Song-man's file from the floor, righting a page that was upside down. 'But Jun-an. Your mother. If there was no car crash... what happened to your mother?'

He took the file from her. 'I think I know how to find out.'

'A Cowboy Town'

The outskirts of Chongjin, 16ᵗʰ July Juche 89 (2001)

They had been driving nearly five hours through the night, and it had been three since Song-man had seen another set of headlights. Not many people who made it as far north as Chongjin – the last major industrial city before the border with China – ended up leaving. It was a city of greedy quicksand, quick to absorb people and never return them. Some called Chongjin the last refuge of the desperate, the end of the world. They were now closer to Vladivostok than Pyongyang, two hundred and fifty miles away.

Song-man peered over the steering wheel into the fog ahead that had slowed their progress since descending the switchback mountain passes coming off Mount Chilbo, a descent that had them gulping and stretching their mouths to pop their ears.

Ji-won arched her feet towards each other, then apart, like out-of-sync windscreen wipers. She wore old black sneakers in preparation for having to run at some point later in the day.

'We're nearly there,' Song-man said, seeing trash-can fires on the edge of the city. 'Remember, we don't talk to anyone. The *Inmin Boanseong* are crawling all over this place trying to entrap people.'

Ji-won had sobbed all the way out of Pyongyang, having kissed eighteen-year-old Jun-an goodbye as he slept, knowing she might never see him again. And all because of a few drunken words against the Party overhead by their neighbours. Word had reached Song-man of a dossier on Ji-won's outbursts doing the rounds, and the decision to flee was made suddenly. He didn't see any other way. Song-man had told Jun-an they might not be there when he woke up, but not to worry, he would explain when he returned in two days. He had organised everything, including a forged travel permit for his wife, as well as a few boxes of Marlboro Reds and some bottles of whisky he had saved up, hidden under his seat, in case they ran into any difficult officials that questioned the false name on Ji-won's permit, or any other unforeseen circumstances – the only kind Chongjin dealt in.

Noticing his wife's trembling hand under her nose, Song-man squeezed her leg. 'We agreed,' he explained softly, 'it's for the best.'

The fog cleared around the city limits, as if it wanted to make sure anyone entering could see exactly what they were getting themselves into. It wasn't pretty.

At the break of dawn, under a dark-burgundy sky, the stars still shone brightly and tantalisingly close, the freedom of the open sky a cruel joke to everyone below: one more place they would never get to.

Song-man's headlights illuminated small, hungry children sitting on kerbsides, tossing sticks into the streaming gutter. They didn't chase the sticks. Their heads appeared too large for their necks, as if standing up would complicate their centre of gravity. They looked settled, like they had been there for hours; specialists in conserving energy, remaining still whenever possible. One hung his mouth open helplessly out of some distant motor-memory of the act of eating. None of the children acknowledged each other: hunger was a solo pursuit.

Women vacated cars outside the Stygian train station, the drivers abandoning them as thoughtlessly and remorselessly as they had been picked up. A decent prostitute could find her way to just enough cash to keep her in Chongjin, and, in time, enough to pay a smuggler to get them to Musan or Hoeryong, then over the border into China. There was little other reason to be there. The women who planned on staying sufficed with a quick lay for a small bag of rice or maybe some bread. It was very much a buyer's market.

Song-man brought the car to a gentle stop outside the train station near the main square, wondering if the man holding a briefcase was his contact. There was something incongruous about the triumvirate of the man's street-smart eyes, his Adidas black tracksuit, then the briefcase.

The main square was dotted with lone souls – had they been walking around all night? – with no task or destination, some sitting on benches like the mapless-lost, faces etched with existential dread;

others standing alone, eyes hunting around in confusion like urban sleepwalkers who'd woken before they could return to their beds. Everyone seemed to be carrying a bag of some kind, its contents their only remaining possessions. Eventually everything would be sold. Some even, literally, the shirts off their backs. Men staggered around begging other beggars, shirtless, their ribcages providing a climbing frame for the morning cold.

The man with the briefcase approached the car, walking in long, languid strides as if trying to prove how easy-going he was, checking there were no officials around. He was chewing gum.

Song-man rolled his window down. 'Chol-kang?'

He casually perched one forearm against the top of Song-man's door like he'd known him all his life. 'Welcome to the Wild West,' Chol-kang said, before popping his gum. His teeth were as perfect as any Song-man had seen outside the Party.

'Thank you for doing this.' Song-man rooted around in his door compartment. 'Do you have what I need?'

Chol-kang looked everywhere but at Song-man's eyes. 'Do you have the money?'

'Of course.' Song-man passed him a pack of Marlboros. 'Do you smoke?'

'I'm trying to quit,' Chol-kang said. He flipped the pack's lid open with one hand, and saw a curled roll of notes where the cigarettes should have been. 'But not today.' He smiled in a way that suggested he knew something about life no one else did. He swung his briefcase up onto the car roof, then handed Song-man an envelope from it smoothly and quickly through the window.

'It's all here?' Song-man asked, doing a quick inventory of the envelope's contents.

Chol-kang popped his gum again. 'Rotas for the border guards at Musan, some Chinese Yen, directions once you get over the Tumen River, everything.' He showed Song-man a map where they would be crossing. 'You drive to Musan, follow this road to the fields, you'll hear the river beyond it. The border guards' towers are only every five hundred metres at this point, so if you get lucky they won't shoot at you.' He folded the map and dropped it through the window. 'You're going at night, right?'

Song-man rifled through the contents of the envelope. 'I'm not going over.'

'So who's going?'

'My wife.'

Chol-kang tipped his body from the waist to get a look at Ji-won.

'I only have enough for her right now, and her situation's more pressing than mine. I'm coming back next week with my son. We're all going to meet in Shenyang, then we're going on to Seoul.'

Chol-kang nodded as if he didn't expect any of them to make it that far. 'Seoul, eh? It's better you go like this. If they caught all of you at once they'd give you a tougher sentence. Premeditation they call it.'

'Hopefully it won't come to that.'

Chol-kang asked Ji-won, 'You a fast runner, sweetheart?'

'If I need to be.'

He looked back out over the top of the car, talking like Ji-won wasn't there. 'Tell her to ring her clothes out as soon as she gets over the Tumen – if she gets over the Tumen. Most of them don't die from snipers, they die of hypothermia on the other side.'

'Thank you,' Song-man said, rolling up his window.

Chol-kang walked back towards the station, approaching one of the prostitutes with his cigarette pack full of money already open.

Hungry after the arduous drive, Song-man parked up and he and Ji-won made their way into the market, a shanty town of dilapidated stalls, the streets running through them thick with mud. Gangs of small children roved the tarp-ceilinged stands, smoking cigarettes that looked enormous between their fingers to suppress their hunger, sonar-like eyes attuned for careless adults with bowls of rice or vegetables they could pinch a handful from before running off. They favoured spicy peppers, as the heat gave the false sense of alleviating hunger better. Theft was a risky game, as Song-man and Ji-won witnessed, as a boy no more than eight (but the height of a five-year-old) tried to snatch a few potatoes from under the arm of a seller.

The boy didn't retract his stealing-arm fast enough, relying on slow stealth, but the seller caught him and proceeded to beat him viciously with an open hand in front of the passing public. He threw the boy to the ground, rubbing his face into the mud so the boy couldn't breathe. 'Filthy, dirty thief,' the man shouted as the boy wriggled loose and ran away. Normally the children could shovel some mouthfuls of food into their mouths before receiving a beating. They would lie there on the ground stoic in the face of violence. It was always worth it.

One child wandered aimlessly on her own, the build of a sapling, and no taller than Song-man's waist. She seemed delirious, unsure of where she was, turning in circles, her eyes looking heavenward. She held a handful of watery mud which she took small, birdlike sips from. A woman selling bread called out to her, 'Put that down, little one, you'll get sick,' but the girl didn't hear her. The woman left her stall and grabbed the girl's hand, wiping her hand free of the mud. When she turned round she saw two boys making off with loaves from the front of the stand. 'See,' the woman berated the girl. 'Look what's happened now, you stupid urchin...'

Song-man and Ji-won couldn't see many North Korean goods, as the factories had all but stopped any kind of production. All the clothes for sale were Chinese. Buyers could tell which vegetables were North Korean, miniature-sized, prised too soon out of the ground.

Soldiers wandered freely, demanding whatever they wanted. Nobody could do anything about it: they were the military, and the Dear Leader himself had ordered the country be run by *Songun*: military first. Not that that ideal suggested outright theft, but it legitimised it in the eyes of the soldiers. 'We're risking our lives to protect this country!' they yelled at anyone reticent to hand over what they demanded. The sellers muttered to themselves as they walked away, 'Risking your lives... you'd think there was a war on.'

Having spent half a month's wages on a small loaf of bread for Ji-won to keep in her dress pocket, they spent the rest of the morning in the car, going over plans and contingencies and counter-contingencies and worst-case-scenarios. In the days and weeks running up, Song-man thought they would find some time to sit and reminisce about old times, in case it so happened that they were spending their last day together. He had been preoccupied by some records on Sun that had come into his possession. They detailed faked confessions he'd written up for previous superiors, and systematic attempts to vanquish other senior Party leadership. Song-man was mounting a dossier for safe-keeping. It always paid to have something to bargain with.

Song-man timed the drive north-west to arrive in Musan at dusk, the industrial-mining landscape making way for the wetlands between the border and the edge of the Tumen River.

Song-man wanted Ji-won to cross on a moonless night, and even checked the weather forecast so their journey coincided with wet weather so the fallen winter leaves and corn husks didn't crack and snap underfoot in the forest over the Tumen River. At night, noise was all the border guards had to go on.

Song-man parked the car at the base of a marshy rise, wondering what you're supposed to say to your wife when it might be the last time you see her. It was something of a luxury for most defectors. Song-man knew of many husbands who woke up one morning to find their wives gone in the middle of the night and never saw them again. Lovers would part without so much as a word, for fear they wouldn't support their decision to flee, and possibly give them up before their escape. To keep from thinking about losing her, Song-man found himself turning all utilitarian. 'Remember what Chol-kang said about wringing your clothes out. And don't strip down to your good clothes until afterwards, they might get scratched up in the forest and you'll look poorly when you get out.'

Ji-won looked out into the darkness in front of her, the faint trickle of the Tumen somewhere ahead. 'I don't want to go.'

'I know, love. But you have to. They could arrest you at any moment if you stay.'

They got out and leaned back against the car, just trying to extend the moment. Now that the time had come, Song-man tried to squeeze in years of kisses and a lifetime of loving vows to Ji-won. No longer inhibited by the car seats where they could only hug in semi-profile, from the waist up, Ji-won's embrace now felt satisfyingly full to Song-man. Her body was clammy and sticky under her second layer of clothes: smarter, more elegant clothes she could peel off into once in China. The Chinese could easily spot a North Korean, as easily as the Party's secret police that patrolled border towns with China's permission.

Ji-won's hands clung to Song-man's back like she were hanging from a sheer drop, neither wanting to be the first to let go. 'It's all my fault,' she sobbed. Song-man kissed her cheek. 'You mustn't say that, my love.' It was so dark, she had to take baby steps away from him, leaning back as she descended the marsh on the other side, waiting for her feet to meet the bank of the river. Any loud splashes could be the death of her.

The trickle of the river got gradually louder, and she felt the water filling up the inside of her sneakers. After getting waist-high, she committed to a swim, but was caught off guard by the strength of the current in relation to its benign sound. She could feel herself being pulled downriver, away from the precise marker Chol-kang had starred on the map. The darkness confused her, turning against the current to work out what way was straight across. The current pulled her head under, and she took in mouthfuls of water, trying to make as little noise as possible, but the less she struggled the harder the current pulled. She started to flail to keep herself afloat.

Back from the side she had come from, frantic voices and directions were called out. After a few moments' silence, with Ji-won swimming strokes just to stay still, shots were fired indiscriminately into the river, the short whoosh and burst of bullets piercing the water getting ever closer to her. Her strokes grew more and more frantic, covering less distance as she gulped for air that wasn't there. Her legs lowered in exhaustion from kicking, in the vain hope that they would meet solid earth underneath and she could walk the rest of the way. Then a current, intertwining with another, turned her upside down and into a spin under the water's surface. The shots were constant now, but she had no concept of where they were striking. She angled her body, swimming through the current rather than against it, and somehow righted herself. Back to the surface, she crawled as hard as she could against the water, feeling the backsplash of bullets only inches from her head. The soldiers back on shore had no idea how close they'd been.

When she couldn't kick any longer, her feet drifted down and felt miraculous ground below, stepping in slow motion until the ground rose up high enough to reach the shore with her hands. As her ears cleared of water, the gunshots sounded deafening to her, the soldiers aiming at the noise of water cascading off her onto the rocks on the other side, bullets cracking against tree trunks and piercing leaves all around her. She kept awaiting the sharp agony of one hitting her, but it never came.

A torchlight panned across the water, looking for signs of rippling, but Ji-won was already across. She hobbled into the woods without looking back, disappearing into the trees. Only when the gunshots stopped and she trusted herself to stop running and scrambling over the prominent roots in the ground, did she realise: for the first time in her life she was somewhere other than North Korea.

Song-man had heard the gunshots as he drove carefully away. He thought about going back, but knew the guards would be there now. He waited until he was a safe distance away from the border, pulling over at the side of the road before yelling and screaming, 'What have I done? What have I done? What have I done?' Wondering if he had just heard his wife be killed.

'A Special Announcement; John Cheever; Victory Station'

Chollima Street, 18th December

Mae returned with her knapsack double-strapped over her shoulders, her hair scraped back into a practical bun. Han was on the couch, his bag on the floor by his feet.

'What about your books?' she asked.

He tapped the side of his head. 'It's all up here now.'

She handed him his notebook. 'You should take this in case anything happens and we get separated.'

He'd forgotten all about it. 'Did you read any of it?'

'Enough to know you're the only person I'd do this with.'

'We should go.' He noticed the single bag she had brought. 'I'm sorry you have to leave your cello.'

'I think the last thing we need is a cello slowing us down.'

'I'm sure they sell good ones in China.'

Mae surveyed the empty room, the broken portraits on the floor the only evidence of habitation. 'It'll be like we just disappeared.'

Han put his notebook down, and went to the paint can across the room. 'Let's leave a message then.'

'What are you going to write?' she asked.

A smile stretched across his face. 'Something a dear friend told me.' He pried the lid off, and slapped the paint on viciously across the wall, writing over the space where his pictures of the Two Leaders should have been, the letters on the top row dripping down into the ones below.

Han stepped back to admire it, sliding seamlessly into Mae's outstretched arm like two matched jigsaw pieces. 'I wish I could see their faces when they find it,' he said. He took his notebook to the bedroom and slid it into *A Great Mind*, placing it on top of the other books under the floorboard.

'Are you sure you want to leave that behind?' she asked.

Han didn't bother replacing the floorboard. 'I want them to find it. They're finally going to know who I really am.'

Room 422, Koryo Hotel

Ben and Hal sat up in their beds, unable to sleep. They had packed their bags together at Ben's insistence so as to stick to their old superstition. Hal was all drumming hands on his thighs, nodding to a song in his head as he smoked a cigarette. This was what he lived for: going off-map, ready to roll. He broke a long silence by saying, 'On the plus side, we'll be able to give first-hand accounts of what a North Korean concentration camp is like.'

'The camera's still got enough memory for a few weeks, right?'

'That's what you're worried about? We'll need to stay alive if anyone's ever going to see it.'

'We're not doing it, Hal,' Ben murmured.

'What, I didn't say anything!'

'We're not recording goodbye messages in case we get caught.'

'Come on, admit it, you were hoping this was going to happen all along. It would make great television if we get killed on camera.' The impracticalities started unravelling to Hal. 'We'd need to make sure we got killed on friendly territory, of course, otherwise the video would never make it to air. Then we'd just be a couple of idiots that got killed in North Korea.'

'If Mr Han knows the right places, we can make it. I've seen videos of people crossing over the border. They do it all the time. They go into China, make some money in the markets and come back across.'

Hal clicked his fingers as he sang. 'Daaa-aaa-aytripper.'

'We've got nearly two hundred dollars on us for bribes. They'd let us kip down in their checkpoint with their sisters for that.'

'You're forgetting one thing.'

'What's that?'

'How do you bribe a sniper to stop shooting at you from three hundred yards away?'

Ben put his hand out for a drag of Hal's cigarette. He said nonchalantly, 'We've been shot at before.'

Central Party Offices, The Forbidden City, 19th December

Secretary Sun stood at his desk smoking a cigarette, watching the sun about to rise over Pyongyang Square. Han's personnel file lay open on his desk, next to a completed arrest warrant with Han and Mae's names on it.

Miss Lee buzzed him. 'Mr Ryong is here as you requested, comrade Secretary.'

Sun waited until he was done exhaling before replying. 'Send him in.'

Ryong came in, bleary-eyed, but immaculately dressed, as if he were always ready to be called for early in the AM. He stood to attention in front of Sun's desk and before he could finish saying, 'Good morning, comrade Secretary,' Sun spoke over him, 'What's the meaning of this?'

Ryong was sure his chest could be seen vibrating through his military jacket. 'The meaning of what, sir?'

Sun waved Han's file at him then threw it down in disgust. 'Did I not make my instructions perfectly clear last time? That you were to watch Mr Han closely.'

'Sir, I have, sir.'

Sun stared back, spreading his hands across the desktop to make himself as wide as possible.

Ryong gulped hard and tried again. 'I *believe* I have, sir.'

'You believe so,' he repeated derisively. 'You were with him and the tourists last at the Victorious Liberation Fatherland War Museum, were you not?'

'Yes, sir.'

'Tell me, the female corporal there showing round the other Westerners. How nice were her legs?'

'Sir?'

'Her legs, how nice were they? Because I have it on good authority that they were about the only thing you were paying attention to when you were there.'

'Sir, I... I was trying...' He couldn't think of a defence.

Sun straightened himself. 'She told me you left the three of them alone, that they were sitting on the floor playing cards.'

'I wasn't... overly concerned with Mr Han's—'

'I told you not to leave him alone, Ryong!'

Ryong couldn't help but notice Sun had dropped the 'Mr' preceding his name now.

'I think I'm starting to see why you haven't progressed very far in this Department. Maybe Hwang wasn't so stupid after all. I can't even trust you to follow leads in this graffiti case. I've got some old crow across a landing handing me suspects faster than you.'

'I'm glad you have apprehended a suspect, sir. I hope this lack of foresight won't tarnish my reputation or bring into question my loyalty to the Party.'

'Your loyalty? This is the problem with your generation, Ryong. There's no revolutionary spirit left in you. You're all too busy chasing women and American booze.'

Ryong gripped his hands behind his back as anger welled up inside him. 'Sir, with all due respect, I feel I have done my best to obey your orders, but in fairness to Mr Han, yes, he appears to have an unfortunate affinity to the Westerners, but I have seen no evidence of any... subterfuge or any other unseemly behaviour.'

Sun rifled through his notes. '"Loyalty isn't everything. One has to be smart too." That is an accurate quote of what Han said to you in the DMZ, is it not?'

'In hindsight I don't feel that—'

'Did he say it or not?' Sun yelled. 'Yes or no!'

'Yes, sir.'

'The woman they brought in earlier who was hiding foreign literature in her home, she's just told us an hour ago he was part of a clandestine group that's sharing this material.' He waved Ryong's own notes back at him accusingly. 'Him and some other woman that I sent to watch him. I can't trust anyone around here!'

All the years of patient service, all the promotions he had stepped aside for on superiors' orders, all the deathly-dull meetings, the constant praise for the leadership, felt like wasted time to Ryong now.

'I'm sorry if you feel I've let you,' he tried not to grit his teeth, 'or the Party down, and I hope I can be given time to set this right, comrade Secretary.'

Sun dropped back into his seat, springing forward then back in slowly decreasing pumps of the chair's suspension. 'It's been taken out of your hands. They'll be in custody within the hour.'

Ryong tried to reassert his posture. 'And what of Mr Han's position? Will I still be assuming his role when this is over?' He paused before adding, 'As we agreed.'

'You really think you've proven your worth to me in the last twenty-four hours?'

It was clear to Ryong now that Sun had never planned on giving him Han's position once he was in custody. 'My loyalty, sir,' Ryong said, feeling his world diminishing by the second. 'You asked for it and I gave you it.'

'We have bigger problems.' Sun's voice dropped an octave. 'Something's going to happen today, Ryong, and I need you to be on top of your usual Departmental duties. There's going to be a special announcement on television at noon today.' Sun gestured as if the meaning of his sentence were obvious. 'So you understand?'

'A special announcement, sir?'

'A *very* special announcement. Keep it under your hat, for heaven's sake. Party leadership and senior officials are being briefed upstairs as we speak. So statements will need drawn up between now and noon. For now, I need you to take Han's tourists to the airport. They're not going to the Great Leader's Hall of Gifts. They're on the next flight to Beijing.'

Ryong remembered what happened after the last special announcement. Mass grief. A ten-day mourning period. Panic. Chaos. Purges. Party members disappearing. It was like the end of the world. And now it was going to end all over again. 'How did it happen, sir?'

Sun sniffed, without a hint of regret. 'Heart attack, the doctors say. Not like it's not been coming for the last ten years, of course. But he's gone now and we're going to have to make sure the Department is in line with whoever replaces him.'

'Will it be Comrade General Kim Jong-un?'

Sun looked up witheringly, and after a pause, nodded. 'It appears so. But frankly I don't see any reason why we should go through another Kim coronation.'

It took Ryong a few seconds before he realised what Sun had just said: open treason in the Forbidden City. 'But... comrade Secretary. You're talking about...'

Sun was unflappable. 'Why shouldn't I? A dynasty of two is embarrassing enough for a socialist state. They've had their run, and now it's over.' He hit his buzzer. 'Miss Lee, I asked for the file on Han Song-man earlier, I still haven't got it.'

Miss Lee replied. 'I couldn't find it, sir.'

'What do you mean? Come in here and find it.'

Ryong unclasped his hands behind his back. 'You only care about yourself.'

At first Sun didn't think he heard correctly. 'What did you just say?'

'You don't even grieve for the Dear Leader who has done so much for us. You just sit there, plotting and scheming for your own ends.'

Sun started to rise in his chair. 'I'll have you arrested you useless, washed-up Jap! You fucking Yankee!' All the shouting was sending Sun's bird into a flapping frenzy, the cage rocking as its wings collided with the bars.

'You don't give a damn about the Party, the people, or anyone but yourself!'

Sun leered at him through narrowing eyes, his speech slowing. 'Do yourself a favour, *comrade*, and get out of here. And you can forget about any promotion. Once this is all over with you can consider yourself suspended. Dereliction of duty.'

'After all I've done for the Party. For the country?'

Sun stuck out his lips, sizing up Ryong's resolve. 'You surprise me, boy. I didn't figure you for the self-pitying type.'

Ryong looked at the bird flapping from side to side. 'The only thing in here I feel pity for is your damn bird.' He took off his hat and stormed out.

Downtown Pyongyang

Mae and Han had spent the night parked up in a secluded alleyway between two dumpsters, sleeping together in the backseat like runaway teenagers. Han's coat was wrapped one and a half times around Mae. While she slept, he read through his father's file, returning constantly to the mug shot on the first page. Each time a military jeep drove past either end of the alleyway he sprang forward. He had left the keys in the ignition, ready to go at any moment.

He was woken at dawn by a garbage man emptying the dumpster behind the car. A man peered in through the windscreen then quickly retreated to his truck when he saw Han stirring inside. His father's file lay on the floor near his outstretched hand.

'What time is it?' Mae asked, stretching herself awake.

Han had slept so lightly his vision was perfectly clear. 'Seven. We better get moving.' He kissed the back of her head because he had seen men do it in American movies when they wanted to be tender. It was all new to him. 'Ryong and So are supposed to pick up the men at the hotel at nine.'

Mae yawned. 'Plenty of time to get ahead.'

'It's not time I'm worried about. It's the description of this car that might be floating around police frequencies right now.'

The streets were clear all the way to the hotel. The army vehicles had been recalled back to their depots, and the traffic wardens were back on their posts, directing invisible traffic again.

Mae handed Han some bread from her bag. 'You should eat something. I heard your stomach rumbling in the middle of the night.'

'Save it for later. It's going to be a long day.'

They pulled up in front of the hotel and Han got out, leaving the engine running.

He said, 'If I'm more than ten minutes, leave without me,' then he kissed her and shut the door.

'What? Wait...' Mae called out, unprepared for the eventuality. 'I can't drive,' but he was already away. She cursed, '*Eminai.*'

223

The men were already in the lobby with their luggage, fed terribly in BH 2 but ready to go. Hal was a little shaken to see Han looking so serious.

'Good morning, Mr Han,' Ben said, trying to greet him in the same manner as previous days.

The receptionist noticed the baggage with the men and asked with a hint of suspicion, 'Are you checking out, gentlemen?' She seemed in some kind of emotional distress, her voice quivering, used tissues lying in front of her.

'*Overnight trip to Dandong,*' Han said. He figured if she ended up talking to the police, it wouldn't hurt to send them to the wrong side of the country.

'*Oh,*' she said, examining her book. '*Because the Ministry has them down here for the Great Leader's Hall of Gifts.*'

'*Change of plan,*' said Han, signing them out. '*And I need their passports?*' he tried to add as casually as possible.

'*For Dandong?*'

Han didn't falter. '*Headquarters wants to run a security check.*'

She returned with Ben and Hal's passports, then reached for a tissue. '*Probably wise given the circumstances.*'

'*What circumstances?*'

She checked no one else was within hearing distance. '*There's a special announcement on the news at noon. They're saying...*' She leaned as far forward as the desk allowed. '*They're saying that the Dear Leader is dead.*'

'*Nonsense. It'll be another missile test. Or maybe Jimmy Carter's coming to visit again.*' His smile did nothing to disarm her.

'*A friend of mine works at the Foreign Ministry. He was asked to cable the foreign consulates in Asia that the Dear Leader died of a heart attack on Saturday morning.*'

Han couldn't believe their luck, but had to hide it all the same. '*My goodness. What terrible news. I will keep the car radio on in that case. In the meantime we must remain professional. The Dear Leader would wish it.*'

She bowed gracefully then wiped a tear from her eye. '*Yes, sir.*'

Han motioned for the men to follow him outside.

'What's going on?' Ben mumbled to Han. 'Our television this morning was running a message saying to stay tuned for a special announcement.'

'We have just won the lottery,' he replied.

As they filed into the car, Han introduced the men to Mae, who had been sitting in the passenger seat.

'This is Mae. She does not speak English, so please for me to translate her. *Mae, this is Ben and Hal I told you about.*'

She waved to them and timidly said, 'Hi.' She had never spoken to foreigners before. Yet another thing to add to her growing list of crimes.

Han turned and smiled mischievously. 'I think that's all she knows.'

Ben asked, 'What do you mean we've won the lottery?'

Han flicked his hand playfully at Mae's leg, his smile growing. '*You'll never guess what the receptionist just told me. The special announcement?*'

'*What is it?*' she asked.

'*The old man's dead.*'

She jumped up in her seat. '*He's dead!*' She whipped around in her seat and slapped the headrest, telling the men in the back, '*He's dead, Kim Jong-il's dead!*' She bounced around, colliding with Han who struggled to keep the car in a straight line.

Ben covered his mouth.

Han laughed. '*They can't understand you, Mae. Well, Ben can, he speaks Korean.*' He looked back at the men in the rear view mirror. 'Did you get that, Ben?'

'I got it,' Ben cried out joyously, raising his hand to high-five Hal.

Hal high-fived back without knowing why. 'What's going on?' Hal shouted, feeling left out of the celebration.

'Kim Jong-il's dead! They just told Han at reception.'

Hal didn't understand why he wasn't as excited as the others. 'But... wait, what does that mean, why is that so good?'

Ben could barely keep still. 'Because every soldier, policeman, and border guard in the country isn't going to be doing their job properly today. There will be a national, I don't know, maybe a week of mourning? It's going to make getting over the border a million times easier.'

'A good time to leave the country,' Han said.

Ben said, 'We're going to go down as the only Western journalists in North Korea when Kim Jong-il died.'

Han smirked. 'Is true.'

Hal leaned forward in his seat. 'Forgive me, Mr Han,' he said. 'But didn't you say something last night about some chick of yours that was an informant?'

Ben's arm froze around his seatbelt, which he had forgotten to put on in the excitement. 'Mr Han?'

Han shook his head like it was nothing. 'It's fine. A misunderstanding.'

'That's a hell of a misunderstanding,' Hal suggested.

Han drove calmly out the car park, not noticing Ryong passing them on the opposite side of a roundabout, entering the hotel grounds at high speed.

The four turned quiet as they made their way through Pyongyang centre, Han getting giddy at the clear road ahead.

'*This is it, then*,' Han said to Mae, who covered his hand on the gearstick.

Pedestrians made their way to work and the markets, unaware of how their lives were about to change in incalculable ways in a matter of hours.

Han slowed as a traffic warden ahead directed him to stop, putting her white glove out. 'Is OK,' Han said to the men. 'Is routine stop.' When they got closer, Han recognised the warden as the same one that had welcomed him into the city just five days before.

'*Mr Han*,' the warden said mournfully, removing her sunglasses, finally revealing eyes which were tear-filled.

Han rolled down his window. '*Are you alright, comrade?*'

'*I suppose you must have heard the news from the Ministry already.*

226

My boss told me. He trusts me not to tell regular citizens.'

Han played along. *'Of course. They woke me early to tell me.'*

The warden shook her head in despair. *'However will we go on?'*

'The same as we did when the Great Leader passed.'

'I wish I had your strength, comrade.' She looked at the surrounding streets and put her sunglasses back on, pointing Han forward.

Ryong came haring out of his car, abandoning it by the front steps of the hotel, the front door flapping open behind him. 'Are they still here?' he shouted across the lobby floor.

The receptionist rose out of her chair. 'Sir?'

He made for the elevators. 'The Yank and the Brit. Are they still here?'

She couldn't fathom what the import was on such a day. 'They already left with Mr Han.'

'Mr Han?'

'Yes. For Dandong.'

He lunged over the counter. 'Show me the log.'

She stood back out his way. 'He signed them out already. They just left.'

He turned to the previous day's page and sighed. 'He signed them out after curfew last night. What about the tourists' passports?'

'He took them too.'

'For a trip to Dandong!'

'He's allowed to. He's a senior officer in the Ministry.'

'Not anymore, he's not,' Ryong grumbled, tossing the book back to her. He ran back to his car and sped out the car park, back wheels spinning on the tarmac. 'Damn you, Han!' he yelled, banging his steering wheel with his fist.

He ignored the traffic wardens telling him to stop at three separate interchanges, blasting his horn at the lugubrious traffic, nearly colliding with a truck carrying wooden crates, that had to swerve to avoid him, which went into a tailspin, spilling its load like toppled poker chips all over the highway.

He was outside Han's building in a few minutes in a journey that should have taken ten. Police cars were already waiting outside, as well as a van with blacked-out windows: a special unit of the *Inmin Boanseong*.

'There's nobody there,' said a junior officer exiting the front door.

Ryong ran to the elevator anyway, battering the button for the eighteenth floor.

'It's out of order, comrade,' the officer shouted to him.

Ryong galloped up the stairs, and by the time he reached Han's floor he was breathless. Sunlight spilled out of Han's open front door where a policeman stood with his hands in his pockets. He pulled them out quickly when he saw Ryong running towards him.

Ryong flashed his ID at the policeman from a distance too far away to possibly read. 'Ryong, Communications. Is he still here?'

The policeman just pointed him inside.

Officers were lethargically rooting through the remains of Han's things in his bedroom, a trio of them standing staring at the living room wall like they were in a gallery, trying to work out what the painting meant.

'What does it say?' the Chief Officer complained. 'I can't read English.'

Ryong caught his breath as he read what was written on the wall in large white letters:

"I'VE BEEN HOMESICK FOR COUNTRIES
I'VE NEVER SEEN
AND LONGED TO BE WHERE I COULDN'T BE."

Han had signed it:

"JOHN CHEEVER".

The men all turned to look at Ryong.

'Who are you?' a sergeant asked him.

The officer next to him wisecracked, 'Maybe he's John Cheever.'

The sergeant snapped, 'Get back to work.' He took out a notepad as if to question Ryong. 'I'm Sergeant Kim. Do you know this Han?'

'He was my boss at the Ministry,' Ryong said, somewhat

228

embarrassed, sensing the sergeant assessing his age against Han's.

He scribbled this down in his pad. 'He's going to the firing squad for this one.' He walked over to the wall and pointed at the remains of the pictures of the Great- and Dear Leaders, now speckled with white paint. The sight of them had been upsetting the men.

'Do you have him?' Ryong asked, averting his eyes from the portraits. 'The suspect and the girl.'

'We got a call from the Koryo Hotel security. He picked up his tourists about ten minutes ago. We're dropping the net.'

'They're going to Dandong,' Ryong said, trying to appear helpful.

A radio left on the coffee table buzzed with white noise.

An officer ran through from the bedroom holding up his radio. 'Sir, they're on the west side of the Taedong. We can set up a block at Yonggwang, near the Glory metro station.'

Kim pushed past Ryong, saying to him, 'Doesn't look like it now, does it.' He took the radio, speaking to the officer at the scene. 'Do it. But keep them there. Secretary Sun wants to see the suspects taken in personally.'

Static crackled from the other end. 'Sir, we have a lot of commuters on foot around the area.'

'I don't care. Keep them there.' When Kim turned round Ryong was already running back to the stairs, the radio from the coffee table gone.

'Sergeant,' one of the officers called solemnly from the bedroom. 'You'd better come take a look at this.'

Kim found him standing over the open floorboard, rooting through Han's novels. 'There's dozens,' the officer said. A copy of *A Great Mind* sat on top, open at the hollowed out pages where Han had left his notebook.

Loudspeakers lining the west bank of the Taedong River, approaching the last major interchanges at the city limits, relayed messages from an ethereal female voice of 'the special announcement' at noon, and that breaks at workplaces would be given to watch it on the television or listen on the radio. Recordings of the Mansudae Art Troupe performing "We Shall Follow You Forever", and "No Motherland Without You" played between the pre-recorded messages, prompting some pedestrians to stop in the street, beating their fists over their hearts and singing the lyrics as loud as they could, hopeful someone would notice their revolutionary pride. Hal rolled his window down to catch some of their audio in the camera mic, struggling to make themselves heard over the loudspeakers.

'We will be out of the city soon,' Han told the men.

Ben gripped his bag in his lap a little tighter as Han slowed, seeing a police van pulling side-on at a crossroads ahead of the Glory metro station, what looked like an elegant roadside restaurant cut into a small copse of trees. The van blocked the entire lane, and the traffic on the opposite side blocked the other lane.

'*Hold on,*' Han said to Mae. '*We might have a problem.*'

Hal quickly turned the camera to face out the windscreen. He moved his head to the side of the mic. 'What's happening?'

'Shit, shit, shit,' Ben said, creeping forward in his seat, holding onto the back of Han's headrest as he saw the police blockade ahead, the van being joined by two others.

Policemen ran to cut off the station entrance, their hands up indicating them to stop.

'*OK,*' he said to Mae, exhaling the mounting panic in his chest, trying to think of alternatives, but at a few hundred metres away there was nowhere to go. '*OK, we have to make a run for it. Get your bag on.*' He took a deep breath, saying, 'Put your bags on, gentlemen. We run for station!' He floored the accelerator, pushing everyone back in their seats. He shouted over the straining engine, 'Get ready!'

Ben clutched Hal's wrist, shouting, 'It's been a hell of a ride.'

Hal yelled back, 'If they catch me just make sure you get the camera.' He offered Ben his hand, upright.

Ben slapped his hand into Hal's. 'Whatever happens—'

'I know, man...' Hal lowered the camera, but kept recording.

The police scattered as Han drove straight at them, then pulled up the handbrake to slide the car side-on so Mae's door faced the metro. He shouted, 'Out, out, out! *Out! Into the station!*'

The police had run to the far side of the blocked lane, giving Han and the others just enough time to make a break for it. The call went out over the police radio: '*They're going for the station. All hands to Glory station!*'

Han grabbed Mae's hand, running towards the stairs leading down into the metro. Ben and Hal sprinted behind, the camera viewfinder a vertigo-inducing shot of shaking pavement.

Two male commuters, urged by the police yelling '*Stop them!*', held their arms out feebly, thinking better of it as Hal charged ahead, swiping his free hand to the side. 'The fuck out the way!' he shouted, while heavenly, choral music played through the station's speakers, as if they were entering some kind of North Korean afterlife.

Ben and Hal vaulted the ticket gate, waiting for Han and Mae who were trailing behind with their much shorter legs. Two police officers picked their way through the confused crowd watching the chase. Ben joined Hal in shouting at the terrified commuters to clear a path down the acutely angled escalator that ran two hundred metres below street level, relying on sheer volume to get the message across. Hal, sounding like someone hitting an oil drum, banged his fist on the separating partition running between the opposite escalator. The crowd hurled themselves left and right to get out the way.

'Drop the bags down!' Ben shouted back to Han, throwing his bag down the partition, sliding off down into the murky bunker.

As the four bounded past, now unimpeded by heavy bags, the commuters filtered back into the centre of the steps, not realising that police were in pursuit behind, slowing their advance. The officers shoulder-barged their way through, shoving people to the ground in order to catch up.

At the last fifty metres of their descent, Han looked back up the escalator and, sensing a chance to get further ahead, climbed up onto the partition, and beckoned Mae up. '*We can slide down!*'

Ben and Hal saw them sliding past, and joined them, screaming all the way down, out of control as their momentum sent them careering past the other passengers. The three copied Han's method

231

of using their hands as brakes before sliding off the end, landing in a heap on their bags that had arrived some time before them. Ben and Hal landed together, crashing into Mae and Han, the four of them scattering like tenpins.

Dazzling chandeliers hung from the ceiling while neon lights shimmered between them like an indoor fireworks display. Marble arches and pillars lined the two platforms on either side, looking more like a ballroom than a metro station. Mae, glancing behind, noticed Hal had struck his head. '*Come on*,' she told him, hooking an arm under his. In the confusion of the fall, Ben and Han ended up picking up the wrong bag, Han ending up with Ben's, which was much lighter than his own, letting him run faster. Mae mounted Hal's bag onto her back, and pulled Hal away.

'Are you OK?' Han asked Hal.

He nodded in a daze, giving Mae's arm a thankful squeeze.

Ben started moving towards a train on the left track, then saw another pull in on the right as well. 'Left or right?' he yelled at Han.

'This one,' Han yelled back, taking them to the west-bound train with its doors open, an antiquated box-shaped carriage with a tiny man in Party uniform in the driver's seat sitting behind a Perspex window. The train looked like an oversize toy.

They ran through the nearest open door, where terrified passengers huddled up against the windows, edging away from Han and the others.

The train sat stationary on the rails, its ancient engine chugging away. Han kept a close eye down the marble corridor, waiting for sight of the police who were only just emerging from the escalator – their attempts at copying the others' slide down the middle partition hadn't gone well, tipping onto the wrong side of the elevator, landing harshly on the metal steps. As they ran towards the carriage, the officers called out in vain for the driver to stop as the doors closed at a narcoleptic pace.

The train pulled away and the four of them collapsed around the floor, the portraits of the Two Leaders staring down at them from high on the carriage wall.

The police back on the platform called on their radios: *'They're heading west to Sungni! Send a team to Victory!'*

Sun clung to the handle above the backdoor of his Mercedes, his convoy from the Ministry following a police car with its siren blaring. A radio by his side kept him in constant contact with the police, stressing he wanted Han held at the scene until he got there.

The convoy pulled up outside Victory Station, the police forming a line outside the entrance. Sun stood back next to his car, in a brown overcoat, smoking a cigarette.

'We've got officers at Triumph in case they stay on,' a captain in aviator sunglasses told Sun.

Sun swaggered to the front of his Mercedes, smoking a cigarette. 'Tell your men to keep their guns holstered. I want him alive.'

Two hundred metres below, the four ran across the Victory Station platform. Normally out of bounds to tourists, the station comprised a bare hallway without any of the lavish murals of Glory, while sparse, dim lights hung far apart from each other from a warehouse-like ceiling.

At the top of the static stairs, they could barely jog let alone run, but adrenaline and terror forced them on, only to find Sun and half the Pyongyang police force waiting out on the street for them.

'You're under arrest,' the captain shouted, hesitating when he saw Ben and Hal. *'All of you.'*

'Mr Han,' Sun called out, stepping forward. *'You've no idea the satisfaction it gives me to do this.'*

Ben and Hal could finally catch their breath. They rolled their heads back and looked up at the grey, vacant sky: they knew it was over.

Han put his arm out in front of Mae to keep her back, his chest heaving for air. *'You killed my father.'*

Sun tossed his cigarette away. *'I always knew he was no good. Just like you.'*

'People like you... your days are coming to an end.'

Sun looked around him and laughed. *'Is that right? And who's*

233

going to tell them? You and your Yank and Brit friends are going to the same place you and your informant whore are. I'm going to have you all lined up in a neat little row in front of the firing squad. That way you can beg for your life, just like your father did.'

'*My father would have begged for no one.'*

Sun looked to the captain and said, '*Take them in.'*

Ryong held the police radio to his ear whilst tearing through the streets, swerving wildly, and blasting his horn almost the entire way. When he heard the call to Victory, he made a reckless ninety-degree turn down a side street to try and make up time on them. He could see a crowd gathered at the end of the street, flashing police lights somewhere beyond. He shouted to himself, 'Do or die, Ryong, do or die, just like a soldier!' and floored the accelerator, his hand pressed on the horn all the way.

The radio said, 'They've just come out the station doors... we have them, we have them...'

People threw themselves out the road when they saw Ryong racing towards them, a traffic warden desperately tried to halt the huge build-up of traffic he had just waved through at the crossroads.

Ryong pointed his car at the blockade, speeding up the whole way, trying to overtake a line of open-top military trucks carrying metal barriers to Pyongyang Square in preparations for the special announcement, travelling too fast to stop for the warden's urgent signals. A shout rang out as an officer spotted Ryong's car, 'Look out!' Ryong jerked on the steering wheel at the last moment, aiming for Sun's Mercedes. The trucks swerved one after the other to avoid Ryong coming from their left side, throwing the metal barriers over the top, streaming down the middle of the road towards the blockade.

The policemen scattered in all directions leaving Sun standing himself, right in the path of the barriers. The first wave swiped his legs from under him, tossing him head over foot. A snapped stanchion in the second wave pierced his head at a forty-five degree angle, coming out the other side. The officers still on their feet were collected by the second wave of barriers streaming off the next truck, blocking them at Victory's entrance.

Ryong threw open the passenger door, blood pouring down the side of his face where it had hit his side window. '*Get in, get in*!' he screamed at the four cowering behind the wreckage of a police car.

Ben emerged first and hunted around for the others. Han was crouched over Mae under a broken-off police car door that had scissored through the air. Hal looked at his empty right hand and realised he had dropped the camera in the dash-and-tumble for cover. It sat on its side on the ground next to a bloodied policeman on his back several strides away. The others screamed at Hal to come back as he ran towards the camera, snatching it off the ground. The policeman grabbed Hal's ankle and pulled him back, slurring in English, 'Yankee bastard.' Hal stamped on the policeman's hand with his other leg. 'Commie bastard,' Hal spat back, and broke free.

Screeching back towards Hal, Ryong spun his wheels in reverse to release his car from the side of Sun's Mercedes. Ben threw the door open and held his arms out. Hal landed in Ben's lap, his feet still sticking out as Ryong hit the accelerator.

'*Let's go, Ryong*!' Han shouted, as the police finally untangled themselves and opened fire. As the car got away they realised they had no cars left to give chase. All either overturned or buried under an avalanche of barriers and twisted metal.

Ryong slalomed them out of the stranded traffic to the nearest exit-way. '*Is everyone OK?*'

Ben was the only one who could speak, everyone sprawled limb-over-limb in the backseat. 'Yeah...'

Ryong craned his neck back at Ben and Hal. 'So that was the Victory metro station, gentlemen.'

'*Thank you, comrade*,' Ben said to Ryong in Korean. '*You saved our lives.*'

Ryong did a double-take before replying, '*You're welcome.*'

'*What are you doing here, Mr Ryong?*' Han asked, wiping blood from his forehead.

'*Loyalty, comrade.*'

'*I thought I told you loyalty isn't everything.*'

Ryong smiled. '*Yeah, you were wrong about that.*'

Knowing from the radio that the remaining Pyongyang police force had been sent to Triumph station, Ryong took them east, where the road was clear all the way to the Arch of Reunification at the city limits.

Ben and Hal gave each other a pound-hug, their intertwined hands separating their chests. 'You stupid son of a bitch,' Ben said, breaking into an adrenaline-fuelled, giddy laugh.

Hal showed him the camera which was still recording. 'Wait 'til YouTube gets a load of this.'

Ryong was the calmest person in the car. '*Where do you want me to go, Mr Han?*' he asked.

Han threw his head back in relief as Mae draped herself across him in exhaustion. '*Chongjin. We need to get to Chongjin.*'

'Camp 22'

Song-man hadn't seen the police car pull up behind him, his forehead resting at twelve o'clock on the steering wheel.

They had gotten an anonymous tip from the Chongjin office about an illegal border crossing on the Tumen, a crossing aided by a car fitting the description of Song-man's. Song-man hadn't struggled when the police told him to get out the car and spread his hands across the bonnet. All he could think about was whether Ji-won was dead, and what would happen to Jun-an now, all the way back in Pyongyang, sleeping in his bed, alone for the second night in a row.

The arresting officers couldn't make out what Song-man was mumbling all the way to the prisoner-processing station in Hoeryong, writing it off as post-arrest delirium – the prospect of the prisons had that effect on people. He was mumbling, 'Jun-an. Jun-an.'

The sign above the entrance to Camp 22 read:

김정일 수령님께 목숨을 바쳐 충성을 다하자

('GIVE UP YOUR LIFE FOR THE SAKE OF THE DEAR LEADER KIM JONG-IL')

The camp was set at the foot of a mountain so tall it was crowned with snow almost the entire year. Camp Hoeryong was on no map, at least in North Korea. Everyone knew it by its number: 22.

The camp was surrounded by a two and a half metre fence electrified with thirty-three hundred volts, enough to kill a well-fed ox. The lights in Pyongyang went out before darkness had a chance to descend, but there in the middle of a mountain range the State found a way to source power twenty-four hours a day. On the other side of the fence, spiked moats angled towards anyone who somehow managed to climb the fence. They said the only way to escape Camp 22 was to die.

The charges were a formality – not that anyone presented them to Song-man. He was taken straight from processing into a cell with ten other men lying on their sides, so the bare minimum of flesh contacted the freezing cement floor.

'Lie on the ground like them, and shut the hell up,' a guard told him.

The slightest movement was punished with as many lashes from a bamboo cane as the guard had the energy to mete out: a lesson inmates learned the hard way. If anyone spoke, the guard would drag them out the cell and they wouldn't be seen again for days. The guards called it 'Caterpillar Time' – the closest any of them got to a bed, the prisoners resembled caterpillars that had their legs cut off and couldn't move they were so squashed together. It was some hours before Song-man realised this was where they were meant to sleep.

After 'Caterpillar Time', the men were allowed outside to clear the toilet huts. They had to bring a barrel each across the cornfields running up the hill towards the foot of the mountain. The barrels were filled with prisoners' excrement, the first smell of which you never forgot. The men that had been there more than a few weeks didn't seem bothered by it. Olfactory hardship was the least of their worries.

Song-man worked next to a man with a deep purple bruise around his windpipe. 'I'm Song-man,' he said.

The man wasn't interested. 'You think telling me your name matters?' He hoisted down the large barrel he had been carrying, the watery excrement sloshing over the top with the sway of his uneven movement, running down his front and back. 'I'm Lo-chang,' the man said.

Song-man looked at the hand Lo-chang extended to him.

He chuckled. 'Worried you're going to catch germs?'

Song-man shook his hand. 'How long have you been here?' he asked, the pair taking up their barrels. Song-man recoiled at the warm liquid dripping down his back.

'About seven years, I think.'

'What did you do? Or what did they say you did?'

'Oh I did it alright! I stole a bag of rice.'

'They gave you seven years for stealing a bag of rice?'

'No. Fifteen.' Lo-chang jerked his head to the side, like the sentence had been reasonable. 'It was a pretty big bag of rice.'

The men were to use the excrement as fertilizer for the crops, not that it seemed to be working much. The field was dying because none of the prisoners knew how to sow seeds properly, and neither did the guards. The promise of being fed whatever was grown was meant to be the men's motivation, but they knew it was bullshit. Eventually everyone stopped trying, happy to do just enough work to not get a beating, or a few days visit to the Wet Room. 'You don't want to go there,' Lo-chang told Song-man.

'What's it like there?'

'Would you be happier if you knew?'

The prisoners worked incessantly from seven in the morning until seven at night, without food. An armed guard would parade up and down outside the cell, brushing the barrel of his pistol across the bars like he were playing a güiro. If someone was slow to get to their feet, he would reach in and shoot them, which only created more work for the other prisoners close by, because they would then have to drag the body outside and help dig the grave, often by hand. The men formed a habit of 'encouraging' everyone around them to get up quickly.

All day, surrounded by armed guards, they were forced to dig up earth with shovels blunted by the rocky ground. The impact of striking a rock would send a crippling tremor up their arms, and shook all through their bodies. The pain had a tendency to linger in their weakened gums where bacteria festered throughout the warm summer, making the roots more vulnerable to pain and shock.

Every day there was another explanation for why they were digging: 'Air raid shelters', 'latrine ditches', 'service roads to the gas chambers'.

'You've got to remember,' Lo-chang reminded him, as they dug, 'we're enemies of Socialism in here. Another barrier against total victory. We stopped existing as soon as the gates closed behind us.'

'We wouldn't be here if the Party were able to feed us. That's why my wife and I wanted to escape.'

Somewhere behind them several shots rang out from a sniper's watch tower, taking out three prisoners who had been digging earnestly. The random executions became more common later in the afternoon, the drunker and more bored the guards became.

There were so many hastily dug unmarked graves, sometimes a prisoner would accidentally unearth a corpse someone else had buried weeks or months before. They'd casually kick the soil back over and start digging a few feet away. In an empty field, there was no telling how many bodies lay under the ground.

Song-man was about to turn around to see what the gunshots were about, but Lo-chang pulled him back to face his work, saying, 'Don't.' At the end of a shift, it was one man's job to go around the field with a wooden cart, and collect the bodies of prisoners that had died throughout the day from starvation or exhaustion, or whatever it was that happened to have made their hearts stop beating.

'I was hungry,' Lo-chang tried to explain, the executions moments ago already forgotten, 'but I wasn't starving. Starving is a whole other area. Hungry makes you steal; starving makes you do things you can't imagine.'

Song-man struggled with his digging, his dehydrated body unable to sweat. 'What happened to your neck?' he asked.

'I tried to hang myself in the tool shed. I took off my trousers to use as a rope, but the guards caught me. They aren't going to let you just kill yourself.'

Song-man wasn't even feeling the spade in his hands anymore they were so raw with cold, the wind swirling off the face of the mountain, cutting right through the loose-weave rags he was wearing that had all the insulation of a potato sack. 'Did you ever eat tree bark? We were living – my family and I – out in Kosong. My daughter starved while I was working for *Rodong Sinmun*.' Tears filled his eyes at the thought.

'They stopped paying me... she died with a piece of tree bark in her hands.'

Lo-chang didn't bother trying to comfort him. Nothing shocked him anymore, he was always able to find a more horrendous anecdote. 'I was travelling through a village outside Tanchon, this ramshackle old village, and I heard these cries behind me. People waving sticks in the air and hurling stones at something. I stopped and watched this dog limping past me followed by this long train of people running after it. An entire village chasing after a dog so they could eat it. I couldn't do that.'

'Me neither.'

'Of course, you've got some cannibals in here too,' he added. 'Some guy from Kimchaek smothered his mother-in-law in her sleep. The police found him on the living room floor eating a *sinsollo* stew made out of her thigh. The old woman was sitting in chopped up piles in the kitchen sink. Crazy bastard had worked her out into portions.' He shrugged, 'That's what happens. Death doesn't mean anything. Not anymore. Not here.'

An armed guard hurried over to Song-man, and jabbed him in the back of his head with the butt of his rifle, sending Song-man to the ground.

'You want to talk, join a knitting circle,' the guard said calmly, then turned to Lo-chang and hammered him several times in the back of the head. The last three blows, delivered when he was already face down on the ground, had the dull, reverb-free sound of wood impacting bone.

Song-man apologised, putting his hands up as he got to his knees. 'I'm sorry, comrade.' It was the "comrade" that really irked the guard, plunging the butt of his rifle several more times into Song-man's head.

'You don't know the meaning of that word,' the guard said, still perfectly calm.

Lo-chang didn't move.

The guard booted him in the ribs. 'Get up, you piece of shit!'

As Lo-chang's body jerked to the side, the wounds opened up, a tide of blood pouring out the back of his head.

'Damn it,' the guard groaned and, after a brief pause, handed Song-man Lo-chang's spade. 'You'd better dig him a grave.' The guard pulled out a small bottle of whisky and took a swig. He turned to the other prisoners and, chugging his arm back and forth, led them in a rousing rendition of "Let's Defend Socialism". The prisoners croaked out the words, exhausted and defeated.

Sometimes out in the fields, when the guards' attention was elsewhere on a slow or dead prisoner, Song-man would find himself looking up at the mountain (the prisoners nicknamed it 'Mother') and the surrounding hills, and he would catch sight of a civilian plane flying overhead. He thought about the passengers eating their bags of peanuts and watching Hollywood movies, unaware of the horror going on below them. They could have been serving time on the Moon for all it mattered. The empty sky above was the worst thing: one should never be able to lay eyes on places one would never go. It deadened the soul knowing there was nobody watching.

The prisoners were fed at night, sat at long wooden benches slurping clear soups, and eating dried maize cobs, which hurt their teeth with the pressure required to chew them off. The older prisoners picked the maize off by hand rather than risk losing more teeth. They knew all the tricks: if tiny sprigs of rice straw or crushed corn cob from the soup got stuck between the gaps in their teeth, and they couldn't prise them out with their tongues, they just left them. Their fingers were always so black they daren't put them in their mouths for fear of catching typhus. Such depressing epiphanies made Song-man feel that his entire body had turned into a vessel he no longer wanted to be stuck inside.

The diet had an obvious effect on the longer-term prisoners, their skin flaky from malnutrition, their legs turning inwards when they walked (hobbling was more common), unable to support even the slight weight of their torsos. Many of them had no fingernails, snapped back by bamboo shoots forced under them during vigorous torture sessions that sometimes lasted days. Veins popped and throbbed in their temples, their foreheads jutting out, their cheekbones shrinking in, as if their bodies were slowly turning inside out.

The worst were the teenagers who had been born in the prison: the 'Descendants of the Sinners'. Kids who had never set foot on free land, all because their grandparents had been caught tuning in to South Korean radio stations, or were overheard by a prying neighbour denouncing the Party. To the State the child's life was worthless, a meaningless husk to be whittled away as soon as possible in order to re-purify the bloodline for the Three Generation Rule. For the Party, something magical and arbitrary happened in the fourth generation of a family, whereby no further traces of dissent would be possible, and a normal North Korean life would be granted to them. Only in North Korea was being born a crime: the ultimate original sin.

Song-man watched the teens in the washroom, struggling to walk or talk properly, those basic mechanics taught by loving parents, or learned from the world around them. Some of them still crawled around on all fours at the age of seven, semi-amphibious, abandoned in dank shed-like kindergartens, left to work it all out for themselves.

Song-man tried not to sit too close to any other prisoners, as their clothes were crawling with bugs and fleas that thrived on the mix of the warm moss underground and cool mountain air. In the fourth week, he found himself infested like the others, which came as a slight relief: his proximity to the most dire hygiene cases no longer worried him.

He kept waiting for Jun-an to arrive one day, and couldn't understand why it was taking so long for them to arrest him, knowing the authorities would house families in the same prison for clerical simplicity. Then one day, while he was helping repair a broken sewage pipe out in the early-October snow, he was dragged by the neck (his weight was already down to a paltry seven stone) to the commandant's office.

Song-man was led into a small sparse box room and told by the guard to stand at attention in front of Commandant Cho's desk. The guard stood behind Song-man, staying within baton-striking distance. Cho was eating a bowl of hot noodles with a starched-white napkin tucked under his collar, the steam rising up in plumes with each shuffle of his chopsticks. He wiped noodle oil from his mouth in an overly fussy manner, finishing chewing before asking, 'Where's your wife, Song-man?'

Song-man replied quickly, already cowering from the guard who was out his eye line. 'I don't know, sir.' He closed his eyes, realising Ji-won must have made it. They wouldn't have been asking if she had been killed at the Tumen river.

Cho turned the front page of Song-man's arrest report. 'Says here you helped smuggle a woman over the border at Musan. Your wife isn't at home with your son, so where is she?'

Song-man couldn't stop staring at Cho's bowl, his pupils dilating.

The guard behind gave him a sharp jab in the kidneys with his baton. 'Answer the Commandant, fucking Yankee.'

Song-man bent slightly at the hips as if he were contemplating falling over. 'I left her at home with the boy,' he groaned. He didn't care anymore, now that he knew Ji-won was alive somewhere.

'You know we'll bring him here, too.' Cho briefly turned his palms up. 'I have no choice: you know how the three generation rule is. Your drunk of a wife's been slandering the Party. Tell us where she is and we'll go easy on the boy. He'll only get a few years in the *kyo-hwa-so*.'

Song-man knew this was a lie.

'Political re-education, that's all. No hard labour. No latrines, no back breaking digging, no typhus. You can still give him a life. All you have to do is tell us where your wife is.'

When Song-man turned his head down the guard struck him in the kidneys again, harder this time. Song-man had no strength to stay on his feet now, his legs buckling.

'Where is she?' Cho repeated, starting to eat his noodles again.

The guard drew his baton back above his head and battered Song-man across the stomach.

Cho peered over his desk, then gave a desultory flick of his hand towards his door. 'This is pointless. Take him to the Wet Room.'

Delirious with pain and starvation, Song-man hallucinated Lo-chang standing beside him, his head-wound pouring blood. 'What's in the Wet Room, Lo-chang?' he kept saying as the guard dragged him away.

The Wet Room was a windowless cell with a sheer ledge flush against the door. Over the ledge was a small pool filled with ice-cold water. Two guards hurled Song-man underarm into the water like he was a rolled-up rug. Once the shock of the cold made tenuous peace with his body, Song-man's feet found the ground, the water coming up to his waist. There was nothing to sit on or hold onto.

The guards slammed the door shut and Song-man was left in darkness, shuddering in the water.

After the third day, the door flew open, letting in a flash of light that was brighter than anything Song-man had ever seen. He was slouched against the wall, the only relief he could find. He had tried to relieve his legs' pain by dropping to his knees and letting the water lap up to his chin, but the freezing water was worse than any leg pain. He had been hallucinating wild LSD-type bursts of light for the past day, groaning barely audible alternating cries of, 'Jun-an... Ji-won...'

He shielded his eyes from the light at the door, seeing the silhouette of a body standing there. 'How long have I been in here?' he asked. 'Two weeks?'

'We're going to let you go,' Commandant Cho informed him. 'There's no point. Wherever your wife is, she's long gone.'

Song-man mumbled something incoherent, speaking in tongues like someone overwhelmed by a religious vision.

Cho turned his head to try and hear. 'What on earth are you saying, man? Speak up!'

Song-man took a deep breath and managed to form the sentence: 'Please... kill me.'

Cho turned to the guard behind, and said, 'You heard the man.'

Outside, Song-man could make out through the crack of his eyelids that it was either early evening or early morning. A lone wooden post stood at the end of a field hardened with frost. Fifty metres back stood a line of guards, rifles at their sides. Song-man couldn't feel his feet on the ground as he walked, like he had already left the earth's surface. *So this is what dying is like*, he thought. All he could feel was relief that Ji-won and Jun-an were being spared, still part of the world, *out there* somewhere.

The guards tied him to the post to keep him upright. His impending death meant nothing to them. To grieve for him was to grieve for taking out garbage to a bin.

Staring exhaustedly at the ground, Song-man heard the crunch of footsteps approaching him from the side, a pair of well-polished tasselled loafers appearing at the top of his peripheral vision.

A voice tutted. 'Do you remember that day we were sitting in the field at school. You told me the best way to get on in the Great Leader's motherland was to pretend you were loyal to the Party.'

Song-man somehow managed to lift his head, meeting Sun's eyes.

'How is that working out for you, comrade?' Sun asked, keeping Song-man's head up with a hooked finger under his chin. 'I was only a boy, but I swore then I would one day see you in front of a firing squad. I've been waiting nearly thirty years for this day. Tell me. How does it feel to have wasted your life?'

Song-man took a deep breath to get the words out. 'Sun... I want you to know... Wherever you are, wherever you go... know that you never made me beg.' Song-man started to laugh.

Sun retreated, saying to a guard. 'Finish him.'

The guard pulled a black hood over Song-man's head but it didn't stop him shouting after Sun, 'My son'll outlive you, you son of a bastard! You hear me, Sun? He'll outlive you!'

Sun made to go back to Song-man, but Commandant Cho stopped him. Cho signalled to the firing squad to take aim.

Song-man kept shouting, 'Do you hear me, you son of a bastard! He'll get out of this godforsaken country! He'll—'

The men fired, and Song-man's torso gave a series of startled thrusts, then his head dropped towards his chest.

Sun marched towards him, pulling out a pistol from his inside coat pocket. 'You Yankee bastard!' Sun screamed at Song-man's body, firing as he went. After emptying the gun's chamber, he threw the gun aside and untied Song-man from the post, kicking him in the chest before his body had reached the ground, 'Yankee bastard!'

Cho had to pull him away, trying to reason, 'He's dead already, comrade director. It's over.'

Two guards picked up Song-man's body and took him to the perimeter wall, ready for collection with the others.

One of Sun's aides asked him, 'What about the boy, Director? Will we take him in?'

Sun kneeled down to wipe Song-man's blood from his loafers. 'No. And keep his record clean. I want him where I can see him.'

'A Good Man; Homeland'

News of the special announcement gradually spread through the north-east countryside. A slow chain of whispers began between fishermen along the coastline, their radios sitting next to them on the docksides. The children who had long since abandoned school went bounding out the harmonica villages, wading from field to field to inform the farmers to come in before noon.

Farther north, people were less interested in politics. The social order wasn't like it was in Pyongyang and the major cities: you were just as likely to be robbed of food by a soldier than a citizen there; they stopped going to work at the ceramics and iron factories; so few workers showed up at the oil processing refineries they couldn't physically keep the machines running. The ones who did show up mostly used the diversion as an opportunity to further plunder the stock, selling it on in the Rason Free Enterprise Zone near the Sino-Russian border. Han and the other fugitives weren't the only ones using the day's events to their advantage.

Han had climbed into the front passenger seat, letting Mae, knocked out as the adrenaline left her body, sleep against his balled-up coat pressed up against the window. Hal sat in the middle, holding a rag to his bleeding forehead, scrolling through the chase footage from the Glory metro, wincing a little at his terrified squeals as they slid down the escalator partition.

Ben had a pad of foolscap out, scrawling notes on possible edit sequences and timelines for the finished documentary, pausing every so often to look out at the mist rolling off the rugged, craggy peaks along the Paektu Range in the distance, thinking his work to be somewhat premature. He had managed some talking heads with Hal about their desperate escape, but Hal wanted to save the camera battery for the trip over the border.

Ryong had been quiet since getting on the highway, asking Han only for confirmation of directions: the roads they were on were new to him.

Han had his father's file open in his lap, but wasn't reading it. '*I assume Sun told you about my crimes, Ryong?*' Han said, ashamed at having dragged Ryong into such a mess.

After nearly two hours on the road, Ryong still couldn't stop checking his wing mirror for a tail. '*Honestly, Mr Han. Reading foreign books. I thought you were smarter than that.*'

'*You don't disapprove?*'

'*I disapprove very much – a man in your position. Then again, loneliness can make a man do silly things.*'

'*I'm not lonely, Ryong.*'

'*I was talking about myself.*'

'*I had no idea you were lonely.*'

'*How could you. After a while you get good at hiding it. I've always been a joke to the Party. I really thought if I did a good job, and loved my country I would be rewarded. Secretary Sun and Secretary Hwang. They're all the same. They use you then they throw you away.*'

Han looked out his window, not wanting to see Ryong's reaction. '*We're going over the border tonight.*'

'*I suspected as much.*'

'*What will you do now?*'

'*I'll take the consequences.*'

Han cracked his window open and lit a Commie Marlboro. He put his elbow up on the ledge and rested his head against his palm. '*Come with us, comrade.*'

'*And leave the homeland? No. This is where I belong. For better or worse.*'

'*Don't you want to live in the Real World? Don't you want to be free for once in your life?*'

'*I have everything I need here,*' he patted his heart, '*and in here,*' then tapped his head. '*What more is the outside world going to give me?*'

Han dragged on his cigarette in lieu of an answer he didn't have.

Ryong angled the rear view mirror in Ben's direction. '*So you speak Korean, comrade?*'

Ben looked up from his notes with a start.

'You thanked me in Korean earlier.'

'I'm sorry, Mr Ryong.'

Ryong had been replaying all their conversations together in his head, feeling himself blush at how all his little deceits must have played out. *'Yeah, well. Your friend's still a dumb Yankee.'* He smiled, calling back to Hal, 'Right, Mr Hal?'

'Is he talking shit again, Ben?' Hal asked, pulling his jacket further up Mae's chest to keep her warm.

Up front, Han switched on the radio a few minutes early in anticipation for the special announcement, the static followed by sombre military music stirring Mae awake. She looked down at the jacket draped over her and smiled at Hal.

'Thank you,' she said.

A mixed chorus sang the *Song of General Kim Il-sung*, then a male chorus for *Song of Kim Jong-il* followed, absurdly, by a regular news broadcast as if everything were fine. Then there was a long pause of dead air. It went on so long, Han thought they might have delayed the announcement, then a female voice came in.

'Hey, that's Ryong Chun-hee,' Ryong said excitedly. *'I've seen her on television.'*

Han turned up the volume.

The announcer was already on the verge of tears: *'The Central Committee and the Central Military Commission of the Workers' Party of Korea, the National Defence Commission of the DPRK, the Presidium of the Supreme People's Assembly and the Cabinet of the DPRK notify with bitterest grief to all the party members, servicepersons and people of the DPRK that Kim Jong-il, general secretary of the Workers' Party of Korea, chairman of the National Defence Commission of the DPRK and supreme commander of the Korean People's Army, passed away of a sudden illness at oh eight thirty, on December seventeen, Juche one hundred, on his way to field guidance.*

'He dedicated all his life to the inheritance and accomplishment of the revolutionary cause of Juche and energetically worked day and night for the prosperity of the socialist homeland, happiness of people,

reunification of the country and global independence. He passed away too suddenly to our profound regret...'

The announcer went on to list – in hyperbolic fashion – the Dear Leader's accomplishments, which were many.

Han noted the inclusion of the same old myths about Kim Jong-il's life – that he was born at the foot of Mount Paektu (when he had actually been born on Russian soil in the village of Vyatskoye) – that had been hammered into him since he was a child. Discussion moved on rapidly to his son and successor, Kim Jong-un, whose leadership *'provides a sure guarantee for creditably carrying to completion the revolutionary cause of Juche through generations.'*

'And so it continues,' Han said dismally, and switched off the radio.

Darkness had fallen by the time they reached Chongjin. Ryong's headlights illuminated people out in the streets, some on their knees on the pavements, weeping, beating the ground with their fists, petitioning the sky for answers why their Dear Leader had been stolen from them so soon. The local *inminban* leaders were out too, keeping track of who was missing from the public ululations.

In the city centre, children played in the street, making sailboats out of litter, racing them down the rainwater in the gutter. Some prostitutes who hadn't watched or listened to the broadcast, and didn't care either way about what it had to say, stood by a brick wall around the corner from the train station, where three dead bodies lay on the steps. All the prostitutes smoked cigarettes while scouting possible clients. Every few seconds little orange dots of burning tobacco would glow then fade, like some lugubrious Morse code. It would prove to be a slow night for them.

The city was coated in a very fine dust from the smokestacks, which had blackened the buildings over time and would never be reversed.

Han directed Ryong to pull up in an alleyway round the corner. He gathered up his father's file and opened his door.

'Where are you going?' Mae asked.

'I need to check on something,' he replied. He went over to the

prostitutes by the wall and showed them a Polaroid from the file.

One of them put her hand out, as if asking for money before she said anything.

Han handed her two hundred won – about US$1.

Ryong kept lookout for police, telling Ben and Hal, '*Stay down. They don't get a lot of Westerners through here.*' The longer Han talked to the women, the more agitated Ryong became, his leg tapping rapidly on the floor, heel-down, like he was playing a drum kit's hi-hat.

The women crowded around Han, shaking their heads in turn at what he was showing them. Then one of them pointed towards the station entrance.

Han flicked his jacket collar up against the wind and jogged back to the car. '*They said he shouldn't be long,*' he said. He slouched in his seat, staking out the station entrance. Hal, with the camera on night vision, filmed children nearby rummaging through the pockets of the dead on the station steps. Ben couldn't think of anything to add to the scene, sitting in abject silence.

Mae, Han and Ryong shared pieces of Mae's bread while they waited, bread Ben and Hal had to politely but strenuously decline, figuring their energy reserves were far greater than their DPRK counterparts.

Half an hour later a man in his fifties with an aggressively rotund belly – he looked like he was smuggling a basketball underneath his red tracksuit – and wearing all-black retro sunglasses emerged from the station entrance, carrying a briefcase. Han crept up in his seat, comparing a photo in his father's file with the briefcase man. Han was about to get out, when Ryong suddenly put his hand out. '*Wait,*' he said.

A police car ambled past across the road with their rooftop lights whirling but no siren, both the officers hanging out the windows, smoking. They pulled up beside the group of prostitutes who descended upon the car like moths to a flame, hitching their skirts up a few inches. The rooftop light was switched off, and officers drove away with three of the women, each hoping they would be the one who did the least work.

'*That's him,*' Han said, watching the briefcase man stop on the steps to light a cigarette, not even noticing the dead bodies. Han set off after him, cornering him at the side of the station. When the man pushed Han up against the wall – forearm across Han's windpipe – Ryong opened his door as if to intervene. But once Han showed the man the contents of his father's file he let Han go. After a few minutes of conversation, the man was all toothless smiles and hugs. Han ran back to the car as the man swaggered coolly across the street, shielding his eyes from Ryong's headlights. The man gestured violently for Ryong to shut them off. '*You want to get us all pinched?*' he scowled, taking up a position hanging over Han's passenger window.

Han handed him an envelope from the dash with five hundred won inside. '*You'll show us where to go?*'

In one long breath, with the cigarette dangling from his mouth, the man counted the notes to himself, then, satisfied with his bounty, finally smiled. He had no teeth except a few molars. '*I can't believe you're actually his son.*'

'*It's me, alright,*' Han assured him.

'Mr Han,' Ben asked, getting a nudge from Hal who was preparing the camera. 'Can you ask if we can film him?'

Han explained to Chol-kang, who replied, '*Tell them to blur my face.*'

With the go-ahead, Hal started recording.

Ryong, playing the protective older brother, asked sternly, '*Who is this, Mr Han?*'

'*This is Chol-kang, everyone,*' Han answered, turning to the others. '*Ten years ago my father paid him to get my mother over the border into China.*'

Chol-kang opened his briefcase and put the envelope inside. His voice was a husky croak of a forty-Commie-Marlboros-a-day man. '*I'm the only one in Chongjin you can trust for maps over the river. They all come to me,*' he said proudly, and absurdly, as if expecting repeat business.

'*The records on my father said an informant in Chongjin tipped the police off about what he was doing.*'

'*A so-called business partner of mine,*' Chol-kang said, turning to one side to spit. '*I didn't even make it back to the city, the police were waiting for me. I doubt your father made it much longer.*'

'*The arrest report named you as an accomplice to my father's crime. They gave you five years.*'

'*Five years is a long time to think about how not to get caught next time. Long enough to lose your teeth.*'

'*How did you get off so easy?*'

Chol-kang shrugged. '*I ratted out my boss. He was taking business away from local Party delegates selling-on food aid. They warned him so many times but he wouldn't listen. There's nothing quite like an idiot's pride in his own idiocy. I felt bad for him, but hey, it's every man for themselves right?*'

Ben and Hal recognised his type. Every city had them: the cowboys, the free-marketeers, the alleyway-merchants. They had a tendency to thrive while all around them withered. If war was good for morale, famine was good for business.

'*He was ripping me off anyway,*' Chol-kang said. '*I'm smarter now. I don't work with anyone else. I pay off the border guards and a cop in the city to keep me out of trouble. I'm never going back to that penal colony, not as long as I have money in my pocket. I want to keep what few teeth I've got left, know what I mean.*'

'*You said you spoke to my father.*'

'*Sure did. I thought he was crazy. Said he was getting his wife over the border. That he was going to come back with you the next week and meet up with your mother in Shenyang. Said he was trying to get you all to Seoul.*'

'What's going on?' Hal whispered to Ben.

He couldn't follow Chol-kang's swarthy dialect. 'He helps people get across the border. I think Han's mother was trying to get to Seoul.'

Han asked, '*Did she look frightened, my mother?*' He felt Mae's arm suddenly reach over onto his shoulder.

'*Not nearly enough,*' said Chol-kang. '*How scared should you look running through a shooting range in the dark?*'

'We all need to get over the river tonight. Do you think we can make it?'

Ryong was visibly uncomfortable about what was being discussed.

Chol-kang exhaled like it was a tall order. *'The tide's pretty high at this time. If you keep together you should make it.'*

Mae wished he hadn't used the word 'should'.

'Are you ready?' Han asked Mae.

'It's this or we go back to Pyongyang,' she replied. *'I'm ready.'*

Han looked at Ben and Hal. 'Gentlemen?'

'We're in,' Ben answered.

'Let's go,' said Hal, itching to get started.

Han smiled at them, taking out their passports from his jacket pocket. 'You might need these later.' He nodded at Chol-kang. *'OK, we're in.'*

Chol-kang took out a map, and showed them where they needed to head. *'There's a spot nearly a mile downriver where they don't have any guard posts. But there are still foot patrols, so keep silent and you should be OK.'* That awful word again.

Ryong leaned over to see the map. *'How recent is this?'* he asked Chol-kang. *'I don't want to get there and find a post has been set up three months ago.'*

Ryong's tone was a little too strident for Chol-kang's liking. *'What's with the stiff?'* he said to Han.

Ryong retorted, *'Hey, I'm not putting my friends' lives in the hands of some pimp off the street without asking some questions.'*

Chol-kang ducked under the window frame, huffing cigarette smoke towards Ryong. *'The maps are good, partner.'*

'You trust this guy?' Ryong asked Han quietly.

'I've got to trust someone right now,' said Han.

Chol-kang gave Han another map. *'This will show you where to go once you're in China. After that, it's up to you.'*

Han put the map in with his father's file, and appeared ready to go. *'Did he say anything about me before he left? My father.'*

Of all the pleas and messages Chol-kang had heard over the years by the wetlands, all he could ever recall were instructions to tell people if they didn't make it that they loved them. '*All I know...*' He paused. '*He was willing to risk his life to get you and your mother out of here. Would words make any difference to that?*'

Han nodded, knowing he was right. '*And what about you? You know the way out better than anyone else, why do you stay?*'

'*What the hell am I going to do out there? The Real World's none of my concern.*'

Han held his hand out. '*Thank you for everything, Chol-kang. You're a good man.*'

He spluttered a surprised laugh. '*That's the first time I've ever been called that.*' He tossed his cigarette away, then reached into the car, offering his hand to the others. '*Godspeed, comrades,*' he said, then slapped the roof of the car affirmatively before straightening his tracksuit top. '*Let me know if the Real World's as good as they say.*' Then he wandered back into the night. By the time Ryong switched the headlights back on, Chol-kang was already gone.

Nobody spoke during the ninety-minute drive to Musan, giving each of them plenty of time to entertain their worst fears, thinking about how far they had come, and how far they still had to go. Mae wished desperately that Han had been in the backseat with her, and had been holding his hand firmly enough to whiten her knuckles. Hal made sure he got a long shot of it.

Ryong had shut off the headlights since the start of the wetlands outside Musan for fear of drawing attention. Light could travel for kilometres at a time in such pan-flat countryside. Han had navigated by hanging out the window, pointing a torch at the ground only a few feet ahead. When the dim light found a cattle grid Chol-kang had noted on the map, Han put his hand up for Ryong to slow. '*This is it,*' he said.

Ryong shut off the engine, and laid his hands on his thighs. Han got out first, prompting everyone else to follow. The gentle sound of the river could be heard just over a short rise in the marshes. The sky was no help, it was overcast and moonless, but their eyes slowly adjusted to the dark. Ben could see Mae was already feeling the cold, and held her, trying to tease the blood flow in her back with his hands.

Han hated how he had to whisper his goodbyes. '*I suppose this is it, Ryong*,' Han said, coming round to Ryong's side of the car to make one last plea. '*Come with us, comrade.*'

'*I... I can't*,' he stammered. '*My family. They're still in Pyongyang. They'll take my family if I don't go back.*'

'*Ryong, either way—*'

He shooed them on, pretending it was fine. '*Go, it's alright. Don't worry about me.*'

Han embraced him one last time, knowing the punishment Ryong would receive for helping them. '*I'll never forget what you did for us. None of us will.*'

Ryong let him go. '*I'll stay here until you're all across the river.*'

Ben shook his hand. '*Good luck, comrade.*'

'Mr Ben.'

Hal put out his hand, then threw his bag down and hugged him, taking Ryong by surprise. '*God bless, comrade.*'

'Yankee bastard,' Ryong said with a smile.

Then Mae kissed Ryong on the cheek, and he turned away, embarrassed by his tears.

They started across the marsh, the squelch of their steps still audible to Ryong after they had disappeared from view. He sat against the bonnet of his car, crying into his hands. He had never felt so alone.

The group held their bags over their heads as they softly waded into the river, Han leading the way. Hal had wrapped his laptop bag with bin liners to keep the water out, but all he cared about was the camera in his hand. The water appeared calm on the surface, but flowed briskly underneath. Mae was the first to feel her body be pulled downriver when her feet could no longer touch the ground. She held onto Han's outstretched arm then trusted herself enough to let her body drift into a swim. Hal had to swim with only one hand, keeping the camera out of the water, and he drifted down farther than the others. Their clothes turned heavy and baggy, weighing them down, and found it hard to kick against the current, relying mostly on their arms.

Farther upriver they suddenly heard splashing from a group of teenage boys returning from China, a crossing they had made dozens of times to go and trade in the markets. But one of the younger ones found himself in distress, unable to withstand the high tide, and started flapping ever louder, his hands making thick slap sounds on the water's surface. The guards at the nearest watchtower, who had fallen asleep drunk with empty bottles of *cheongju* next to them, stirred from the noise. The sound of the younger boy calling out for help prompted the guards to race downstairs, and they fired towards the yelling. A guard had brought a spotlight, and shone it across the river, catching sight of the boys, and then Han and the others a short distance away.

Ryong, hearing the commotion, threw his car door open and blasted his horn, flashing his headlights in the direction of the shots. '*Hey! Hey, over here!*' he yelled, waving his arms in the air.

The guard with the spotlight turned it away from Han's group, just as another guard was about to shoot, fixing his crosshairs in Ryong's direction instead. Ryong had grabbed the torch and ran towards the riverside, waving it as wildly as he could, still shouting, '*Over here!*'

Han, treading water near the other side, screamed, '*Ryong, no!*'

Mae, Ben and Hal shouted at Ryong as well, but Ryong kept yelling at them, '*Keep going, you can make it!*'

More shots rang out from the guards' post, the spotlight now fixed on Ryong. As Han scrambled to the shore with Mae, both of them heaving for air, he turned in time to see Ryong hit in the shoulder by a bullet, spinning him a half-turn.

Han screamed out, '*Ryong!*' as two more bullets hit him in the chest, and Ryong sank to his knees, as if in prayer.

Ryong's face turned calm before his eyes closed, and another bullet in his chest pushed him onto his back.

'*No!*' Han screamed, who had to be held back by Ben and Hal from swimming back across. '*No,*' he said, fighting them off, '*we have to go back for him...*'

A few of the guards ran to the shore, pulling the boys into custody, while the firing guard kept ploughing bullets into the leafless trees on the other side of the river, hoping to get a lucky hit.

The others had to drag Han away into the woods, before the guards could mount a chase. They scrambled into the cover of the trees, not wanting to stop until they found the Chinese village Chol-kang had put an asterisk next to on the map, running between tree roots and loose rocks, running to keep warm.

After an hour, Han slowed to a stop, holding Mae's hand. None of them could run any longer. Ben, who had taken control of the map, said, '*We must be out of North Korea by now.*'

Hal got them all to take their clothes off and ring them out as best they could, before hypothermia set in. Hal had to do Han's shirt and jacket, as ten years of grief finally exited Han's body, and he sat crying in Mae's arms. '*It's over,*' Mae told him, '*it's over.*'

He looked up at Ben and Hal, his eyes overflowing with tears at the people who had rescued him. 'Thank you,' he cried, standing up to embrace them. And for the first time in ten years he didn't feel alone.

'I Am In Here And You Are In There'

Upon arriving in Seoul, compared to the trendily dressed South Koreans Han and Mae felt like peasants in their surroundings. They were confused by the couples who dressed in matching outfits, the same coats, glasses, even the same shoes. It seemed like everyone was holding someone else's hand: it was a city for lovers.

Ben and Hal took them to the fashionable Apgujeong-dong ward to buy them some more modern clothes, the streets ablaze with Christmas lights and trees, the churches with neon crosses lit up on their spires. Each shop they went into seemed to have Mariah Carey's "All I Want For Christmas Is You" pounding out the speakers. It was music unlike anything Han or Mae had ever heard. Han tried to speak English when other Koreans were around, scared his rougher accent would give him away. Mae would only whisper in Han's ear whenever she wanted to say something. She watched women clawing at dresses and shirts on the rails before dismissing them momentarily. The shoppers bought donuts and chips from street vendors outside, money passing hands like it was worthless. Mae felt ugly and blank compared to the women lined up at the cosmetics counters, trying samples of eye makeup and lip gloss. Mirrors designed to make you look slimmer hung from every wall.

Han watched with baffled fascination at Ben paying for their clothes with his American Express card, wondering how the payment operated.

All their new clothes felt too small for Han and Mae when they got out into the street. 'This is how clothes are supposed to fit, Jun-an,' Ben told him.

'Very nice, Soon-li!' Hal gave her an impressed look with a thumbs up, gesturing for her to give him a twirl.

She grabbed at the tails of her white and black polka dot dress under her coat, covering her mouth as she laughed.

Han kept pulling the collar of his sports jacket away from his neck. 'Is OK, Hal?' he asked him.

Hal adjusted Han's collar and playfully slapped his cheeks. 'Very cool.'

'*We have to find a music shop*!' Mae exclaimed, dancing in circles around Han.

Han seemed distant, overwhelmed by the neon signs and video screens flashing and blinking above the shop fronts, and the constant sound of laughter setting off in surround sound around him. Everything about the city was exorbitant. The more he looked at the couples, the more he could see little schisms between them. They all seemed to be talking on mobile phones or tapping on their screens as if they were trying to summon them to life. They wore headphones which cut out the sound of the city around them, lost in their own little worlds, music streaming into their ears, and movies on their phones, and checking their Facebook and Twitter notifications from people they only knew trivia about but called them friends. They browsed YouTube, skipping songs after only a few seconds, clicking links on the sidebar, always trying to find something newer, something elusive, and never satisfying in the way they hoped. And the billboard- and bus shelter adverts: all about how to make yourself more attractive, or to communicate faster and in more ways, to have more fun and entertain yourself, and make more money. There was nothing about being vigilant of counter-revolutionaries, or helping the state overcome foreign terrors; no billboards of soldiers holding rifles, or nuclear missiles with pro-Party slogans on them. It was all about constant entertainment and onanistic pleasure: the triumph of the individual, the Self.

We are not just bodies; we are machines made of feelings.

Han couldn't fight off the creeping feeling inside him, the same sadness and loneliness he had felt in North Korea. It terrified him: if he couldn't be happy here, how could he be happy anywhere? All this time, he had thought it was something inherent about North Korea that made it so hard to be a human being. But now he was wondering if maybe it was just hard being a human being, period. Because no matter where you are, you are always inside.

'The world's no longer a thing remote, Jun-an,' Ben said, while Hal recorded cutaways of them walking the street ahead.

'It appears so,' Han replied, looking in glazed awe at a bookshop across the street. There was something about the bookshop's doors being wide open that broke Han's heart. 'Do you want to go in?' Ben asked, gesturing to the shop. 'We have time.' Han seemed reticent, but Ben led him over. While Han browsed the fiction shelves, noting all the books he had left behind under the floorboard, Ben came back from the till holding a bag. He handed it to Han. 'He escapes in the end too.'

Han took the book out the bag, holding his first ever legally bought book since *A Great Mind*: *Robinson Crusoe*.

Back over the street, beside Mae who was peering at cellos in the window of a musical instruments shop, Hal was talking on a mobile phone, holding it up to Ben and giving a thumbs-up.

'It looks like we're on,' Ben said to Han, who suddenly looked scared. 'Do you still want to do this?'

Hal sat next to Han and Mae in a seating area on the ground floor of the South Korean embassy. Much like a hotel lobby, it had leather banquettes running the length of the windows looking out onto the street.

Ben was on the phone at reception to his producer in London, struggling to recount the journey they had been on for the past week: hiking through the forests in the Chinese countryside, bribing farmers and truck drivers, hiding in the back of their cabs to get them to Shenyang, buying fake passports for Mae and Han from North Korean dissidents operating in the backstreets of the city. Even there they had to have their guard up, knowing there were secret police and informers operating in the area. They ate at a noodle bar, where Han and Mae feasted on beef, chicken, and pork dishes until they couldn't move, sliding down in the booth, exhausted by so much carbohydrate and protein. Then from Shenyang they took a flight to Da Nang International in Vietnam, and finally to Seoul.

'*Are you alright?*' Mae whispered.

Han was holding a bouquet of *moogoonghwa*, pink hibiscus, wrapped in plastic, nervously turning it in his hands. He pursed his lips together at Mae. '*I was just thinking about Secretary Sun's bird.*'

'No, we've got it all on camera,' Ben said boisterously. 'The chase through the subway, Chongjin, the border... yeah, Hal got everything.' He looked over at him. 'I know, I couldn't have done it without him.'

Hal was hunched over his laptop, enjoying his first Wi-Fi feed for over a fortnight, the outside world back in his grasp. 'You'll never guess what I've found on *Chosun Ilbo*,' he said.

Han budged across to see the screen.

'There's a report about Sun. The Party's saying that "overwhelmed with grief at the sudden and shocking passing of the Dear Leader, Kim Jong-il, Secretary Sun, Minister of Communications, died a brave warrior's death after being struck by a military convoy."'

It was the sort of report Han's father would have been asked to draft back at *Rodong Sinmun*. 'There nothing they can't do, Hal,' Han told him.

An embassy official descended the stairs into the lobby, holding a thick dossier under his arm.

Ben broke off his phone call and beckoned Hal over with the camera.

'*Jun-an,*' the official said. '*I believe you've been waiting for someone.*'

Han stood up, seeing a woman following behind.

The official turned towards the woman. '*Ji-won...*'

She was toying with a pair of sunglasses in her hands. Han thought she looked like a film star. Her hair long and flowing down over her shoulders, wearing a fitted cream suit.

Mae let go of Han's hand and he rushed towards his mother. What they said to one another was indistinguishable, their faces buried in each other's shoulders.

We are not just bodies; we are machines made of feelings.

She tried several times to speak, when she pulled back. *'Jun-an, my dear Jun-an! I'm so sorry, I'm so sorry I left you, my son. I knew you would come back to me.'* She scoured the rest of the room behind him. *'Is your father with you?'*

The question stalled somewhere in his brain before he could make sense of it. Han bowed down at the flowers he forgot he was holding. *'They arrested him, mother. He didn't make it.'* He raised the flowers weakly, wanting something between their bodies when he told her. *'They killed him... my father's dead.'* It only occurred to him then that it was the first time he had said these words out loud.

The embassy official looked on helplessly, flattening the pages of the dossier he was holding. Too many times had he been the conduit for bad news.

Ji-won had prepared herself for such an eventuality, but the confirmation that her husband who had risked everything to save her life was never coming back, never to walk the earth again, made her stomach somersault in a way she hadn't felt since running through the woods out of Musan. *'They were going to arrest me, son. But your father did everything he could to keep us together.'* She broke off. *'I'm so sorry...'*

Han gave her the flowers and led her over to the couches where Mae was standing. *'Mother, there's someone I'd like you to meet. This is Soon-li.'*

Ji-won put her hand, wet with tears, to Mae's face. *'You've been looking after my son?'*

'He's been looking after me,' Mae replied.

Ji-won brought Han closer to her and held the pair of them together, one on each side. *'I have my family back,'* she said.

Hal lowered the camera for a moment to get them all in shot.

'How's that for a third act?' Ben mumbled to him.

Hal took up the camera again, panning around them so the people walking past on the street outside were in frame, video screens of a South Korean news channel showing pictures of Kim Jong-il's funeral, so close and so far away. The people outside had no idea what was taking place only just through the glass, even though they could see in. It was the same out there, in the Real World, that place Han had dreamt of for so long: all those people going about their lives with little idea of what was going on in anyone else's head. Did it even occur to them to think such things? Han wondered. Now he was also part of the Real World, he wanted terribly to be able to lift the veils off their cages and really find them, every single one of them. Was it possible to still feel lonely surrounded by so many people, where happiness was so abundant?

Given that ten years had passed since he last saw her, Han had expected to feel distant from his mother but for some reason it was like she had never left him. And as she began telling him her story, he realised it was because he had been carrying her with him all this time, preserved in memories that no external agency could destroy. It was all inside him.

Pyongyang Metro Police Station

A guard swung his head round the dangling light bulb hanging from the basement ceiling. He scanned the evidence shelves until he found the box of books he had been sent down to find. He wrote on the blank ID tag, 'CASE NO.7677AB – Han Jun-an', and was about to seal the box up, but curiosity got the better of him and he opened the box. Noticing Kim Il-Sung's *A Great Mind* inside, and wondering what it was doing among the other illicit material, he opened it up, finding Han's notebook in its hollowed centre. After checking no one else was around, the guard sealed up the box with silver tape, then slipped the notebook into his coat's inside pocket.

Later that night, sitting in his empty apartment, the guard reached the last page of the notebook. Han's final entry: "And even though 'I am in here' and 'you are in there', someday, in any given place, a stranger might play a piece of music that lifts the roof off the world, or writes a book that dissolves the bars of a cage, or drops a foot in the

265

ocean and raises the water just slightly enough on the other side of the world for them to notice, and that stranger will no longer feel like a stranger. And as you read these words, you might know who I really am. They are the only door I can open, the only cage I can unlock. The limits of everything I am. The limits of the world."

Acknowledgements

Do people still read these? I hope so.

Trent Kim provided me with invaluable advice on Korean translation, given- and family names, and all manner of crucial cultural information for no other reason than believing in the story I wanted to tell. Although every effort has been made to translate Korean phrases and slogans etc accurately, any errors or mistranslations are entirely mine.

Gill Tasker and Helen Sedgwick at Cargo Publishing, for their editorial nous. And seemingly infinite patience.

Naturally, North Korea is a daunting research project. The following are some of the books that got me a little closer to the Hermit Kingdom:

Nothing to Envy by Barbara Demick (Granta); This is Paradise by Hyok Kang (Abacus); The Aquariums of Pyongyang by Kang Chol-Hwan & Pierre Rigoulot (Atlantic); Under the Loving Care of the Fatherly Leader by Bradley K. Martin (Thomas Dunne Books); The Cleanest Race by B.R. Myers (Melville House).

I am also particularly indebted to the documentaries:

'Inside North Korea' – VICE News, producers Shane Smith and Eddy Moretti; and BBC Four's 'Holidays in the Axis of Evil – North Korea', produced by Ben Anderson.

Thank you, EP. Who made everything beautiful and nothing hurt.

I dedicate this book to my family, both gone and rediscovered.

THE LIMITS OF THE WORLD

ANDREW RAYMOND DRENNAN

Cargo Publishing